About the A

Maisey Yates is the *New York Times* bestselling author of over 100 romance novels. An avid knitter with a dangerous yarn addiction and an aversion to housework, Maisey lives with her husband and three kids in rural Oregon. She believes the trek she makes to her coffee maker each morning is a true example of her pioneer spirit. Find out more about Maisey's books on her website: maiseyyates.com, or find her on Facebook, Instagram or TikTok by searching her name.

USA Today bestselling author **Joanne Rock** credits her decision to write romance to a book she picked up during a flight delay that engrossed her so thoroughly, she didn't mind at all when her flight was delayed two more times. Giving her readers the chance to escape into another world has motivated her to write over 100 books for a variety of Mills & Boon series.

Joss Wood loves books, coffee and travelling – especially to the wild places of Southern Africa and, well, anywhere. She's a wife and a mum to two young adults. She's also a servant to two cats and a dog the size of a small cow. After a career in local economic development and business, Joss writes full-time from her home in KwaZulu-Natal, South Africa.

Opposites Attract Collection

Opposites Attract:
Rancher's Attraction

MAISEY YATES

JOANNE ROCK

JOSS WOOD

MILLS & BOON

First Published in Great Britain 2025
by Mills & Boon, an imprint of HarperCollins*Publishers* Ltd
1 London Bridge Street, London, SE1 9GF

www.harpercollins.co.uk

HarperCollins*Publishers*
Macken House, 39/40 Mayor Street Upper,
Dublin 1, D01 C9W8, Ireland

Opposites Attract: Rancher's Attraction © 2025 Harlequin Enterprises ULC.

A Forever Kind of Rancher © 2024 Maisey Yates
The Rancher © 2021 Joanne Rock
Rich, Rugged Rancher © 2020 Harlequin Enterprises ULC

Special thanks and acknowledgment are given to Joss Wood for her contribution to the *Texas Cattleman's Club: Inheritance* series.

ISBN: 978-0-263-41732-6

This book contains FSC™ certified paper and other controlled sources to ensure responsible forest management.

For more information visit: www.harpercollins.co.uk/green

Printed and Bound in the UK using 100% Renewable Electricity
at CPI Group (UK) Ltd, Croydon, CR0 4YY

A FOREVER KIND OF RANCHER

MAISEY YATES

Chapter One

She was the most beautiful woman he'd ever seen. A vision dressed in pink, and somehow it made him think of strawberries, which got him to wondering if her skin tasted like strawberries.

She wasn't dancing, and she should be. Hell, Boone was wearing a suit, and he didn't much care for that shit. He didn't much care for dancing either, but this was the kind of thing you wore suits to, and danced at, so it felt like a crime she wasn't dancing.

It was his brother's wedding after all.

And he was damned happy for Chance. Really. He'd fallen in love and all that. Boone was in love too.

Had been for years. In a way that had left him cut open, hollowed out and embittered.

He respected the hell out of love for that very reason. He knew how intense it could be. How long-lasting.

He decided to remedy the fact that she wasn't dancing, because hell, he was in a suit after all.

He knew better than this. He stayed clear of her, except when he couldn't. He knew better than to approach her. She was forbidden. Because of what he wanted to do with her. To her. If all he wanted was a chance to say hi, a chance to shoot the breeze, they could be friends.

But it wasn't what he wanted.

It never had been.

Tonight this place looked beautiful, and so did she, and she was standing there alone, and that was wrong.

He ignored the warning sounds going off in the back of his head and crossed the old barn that had been decorated with fairy lights and flowers for his brother's big day.

"Care to dance?"

She looked up at him, and he saw it. That little spark of awareness that always went off when they were near each other. They saw each other way too often for his taste, and hers, too, probably. He loved it, and he hated it. He had a feeling she only hated it.

It only ever ended one of two ways. With her turning red and running in the other direction or getting pissed off and getting right in his face. As if one or the other would hide the fact that she wanted him. She did. He knew that.

Not that either of them would ever do anything about it.

They were too good.

Boone hadn't often been accused of being too good. But when it came to her...

He was a damned saint.

She lifted her hand, and the diamond there sparkled beneath the light.

"If he's not going to dance with you," Boone said, "you might as well dance with me."

And he could see it. That it was a challenge he laid out before her, and she wouldn't back down.

Wendy never backed down from a challenge. It was one of the things he liked about her.

That diamond ring was the thing he didn't much like.

And the fact that it meant she'd made vows to his best friend. Wedding vows.

Boone wanted his best friend's wife. And it felt so good he couldn't even muster up the willpower to hate it.

He didn't wait for her to answer, instead, he reached out

and took her hand and pulled her up from her chair, led her to the dance floor, and tugged her against his body like they were friends, and it was fine. She looked over her shoulder, her expression worried. And that spoke volumes. Because they were friends, as far as anybody here was concerned. Because there was nothing between them, not outwardly.

But they both *felt* it. And that was what made dancing with her dangerous. He had known Daniel for a long time. He loved him like a brother. At least, he had. Before he'd married Wendy.

Daniel, as a husband, sucked. Witnessing that had started to damage their friendship. Boone had never been satisfied that Daniel valued that marriage.

He'd never witnessed anything concrete—if he did he'd be the first one to tell Wendy—but Boone had always had the feeling Daniel took his marriage vows as suggestions when he was on the road with the rodeo.

Not only that, Daniel missed a lot of his kids' milestones, not that Boone had any kids. Not that he was in a position to judge. It was only that he *did* judge.

Because he wanted what his friend had so very badly.

"What's wrong?" he asked.

He knew she wouldn't answer that. Because she wouldn't admit it.

Never.

And maybe they never danced. But they knew this particular dance well. They'd been doing it for fifteen years.

"Nothing is wrong," she said, linking her fingers behind his neck, and he wasn't sure if she was preparing to strangle him, or trying to keep herself from moving her hands over his body and exploring him.

"You look beautiful," he said.

She paused for a second. "Boone…"

"Where is Daniel?"

"Drinking," she said, looking up at him, her eyes defiant, as if she was daring him to comment.

He didn't have to. Instead, he moved his hand just a little bit lower on her back.

Her nostrils flared, and he even thought that was hot.

"If he's drinking, then he won't miss you."

And why the hell should Daniel have her anyway? He didn't fucking care about her. Boone was almost certain that every time he went out drinking with the guys, Daniel was screwing around with buckle bunnies. There was no way he was only dancing with them at the jukebox. Boone could never bear to stick around and find out, because he would have to tell Wendy, and his loyalty was supposed to be to Daniel, but he was at a point where he didn't feel like it could be. Not anymore. And he'd told himself he could not feel that way, and he couldn't act in the way he wanted to, because he had an ulterior motive. But now he didn't care. Right at this moment, none of it mattered.

"Come with me."

"Where?"

"Does it matter?"

Slowly, very slowly, she shook her head no. And he led her off the dance floor, out of the barn and into the night. And in one wild, feverish moment, he pushed his best friend's wife back against the side of the barn and pressed his mouth against hers.

Boone woke up with sweat drenching his body.

Dammit.

For a second, he let the dream play in his mind over and over again.

It was the sliding door. The other path.

The one he had decidedly *not* taken at his brother's wedding, when he had gazed across the barn and seen Wendy looking like a snack that night.

He hadn't even danced with her. Why? Because he'd known he was too close to losing control. But in his dreams…

In his dreams he held that pretty pink slice of glory in his hands. In his dreams, he had pushed her warm willing body up against that barn and tasted her mouth.

It was so real. It was so real he could scarcely believe it hadn't happened.

Damn it and him, to hell.

He was wrung out. It was all the sleeping in cheap-ass motels.

He missed home or so he told himself. Because it was better than missing a woman he'd never actually held in his arms.

He had bought himself a ranch, one that currently had no animals on it, with a damned comfortable bed in one of the rooms—a bed he hadn't brought a woman back to yet—in preparation for his life changing. He was on the verge of retirement, because… Hell. His brothers were all out of the rodeo, so he didn't understand why he was still in. He was the last one standing. The last one who hadn't left, who wasn't with the person that they…

Well. He had no idea what the hell Buck was doing. So maybe that wasn't fair.

Buck wasn't in the rodeo—he knew that much. But he knew nothing else since Buck had cut all ties with their family.

You have to face it, Buck. It happened. There's no use sitting down and crying about it, there's no use falling apart. You have to be realistic.

Not his favorite memory. The last time he'd seen his older brother. Eighteen months his senior and the heir apparent to the Carson Rodeo empire.

Not now, though. Now the heir was Boone.

Someone had to keep the legacy going. It was in his blood.

Because, after all, the Carsons were rodeo royalty.

He nearly laughed.

Rodeo royalty in a shitty motel. Oh well. That was the life. The royalty part came from the fact that they all had trust funds, something Boone had sat on until he got his ranch outright in Lone Rock, Oregon, where he would be near his parents and his brothers... Where he would finally settle... He supposed, because there was a point where the demands of the rodeo would get to be a little bit much, and he wasn't going to be bull riding past his fortieth birthday. He could, he supposed. He could keep going until he gave himself more of a trick back than he already had.

He could downgrade himself to calf roping, keep on keeping on, because he didn't know what the hell else to do, but he did feel like maybe there was a fine art to just quitting while he was ahead.

Except when his brothers had quit there had been a reason. There had been a woman.

He got out of bed and looked at the bottle of Jack Daniel's on his nightstand. Then he picked it up and took a swig. Better than coffee to get you going in the morning.

He grimaced, his breath hissing through his teeth, then he threw on his jeans and his shirt, his boots, and walked out of the hotel.

It was the third night of the championship, and he would be competing for the top spot tonight. Finally, for the first time in a long time, not competing against one of his brothers.

Not that he minded competing against them. It was all fine.

He wondered if Wendy would be there, or if she would have to be home with the girls.

And he had the feeling he had put more thought into Wendy's whereabouts than her husband probably had.

He spent the day doing not much. Had breakfast at a greasy

spoon diner near the rodeo venue and didn't socialize, stayed in his own head, like you had to do.

He got to the arena right on time and cursed a blue streak when he drew the particular bull that he drew, because that bull was an asshole, and it was going to make his ride tonight a whole thing.

And then he saw Daniel from across the way, his friend tipping his hat to him, the ring on his left finger bright.

That was when Boone decided he wasn't going to let Daniel have *two* things that he wanted. He couldn't do much of anything about Wendy, but he'd be damned if he wouldn't get this buckle. It was only when it was his turn to get in the shoot that everything felt clear. That everything felt right. The dream finally wasn't reverberating inside of him when he got on the back of the bull—the bull who was jumping, straining against the gate.

Eight seconds. That was all it took. He couldn't afford to blink. Couldn't even afford to breathe wrong. Couldn't afford to have his heart beat too fast. Adrenaline could take him after, but not before. Before was the time for clarity.

Before was when everything became still. It was when he was at peace. At least, the most that he ever was.

It was damned near transcendental meditation.

He didn't question it.

And when the gate opened, the animal burst forth in a pure display of rage and muscle and he clung to the back of him, finding a rhythm. Finding that perfect ride. Because it was there. In every decision he made, and the way he followed all the movements of the animal. In the way he made himself one with him.

And maybe no other cowboy would relate to that way of thinking about it. For sure his brother Flint would laugh his ass off. But Boone didn't care.

There was a reason he was the last one in the rodeo, and it

wasn't just because he hadn't gone and fallen in love. It was because no matter what he loved, part of him would always love the rodeo in a way he didn't think his brothers ever had.

Part of him would always know he found purpose there. And if he won tonight, he could leave being the best. And that was what he wanted more than anything. Quit while he was on top. Quit while he could still love the rodeo with all that he had, all that he was. To leave it wanting more. To leave himself wanting more. Because what the hell was worse than overstaying your welcome?

He couldn't think of much.

He'd set out to prove himself, and he was doing it.

So he rode, and he rode perfectly. And when that eight seconds was up, he jumped off the bull. He wasn't unseated.

And the roar of the crowd was everything he could have asked for. Except the one thing he really wanted. So he let it be everything. He let that moment be everything.

Nobody was going to outride him. Not tonight.

He was number one on the leaderboard and he stayed there, for the whole rest of the night, and damned if he didn't give the people kind of a boring show. Because nobody could touch his score, and he loved that.

In the rodeo, Daniel Stevens was second.

And hell, for Daniel that was probably enough. With the Carsons, all except Boone, moved out of the way, that was a damned high ranking for Daniel.

But Boone felt mean about it. Because he was number one, while Daniel was number two, and if Boone couldn't have the other man's wife, then it seemed like a pretty good alternative prize.

There was no question about going to the bar after, because the mood was celebratory, and the women were ready to party, and Boone figured it was just the right night to find himself a pretty blonde dressed in pink, one that would make the fantasy easy. He would lay her down in that bed he'd slept in last night, and he'd find himself back in that dream, make it feel real.

He didn't feel guilty about the fantasies anymore.

He'd been doing it for too long.

But when Daniel came up to him just outside the barn and clapped him on the back, he felt a little bit of guilt. Just a little.

"Hell of a ride," said Daniel. "You made that bull your bitch."

He frowned. "I don't work against him. I work with him."

"Whatever. Seems to work for you."

"It does."

One of the other riders, Hank Matthews, sidled up to both of them as they made their way into the bar. "Does that thing weigh you down?" Hank asked, pointing toward Daniel's ring.

"Oh, hell no," said Daniel, holding his hand up. "If anything, there's a certain kind of woman who likes it."

Boone let his lip curl when he looked at his friend. "Is that so?"

"Hey, don't worry about it," said Daniel. "Just having a little fun."

And after that, the intensity of the excited crowd broke up their group. Fans, male and female alike, were all over the place, and this was their moment of glory. There wasn't a medal ceremony, instead, they were showered with praise in the form of Jack Daniel's and Jesus. Free shots and a whole lot of glory to God.

It was normally the sort of thing he loved, but he was still distracted. That dream was in his head, and then what Daniel said about the wedding ring had gotten under his skin and stuck there.

He hadn't seen Wendy tonight, and it was kind of odd, because it was a championship ride, although they were pretty far off from their home base.

Still. He would've thought she might show up.

And there were women all over her husband.

Normally, Boone would be determinedly paying attention to his own prospects. Not tonight.

There were two women on either side of Daniel, both of them touching him far too intimately for Boone's liking. And then Daniel turned his head and kissed one of them, and Boone saw red. He was halfway across the bar, on his way to do God knows what, when a car alarm cut through the sound of the crowd and the music in the bar. The door opened and some guy came running in like the town crier. "Some bitch is going crazy out there on a pickup truck."

That was enough to send half the bar patrons pouring out into the night. And when a loud smashing sound transcended the noise of the alarm, Boone found himself moving out there as well.

He stood at the door, stopped dead in his tracks by what he saw. A black pickup truck seemed to be the source of the sound, the headlights on, casting a feminine figure into sharp relief. A slender silhouette with a blond halo all lit up by the lights. She was wearing a short, floaty-looking dress, and she was holding a baseball bat. Then she picked up the bat and swung it, and made the headlights go out, casting everything into darkness like a curtain had fallen over the star of this particular show.

"What the *fuck*?" It was Daniel, behind Boone, who shouted that. "That's my truck," he said.

"And I'm your *wife*," came the shouted replied, as the bat went swinging again, and dented the truck right in the hood. "I got you the deal that got you gifted this truck, by the way, so I think it's fair enough for me to vandalize my own property."

Wendy.

Somehow, he'd known it was Wendy. Or at least, his body had.

An avenging angel, looking beautiful and dangerous, and hell…he'd never wanted her more.

Daniel pushed past him, his jar of whiskey still in his hand. "You're being a fucking psycho," he said. "What the hell?"

Wendy advanced on him, her chin jutted out, fury radiating from her. "Tell me you weren't in there with another woman."

Daniel backed up, his face going bland. "I wasn't with another woman."

"I got the most interesting series of pictures texted to me today, Daniel. And it's definitely you, because I'm intimately familiar with your *shortcomings*."

"What the hell does—"

"Pictures. Of you. Screwing someone else."

"I never…"

"Save it. What's the point faking it? You don't have a reputation big enough to try and save it. Like I said. I know every detail of you just a little too well for you to try to tell me it's Photoshop."

And then Wendy stormed right up to Daniel, pulled her rings off and dropped them in his glass of whiskey. "Keep them."

"Baby," Daniel said, reaching out and wrapping his hand around her arm, and that was when Boone lost it.

He was right between them before he even realized he'd moved. "Get your hands off her."

"Boone?" Daniel asked, looking at him like he'd grown another head.

"I said," said Boone, reaching out and putting his hand around his friend's throat. "Get your fucking hands off her."

"She's my wife."

"And you put one hand on her while you're angry and I'll make her your widow. Step back."

"You should be defending *me*," Daniel said, as he moved away from Wendy. "You know I'd never—"

Boone growled. He couldn't help it. And it shut Daniel up good.

Wendy looked high on adrenaline, her eyes overly bright.

And Boone wanted to grab her and shield her from all of this. From the onlookers, from everything. From the truth of the fact that Daniel just wasn't the man that he should have been for her.

Like you are?

No. But he hadn't made vows to her. And if he had, he would never have…

"I can't defend you if there's nothing to defend," he said.

Wendy looked around, and it was as if the reality of everything crashed over her. As if she suddenly realized what she'd done, and how publicly she'd done it.

Yeah, this was the kind of thing that got you on the news. And it was likely she'd only just realized that. And he wondered if she had driven all the way from California to Arizona riding high on anguish and anger.

He wondered if she'd even given it a second thought.

And now she was giving it a second thought. And third. And probably fourth.

But for what it was worth…

He moved near her, and she looked at him like she wished he would disappear. He didn't take it personally. She kind of looked like she wanted the whole world to disappear.

"Whatever you do," he said. "Don't regret *that*. Because it was damned incredible."

And he meant it.

"I don't have anywhere to go now." She looked numb.

"Sure you do," he said. "You can always come to me."

Chapter Two

Three weeks later...

If there was one thing Wendy Stevens did not want to do, it was depend on another cowboy. She'd learned her lesson. Some fifteen years and two kids too late, but she'd learned it.

She tried not to think about that night. The one that hadn't exactly covered her in glory. But it had covered the ground in shattered glass, and for a moment, it had made her feel satisfied.

For a moment, the images of her husband with another woman had felt dimmed, dulled, because all she had seen was the destruction she had caused to his truck. Technically, her truck.

Except you bought it with his money...

Well. That was the problem. She had given up her life in service to that man. She had acted as his agent, essentially, getting him endorsement deals and other things. He was good-looking. It had been easy to do. He was charming, that had made it easier.

Both of those things had likely made it easy for him to get women into bed too.

She was still reeling from the truth.

For a few days, she'd clung to the belief that he'd only cheated on her the one time. The time that had come with photographic (emphasis on the *graphic*) evidence.

She knew it was naïve. But it was deliberate. A form of protecting herself.

It hadn't lasted long.

Because once the floodgates of truth had been opened up, more truth had kept on coming.

Fast and swift.

More women had stories. Texts. Photos.

He'd *never* been faithful to her. Never even once. Their entire marriage was a lie. Everything they'd ever built in their relationship was a lie. She supposed the one thing she had to be grateful for was that he had been judicious in his use of condoms. One of the first things she had been worried about was what hideous disease the man had given to her, but he had sworn up and down that he'd had protected sex with all those other women.

As if that earned him some sort of commendation.

I would never do that to you, he'd said.

She hadn't even known what to say to that.

But she hadn't known what to say for a good three weeks now. That was the amount of time she'd given herself to clear up her life and find another place to go.

She had given everything to that man. When his career in the rodeo had started to take off, she'd discovered she had skills she hadn't known she possessed. She'd brokered all the endorsement deals that he'd gotten over the years. Her reputation was tied to his. Her career had been all about making money for him, and they'd put it all in one pot rather than having an official split because why would they ever need that? They were in love. They were forever.

The phrase *all your eggs in one basket* was suddenly far too clear for her liking, and yet there was nothing she could do about it.

Her eggs were in Daniel's basket.

She made a face. She did not like that.

"Mom?"

She turned to look at her daughter. "What?"

Fifteen-year-old Sadie looked at her from the passenger seat, and then twelve-year-old Michaela—Mikey for short—leaned forward. "Are we going?"

Wendy was at the end of a long dirt driveway. The one she knew would take her to help. The one she didn't want to drive down.

"Yeah. In a second. I'm just sitting here thinking about how little I like any of my options."

"You have our support," said Sadie.

"Yes," said Mikey. "It isn't your fault that Dad's an untrustworthy blight on humanity."

"Your vocabulary," said Wendy, rolling her eyes, but she was actually very proud, and beamed a little every time Mikey opened her mouth.

"It's because I read," said Mikey. "And also, because I binge-watch TV shows that are probably above my age rating."

"Let's just leave it at reading," said Wendy.

"I thought Boone was Dad's friend," said Sadie.

"He is," Wendy said slowly.

And she left out all the complications that Boone made her feel. She made sure to keep the pronunciation of those words as simple as possible. She made sure to leave any kind of subtext out of what she said. Because she had to. She had no room in her life for subtext. Not right now. And never when it came to Boone.

"So, why are we going to stay with him?"

"Because he offered." And he'd offered her a job. It was humiliating. But she didn't really have another choice. The one thing she had any kind of experience with before marrying Daniel was housecleaning. Boone said now that he was back from the rodeo, he needed a cleaner, and he had more than one house on the property, and more than enough room for her and the girls. She was in no position to turn it down. She had to take the offer.

Anyway, that night…

She kept seeing it. Over and over again. She'd been unhinged. But brave. And she couldn't help but admire herself. But also, she kept seeing the way Boone had put his body between hers and Daniel's. The way he'd been. Like fire and rage, and completely on her side.

And then the way he told her…

Don't regret it.

So she hadn't. Because Boone had told her not to, and maybe that wasn't healthy, but dammit all, she didn't have a whole lot of healthy available to her right now. Mostly she had disillusioned and confused.

"He didn't take Dad's side on this."

"Good for him."

"I admire his willingness to break with traditional toxic masculinity," said Sadie.

"Well, don't go giving that much credit," Wendy said. "He *is* still a rodeo cowboy. He just happened to…bear witness to some things."

The brief text conversation she'd had with Boone after her grand performance in the parking lot had confirmed that Daniel had been well on the way to cheating on her that night too.

At that point, she had known it was a routine thing.

Any guilt she might have felt eventually over smashing up the truck had been effectively squashed at that point.

There was no room for regret in the well of rage created by Daniel's own actions. If he didn't like the way she behaved, he should have been different. From the very beginning.

"I need something to get back on my feet. And I think we all need a fresh start. This isn't where we're going to stay forever but…"

"It's pretty," said Sadie.

She had expected her daughters to be a little bit angrier about leaving California than they were.

They'd lived in Bakersfield, and it didn't often feel like there was a lot happening there but heat and drought. They complained about both, often. And they seemed to be in places with friends where they were glad for a fresh start and a change of scenery. She couldn't help but wonder if some of it was the pain of having Daniel break up their family. And maybe leaving rather than having to tell everyone about it was easier. At least, that's how it was for her.

Their life had been quiet and stable. He might've been out chasing glory, but she hadn't been. To her, their life had been glory.

But it hadn't been enough for him.

She should've known.

He wasn't home all that much. When he was, they'd had a healthy sex life, but she had honestly just imagined that he was like her. That he turned it off when she wasn't there, like she did with him.

That's oversimplifying things, isn't it?

She gritted her teeth.

Maybe.

Maybe it was.

But she was happy for oversimplification right now. She needed it.

As if simplification didn't cause some of this mess in the first place.

So she started up the car engine and continued down the road that would take her to Boone's house.

When the house came into view, her stomach twisted. It was weird, because it was Boone. And she didn't need to go getting wound up about her own inferiority complexes, or her memories of growing up poor. Her memories of being a have-not in a sea of haves. Of her mother being the one who cleaned and now she was...

It wasn't the same.

Not because she was ashamed of her mother. She wasn't. She never had been. The difference wasn't in the work, it was in the person needing the work done.

Those people had all fancied themselves better than her mother. And that wasn't Boone. And it never would be. It wasn't why he had asked her to come.

He felt guilty, she knew that.

She also wondered how much he had known for all those years...

Well. You have plenty of time to talk.

Seeing as she would be living on his property and cleaning his house.

"Wow," said Sadie.

The house was beautiful. Even more beautiful than the one they had left behind in Bakersfield.

Their house had been elaborate. Because it was the kind of fancy Daniel liked. It had been positioned across from a field that was just empty.

And now she kind of felt like it was a metaphor. A dream house surrounded by a whole lot of nothing.

Empty. Like his promises.

She ached, and she couldn't quite work out exactly what she was feeling. If it was heartbreak or the sting of having been tricked. If it was betrayal or the loss of her marriage. Or simply the loss of her life.

She didn't know. Maybe it was all those things. It seemed like each moment one of those things felt more prominent than another. And then it would shift.

She didn't have time to think about anything shifting at the moment. What she needed to do was get her game face on.

She pulled the truck up to the front of the house and turned the engine off.

Okay. It was just Boone.

And something about that made her feel every inch a liar.

There was no *just Boone*. There never had been.

He'd been a particularly problematic thorn in her side for years.

Mostly because…

Of one moment. A very clear and terrifying moment—the minute she had first seen him.

She and Daniel had only been married for two weeks. It had been a whirlwind romance, and she'd been head over heels, and pregnant far too quickly, so they'd had a shotgun wedding, though Wendy had never felt forced.

She'd wanted it. She'd wanted to secure that life. She hadn't wanted to be a single mother. She'd found an easy man. A fun man. A happy man.

Her life had felt lacking in those things, growing up with scarcity was a feeling Wendy was very sensitive to.

Daniel had felt like excess. Excessive joy, excessive drinking, eating, happiness. She'd loved it. And when their love affair had had consequences…he'd been kind and he'd done the right thing.

He'd told her he loved her.

She'd said she loved him, because it was best if they did, and eventually she was sure she'd meant it.

And then she'd gone to the very first cowboy thing she'd ever done with him, and Boone had walked in, and it was like everything in the world had fallen away. Like something inside of her had whispered, *This is him*.

She had never in her life believed in the concept of the one. Ever. But right when Boone had come in, it was like the universe had whispered across her soul. That it was *him*.

She had never been so completely devastated by the impact of another person in all her life. He was ruinous. And glorious.

And the moment she had first seen him, she had wanted to *not* see him just as quickly.

Had wanted to go back to living a life where she had no idea Boone Carson existed in the world.

It was just easier if she didn't know.

When she was married to another man. Pregnant with that man's child.

She had told herself that all of it was silly. Boone was handsome, that was all. And she'd been surprised by the impact of him.

You didn't expect to see a normal man like that just…out and about in the world. That was all.

She was very, very good at telling herself that story.

She loved Daniel.

She had loved Daniel.

Did she still love Daniel?

Right now, she felt hollow.

She loved her daughters. She knew that much.

She let out a long, slow breath.

That was going to have to be enough, because it was going to be the thing that was driving her now.

She missed her anger.

It had been so bright and glorious and wonderful. And far too fleeting.

But it had fueled her for a while there and now she was just…

Well, she was at Boone's house.

She sucked in a sharp breath and killed the engine on the truck. She got out and the girls followed suit. Then she went around to the bed of the truck to start gathering their bags.

Boone walked out the front door.

"You made it," he said.

She stopped, and she wished she didn't feel like she'd been hit by a train, because she did. Just looking at him. She'd known him now going on fifteen years, and she couldn't understand how or why the man still did this to her.

"Yes," she said. "We did. Kind of a long drive."

"Not as far as Arizona." The corner of his mouth lifted.

She didn't smile back. "Yes." She moved to the bed of the truck to grab her bag, but he started moving toward her purposefully.

"You don't need to get anything," he said, and then he reached into the back of the truck and plucked up her bag, her daughters' bags and a suitcase, which he lifted up over his shoulder. "Your place is just a walk out back here," he said, gesturing behind his grand house.

She stared at him. At the way he held all her baggage so easily.

It was a very weird metaphor to be confronted with right in this moment, and was it bad that she wanted him to carry it all? Was it bad that she was tired? That she wanted him to carry her worldly possessions in his strong arms and over his shoulders because she was just so damned tired of…everything?

Yes, it's bad. You need to figure out how to stand on your own. That's your problem. You let a man carry you for too long.

Well, that wasn't fair. Daniel hadn't carried her, but she'd wound herself around him so tightly that cutting ties was painful.

Difficult.

But it wasn't the same as being carried.

But she figured she could also chill out and not see her literal baggage as a metaphor. Because physically Boone was stronger than her and he knew where the house was, so why not follow him?

"How was the drive, girls?"

"Good," said Mikey, "we played the alphabet game and also discussed elaborate ways men should die."

"We didn't do that," said Wendy quickly.

"Wouldn't blame you if you did," said Boone.

"Not *you*, of course," Sadie said.

"Appreciate it, Sadie," Boone responded.

Boone had always had a decent rapport with the girls. It was weird that right now it made her feel…lightheaded.

But Boone had been that fun uncle figure when he'd been around, which had been often enough, and of course the girls enjoyed him.

It turned out their dad also thought of himself as a fun uncle. Which really didn't work when you were supposed to be a husband and father.

The path behind the house led to a cottage. It was small, with freshly planted flowers all around the front, and two hanging baskets with flowers on the porch.

It was beautiful. Small, she wondered if the girls would see it as a major downgrade. But right then…she saw it as salvation.

It was hers.

Theirs.

For now.

"Thank you," she whispered, her throat going tight.

She looked up at him, and her breath caught. His blue eyes were startling, arresting, there in the sunlight, and the way the gold played against the whiskers on his face did something to her stomach, low and intimate. His face was just…perfect. As if an artist had lovingly sculpted him by hand with the intent of making him the perfect masculine figure.

His jaw was square, his nose straight, his cheekbones so sharp she could cut herself on them. And then there was his body, which she'd spent a lot of time not contemplating and she surely wasn't doing it now, with her daughters present.

She freed the breath from the little knot in her throat and got herself together. She didn't need this kind of drama. Not now.

"This is so cute!" said Sadie, her voice going high, and the delight in her tone shocked and pleased Wendy.

"It's like a fairy house," said Mikey.

Wendy had to wonder if her daughters were being overly happy for her benefit, but then she decided she didn't care.

They'd been so supportive of her through everything.

If they'd been younger, she'd have tried to shield them. But the thing was, she'd sort of made the news.

"Scorned Wife Goes Full Carrie Underwood Song on Cheating Husband."

It was all over the country music news sites, given the rodeo circuit was sort of adjacent when it came to industry interest crossover, and also because, indeed, she had *sort of* had a certain set of song lyrics in her head when she'd driven across state lines.

Lucky for him it was more "Before He Cheats" and less "Two Black Cadillacs."

The article had actually made that point.

But because of that there had been no shielding the girls from the truth. She could have handled herself better, though she had a feeling there would have been some news about it anyway since Daniel was a minor—very minor—celebrity who both rode rodeo and had done some reality TV, so the breakup would never have stayed entirely between them.

"I'm glad you like it," Boone said.

He walked up the steps and pushed open the door and revealed a house that was immaculately put together. Everything in it was new. And she had to wonder if it had been furnished like this when he bought the place or...

She decided to stop wondering.

And just enjoy the experience.

Tomorrow she was going to get the girls off to school,

and she was going to start work. She would give herself four weeks of this. Of taking Boone's help, and then she was going to need a plan. A real plan.

She was resourceful, and she was a hard worker, so she knew she would be able to come up with something. But it was hard to do when you also had deep wounds that needed a little healing.

And also had to be an adult and a mother when you just wanted to keep on being subject to the whims of your emotions. Being that woman, the one with the baseball bat, had been easier than being this woman. The one making plans and trying to hold it together.

But that was what she needed to do; it was who she needed to be.

For her girls if nothing else.

"I'll leave you to get settled," he said. "If you need anything, just give me a holler."

And then he put their things down and left them, shut in the little house that felt somehow indescribably safe, secure and...wonderful.

Like shelter from a storm she hadn't realized she'd been in.

Right now, she could rest.

Even cleaning his house for a few weeks would feel like rest.

And then she would have to figure out what to do with her life.

But until then, she was going to take the shelter he was offering. Since the man she'd made vows to had kicked her out into the elements.

So why not have this? Even just for a time.

"Why don't we get our things put away and then explore town?" she asked.

She knew Lone Rock was small, and the exploration wouldn't take long, but they needed to find some food, and a distraction would be good for everyone.

Her daughters smiled at her a little too bravely, and right then she hated Daniel. Because he'd done this to them.

"Great," she said. "This will be great."

"You did *what*?"

"I gave her a place to stay," said Boone, looking down the bar at his brother Jace, who was staring at him incredulously. His sister-in-law Cara leaned over the bar and stared at him as if she was waiting for more details.

"What, Cara?" he asked. "There's nothing to say."

"I don't believe that," she said. "The whole breakup was headline news, and he's your best friend."

"He is *not* my best friend," said Boone. "I *was* friends with him. More importantly, I was friends with the man I *thought* he was. But I didn't think he was out there betraying his wife every week out on the road."

"You really didn't know?" Chance, his other brother, who was seated next to his wife, Juniper, asked.

"No," he said.

And he left off the part about how he'd never *wanted* to know because it wasn't simple and never could be.

"Sounds unlikely," said Shelby, his other sister-in-law, from beside her husband.

Shelby and Kit had recently had a baby, but Boone's mother was always so happy to babysit that the happy couple could go out whenever they wanted. And were practically forced out by the well-meaning grandma even when they didn't want to go.

All his siblings—except Buck, as far as he knew—were coupled up now. And the only couples *not* present were his younger sister Callie and her husband, Jake, who lived out of town, and his brother Flint and his wife, Tansey, who was a famous country singer currently on tour. Flint was with her.

Talk about revenge songs, Tansey had written a hell of a song about her and Flint's first go-round that had made him infamous. Flint would probably have measured words for the whole situation since he knew how the media could whip up personal issues.

But Flint wasn't here, so no one was being measured.

"Good for her, I say," Shelby said to her husband. "But I'd leave your truck intact and take it. Your dick on the other hand…"

"Same," said Juniper.

It served his brothers right for marrying sisters who were as pretty as they were badass. Boone loved them. He loved it even more when they gave his brothers hell. His brothers seemed to get something out of it too.

His brothers had all married pretty badass women.

Bar owner Cara was no shrinking violet. And Tansey, well she'd gotten rich with her revenge, and made his brother infamous in the process.

He thought of Wendy and how fragile she'd looked today. He'd wanted to tell her he'd done all that for her. The flowers, the new paint, the new furniture. He also hadn't wanted to say a damned thing because he didn't want her to think she owed him, and he didn't want her to thank him for something a man ought to just do for her because she was there and breathing and *her*.

He didn't want to do anything to crack her open when she was working so hard at holding it all together.

She was badass too. Hell yeah, she was.

She'd smashed the hell out of Daniel's truck.

But she was also wounded. And she needed to be taken care of.

He couldn't say he'd ever had experience with that, but if he was going to push the boat out on caregiving it was going to be now and it was going to be her.

"Did it really go down like they said?" Jace asked.

"It did," he confirmed. "But if you see her around, don't ask her about it."

Cara snorted. "We aren't feral."

Jace gave her a long look. "Well…"

"Okay, but we do know how to behave and not hurt people's feelings," Cara said.

"I know," Boone said. "But she's not going to be here forever. I'll talk to her more tomorrow about her plans."

Because if there was one thing Boone was certain of, it was that no matter how much he might want it to be, this couldn't be forever.

He might love her. He did love her.

But she was still married, and he didn't have the first clue how to…

He'd never had a real relationship, and there was no way this would ever be what she needed.

She had kids.

He had a ranch, which was a step into adulthood, but he didn't know how to do feelings and all that. It was one thing to carry a torch for a woman he couldn't have.

He was good with not having her.

One thing he wouldn't do was leave her uncared for.

He would make sure everything in her life was set to go just as she needed it to be, and then he'd let her go, because it would be the kindest thing.

She didn't need another project.

He wouldn't be the cause of any more pain for her.

If he was certain of anything in this world, it was that.

"She's with you?"

He regretted answering his phone as he walked out of the bar.

"Yes," said Boone. "And if I see you, I'll run you right off my property."

"What the hell, Boone? I thought we were friends."

"And I thought you were a husband, but it turns out you're just a little boy who can't control his dick."

"Boone… I'm sorry, I have to get her back. I royally screwed this up. I can't live without her and the kids."

The change in tone did nothing to sway Boone. Because he just didn't care. He wondered if Wendy would, though. Daniel was the father of her kids and all that. Boone didn't have kids, and the thought didn't sway or soften him at all. But he figured that could be because it was a connection he didn't especially get.

It maybe wasn't up to him to decide that Daniel should never speak to Wendy again. But he wasn't going to facilitate it, that was for damned sure.

"You should have thought of that before you cheated. Extensively, from what I understand."

"It was separate to me," he said. "I never thought of it interfering with what we had as long as she never knew. When I was home, I was always with her."

And I'm with her every time I'm with anyone.

I'm with her when I'm home. When I'm on the road.

Always.

He didn't say any of that. But he wanted to jump through the phone and strangle Daniel.

"She deserves better than you," Boone said, his voice rough.

"What? She deserves you?"

And that cut him deep because right then he knew Daniel wasn't as oblivious as he pretended to be. He only played like it when it suited him.

But of course he couldn't be as dumb as he played. He was a pretty big success and that didn't come on accident.

"No," Boone said. "But she does deserve someone who's honest with her."

"Is that why you brought her out to your place? Have you been screwing my wife, Boone?"

"When the hell would your wife have time to screw around on you, Daniel? She's busy raising your kids and holding your life together. Say what you want about me, slander me all you want, but don't project your bullshit onto her."

Boone hung up then.

He shouldn't have, maybe.

Because if Daniel was going to make up a story about him and Wendy it would probably only be reinforced by him hanging up like that.

But he just didn't care to speak to that asshole for another second.

He couldn't bear it.

Instead, he drove home, and when the phone rang again, he ignored it.

Chapter Three

The alarm went off too early and Wendy wondered at the wisdom of making the girls start school right away. Or at all.

If they were only going to be here a month...

But maybe they'd stay in Lone Rock for longer. Or maybe not. But it would be normal for them to have a school day and ultimately, that was what she wanted. For them to have something that felt normal.

She couldn't promise them a long time here, or forever or anything close to that, but she could give them something that felt like childhood.

She'd discovered last night that the fridge was fully stocked, and she wondered who had done all this. Boone? It didn't seem likely since he'd said he needed a house cleaner and had acted like he couldn't perform basic tasks without help because he was so slammed with setting up the new ranch.

Maybe one of his sisters-in-law had helped.

She'd have to thank someone for it. For the miracle of waking up to having coffee in the house and having bacon and eggs to fix the girls.

And she really didn't count on Boone showing up right when they were about to walk out the door.

"I thought, if you'd like, I could drive you because I know the way to both schools."

And she could have figured it out with GPS, she knew, but she very dangerously wanted to take this easier option.

Couldn't she? For just right now?

"Okay, if…if the girls don't mind."

"Sure," said Sadie, casually.

Because why would she care? This was definitely Wendy's issue, not her kids'.

"Yeah," Mikey said, reinforcing that thought.

The girls climbed into the back seats of the crew cab pickup, and Wendy got into the passenger seat. Suddenly, when he closed the door, the cab felt tiny, and she tried to remember if she'd ever been in such close proximity to Boone before.

She hadn't. She'd remember.

She did remember being at Juniper and Chance's wedding, because Daniel knew Chance from the rodeo and they'd been invited, and it had an open bar, he'd joked. She'd been sure then that he really wanted to support his friend's love and happiness. Now she thought it might have really been about the bar.

She remembered Daniel being out drinking and being alone at the big wedding reception.

She remembered looking up and seeing Boone. Looking at her.

Not just looking at her, though, it had been something hotter. Something deeper.

It had stolen her breath and made it impossible to breathe.

It had made her feel…

She had to stop thinking about that now.

She had to.

She kept her eyes fixed on the two-lane road and tried not to let the silence in the truck swallow her whole.

"Well, if you need anything or you need me to come get you, you can text me," she said, addressing both her daughters with an edgy desperation because she needed something to take over her awkwardness, even if it was a random comment she hadn't needed to make.

"Thanks, Mom. I'm sure we'll be fine," said Sadie.

"Or we won't be," Mikey said. "And it will either be a story of great triumph of the human spirit, or our villain origin story."

"I think we know which one it would be for you, Mikey," Boone said.

"Villain, for sure," Mikey said, happily.

The middle school came first.

As they drove away after Mikey got out, Wendy was struck by a feeling of loss and a sense of weird wrongness. She always felt that after summer break, and apparently a new school did that to her too. This weird feeling that she was leaving her kids with strangers. They weren't strangers. She'd had video meetings with the teachers before they'd come here, and the kids had had a chance to meet them too. But it didn't make it feel less weird.

She had the same feeling after dropping Sadie off.

But it was replaced instantly by the electric shock of realizing she was alone with Boone.

Alone with Boone, without her wedding rings. Without her kids.

Without anything keeping her from…

"So, what do you need done today?" she asked, because filling the horrible silence with words, any words, was all she knew to do.

"Oh, I'm easy," he said, slow and lazy and she felt it between her legs.

What was wrong with her?

Was this a trauma response to discovering her husband was a ho?

She would be able to write it off as that much more easily if Boone wasn't a preexisting condition.

Something that made her feel, deep down, like maybe she'd deserved for Daniel to betray her.

The thought made her feel like she'd been stabbed.

She hadn't realized she'd been holding on to that feeling. But she had been. Deep down.

She'd been attracted to Boone for years, and she'd done her best to avoid him. Not that avoidance had done anything to make the feelings go away.

She'd done her best to keep it hidden.

Maybe Daniel had known, though, that part of her had always been tangled up in Boone.

She needed to stop thinking about that.

Why did you come to him, then? Knowing it was this complicated, why did you choose this?

Because he'd offered.

That was all.

It was never all. It was never that simple with him.

She took a sharp breath. "I just want to make sure that I'm paying you back, because you're being so kind to me and..."

Tears welled up in her eyes and she hated that. Now she was crying? What was happening to her?

Why couldn't she just take what he'd offered, which had been work. And she'd been grateful he'd done it that way because if he'd just given her a place to stay it would have felt loaded, and like charity she couldn't afford to take, and he hadn't done that because he'd known. She knew he had known. That she couldn't take his charity, that she had to earn this fresh start.

That she couldn't feel like she owed him.

So why was she now falling into crying like it was a favor? Like it was personal.

They were both trying so hard to not make it that and now she'd gone and made it very, very weird, and she couldn't stop her throat from tightening, couldn't stop a tear from falling.

She hadn't cried.

Not once.

She'd gone from rage to determination and she didn't want to weep now. But it was the kindness of it all.

From a man she'd love to call just another rodeo cowboy.

A man she'd love to lump in with her husband.

But she just couldn't do that.

"I need to know what you want," she said, trying to get a handle on her emotions. Her breath. Everything. "Because you offered me work, and I do know how to keep house. Do you need a meal? Do you need something organized?"

"I just moved in, and there are a lot of things yet to unpack."

But the little cottage was perfectly set up.

"I can do that if you don't mind me deciding where things go."

"As long as you tell me where they end up, I don't mind."

"Okay, so what do you like to eat?"

"If you want to make me dinner I won't complain but do something you and the girls like and just make an extra portion."

She almost wished he was being high-handed. So she could get ahold of herself.

The kindness was almost too much.

You really can't be pleased.

Well, maybe in her position that was fair?

They pulled up to the house, and she realized she hadn't been conscious of where they were at all.

He killed the engine, but didn't get out of the car, and she did something foolish. Very foolish.

She turned her head and looked at him.

And it was like all the space around them became less. Like it contracted and sank beneath her skin. Shrinking around her lungs, her heart, her stomach. She couldn't breathe. She couldn't think.

She could only see Boone.

His blue eyes.

That moment at his brother's wedding when they'd seen each other across the room was suddenly alive again in her memory. Because they'd seen each other that night. They hadn't simply looked at each other for a moment across a crowded space.

The two things were different.

They were so different.

She hadn't truly realized it until now.

She tried to breathe, but she couldn't. Because everything in her was too tight. Too bound up in him.

Bound up in him…

And that did it. Like scissors cutting a string. Everything in her released.

Because she'd thought about being tied up in someone just recently.

It was the very way she'd thought about her relationship with Daniel.

She hadn't left to get tied up again.

She couldn't afford that, not ever.

She found herself practically dumping herself out of his truck, her boots connecting with the dirt and sending a cloud of dust up around her.

"I'll go get changed and then start work," she said, trying to sound bright, and like nothing had happened.

"Okay," he said. "Do you need me to show you the lay of things?"

"No. No you go ahead and get started on your day." She didn't want to wander around the house with him.

She wished she could pretend.

She wished she could pretend that her strange moments of attraction were indigestion. Or at the very least that they were infrequent, or one-sided.

But if she'd ever been able to trick herself into thinking her attraction to Boone wasn't mutual, he'd destroyed that with a glance the night of his brother's wedding.

Because that moment had contained so much deep truth, she'd had to turn away from it.

Because that moment had been filled with an acknowledgment they'd both spent fifteen years turning away from.

They'd been two seconds of prolonged eye contact away from admitting it, for all those years. Never speaking of it wasn't enough. Because their eyes were determined to give them away.

Then the hitch in their breath.

And Boone…

She remembered him looking like the big bad wolf and the savior of the universe all at once. She'd wanted him to take a step toward her, and she'd wanted him to turn away. She'd wanted him to come for her, and she'd wanted to pretend she'd never even met him.

He'd taken a step.

And she'd taken one back.

And he'd stopped.

He'd listened to her. To everything she couldn't say. To the single footstep that had been her begging him to stop. To not take them another step further because it would be too far to turn back, and she'd wanted—she'd needed—to be able to turn back.

Just like she'd needed to jump out of the truck now, and he'd let her. She appreciated that.

The way he listened, even when she didn't speak.

"I'll just… I'll just go change," she said again. "And then I'll get started."

His face was like granite. Like at the wedding. "Okay. See you later."

She couldn't have made it any clearer that she didn't want him in her space today. She also couldn't have made it any clearer that she was attracted to him.

Attracted was a crucial descriptor. Because it was different from wanting.

He wanted her.

He wanted to take her into his arms and kiss her. He wanted to take her to his room and strip her naked and have his way with her.

He wanted her.

Like breathing.

More of a need than anything else.

She was attracted to him, and she did not want it. Not at all.

And he…well, he knew his place here. He was helping her. He cared about her, dammit all. And he was far too familiar with the fallout that happened when people didn't fulfill their obligations to the ones they were supposed to love.

She'd trusted Daniel and he'd betrayed that trust. Boone would never do that. He would never put her in a position where she felt obligated to him.

That wasn't why he was helping her.

He never shirked his responsibilities. Not ever.

He didn't leave people to fend for themselves.

That might be his oldest brother's way, it might be Daniel's way. But it would never be Boone's.

Some people might live in a fantasy world, and others lived with their heads up their asses. Not Boone. He was a realist, and he handled things. He didn't need to lie to himself or anyone else to get through life.

He'd been like that once. Someone who couldn't face the hard truths. It caused more harm than good, that was for sure.

He thought about that, a whole lot. The lines between attraction, desire, want, need and feelings. Obligation. All while he worked. Mostly he thought about her. Because she was in that house behind his, and it was the kind of proximity he'd wanted with her for a long time.

His phone buzzed in his pocket.

He pulled it out and saw Daniel's name again. "What?" he growled.

"Can you just ask her what I can do?"

"If she isn't answering your calls then there's not shit I can do for you."

"We went through hell together, Boone. Who was there for you when you were crying drunk over your brother taking off, huh? When you were the one who had to deal with your mama's broken heart because her firstborn ran off, after all the pain she went through losing her baby girl..."

"Don't talk about my family," he said. "Yeah, you were there for me when Buck ran off, I'll give you that. You were there when I was feeling squeezed by the family obligation he left for me, but here's what you're missing, Dan. Buck and I will never have a relationship again because he had a duty to this family, and he chose himself instead. I don't like it when people misuse and mistreat people in their lives. When they fall down on their obligations. I can't respect weak men, and if you don't live up to your responsibilities, you're a weak man." He breathed out, hard, and his breath was visible in the early evening air. "You're a weak man, Daniel Stevens."

Then he hung up, because honestly.

He got into his truck and drove back toward the house. It had been a long day of chasing up permits at the county, making arrangements with contractors and going over the sections of land he could use for grazing, what he could irrigate and a host of other things.

Setting up the ranch wasn't going to be easy. But until his dad retired...

Well, he supposed he'd be taking over as rodeo commissioner in a few years. And he had to do something until then. Maybe after that he'd do what his dad had always done and hire out workers.

Buck had been the one who was supposed to do all this.

But Buck was gone.

Boone knew his brother had been through some shit, he did. But it was no excuse. At least not in his mind.

Even if you were going through something, you should be there for the people in your life. Your responsibilities didn't just...go away.

He'd told his brother that, the night before his brother had split town for good. Buck had been drinking, far too much. Like alcohol would erase the accident he'd been in. Like it might take away the horror of that night.

And Boone had snapped.

"You have a family, and you aren't dead. Stop acting like you're six feet in the ground with your friends. You aren't."

"It should have..."

"It wasn't! You're alive. Have some gratitude and get back to it. You have responsibilities."

And then he'd gone.

Boone had felt guilty about his brother leaving until he'd realized guilt was a waste of time. Time he didn't have to waste. It had been Buck's choice to leave. It was Boone's choice to deal with it.

There was no use getting lost in what-ifs.

Boone knew, from the outside looking in, people would probably think of him as a guy who didn't take much seriously.

They saw a cocky bull rider who could have a different buckle bunny every night when he was in the mood for that. They didn't see he was the one who held his mom while she wept on difficult anniversaries.

He was the one who took the brunt of their father's expectations onto his shoulders as the de facto oldest in the absence of the eldest son who had gone off to lick his wounds. A car accident the year Buck graduated high school had resulted in the loss of three of his friends, with Buck as the sole survivor.

It wasn't that Boone didn't get why that had fucked him up.

It was just…

They were all a little messed up. They'd watched their baby sister die when they were kids. So why not band together? Why not try to support each other?

That was what he'd never understood.

They'd been a support system, the Carson Clan, and never as close or as stable once Buck had taken his support away.

But his issues weren't the order of the day.

Today Boone wanted to make sure that Wendy was doing all right.

He pulled up to the front of the house and he smiled, just a little bit, when he saw the lights on in the kitchen. He wondered what it would be like to come home to her, and then he pushed that aside because it was a pointless little fantasy, and if he was going to have a fantasy it was going to be a big, dirty one, not a little domestic one about her in an apron holding a casserole pan.

Except he wouldn't even let himself have a dirty fantasy about her, not right now. She was too vulnerable, and he wasn't that guy. Not when her husband had proven to be such a horndog.

He wouldn't even go there in his head.

He walked up the front steps and into the warmth. This was his house. His home. He hadn't had one before, not really. It had been a place on his parents' property, and places on the road all these years, and it was all fine and good, but there was something surreal about walking into something permanent.

Nothing is permanent, Boone.

Yeah, he knew that. Not relationships with older brothers, or little sisters, or anything.

You couldn't trust a damned thing.

But when he walked in his house it smelled like heaven. And his kitchen was empty.

There was a plate sitting on the counter with foil over the

top, and he assumed she'd done the cooking here, but took the rest back to her place and then vacated before his return which…was about right.

Attracted. Not wanting.

He lifted the corner of the tin foil and his stomach growled when the smell of roast and vegetables hit him.

Wendy might not be here, but a home-cooked meal was a close second. And when it made his mouth water, he could have it. So, there was that.

He opened the drawer in the kitchen island and took out a fork, and hunched over the counter, taking bites of food. And then there was a knock at the door.

His stomach went tight, and his heart did something he couldn't recall it doing before except when he was about to ride a bull in competition. "It's open," he said, around a piece of roast, and without moving from his spot.

"I didn't know if you'd be here yet or not."

Wendy. And she was lying. Because she'd probably seen him come in and that was why she was here. Because she'd wanted to avoid him. Except she didn't really.

He could relate.

She came into the kitchen, and she was holding a plate with something on it, but he couldn't look away from her for long enough to take in what it was. She was wearing pink. The same shade as the dress she'd had on at the wedding.

Her blond hair was in a ponytail, and she had on just a little makeup. Her cheeks were the same color as her dress, and so were her lips. Like a strawberry fantasy just for him.

Even though she wasn't for him.

There was something about it that made him want her more, and he had to wonder if that was just his body pushing back at years of being good.

Very few people would characterize Boone Carson as good. He understood that and he understood why.

Again, it was the bull riding, drinking, carousing, and on and on. But they didn't see all the shit he did *not* do. Like turn away from hardship in his family. Like running away. Like kissing his best friend's wife at his brother's wedding.

He deserved a damned Boy Scout patch.

Did Not Fuck My Friend's Wife.

Also knot tying.

He was good at knot tying.

He didn't get credit for the things he deserved to.

"I baked a cake over at the cottage while the girls and I had dinner, so I figured I'd bring you some."

Oh. Cake. That's what it was. He could see it now, even if it was fuzzy at the edges because he'd rather look at her hands holding the platter than at what was on it. But she'd made it, so he would eat it.

"Are you really eating standing hunched over a counter like a rabid wolf?"

"I don't think rabid wolves eat pot roast, I think they eat pretty women carrying cake."

He shouldn't flirt with her. But her cheeks turned pinker. So he considered that a win.

"Maybe just a regular wolf, then."

He grinned, making sure to flash his teeth. "Hard to say."

"You should sit down. There are studies on how you shouldn't eat standing up."

"Are there?"

"I'm pretty sure. It's something I'd say to my kids, anyway."

"Oh, well, then, I guess I'll consider myself chastened."

She glared at him. "I don't think you are."

"No. You need shame to feel chastened, I think."

"And you don't have any shame?"

He made sure to grin even wider. "None whatsoever."

If only that were true.

If only he didn't care so damned much about doing the

right thing, and at this point it had nothing at all to do with Daniel. It was about her.

And that was immovable, as far as he was concerned.

"I really..." She closed her eyes for a moment, and he looked at how her lashes fanned out over her high cheekbones and felt a bit like his heart had lifted to the base of his throat, and his lungs right along with it. "I appreciate you doing this," she said, opening her eyes, letting out a breath.

It was like she released his breath along with it.

Then she walked over to the kitchen island and set the cake plate on it. There was nothing more than a slim length of counter between them now.

She put her hands on the counter and examined them.

He did too.

Her hands, not his.

"Why wouldn't I?"

"Daniel has been your friend for longer than you've known me," she said. "You didn't take his side."

"There's no side here," he said. "To be very clear, I was done with him the minute I...that night, before you got there, he kissed another woman. I had never seen that before, I swear to you. And I looked the other way, I'll admit that. There were things I didn't want to know, because..." This was dangerous ground. They both knew it. "You know why."

"Do I?" she asked.

The words were too loud in the silent kitchen, even though they were practically a whisper.

"Yes," he said. "You do."

He cleared his throat. And took another bite of roast. Then he looked at her again. "I tried to keep myself out of your marriage. But I wouldn't have after I saw that, okay? I want you to understand. I was outright done with him the minute I knew he wasn't faithful to you. I told him so today."

"You...talked to him?" Her blue eyes went round.

"Yeah. He called. He wants you back."

She laughed. "Of course he does. I cook, clean and manage his career. I am an idiot who devoted years of my life to him and gave him two kids and asked for very little and when he wasn't with me, he was able to pretend I didn't exist. Who wouldn't want that woman back?"

She shook her head. "I'm not going to be her anymore."

He didn't have any place in this. Didn't have the right to lecture her, but he was going to do it anyway.

"Don't blame yourself. I didn't see it either. Like I said, I had some suspicions I shouldn't hang around and watch to see what he did with his evenings, but that's different than actually believing someone is a serial cheater. It's about him, and what he thinks about the people around him. How much he values them. Not how much value they have."

"Thank you, Boone," she said, though she didn't look at him when she said his name.

How many times had they circled each other like this?

There were so many moments over the years.

So many barbecues where they talked with a table between them and very little eye contact. So many rodeo events where Daniel would leave to get a drink and they'd be standing there, and it was like electricity. But the thing was, they'd never moved toward it.

They both knew it was there.

And that was the most unfair thing of all.

Daniel was the kind of guy who'd hump a table leg. He strayed just because he could.

Boone wanted Wendy in a way that went beyond anything normal, average or everyday. What he felt for her had been instant. It had been ruinous.

It had destroyed something in him he'd never built back up.

Desire like that wasn't common. It wasn't typical.

And the man standing in their way, the man who was still

in their way because of the position he'd put Wendy in…didn't deserve the label of roadblock because he wasn't important enough. Because she hadn't meant enough to him.

What they'd resisted for the sake of responsibility was something you could write a song about.

And Daniel didn't resist a damned thing.

But even without any loyalty left to him, Wendy was facing starting over, with her girls. She was in Boone's care, and Boone would never take advantage of that.

"You're welcome. I promise when I eat the cake I'll sit down."

She did look at him then. "Good."

He started to move around the side of the island, he didn't even think about it, but then he watched her eyes get round, watched her posture go stiff, and he stopped.

If he got too close to her…

"Good night," he said, firmly.

"Good night."

Attraction wasn't the same as wanting.

He had to remember that.

Chapter Four

She felt breathless still the next morning, and all the way through taking the girls to school, and definitely when she walked cautiously into Boone's house to begin the day's chores.

There was quite a bit to do because the man wasn't settled into his house at all. There were boxes to unpack and things to organize and it was nice to lose herself in the satisfaction of a small task, easily completed in a short amount of time. Each little section—kitchen utensils, plates, cups, clothes, toiletries—was its own kind of satisfying.

It was also intimate, though, and she had to stop herself from running her fingers slowly over his T-shirts as she put them away.

Which was perverse behavior and she needed to quit.

She needed to focus on the fact that at least today, right now, there were small things she could make better.

Because Lord knew everything else felt like too big of a mess to even look at right now. So she closed the door on what she'd left behind, and what was up ahead, and she focused on folding Boone Carson's laundry.

That should demystify him.

He was the sexiest man she'd ever seen, and when he'd looked at her last night across the kitchen island and taken a step toward her, in the space of a breath she'd gone from being in that moment, to imagining what it would be like if he took her in his arms and…

Folding his socks should make that go away.

It was all fine and good to look at a man and think he was a sex god when you weren't handling his woolen boot socks.

Though here she was, socks in hand, still breathless.

This should be exposure therapy. She and Boone had had no choice but to try and avoid each other through the years. There were moments where she'd felt guilty for sharing a long look with him, because sometimes those looks were so sexually charged, they left her feeling more aroused than actual sex with Daniel.

It was a terrible thing to admit—or at least it had been.

And so she'd done her best to avoid ever acknowledging that sticky truth.

Part of her had wondered, though, if some of his appeal was that he was a fantasy. Daniel had always seemed affable and easy. She'd never thought of her husband as a bad boy—ironic—but Boone had seemed…edgy.

Raw.

There was something about him that called to unhealed places in her. To darkness she'd never felt like she could express with Daniel. He wanted his life to be easy. They had money and security in the grand scheme of things, so he didn't much want to hear about the way hunger pangs sometimes gave her flashbacks to a childhood of occasionally empty pantries.

How she'd had to mend the holes in her hand-me-down clothes.

How she'd spent her summer days alone in an overheated house because her mom had to work and there was nowhere else for her to go.

How, on those long hot days, she'd gotten good at hiding when the landlord came trying to chase down rent.

Daniel didn't like to hear about those things. They didn't matter. They were in the past.

She'd thought—more than once—that Daniel couldn't handle the idea that there were issues inside her that weren't solved by being married to him. He wanted to be everything to her. To have fixed everything.

It had never really occurred to her what narcissistic nonsense that was until that very moment, with Boone's wool socks in her hand.

She thought of Boone. The way he had looked last night. Intense and close. He was always intense. But there was usually something between them. Something other than a countertop. Her marriage. Her dedication to her vows. Her love for her husband. Because for all that she had wanted Boone from the first moment she had laid eyes on him, for all that it had felt significant and real and like something bigger than she was the first time she'd seen him, she had always loved Daniel.

She sat there, feeling the silence of the room pressing on her. Did she love Daniel?

No.

And it wasn't the infidelity that had done it.

Suddenly, it was like the truth was raining down on her, as if invisible clouds above had opened up and let it all come down.

They had been disconnected for a long time. She loved her life. She had loved their house in Bakersfield, even though it was hot there. Even though there was a big empty field across from them.

She had loved her routine of taking the girls to school. Of bringing them home. Cooking them dinner. She loved the freedom she had, the financial security that had come from his career as a bull rider and the way she had managed it. She had loved that her daughters didn't have empty pantries and long days at home by themselves. In that sense, she had been the happiest she'd ever been. But she didn't think she had been the happiest she'd ever been when he was home. It wasn't that she'd been unhappy when he was around, she just didn't think he was the main part of that happiness.

When he was away she could do whatever she wanted. She got to binge-watch TV shows and wear ratty pajamas. She had ice cream out of the carton and she took up the middle of the bed.

She was content with her fantasy life when he was away, and she didn't mind being by herself.

And none of those things were signs in and of themselves that she didn't love her husband. It was only that she could be a little bit more honest in this moment than she'd been able to in those first couple of days. She wasn't heartbroken. She had felt deeply wounded by the fact that she had lost her life. That she had lost these things she cared about so deeply. That her life had been compromised and shaken.

That she was thrown back into the space where she didn't know how she was going to survive. And she had never wanted her daughters to experience that.

She had never wanted them to feel any instability, and she was the most upset about that. And being betrayed. That had been a knife wound straight to her chest. That had been unconscionable. She really and truly hated it. She didn't like that she had been lying next to a man, making love to a man, telling a man she loved him, while he was able to take those hands, that mouth, that body and make love to another woman.

She would never have cheated on him. Not ever. She would've coasted along in this marriage that functioned primarily because…

Even though she had never betrayed him, she was in many ways functioning as a single woman when he was gone. And she had a feeling that was part of why their marriage had worked as well as it had.

He pretended she didn't exist when he was away, and she sort of did the same to him.

That didn't make her feel guilty, it just made her recognize that some fundamental things were missing from her marriage. And maybe that was why Boone had loomed so large in her fantasies.

She had done her best—her very best—to never fantasize about Boone.

She was *attracted* to him. But she didn't lie in bed when Daniel was away and think about Boone intentionally when she lay there and put her hands on her own body while imagining they were his.

Now sometimes he popped into her head, and she replaced him with Captain America because it was totally fine to fantasize about a man you weren't married to, but he really should be a man you also didn't know in real life. At least, that had been her arbitrary set of rules.

Every woman needed an arbitrary set of rules.

She did not need to follow those rules now.

Daniel had rendered them void.

That made her feel hot. She shifted, and she put Boone's socks down a little bit too quickly. Yes, she could fantasize about Boone now if she wanted to.

She didn't love her husband.

Suddenly, she felt dizzy. She didn't know if she was elated or if she was crushed by that realization. But she had been living a life she hadn't intended to find herself in. Daniel's betrayal was not the biggest issue with her marriage.

The problem was, they had met and they had fallen in love quickly. And Wendy had always been guarded. But he had gotten through her defenses with his charm. She hadn't been one for casual sex. She'd been waiting, and not because of any great moral reason, but because she was afraid.

He had gotten past all of that, and when he had asked her to marry him two months into their affair, she'd said yes. She didn't have anything else. Her mother had passed away the previous year, and she'd just felt so alone. So being with some-one... To make a family, she had loved that.

And she had to wonder how much of it had always been loving that. Loving that she had someone. Someone she was attracted to, someone she genuinely liked—most of the time—but perhaps someone she had never actually been head over heels in love with.

She didn't want him back. She wanted the stability back. She wanted to be comfortable. But...

But if she were being perfectly honest with herself, she was thinking about more than comfort. That moment with Boone in the kitchen last night had been so electrically charged. And the way he had responded to it was... It was unlike anything else she had ever experienced.

Because he had been watching her. And more than that, he had seen her. He had responded to the way she had stiffened up, the way she had resisted.

And it was only because she knew if he had gotten any closer she would've kissed him. And more than that, she knew the minute she and Boone touched it was never going to stop at a simple meeting of mouths. Their clothes would be off in-stantly, and...

That terrified her. Because she was trying to start over, and she was trying to find something new. Because once she had imagined herself in love with a man because she had been at a crossroads in her life, because she had been afraid and inse-cure. Because she had thought it would be preferable to grab hold of the first man she slept with rather than be by herself.

And she didn't want to go from one relationship straight into another.

It doesn't have to be a relationship...

Now she really was being an idiot. She had to stop think-ing about that. She had to.

She picked the socks back up and started folding again,

and then she heard a sound downstairs. She stood up from the bed, the socks still clutched in her hand, and went down the hall, looking over the rail of the staircase down to the front door below.

Boone was in the doorway. He looked up at her, a cowboy hat placed firmly on his head. And right now, at this point in her life, the sight of a cowboy certainly shouldn't make her tremble.

"Hi," she said.

"Hi, yourself."

"What are you doing here?"

"I decided to come back for lunch today."

"Oh. Let me… I'll make something for you."

"You don't have to do that."

"I'm not taking charity from you," she said.

"I didn't ask you to."

"All I'm doing is very slowly folding your laundry," she said, holding up his socks.

"All right. Well, I hate to interrupt the very serious business of sock folding. But if you really want to make me a sandwich…"

"I really do."

She went down the stairs, and every step she took closer to him made her heart start to beat just a little harder.

Damn that man.

And damn her for being so…thrilled by it. She felt like a teenager. The kind of teenager she had never been. Because she had never indulged in flirtations, and she had certainly never experienced that wild, reckless feeling she heard people describe when they were in situations where no one was there to stop them from doing something stupid.

She felt it now. There was nothing to stop her from closing the space between them and wrapping her arms around his neck. There was nothing to stop her from touching him.

Nothing. Except for good sense. And the fact that there was no way she could carry on a physical-only affair under the watchful eyes of her far-too-perceptive daughters.

And there was no way she was going to put them through something like that when their lives had just been upended.

So yeah. Nothing stopping her.

It made her want to laugh.

She had behaved for her mother, of course, who had been deeply afraid of her becoming a single mom and struggling the way she had.

And now she had to behave herself for her daughters. Caught in between a mother-daughter relationship always, she supposed.

It can be a secret.

No. They would figure it out. That was just asking for the kind of sitcom hijinks she did not want to be embroiled in anymore. She'd reached her limit. Dirty pictures being texted to her of her husband's affair, and her busting out his headlights, were either a police procedural or high comedy, depending on how you looked at it, and she wanted no part of either.

"What's for dinner tonight?" he asked.

"Spaghetti," she answered.

He grinned, and she felt like he'd touched her.

She looked away and beat a wide path around him to the kitchen.

"I could get used to this," he said.

"I probably shouldn't stay more than a month," she said, reiterating what she'd told him before. On the phone. Before she had agreed to come.

"The cottage is awfully nice, and it's there for you as long as you want. Don't feel the need to move on quickly."

"I don't think I can stay for too long. I don't want to get… dependent."

"Is that really why?"

"That is the only reason we should discuss."

He nodded slowly. And she could see he was holding back. It was a strange thing to say. Because Boone was strong, and he was fearless. Because she'd watched him ride in the rodeo before, and he wasn't a man who ever hesitated. But there he was, holding back. And she knew it wasn't because of him. It was because of her.

Because he cared about how what he might say affected her.

And that touched her deeper than just about anything. Because she'd been married to a man who hadn't given a second thought to how his actions would affect her.

To what she felt, to what she cared about.

Boone cared.

"There's not a *should* anymore," she said.

Except there were. So many. And they both knew it.

"What's that code for?"

"Say what you're thinking."

"Be very sure," he said.

"I'm sure."

"You don't want to stay because you're afraid of what will happen between us."

She felt like a layer of her skin had been peeled away, but she nodded slowly. "Maybe."

"I don't think there's any maybe about it. It's been two days, Wendy. Two days and I swear to God if I come too close to you…"

"I know." She was suddenly desperate for him to stop talking. And she realized now why he held back.

"I won't, though, is the thing. I need you to know that. I recognize that what he did to you is going to have you messed up for a while. I don't want to be part of that. I don't want to be part of this… Hurting you. I don't especially want to have anything to do with him. You understand that?"

"Yes," she said.

"I would never do anything to take advantage of you right now. Or ever."

His words were raw. And the most real thing she had heard in so long. After so much bullshit.

"I appreciate that."

It was such a weak statement. And it didn't tell the whole truth. Or even part of it. *Appreciate* wasn't the right word for him. It never could be. It was much, much too insipid.

She felt torn apart looking at him. And mostly, it was regret. Regret that she couldn't afford to feel. Because she had the life she had. And the truth was, without Daniel in it, it was so good. She had Sadie, and Mikey, and they were wonderful. She would figure out what to do, and it wouldn't always be a struggle. She had confidence in herself now, confidence she didn't have when she'd been younger, and it hadn't been given to her by Daniel, so it couldn't be taken away by him.

She couldn't regret those things. And yet, she looked back on that moment when she had first seen Boone, and she felt… pain. This deep wish that she could go back in time with two doors in front of her. Two men. That she could walk toward one and not the other. If only those moments had joined up. If only they had been side-by-side.

If only Daniel hadn't been first.

But then she might not have confidence because of him, but she had made the steps she'd made in life in part because of her relationship with him, and she could never take him away and expect that she could have been the same person she was now.

So regret was pointless. But appreciation wasn't the right word either.

Because Boone made her feel bruised. And swollen with need. All kinds of it. And she felt…tired. And where before that exhaustion had made her want to let Boone carry her bags, carry her burdens, now it made her want to let her guard down.

Because it just took so much strength to be near him and not get nearer. She hadn't realized how much strength it had taken all these years, but they were closer now. Closer than they'd ever allowed themselves to be, and that created a situation, or rather it exposed one she hadn't fully realized she'd been in.

She went to the fridge, and she got some mayonnaise. Some lunch meat. Then she got bread and tomatoes. And she began the very mundane work of making the man a sandwich. This was on the heels of having done the very mundane work of his laundry. She had none of the excitement with him. None of the electricity. And all of the chores.

And that should demystify him. It should make this feel as bland and dry as appreciation. As thanks for helping her out, and nothing more.

She got a knife out of the drawer and she began to spread mayonnaise on a piece of wheat bread. Truly, what could be more boring?

"I like a little mustard on that."

"Oh," she said.

She turned back to the fridge and opened it again, hunting around for the mustard.

"You said you wanted to make me a sandwich."

"I do."

"But you don't want me to tell you how I want a sandwich?"

"I didn't say that."

"But you're annoyed."

"I'm not annoyed."

Maybe she was. Maybe she had kind of wanted to intuitively guess exactly what he wanted on his sandwich. She blinked. That was a very odd thing to want. A strange thing to worry about.

"Listen," he said. "At the end of the day, I would probably like it however you wanted to make it. But if you want a little instruction…"

"Who says that I like to take instruction?"

"I'm sure you don't."

And here they were, standing in the man's kitchen in the middle of the day. The sunlight streaming in through the window. There was no sexy mysterious lighting. A broad shaft of light was going across his face. But it only made him look more handsome. He was the sort of man who could withstand being on a big screen with high-def. She was sure of it.

He didn't have a flaw in his features. He was perfect in every way.

And so even the broad light of day couldn't diminish it.

"Tell me, then. Tell me how you like it."

His smile shifted, turned wicked. And they might not be in a bedroom, but his eyes held the suggestion of it.

She took the mustard out of the fridge.

"Just make sure you've got a firm grip," he said.

"For God's sake, Boone."

"What? You wouldn't want to drop a bottle of mustard."

"I guess not."

"Give it a good squeeze."

"Boone," she said, not sure whether she wanted to laugh, or get irritated, or… If she was a little bit turned on. That was ridiculous.

"Just trying to help with best kitchen practices. You can lay it on a little thick."

She rolled her eyes because she decided faux irritation was better than melting into a puddle over this kind of thing.

She turned the bottle over and squeezed a generous helping onto the sandwich.

"Just like that, Wendy."

His voice was like silk, and the sensation it sent along her nerves was glorious.

"I don't need encouragement to make the sandwich."

"All right."

She got the tomato and sliced it, then laid it on along with some turkey. And then she handed him the sandwich with no ceremony. But when he took it from her, their fingertips brushed, and her breath was sucked straight from her lungs.

He looked at her. And he really looked. Saw her. Looked into her. He took a slow bite of the sandwich, and there was something about the way he did it, purposeful, and intense, that made the space between her thighs throb.

She shook her head and turned away from him.

"It's a good sandwich," he said.

"You're welcome," she said.

Doing housework for the man felt like sex. And that seemed unfair. Because it should defuse things. Everything. This reminder that he was normal. That he was a human. That he could never live up to whatever fantasy her body was convinced he would give. Because how could he? No man could. No man could live up to the ridiculous thing she had built up in her mind.

Or rather, tried not to build up.

"So you only want to stay here a month," he said.

"Yes. That was my thought."

"And what do you want to do after that?"

"I don't know."

He set his sandwich down on a paper towel on the counter. And then he grabbed hold of the loaf of bread and took two pieces out. "Do you like mustard, Wendy?"

"No," she said.

"Mayonnaise?"

"Yes."

"Okay."

And then, slowly and methodically, he began to make a sandwich. This one without mustard. And she could only stare at him because she didn't know why it made her want to cry. Because this was such a small thing. Because she was supposed to be working for him, and he was doing things for her, and she had made him a sandwich, and they could've easily made their own, but he was making one for her.

And it just seemed exceptional. Maybe it shouldn't. Maybe that was the biggest commentary on her marriage to Daniel so far.

That she wanted to weep as she watched strong, scarred masculine hands put turkey between two slices of bread.

He handed it to her, and she did her best to swallow the lump in her throat.

"Thank you."

"You're welcome."

She took a bite of the sandwich. "I don't know what I'm going to do," she said finally.

"But not this."

"No," she said. "Not this. My mother cleaned houses. It's a good job. It's a great job. I don't look down on anyone for any kind of work that they do."

"But you've been looked down on."

She nodded slowly. She felt exposed, and he could see that. Quite so easily.

"Yes. I have been. I grew up in a community where being the daughter of a cleaner made me a certain thing to other people. Mostly, the worst part about my mom's job was that sometimes the people she worked for tried not to pay her. And that would create gaps between paychecks. And she was never quite in a space where she could just walk away from that work, not while they were dangling money owed over her head. There was no protection. No rights. No power. It's the kind of thing you never forget. And I never wanted to be in that position. I never want my girls to be in that position. And here I am. We don't have a prenup or anything, and I know he's going to have to pay child support of some kind, but the truth is I earned so much of his money for him. Right now, I don't want it. I want to wash my hands of him and walk away. But I know that in the long run that isn't the best decision. I know it isn't going to serve me. It isn't going to serve my daughters, so it isn't the way I can treat this situation. But I want... I want to find myself. I want to *be* myself. Whatever that means."

"I know who you are," he said. "You're the woman that showed up with the baseball bat and smashed the hell out of that asshole's truck. Even though you could've gotten in trouble for it. Even though it destroyed a perfectly good vehicle. You've got a lot of passion. And you're right, you have a lot of what you have because of that passion. Because you got him all those deals, because you were so good at building him up. And what did he do with that? Tried to tear you down. If you need anger to motivate you, to kind of guide your way... why not use it?"

"Well, the problem is, I'm not all that angry right now. I'd like to be. But anger just implies a level of passion I'm not sure is there. I felt scorned. I felt tricked. And that made me mad. I felt disrupted. That made me mad. I'm not heartbroken, though."

Something in his eyes sharpened. "Really?"

"Really."

This was dangerous. She had tried to steer them back into something mundane. Tried to think about socks and turkey sandwiches, but he had gone and changed everything when he had made the sandwich for her.

Her husband had found it a turnoff for her to talk about her past. And yet here he was, listening to her, and he didn't seem turned off.

"No. Because I think that I love the life I had as a result of my marriage a lot more than I love my marriage. Or maybe seeing a picture of him quite literally sticking it in another woman did it for me. That could also be it."

"I'm sorry. It was a terrible thing."

"It was. But you know the truth… There have been very few moments in my marriage when I haven't wanted another man. You know that."

She was being so dangerous right now. So very dangerous. "And I might not have acted on it… But the truth remains… I was with Daniel and the whole time I wanted someone else."

"Yeah," he said, his voice suddenly gruff and strangled.

"I was poor," she said. "And I've been shaped by that. The way you saw me react to my divorce, it was all the anger that had built up inside me all those years. All that hunger. Because I know what it's like to have an empty pantry and I never wanted that for my girls. Because I didn't have a father growing up and I didn't want that for them either. So I clung to the shape of my life because it was the shape I wanted, even if the content was never quite what I had fantasized about it being. It didn't matter. I found a man, and I thought that was going to keep me safe, so I clung to it. And even though I know better, I've seen better—in all these years I've learned I don't need him to keep me safe, I don't need him to make me money—I was afraid that by walking away from the marriage I was walking away from security. And so, when he ripped it out from under me, I was furious. Because I felt like he was taking from me the one thing I cared about the most. My security. That was why I was so angry."

"As you should be," he said.

"Does it bother you? To think of me that way."

"In what way?"

"Does it bother you to know that the woman you met, the woman who was dressed nicely, who looks like she's never known a struggle, isn't real?"

"Why the hell would that bother me? You're strong. And I like that about you. I always have. Did you really think I was responding to a certain brand of cowgirl boots? Did you think I was responding to the rhinestones on your jeans? I don't give a shit about that. It's your backbone. There are a lot of beautiful women, Wendy, but I haven't spent fifteen years fantasizing about what it would be like to get them naked. It isn't just how pretty your eyes are, or the shape of your mouth, though I think it's beautiful. It isn't just the way your tits look in what I assume is a pretty expensive bra. Though I like that too. It's not your ass. Though again, I like it."

His words were the single most erotic thing she'd ever heard in her life, and maybe that made her simple, but she didn't care. She just did not care.

"It was always the spark in your eyes. It was always that little bit of wicked in your smile. The way your ass moves because of the way you walk, which has nothing to do with the shoes or how expensive they are, but with the way you carry yourself. You're strong. And he never gave you any of that. And he does not have the right to take any of it away. No. Finding out that you were broke when you were young doesn't turn me off. It just explains what I saw in you already."

"He didn't like to hear about it," she whispered.

"He's a weak man," he said, restating it.

"And you're not."

"I'm just a man," he said. "I'm a man who wouldn't dream of turning away from my responsibilities, not on the level he has. But also, I don't take on shit I can't hang on to. I don't try to carry something I can't hold."

That felt like a warning more than a promise. And she should be grateful. Because she knew it was foolish to go straight from a marriage into another relationship. Hell, it was foolish to go straight from a marriage into Boone's arms, but suddenly it seemed like maybe it was a stupid thing *not* to do.

"Fifteen years," she said. "That's how long it's been since I walked into that bar and saw you," she said. "That's how long it's been since I…since I looked down at my wedding ring and wanted to take it off. I didn't want to do that all the time. Not for the whole fifteen years. But pretty much every time I was with you. I wanted to break my vows for the chance to know what it was like to have your hands on my skin, Boone Carson. Do you know what kind of insanity that is?"

He moved closer to her, his blue eyes blazing. And there was no counter between them.

"Yes. Because it's the same kind of insanity I felt since the moment I saw you. Forget friendship and all of that. Because I just wanted you."

"I had kids with him," she said.

"I know," he growled. "Do you have any idea how much I hated that? Knowing… Knowing just how tied to him you were. Your girls are great, don't mistake me. And I'm not saying that I should've been a husband or father or anything like that. But I am saying… Damn, honey, I wasn't gonna go here. I wasn't gonna touch you."

"You still haven't."

"I'm going to, though, you know that."

"It was inevitable. From the beginning."

"Maybe I should thank him. For being the one to blow it up. Because we don't have to."

She shook her head. "We wouldn't have."

"Are you sure? Because I'm not. You've been here two days. And here we are. Being just a little too honest."

"You made me a sandwich."

"So?"

"Yeah, I asked myself that same question. Why should that matter so much? Why is it so damned impactful that a man is showing me basic concern? Because it's what I've been without. Because I had a marriage, but just the framework of one. We were business partners, and sometimes I think we liked each other. We had sex, and it was fine. I gave myself to him when I was nineteen, and that was just that. I thought I had to stick with it. Because I didn't want to be pregnant and alone. Because

I didn't want to have the life I grew up with anymore, and I didn't want that for my kids. I sure as hell wasn't gonna blow it up just because I wanted to tear some other guy's clothes off."

"I want you," he said. "I want you, and I understand that you don't want me."

She was immobilized by that. "What does that mean?"

"You're attracted to me, but you don't want it. You don't want me to take your clothes off. You don't want me to kiss your lips. You don't want me to taste every inch of you. And you sure as hell don't want me inside you."

She couldn't breathe. His words were tracing erotic shapes through her mind's eye, things she was never going to be able to unseat. To un-imagine.

"I don't understand…"

"Because if you did, you'd be across this room already. Because you know what's holding me back. It's you. I cannot be part of hurting you. And I cannot be part of taking advantage of you, and I sure as hell can't have you thinking you owe me. And it doesn't matter that I know you're attracted to me. I know something is stopping that from becoming want, because if it was *want*, then the want is on both sides. And it would be enough to push us together."

"I have the girls. And I just think that if…"

And she knew that it was a lie. The moment those words passed her lips. Even thinking about whether or not it was smart and all of that, it was just excuses. She didn't want to get hurt. She didn't want to get burned by the intensity of the thing between them. She had discounted common sense once for a man, and ended up married to someone who had never been faithful to her. So this was all about fear. It was one thing to want Boone when she couldn't have him. It was quite another to have him and contend with what that might mean.

With where he might fit into her life, or with where she would want him to fit into her life even if he didn't.

But she knew one thing.

That she had fifteen years' worth of complicated regrets. Like trying to pick broken glass out of a piece of cake. And she just didn't want any more of that. There had been good things about her marriage. Even though she was hurt by it now. Even though it wasn't going to last forever. Even though it was over.

She had her girls. She had some work experience. She would find a way to use the things that her marriage had given her. Even as she moved forward without her husband.

But she didn't want Boone to be a regret. Not anymore. He'd been one, deeply, for fifteen years. And that was what she didn't want. More than anything. More than she wanted to be protected. More than she wanted Boone to be a safe space. And yes, when she had first shown up at the house, she had maybe wanted safety more than she wanted him. For a minute.

Because it was wonderful to have him remove the burden. Wonderful to have him give her a place to stay. Wonderful to have him carry her bags.

But she would leave. She would leave in four weeks, just like she'd said, and she would start fresh on her own. But she would know. She would know what she'd been missing all this time, and he would be resolved. She deserved that. She needed it.

"I do want you," she whispered.

She took a step toward him, her heart pounding. Nothing was stopping her. And she was giddy with that. Giddy with a sense of freedom and wildness.

And it was like years had been lifted off her shoulders. Not just the years of marriage, but the years that had come before it. The years of feeling like she had to be good. Better. To avoid ever stepping into the trap of poverty again. To avoid food insecurity and homelessness and all the things she had grown up so terrified of. The things that had shaped her. And yes, they had made her strong, but sometimes she was just so tired of being that kind of strong. She didn't want to do it anymore. And he made her feel, in that moment, like she could just be. Like there was nothing but now. Because there were three hours until she had to go get the girls from school. Because her wedding rings were gone, and her vows meant nothing. Because he didn't look at her and see somebody who deserved to be treated like less because she had been through something difficult.

Because he had listened.

And all those things combined to make her feel free.

And she knew what she wanted to do with that freedom.

Nothing was holding her back.

And for the first time, she reached out and she touched Boone Carson.

Chapter Five

Wendy's hand on his chest was so much more erotic than anything he ever could've imagined. His heart was pounding so hard he thought it was going to go straight on through his rib cage. And then she would be able to hold it in her delicate hand, and that would seem about right. That would seem like the appropriate fee for this gift. This gift of her delicate hand against his body.

They had been foolish to think it wasn't going to end here.

Maybe they had needed to be that foolish, for a time.

God knew he had.

He had needed to construct a ladder made of lies so they could climb up to this moment.

Because the truth would've sent them both turning away.

Thank God for the lies that had brought them here.

He wanted to savor the moment.

This moment *before*. When it was like storm clouds were all gathered up ahead, swollen with the promise of rain, but not a single drop had fallen. Where the air had changed to something thicker, more meaningful. Thick with promise.

The promise of her mouth on his.

In only a few moments he would taste her. And when he did, he was going to part her lips, slide his tongue in deep.

But he hadn't yet.

And it was the promise that kept him poised on the edge of a knife. That kept him on high alert. The promise of strawberries, the forbidden, and the need that had been building in him for fifteen years.

He was in no rush for the first raindrop to fall.

He could live in this moment forever.

Except then her touch shifted. Except then, she moved her hand up to curve around the back of his neck, the touch erotic, purposeful. Glorious. And the minute her fingertips made contact with bare skin, it was too much. It was electric. And all his control snapped.

The rain began to fall.

He wrapped his arm around her waist and brought her hard against him so she could feel him. Feel his need. Feel the way his heart was beating almost out of his chest, feel how his cock had gotten hard.

For her. His breathing was ragged, pained. And he knew she could hear that, feel that. The way his chest hitched, the way his breath tried to cut his throat on each and every exhale.

She swallowed hard, and brought her hand around just beneath his jaw, traced it, down to the center of his chin.

"Wendy," he whispered.

She licked her lips, and that was it. He lowered his head and brought his mouth down onto hers.

The impact of her mouth under his was shocking. He had kissed any number of women. More than he could count. Innumerable.

But that had never been this.

No woman's mouth had ever been this.

It was Wendy, and she was imprinted into every cell of his body.

Her mouth was so soft. And she didn't taste of strawberries. It was indefinable, wonderful her. It was nothing else. It never could be.

It had been the easy way out to imagine there was another flavor to compare her to. Something he could hang on to on late nights when he was unsatisfied. A lie. And one he had needed. The same as he could lie to himself and say that having sex with a gorgeous blonde might do something for that need.

Of course, it didn't. Of course, it never could. Because that was just sex. And this was something else.

It was something more. Much more.

Sex was as cheap as vows that weren't kept. This was precious. Real. Deep.

It pulled a sound straight from the bottom of his soul like dying, like hope, like pain and glory and wonder, all rolled into one.

He cradled her head with the palm of his hand as he leaned in, took the kiss deeper.

His heart was pounding so hard he thought it might be a heart attack, and if it was, he would accept that this was his moment to go and be happy with it.

He'd ridden on the backs of angry bulls intent on grinding him into the arena dirt beneath their hooves. He'd won competitions and lost them. His sister had died. His brother had left. He'd felt his heart pound with adrenaline, ache with loss, burn with anger.

And this was somehow more, and better and worse, all at once.

It was new.

Boone had given up on ever feeling anything new again in his whole jaded life, but this was bright and shiny and wholly unique.

This was Wendy.

Not a kiss.

An event.

His mouth shifted over hers, and it nearly brought him to his knees. He tasted her, deep and long, and as much as he wanted this to go fast, to see her naked, feel her naked, be inside her, he also wanted this moment to go on forever. Just like that breath before the kiss.

He wanted everything all at once. The anticipation, the glory of need and the thunder of satisfaction.

But he didn't have the control to hold back, so he tasted her deep, though he kept his hand firmly on the back of her head, and the other wrapped hard around her waist, because if he let himself explore her...

It was Wendy who moved her hands over his shoulders, down his back, then his chest.

It was Wendy who let her fingertips skim down his stomach, and then skimmed his denim-covered arousal.

His breath hissed through his teeth, and he felt like she'd lit a match against him.

He lifted her off the ground, holding her heart against his body as he continued to plumb the depths of her mouth.

He knew what it was like to desire somebody. He knew what it was like to be physically aroused. This was past that. It surpassed everything.

This was something new altogether. Something intense and raw and more.

It was the thing he had always both craved and wanted to close the door on forever. Something altering and destructive that he felt far too familiar with.

Because how many times in his life had the landscape of his soul been rearranged? Torn apart?

He hadn't wanted to do it with her.

And yet, there was an inevitability to all of it. Something that couldn't be denied. And he wasn't going to deny it, not now. It was only that he was very, very aware this wouldn't simply be sex. But something more altogether. Something he had never experienced before.

It was Wendy.

And there was no use comparing her to anyone else. No

use comparing the way his need for her tightened his gut, made his body so hard it hurt, made him tremble with the need to be inside of her. Because there was nothing worthy of drawing comparison to. There was nothing like her. And there never could be.

He moved his hands down to her thigh, gripped it and lifted her leg so it was bent over his hip, then he moved her back against the kitchen island so he could press himself against her, let her feel, at the center of her need for him, just how much he wanted her. She gasped into his mouth, and rolled her hips forward. "Yes," he whispered against her lips.

And he knew he could get lost even in this. And moving his body against hers fully clothed, like they were a pair of desperate teenagers. And he would find pleasure in that. Because already, he had found more satisfaction in his mouth on hers than any previous sexual encounter had ever brought.

Maybe this was delayed gratification. Maybe this was just the way it went when you wanted somebody for years and couldn't have them. Maybe this was the release of self-denial followed by action. Or maybe it was simply Wendy.

He couldn't answer the question, or maybe he just wouldn't.

He would leave it a mystery. Intentionally. Wound up in a tangle he could easily undo if he pulled at the right thread. He knew where the right thread was.

But there were some mysteries best left tangled.

And that was the truth.

But there was no need for deeper truths than the one passing between their lips now, and there was no need for honesty any deeper than the raw need that coursed through his veins. It was enough. And anything more was likely to destroy them both, and it would be nice if, at the end of all of this, they could stand on their own two feet.

Because he didn't want to reduce her, and maybe even more

than that, he didn't want to reduce himself. He wasn't a saint, after all, and he had never claimed to be.

He was simply a man. One who was held in the thrall of the desire he felt toward the woman in his arms.

And even though he could've stayed like this forever, he didn't want something juvenile and desperate to mark the first sexual encounter between them. He wanted it to be her, and him, and nothing in between.

So he lifted her up again, and began to propel them both toward the stairs.

She clung to him, lifting her other leg and wrapping them both around his waist, holding fast as he propelled them both up, and then down the hallway toward his bedroom.

And he knew he would have to address the subject of barriers, especially because she'd been with a man she couldn't trust, and it was going to take a deep amount of trust to want to be with someone like that again.

And he would never violate her trust. Not out of desire, not out of selfish need. Not for any reason at all.

And he would never be lost enough in his own arousal to lose sight of her.

Because she was the reason. She was the answer to the question. She was the fuel for the fire raging through him now, so how could he turn his focus inward? He couldn't. Ever.

When they got to his bedroom, he set her down gently on the foot of the bed, and knelt before her, lifting his hand to cup her cheek. "I have condoms," he said.

"I have taken every test known to man recently out of an abundance of caution."

He nodded. "I trust you. But you don't have any reason to trust me."

She looked at him, her blue eyes seeming to go deeper than his skin. "I don't have any reason to trust Daniel. But you've never given me a reason to not trust you. You gave me a place to go, and I know you didn't do it so we would end up here. I trust that. I know nothing you did was to manipulate me. To use me. You've never been anything but honest with me, Boone."

"I want you. Without one. I don't want anything between us. But I will do whatever you need to feel safe."

"Well, I'm protected from pregnancy. So if…"

That did a weird thing to him. To his gut. Because the idea of Wendy being pregnant with his baby didn't make him scared or upset at all.

It made him feel something else altogether, and *that* made him a little bit scared. Made him a little bit upset.

"Good. Then we don't need it."

He moved away from her and stripped his shirt up over his head.

This was happening. And it was everything he wanted.

He just had to make sure he survived it.

Chapter Six

Wendy couldn't keep her eyes off his bare chest. He was the most beautiful man she'd ever seen. He always had been. Even with her doing her best not to examine the fine architecture of his body, she had noticed.

How could she not?

He was so glorious. So utterly perfect. And shirtless, he was... He was a phenomenon. He was the kind of stunning that could only be compared to a mountain range, looming in the distance, glorious and transcending all other natural wonders. Broad and brilliant, the musculature of his shoulders, his chest, his stomach...

She had always known the desire between her and Boone went somewhere beyond mere physical attraction, but for the moment, she just marinated in the absolute masculine perfection present before her. For he was something else altogether than she'd seen in person. That was for sure.

She was almost startled by the visceral reaction she had to him. By the wave of need that washed over her. She wasn't a stranger to sexual desire, or arousal. She enjoyed sex.

But it had never been like this. It had never been all-consuming. It had never been a driving need that washed out everything else, washed out her fear. Because she was the kind of woman who had been raised from a place of fear, because her mother had known she would need it in order to make her way in the world. Because her mother knew that a woman had to suspect everything and everyone. That a woman could never fully place her trust in another human being, because the moment she did that person could take advantage of her.

Yes, she had always been afraid. And so nothing had ever been able to carry her away, not completely. She had left herself fairly unprotected in her marriage, but even now, she'd known exactly how she would get away. And she had already made sure she and her girls didn't end up on the streets. And perhaps she was giving herself a bit too much credit when Boone deserved more of it, but still, she felt confident saying she had never let herself get lost entirely in any sort of passion, anytime, anywhere.

Except now.

There was no logical thought. Nothing rational or reasonable about this. It was just need. Raw and aching and torn from the depths of her soul.

She was empty, and she needed, more than anything, to be filled by him.

She leaned back on the bed, looking up at him.

His grin… That edgy, wicked grin she had always longed to have turned on her.

And nothing was holding her back now. Nothing whatsoever.

It was freedom, the kind of freedom that made tears prick at the backs of her eyes, the kind of freedom that made her feel like she might be on the edge of a cliff.

And normally that would scare her. She was afraid of heights.

But not here. Not now.

Everything about this man said he would catch her.

She could jump. With all the wild abandon she never let herself feel, she could jump.

Because he was more than strong enough to catch her.

Because he was more than strong enough to make good on every promise the arousal he built inside of her created.

Yes. He was the man who had engineered this desire, and he was the man who would answer it.

Because Boone Carson was a man who kept his word.

Even when they were words he didn't speak with his mouth.

He moved his hands to his belt buckle, and everything in her stilled. He began to undo the leather slowly, and her body rejoiced.

He pulled the belt through the loops on his jeans, and methodically set it on the edge of the bed, right next to her. He kicked his boots off, the movements there slow as well, removing his socks and placing them next to the boots. He was doing this on purpose.

Because he didn't hurry to get up here, and now he was taking his time. She couldn't even be angry, because it was the single most erotic thing she'd ever experienced. An echo of the denial they'd been experiencing since they had first met, and yet now with the promise of that desire being satisfied.

His hands went to the button on his jeans, then slowly lowered his zipper. His pants and underwear came off as one, and the extreme pulse of desire that rocked through her core when she saw the full, masculine extent of him made her mouth dry. He was glorious. The most beautiful naked man she'd ever seen, even though she'd only ever seen one other in person.

He was perfection. He was everything.

She couldn't help herself. Or maybe she didn't want to. She licked her lips.

And he laughed. Enticing. Husky. He made her feel like maybe she was wicked too.

And for the first time in a very long time, she didn't feel like somebody's wife or housekeeper or household manager. She didn't feel like somebody's mother. She just felt like her. Her, if she hadn't been raised to fear everything, to hoard good things and be afraid of what might come tomorrow.

Just who she might've been. Who she wanted to be.

A woman. A woman with the capacity to desire perfection. A woman with the capacity to let herself hope.

All because of Boone Carson's gloriously naked body.

And if that wasn't a testament to the wonder of a perfect penis, she didn't know what was.

And she hadn't even touched him yet.

She put her hands on the hem of her T-shirt, fully expecting to undress herself, until his eyes met hers. "No." The command, the denial, was rough and hard.

"That's for me," he said.

"Okay," she said, her voice trembling slightly.

But she loved the command in his voice, and she didn't want it to go away.

He took her hand and encouraged her into a standing position, and then he grabbed hold of the edge of her shirt and pulled it up over her head.

His nostrils flared, his eyes going hot. "You're so beautiful. And I'm gonna tell you right now, I'm not going to have any pretty words for you. Just dirty ones. Rough. I'm not gonna write you poetry, because I just want you so damned bad. And that is the most flowery, beautiful speech I have. Everything else is going to get a lot harder. You okay with that?"

"Yes."

Because it was poetry to her since it was said in his voice. Because the heat in his eyes might as well be a sonnet, and the music he called up within her a symphony.

He could say whatever he wanted. He could do whatever he wanted. It wouldn't be wrong. It couldn't be.

And he made good on his word. As the layers of her clothes came off, he affirmed her with rough, coarse speech that made goose bumps break out on her skin. Her husband was a cowboy. He'd used all manner of rough language. He wasn't delicate when it came to words surrounding sex, but it was different from Boone. Because it was about her.

Because his language spoke to a level of desperation that healed something inside of her she hadn't even realized had hurt.

This idea that she hadn't been enough. That giving a man her body hadn't been enough. That loving that man hadn't been enough. That keeping his house, raising his children, managing his money hadn't been enough. That if doing all that wasn't enough to satisfy him, it meant there was a deep shortcoming within her she was never going to fix.

Boone made that laughable. He made it clear, so very clear, even to her, that the issue was Daniel.

Because if Boone could be reduced to trembling over the sight of her bare breasts, then maybe she was beautiful after all.

Then perhaps she wasn't wrong. Then perhaps her husband was just a bad husband.

And she had been a good wife. It just hadn't mattered to him. And never would, no matter what she did.

And so this weight that had been resting in the pit of her stomach from the moment she had found out about Daniel's infidelities evaporated. And then Boone took her pants off. Her underwear. And she was naked in front of him. This man she had wanted for so long, for whom her desiring had become as natural as breathing, so much so that she had managed to carry it around all these years, some days barely noticing it.

And now she could feel it. The way that it made her want to be wanted.

The cascade of all those years was suddenly pouring down over her, amplifying her desire. Her need.

She wasn't embarrassed to be naked in front of him, because she knew she had been thousands of times in his mind, and she could see from the heat in his eyes he wasn't disappointed. Far from it. And then he began to tell her. Just how satisfied he was.

And he was wrong. It was poetry. A field of dark desire

dotted with bright, explicit daisies. And it was more than beautiful to her.

Because it was real. Because it was nothing held back. Because it was as honest a moment as she'd ever had in her life, and honesty was perhaps the biggest aphrodisiac of all right now.

Truth.

Unfiltered, unabashed.

And then he wrapped his arm around her waist and brought her bare body against his. And they were touching, everywhere. Naked, against each other. He was so hard and hot, and her desire for him was like a living thing. Demanding. Exulting. And she indulged.

She wrapped her arms around his neck and kissed him, gloried in the feel of her sensitized breasts moving against his hair-roughened chest. Loving the way his large, calloused hands moved over her curves, the way one cupped her ass and squeezed her hard.

Then delved between her thighs to tease her slick entrance.

She cried out as he pushed a finger inside of her, and then another.

Boone. She would never not be conscious it was him.

It wasn't about generic desire. It wasn't about that basic sort of human need that everyone experienced. This was singular. It was for him. About him.

And when he lifted her up and laid her down on the bed, he looked at her like a starving man. And he pushed her knees apart, kissing her ankle, that sensitive spot right on the inside of her knee, and up her thigh, slowly. His mouth was hot, and his eyes were full of intent, and even as she felt a vague amount of discomfort and embarrassment wash over her when he drew closer to the most intimate part of her, she couldn't look away.

Because she had to see it. She had to see Boone's mouth on her. And then it was. She gasped, arching up off the bed, her hand going over her own breast as she squeezed herself, greedy now with all the heat inside of her. And he began to lick her, deep and with intent, pushing a finger inside rhythmically as his tongue moved over the most sensitive part of her.

She was lost in it. In this new music inside of her.

He was an artist, and if he would make her his muse, she would consider herself fortunate.

She closed her eyes, finally surrendering to the overwhelming onslaught of pleasure, finally unable to keep them open. But still, she saw him. His face. His body.

Boone. She was overwhelmed by him.

His touch, his scent. And that realization, his name, him—that was what sent her over the edge, more than a touch, more than his skilled mouth. Just him.

And when she shattered, he clung to her tightly, forcing her to take on more and more pleasure. As he pushed her harder, further, through wave after wave, through a second climax that hit before the first had even abated.

And she was spent after. His name the only thing in her mind, the only thing on her lips. Perhaps, the only thing she knew.

"Boone," she whispered, as he moved up her body and claimed her mouth, letting her taste her own desire there, the evidence of what they had done.

His smile was more than wicked now. It was something else. Dark and satisfied, and everything.

He moved his hands up to cup her breasts, skimmed his thumbs over the sensitized buds there, then moved both hands down her waist, her hips, beneath her rear as he lifted her hips up off the bed.

"I want…"

"Later," he said, his voice jagged. "I need to be inside of you."

And then he was, in one hard, smooth stroke, filling her,

almost past the point of pleasure into the gray space where pain met need, and it was wonderful.

He began to move, rough, hard strokes that pushed her further and further toward that shining, glorious peak again. Impossibly. Brilliantly.

There was no way she could come again. She had never in her life come twice during sex, and a third time would just be pushing it, except each and every stroke demanded it.

It was Boone. Inside of her. Tormenting her. Satisfying her. Creating within her an aching need that only he could satisfy.

And she could've wept with the glory of it. With the intensity of the new, building need in her that felt entirely separate from the need she'd had before.

Because this was about them. Being one. His body in hers. Intimate. Too much. Not enough.

She met his every stroke, and then he took hold of her chin and pressed his forehead to hers. "That's right," he whispered. "Come for me. For me, Wendy."

It was the desperation there, the fact that he wasn't talking dirty to her for the sake of a game, but issuing a command that came straight from the very center of who he was, out of the deepest, darkest desire. That was what sent her over. That was what shattered her. And it was nothing like her other two climaxes. This was like something sharp piercing a pane of glass, cracking and shattering it into glorious, glittering pieces. Making it into something almost more beautiful than what it had been before.

And then he followed her. On a rough sound, he found his own release, spilling himself inside of her, his body pulsing deep within. And she watched him. Watched as he was undone.

By her. By them. By this.

And all she could do was hang on to him in the aftermath. Clinging to his sweat-slicked shoulders as she pressed her head to that curve right there at his neck, as she tried to keep herself from weeping.

"Boone," she said.

"It's about damned time," he said.

And she laughed. Impossibly, because nothing felt light or funny.

Except it was just the truth.

It had been so long in coming, that it was nearly a farce.

Had it always been inevitable? She supposed there was no good answer to that question. The decision as to whether or not they would do something to violate her vows had been taken away from them. And they had certainly kept themselves away from any sort of temptation they couldn't handle for long enough that they deserved a medal.

But it had been taken away from them, the need to resist. And so they didn't.

Lying there with him felt inevitable.

But maybe it was Daniel's betrayal that had always been inevitable, considering he had never once seen a need to be faithful to her.

Maybe that was the thing that had always been set in stone: the failure of her marriage. Maybe it had been fate that day that had brought Boone into her path and said, *Here is the better choice.*

For all the good it had done. Because she had been so bound and determined to do the right thing, she hadn't taken the destined thing.

Except now, in the aftermath of what had been fairly spectacular sex, she was left with the reality that sex was hardly destiny.

It had been amazing. Surpassing anything she had even thought could exist.

But she still had all the things in her life to take care of. And kids to pick up from school in… She looked over at the bedside clock. Thirty minutes.

For a moment she had felt free of all her responsibilities, but she wasn't. Not really.

She still carried them all. She still had to be Wendy Stevens. Mother, a woman in the midst of a divorce.

She still had to figure out where she went from here, and what she did next. Not even three soul-shattering orgasms could take that away.

Because bodies meeting wasn't a promise. Not forever, not really anything.

And in the place she was in life, she could hardly ask Boone for promises.

He looked at her, and she wanted to.

But she didn't.

They had known exactly what to do.

It was funny that neither of them seemed to know what to say.

"I have to go get the girls. Soon."

"Yeah."

"I can't… You know I can't be over here at night."

He nodded. "Yes."

"I just can't have them knowing."

"I get that." He cupped her chin. "It's not gonna just be the once, though. You know that."

She could resist. She could tell him it had to be once. She could tell him that, for their own protection, they needed to keep it that way. That they had to be smart. But she would only end up back in his bed the next time they were alone in the house, and it would just make her a liar.

She wasn't going to do that. She wasn't going to insult them.

Because the truth was, she wanted him again even now, and if she wasn't on a time limit, she would probably be climbing on him.

Because she hadn't been able to touch him the way she wanted to, hadn't been able to explore him. Hadn't been able to taste him.

And she was just not in the space to build up a host of re-grets. Or even a single new regret.

"I am going to leave," she said.

"You said."

"I'm not even divorced yet."

"You are in every way that counts."

"Except the legal ways. And I have to get through that."

"I get that."

"Thank you. For being here for me. I really appreciate it. I really… This is going to happen again."

"Yes," he said.

And then it was her turn to be bold. Because why get mis-sish now?

"I need to taste you," she said. "I haven't had you in my mouth."

He growled, and she found herself pushed flat on her back, a whole lot of muscled, aroused cowboy over the top of her.

"Careful."

"I don't have time," she said. "Because as wonderful as that was, I can't stop having my life just so I can please you sexually."

"Tease."

"It feels good to tease."

It felt good to be with him.

It was strange how natural it felt, sliding out from beneath the covers and taunting him with her naked body as she went to collect her clothes.

She just wasn't embarrassed.

And she wasn't going to pretend to be. Why take on shame she simply didn't feel? There was no point to that.

Now she just had to get through the rest of the day with her head on straight. She had to pick up her girls like she hadn't just been ravished. She had to get dinner made.

"I'm probably gonna go out tonight," he said. "Don't worry about saving me dinner."

And that felt… It hurt. It felt like he was avoiding her, and maybe he was.

"Oh," she said.

"I'll see you tomorrow, though."

"Okay."

"I can't have you again tonight," he said. "And I get that might sound outrageously selfish to you. But honestly, I'm not sure I have it together enough to be around you in front of the girls, or to… I just need some space."

She was shocked by that. By the honesty. By the blatant truth that had just come out of his mouth, a truth that exposed deeper feelings in him that she had thought he would be comfortable betraying.

"Oh."

She had wanted to be close to him because she felt needy right now. But he had a point. They needed to figure out how they were going to be around each other if the girls were in the middle of them.

And right now, they were on anything but normal footing.

"Okay."

"I don't want you to be hurt."

She shook her head. "I'm not."

"Don't lie to me, Wendy. There have been enough lies all around us, there don't need to be any between us. Not anymore."

"Okay. I was a little bit hurt. I thought you didn't want to be around me if you couldn't have me."

"Yes…but it isn't like that. It's not because I don't have another use for you. It's just because I don't quite know what to do with myself right now."

"Okay. That's fair."

And maybe a little bit more honest than she'd been with herself.

"I will see you tomorrow."

"Okay."

Chapter Seven

Walking away from her had been the hardest thing he'd ever done. But he had work to finish, and she had to get her kids.

Being honest with her about why he needed a little space had been the other hardest thing he'd ever done. Because it came too close to admitting the truth.

This impossible truth that he had no idea what to do with now that they'd slept together.

He had felt like he was in love with her for a very long time.

But that love had been impossible to act on. So it had felt… safe in a way.

Or at least abstract.

The truth was, Boone didn't know how to love somebody actively.

He knew how to do things for them. But he had no idea what being in love entailed.

He looked at the way his brothers had brought women into their lives, the way they'd rearranged themselves to have them. He didn't like the thought of that. Not at all. Because he'd rearranged his life so many times.

And he just couldn't take all that on right now.

Hell, more than that, he knew it was an impossibility. Wendy was going through a divorce. Wendy had kids.

There was something much heavier to the idea of trying to be with a woman who had been through so much, than if it was a woman he didn't know.

He knew her. He knew how difficult all this was.

He knew about her life, about the things that she'd been through. And about the responsibilities she had.

And he took all that shit very seriously.

So he decided to go out. Decided to go to the bar. And wasn't surprised to find his brother Jace there, since Jace's wife was working tonight.

"Hey," he said.

"Hey yourself."

"What brings you out on a weeknight?"

"I need a drink."

He could confide in his brother.

He could. He was still considering it when Jace looked at him just a little too keenly. "Woman trouble?"

"You could say that."

Because he had been considering telling his brother about it unsolicited, so he sure as hell didn't have it in him to lie.

"Wendy?"

"Yeah."

"You know, this just isn't a great time for her, I would imagine."

"It was a fine enough time for her to sleep with me."

"Oh. Well. I guess I shouldn't be too surprised about that."

"It's not a surprise," he said. It really wasn't. They wanted each other too badly for too long for it to be a surprise.

"What's the problem?"

"Life is just really messed up," said Boone. "I don't know how you ever let go of that enough to be with someone. Especially when everything they're going through is as equally messed up as the world around you. It was easy. To carry a torch for her knowing I could never have her. But the rest of it…"

"Yeah. I get that."

"She's in a bad space," he said.

"So you said," Jace commented.

"It's true though. And it's important I remember that. I don't want her to feel obligated to me."

"Bad news," said Jace. "When you have a relationship with somebody you do often feel obligated to them. It's not a bad thing. I think that's somewhere in line with basic human connection and empathy."

"Yeah, but I don't want this to be transactional."

"Fine. I can understand that. But if you do something for her and she wants to do something for you, that's not transactional so much as it is a relationship."

"She doesn't need one of those right now."

"And that's up to you to decide?"

He snorted. "I didn't say that. But I don't…"

"Listen to me, and trust me. I say this as a man who talked himself into thinking he knew better what the woman in his life wanted than she did. That way lies disaster. If you actually care about her, you need to give her some respect. The respect that she knows what's going on in her own mind. At least that."

"I know she does," he said. "But just… You weren't there. You didn't see her marriage. Okay? I did."

"Yeah. You were friends with her husband. If you hate the guy so much then why—"

"I didn't hate him. Not everything about him. When we were hanging out on the rodeo circuit, he was a good guy. The thing is, he kind of taught me how to have a good time. I needed that. You know how things were after…after Buck left. I had to take on a lot. And it was heavy. And I threw myself into the rodeo after that because I knew it was so important to Dad. I found some things there that I didn't expect to. But Daniel is a fun guy. And he kind of gave me something to look forward to. He taught me how to enjoy what had felt like an obligation before. There were good things about him. But when he married Wendy, things did change." And he left out the fact that a huge part of that was the way Boone felt about Wendy. From the moment he'd first seen her. There was no way Daniel could ever have been good enough for her. Even if he'd been perfectly good after all.

It was just that he hadn't been. So that combined with everything else made it kind of an impossible situation.

"Our friendship has had some cracks in it for a while. And in the end, I chose her. I was always going to choose her. I…" He realized what he'd just said.

"How long have you had a thing for her?"

"Too long. But the timing is bad."

"Word of advice. The timing is always bad."

"No, it really is. And I'm… I'm not someone who just hopes because he wants something. Not anymore."

"Boone, listen. I know… I know Sophia—"

"It was a lesson, Jace. When an illness is terminal, hoping for the best is stupid. It's not charming." He took a drink. "It's been a long time. But I changed. I know better. And I can see clearly, without…without being a blind optimist. The timing is bad."

Jace shook his head. "I get where you're coming from. But when it comes to relationships, the timing is always bad."

"What the hell does that mean?"

"Because at some point, caring about somebody means getting over yourself. And that is a really hard thing to do."

He could understand what his brother was saying. But caring about Wendy had always meant denying himself. It had always meant caring more about her than about him. Of course it had.

He'd always been clear on what loving Wendy meant.

He could care, but he couldn't have her.

And if anything, it just reinforced what he had to do. And that was let her go at the end of all this.

Because that was what caring about her meant.

It meant not being like Daniel. Not holding her to him when it wasn't right. When it wasn't the best situation for her. That was what love was.

It was sacrificial.

So there.

"Well, that's the way I feel about her," he said. "Like my feelings can't be first."

"Great. Just make sure you don't decide for her what her feelings are. Okay?"

"Yeah."

Jace raised his hand, and Cara brought over a couple of beer bottles.

"Do you have a designated driver, Boone?" she asked.

"You have my permission to put me in a cab if I have too many."

"Good. I have to look out for you. You're my brother now after all."

It was weird, the way the family kept expanding. Especially after being so conscious of the contractions in their family for all those years.

But Cara was a sister to him. Another person who cared.

That sat a little bit uncomfortably in his chest, and he couldn't quite say why.

"My biggest problem now," he said, lifting his beer bottle and looking at his brother, "is figuring out how to act like what happened earlier today didn't happen, especially when her kids are around."

"Well, not that I know, but I assume kids are a pretty big dampener on the libido."

"Especially teenagers," Boone said. "Little kids you could get that past, but older ones…"

"I don't know, man. Sounds to me like you just stepped your boot into a whole mess of sexual tension snakes."

He laughed. "Yeah." He didn't laugh because it was funny.

He laughed because it was true. He laughed because the mental image that it painted was far too accurate.

He had gone and done it. The nest of sexual tension snakes had been there all along, and he'd known. Full well.

But it was like stepping in it had been the only option. So there he was.

And now he was going to have to get back to the task of taking care of her. And taking care of the girls. All while carrying on a blisteringly hot, temporary affair with her. Because the snakes had been stepped in. So there was no point going back now.

"I'll figure it out."

"Sure you will," said Jace, a little too cheerfully for his liking.

"Why exactly do you seem to be enjoying this?"

"Because a woman completely rearranged my life some years ago, and a few months ago, I was finally able to figure out exactly what that rearranging needed to look like. I'm glad to see you in a similar situation."

Except it wasn't the same. It never would be. But he didn't argue with his brother. He didn't have the energy for it. He had other things to save his energy for. If his time with Wendy was limited, he was going to pour everything into it. Absolutely everything.

She was so distracted. She needed to get her daughters through homework. And then she needed to get herself off to bed.

She managed that, just barely. But then she couldn't sleep.

She was completely consumed by her thoughts of Boone. And what had happened between them that day.

He was gone still, the driveway empty, and she should be completely okay with that. He explained himself after all.

And, anyway, he didn't have an obligation to her.

It wasn't about obligation, though. She just wished he was here. And when she saw headlights pull up into the driveway, she climbed out of bed and, without thinking, went out the side door of the cottage and walked toward his house.

It wasn't a truck; it was a car. And she stopped and stared at the unfamiliar white vehicle, not quite understanding what was going on until she saw the logo on the side.

He'd gotten a taxi.

He got out of the cab, and she saw him stumble into the house.

And without thinking, she went the same way he did.

"Are you drunk?"

He turned. "Tipsy. Not drunk."

"Okay. Why?"

"I was trying to make it a little bit easier to fall asleep, actually."

"Oh, Boone. Come on inside. I'll make you some tea."

"No. That is counter to my objective. Which is to not think about you. And definitely not to fall asleep with you on my mind."

He was a little tipsy. And she didn't usually find that kind of thing sexy. But here she was. She had a feeling she would find Boone's hangnail sexy. And that was a whole other kind of problem she'd never had before.

"In the house."

"I don't take orders."

"Why not?"

He grinned, and she found herself suddenly pressed up against the side of the house. "Because I like to give them."

Arousal crashed through her body. Yeah. She would really like to take orders from him. Though, that wasn't supposed to be what was happening tonight.

"And tomorrow afternoon when you're sober, and you come in for your lunch break, you're welcome to tell me everything your heart desires. But right now, I'm telling you to go in the house so I can make you some tea."

"I think you'd have more fun if you got down on your knees."

"For sure," she said, breathless with the desire that thought infused in her. "But sometimes you can't get what you want."

"I'm well familiar."

"Inside."

And this time, he obeyed her.

So there was that.

She found an electric kettle—which was surprisingly civilized of him, she thought—and plugged it in, flicking on the switch to start up the hot water.

"I appreciate that you got a cab. I feel like sometimes you guys are not so great with the designated-driver thing."

"You guys?"

"You rodeo cowboys," she said.

"Yeah well." He cleared his throat, his expression going stoic. "My older brother was in a drunk driving accident. He wasn't driving. But they were a bunch of boys that had gone out camping and drinking and… Anyway. He was the only one that survived. After something like that you take the whole thing pretty seriously."

"Oh. I'm sorry, Boone, I didn't know."

"Yeah. Nobody knows Buck. Because he took off so long ago. It really screwed him up."

There was something raw and unspoken in his words. A truth buried there she couldn't quite figure out. And he wasn't going to tell her. Not willingly. Not right now.

And that was okay. Because that wasn't supposed to be the point of this. But now she couldn't stop imagining the catastrophe, and the way it must have hurt everyone.

"Was he injured?"

Boone nodded. "Yeah. He was okay, though. I mean physically. But it's a small town. And people will define you by something like that. And everyone will know. You can't outrun it unless you leave. I know that."

"It must've been hard. Having him leave."

"Plenty of families don't live in each other's pockets."

"Yes. That is true. But I expect it feels different when somebody leaves because of something like that."

"I guess. Were you close to your mom?"

"Yes. Until she died. She died when I was eighteen. And then after that, I met Daniel. I expect I was looking for a connection."

"Yeah. Probably."

"We don't often do the best things for ourselves when we're feeling desperate." She closed her eyes. "That isn't fair. He was good to me. As far as I knew. I wasn't openly accepting poor treatment."

"I was trying to remember today, when my brother and I were talking at the bar, exactly why I used to like Daniel. It occurred to me that he was one of the most carefree guys I've ever met. And as somebody who was burdened with a host of care by the time I was sixteen, I liked being around him."

"That's what I liked about him too. I was always afraid. Always afraid of losing what little I had. Always afraid of when the other shoe was going to drop. I was always scared. And he never was. Not of tomorrow, not of his success vanishing, not of our relationship imploding, he just lived. And now, I feel a little bit betrayed. Because so much of that is just arrogance, isn't it? Thinking you're the center of everything, the most important person, and that nothing you do can compromise it. And here I thought I was maybe learning some kind of life lesson from him."

"There's still a life lesson there, maybe. He doesn't have to have had everything worked out for some of it to be true."

"I guess."

"Did he ever make you happy?"

"Yes," she said. "And I guess it was real enough. I guess."

"I can understand why it's difficult. To accept that any of it was real when it seems like he was lying all that time."

"Yeah." She poured the hot water into a mug and put a tea bag in it. "But I guess that's the thing. That was part of his arrogance. He didn't think I needed his fidelity as long as he kept it from me. And I think he didn't much see the conflict there. It's insane. It doesn't make any sense. But I think that's what he thought. And so in his way, I think he loved me. I just think he never really loved anybody as much as he loved himself."

"And that may be why he was so happy," Boone said.

That made her laugh. "That's fair. How happy can you be when you're worried constantly about the happiness of somebody else? When you love yourself most, your joy isn't completely tied to the feelings of others. Like it is when you care about others as much as you care about your own. For Daniel, ultimately your own happiness is what matters…"

"I expect that's the easiest way."

"I wouldn't want to live that way, though. Because I wouldn't have my girls. Makes everything hard. Because as difficult as it is to go through this separation, it's so much harder when you're worried about other people's happiness as much as you are your own. Or more. But then I think at least I know what it's like. To feel an intense amount of caring for somebody else. I think that's the depth of it."

"Yeah. I think that's the depth of it. When I was a kid, my sister died. You might know that."

"I didn't," she said.

"Well. Sorry to bum you out with my family history. But it was a long time ago."

"I'm sorry."

"Thanks. Me too. But you know, that was my first introduction to understanding just how badly love could hurt. But what can you do? You love your siblings. No matter what. And I couldn't turn off my love for my family just because we lost our little sister. So I learned how to kind of move on with it. I learned that you could love even though it hurt. The hurt is part of it. And yeah, I think the way Daniel loves, that's kind of something else."

"Narcissism?"

"Possibly."

"I'm very sorry to hear about your sister. And your brother. Do you see him at all?"

"No. And in some ways that feels harder to deal with than Sophia's death. Because he is still alive. He just doesn't speak to us. He is still alive, he just… He won't come to us for help. After everything we went through. As a family. He put my parents through losing another child, effectively. He lived, but he won't live. And I just can't wrap my head around that."

"This one isn't about me," she said slowly. "It's my mother's story. But she isn't here to tell it, so I'd like to. My father abused her. She loved him, she trusted him, and he abused her. Physically. Emotionally. And I know that the woman she was after him was different. No matter how much she wanted to go back. She just couldn't. And sometimes I wondered why she didn't go home. Why did she go out on her own and struggle? When she could have gone back, because she talked about her family like they were all right. But the issue wasn't them, it was her. She survived something she didn't want to explain to anybody. And she didn't feel like she could go back. And I think there was something sad about that. I never got to know my parents. But I also understand there were things that happened that were so traumatizing she just couldn't face people seeing how they had changed her. And I can't judge her for that. Maybe your brother feels the same. Maybe he doesn't want you all to see who he is. Because maybe in some way he does feel like he died. I don't know. And I'm sorry if I'm overstepping. It's just that I love someone very much who did a similar thing."

He was quiet for a long time.

"This is maybe a little bit of a deep conversation to have when I'm partway into my cups," he said.

"I'm sorry. I didn't mean to overstep. But I—"

"You didn't overstep. Hell. We had sex a few hours ago, I think you can give me some advice."

"It's not really advice. It's just you said you didn't understand, and I hope maybe you might feel less mystified. And even if it isn't true, even if that's not why he left, if he didn't tell you, well, then what can you do? But if having an answer, any answer—one that's about him and his pain and not you—helps, then you might as well choose to believe that one."

"Good point. I can't argue with that."

"You could."

Their eyes met. This felt dangerous. Quite dangerous. Because this was another thing they hadn't done these last years. They hadn't gotten to know each other. They knew each other in the sense that they saw each other around. She knew the quality of man Boone was because she saw the way he interacted with other people. Because they chatted in passing at different things when it couldn't be avoided, and they did their very best to never be self-conscious about the sparks between them. To never draw too much attention to all of it.

But they didn't do this. They didn't sit and have heart-to-hearts. They didn't talk about his dead sister or his missing brother. Maybe she had started it, trying to push him away by telling him about her childhood. It hadn't worked. And now she knew about his, and that was close to having a connection. It was close to something she should be avoiding. And definitely something she shouldn't want.

Definitely not.

"Yeah. But, why? I'd rather kiss you."

"That's probably not a great idea." But she was already lean-ing in, and when he kissed her, it was almost tender. Nearly sweet.

It could never be entirely tender, though, because there was an edge to the meeting of their mouths that she thought not even time would take away.

It was the wanting. And how long they'd lived with it.

But tonight, there was something glorious about it. An ache fueled by how much she wanted him, and by knowing tonight she couldn't have him. Because she needed to get back to the cottage, needed to get back to the girls.

Because one thing she really couldn't afford was for her daughters to discover she wasn't home. For them to wonder where she was.

So he was forbidden again, but only for a few hours. There was something illicit, in a glorious way, about that.

A fun way because it wasn't impossible, it was just delayed.

So she let the kiss get intense, hungry, and she gloried in it.

In the building desire between her thighs, and the reckless heat that threatened to overwhelm her.

His whiskers scratched against her skin, and she liked that too.

Yes. She really did like it.

And when they pulled away, they were breathing hard, and her whole body felt like it was strung out, ready to shatter at the slightest touch.

"Are you going to touch yourself tonight? And think of me?"

It wasn't a question, she knew. It was a command. Because that was who he was.

"Yes."

"Tell me about it."

"Okay."

"Send me a text and let me know exactly what you thought

I might do. Because you know, 'you have not because you ask not.'"

"All right."

He kissed her again, once more, then picked up his mug and stood. "I'll head to bed."

"Me too."

And she did exactly as he ordered, and when her climax hit, she turned her face into her pillow and said his name.

Then she sent off a furtive text letting him know she had completed the task. But when it came to what exactly she thought about? That was a lot more difficult. And in the end, she only wrote one word.

You.

Chapter Eight

You.

He couldn't stop thinking about that. Couldn't stop turning it over and over in his mind. Damn that woman.

Getting up this morning and heading to work felt like a farce because he was living for that afternoon break. He was living for their agreed-upon meetup. He didn't care about anything else. He lost the ability to do it. He just wanted her.

He had waited all this time for her. And then last night she had…

She had managed to stick a ruthlessly sharp knife blade into that wound, and the painful cut had let out some of the poison.

He didn't know how she had done it. How she'd so incisively given him a truth he needed, even if it wasn't what he wanted.

He didn't need for her to understand him in addition to being the hottest sex he'd ever had.

He didn't actually need for her to be anything, and yet, she was doing her best to be everything.

You.

And by the time the afternoon rolled around, his blood was thundering.

He practically tore the door off its hinges when he got into the house, and when he saw her standing in the kitchen, barefoot and wearing a sundress that came up well past her knees he just about wrote poetry. Or perhaps a prayer of thanks to whoever had invented the sundress.

It was a magnificent work of art. The creation he had never fully paused to consider or appreciate until this moment. Until he had beheld the glory of one on Wendy.

And he was done playing. He was done waiting.

They'd set their boundaries, and he'd made it very clear what he was doing, and what he wasn't doing. Because of that, he felt like he didn't need to waste time with pleasantries now.

"You look pretty. I want you on your knees."

"Here?"

"Yeah. Here."

But because he was a gentleman, he went over to the stove and took down a tea towel. Then he put the folded-up fabric onto the floor, cushions for her. Because he didn't want her discomfort. He just wanted a little obedience. He just wanted...

This was a fantasy he hadn't let himself have. And now he wanted it. And he wanted to hold on to it. Tight.

Slowly, she sank down to the floor, her knees coming down to the center of that folded-up towel.

In his kitchen.

Holy hell.

All this trying to stay clear of domesticity, and he was doing a great job twisting and perverting some kind of house-wife fantasy.

But he liked it. He couldn't help it.

What did he want? Just from his life in general. What had he ever wanted? Past the glory of the rodeo. Past being the one who picked up the slack for people who let go of their responsibilities.

What was left for him?

Was he going to live alone forever?

The years, the long lonely years, stretched out before him, and he realized why he never thought past the rodeo. Why he had put off retirement. Why he had put off this—buying a house. Making a life outside the rodeo.

Because he was clear-eyed. Because he wasn't an optimist. Because he didn't do hope, or dreams, and that meant the future was…

He could hardly even see it.

And that was sad.

But *this* wasn't.

So he was going to push all that to the side, and just be here. With her.

Because all she needed was him. And all he needed was her. That was for damned sure.

He moved closer to her and undid the buckle on his jeans.

And he suddenly felt unworthy of the gift she was giving him. It had been a follow-through of the game they were playing last night, and now it felt like something he maybe didn't deserve.

But she was looking up at him with wide, expectant eyes, and he was powerless to turn away.

He shifted the fabric of his pants, his underwear, and exposed himself to her. She wrapped her hand around the base of his cock and slid her elegant fingers along his length. Then she moved in, taking the tip of him into her mouth, before sucking him in deeply. She was confident. And more than that, her enjoyment was clear.

She wasn't shy—her eye contact bold, the sounds of pleasure coming from deep within her throat intense and raw.

He pushed his fingertips through her hair, held her there, held himself steady.

He didn't think he would survive this.

Even in this, he was so very aware it was her. Even in this, it could be no one else. He felt honored. Which was such a weird-ass way to think of a blowjob. But it wasn't just a blowjob. Because nothing with her was ever that simple. And it never could be.

He was close. So close, and he didn't want it. Not like this. He moved away from her, and she looked dazed, confused.

"Didn't you like it?"

"I loved it," he said, taking her hand and lifting her to her feet. And he kissed her, open-mouthed and hot. "A little bit too much. I need you. To be inside of you. Because I've got a month with you, Wendy, and there isn't going to be enough time. I'm not wasting it."

Something that looked like grief danced over her features, and he did his best to ignore that. They stripped each other naked, and made it as far as the living room rug. He pulled her over the top of him, and thrust up inside of her. Let her set the tempo of the lovemaking this time. Let her have control. She flipped her blond hair over her shoulder, planted her hands on his chest and rode him, the view provided by the position making him feel like his heart might explode.

Then she closed her eyes and let her head fall back, small incoherent sounds issued from her lips creating a glorious soundtrack to his need.

Her climax came quick, and he was grateful, because that meant he could give her two.

As she continued to move over him, he pressed his thumb right there, to that sensitized bundle of nerves, and began to stroke her. She shivered, the second wave of her desire cresting as she cried out his name on a shudder and a shout. And then he followed her over the edge. It had been so much faster than he wanted it to be. But it had been perfect.

That woman. Damn that woman.

"Have dinner with me tonight," he said without thinking.

"I have the girls."

"Well, all of you have dinner with me tonight. I missed you last night."

"You left last night on purpose."

"I know I did. But I don't want to be alone in this house tonight, and I don't want to be without you, and I don't care if that makes sense."

"It's the sex talking," she said, throwing her arm over her face and rolling over onto her back.

"Sure it is. But it's great sex, so it can talk as loud as it wants."

"You're impossible, do you know that?"

"Whether I do or don't is sort of immaterial, don't you think?"

"No." She frowned and rolled over onto her stomach, propping herself up on her elbows. "I have a question for you."

"What is that?"

"Does anyone take care of you?"

"What?"

"Your brother left, and you made it sound like you got a lot of responsibility afterward?"

"Not a lot. It's just there were a lot of assumptions about Buck's place in the family. A lot of pressure for him to be great at riding in the rodeo, to help my dad with the ranch. He was the oldest, and then I became the de facto oldest. I had to pick up where he left off. But I already had my own place in the family, and nobody stepped in to fill that. So it was just a matter of doing a little bit of double duty. But I don't resent it."

"You're lying. You do resent it a little."

"Okay. Maybe. But like anything else, what difference does it make if I do or don't? It is what it is."

"Maybe. But if you admit your resentment, it might inspire you to figure out how to live your life a little bit differently, don't you think?"

"There is no different for me."

"Why not?"

"I don't deserve to be upset about Buck," he said, his voice hard.

"Why not?"

"Because I'm the reason he left."

Her eyes went round. "You...you're the reason?"

"I didn't mean to be. But he was...he was a mess after the

accident. Not physically. Mentally. It reminded me too much of other grief. Other times. The thing is, I know life is hard. But you have to be…you have to be realistic. You can't sit around hoping for things to be different, you have to deal with what's in front of you."

"And that's what you told him."

He nodded once. "Yes. It's what I told him. And the next day he was gone."

"Boone…"

"I don't deserve your sympathy, it's misplaced. But I don't feel guilty either. Buck was imploding, and he was going to do what he was going to do. I nudged him, I guess, with some harsh truth. But like I said, I don't wallow. I just deal."

She was silent for a moment. "Except for you dealing means…not even planning your future? Not wanting anything?"

"It's not quite like that. But I take things as they come, knowing there are certain expectations and I'm going to fulfill them."

"You're just going to ride bulls forever?"

"No. I'm retiring."

"Oh. Well. That feels like big news, Boone."

"I'll probably end up being the commissioner. After my dad retires. That's part of the deal. That was kind of supposed to be Buck's thing, but now it's not going to be. Because he's not around."

"What do you want?"

"I'm kind of uninterested in that bit of trivia. I don't care what I want. What I want doesn't really matter. What I want is secondary to what's going to happen. For my family."

"What you want isn't trivial."

He wasn't in the business of being self-indulgent, and there were limits to how deep he wanted to get into a conversation like this. But it was hard to hold back with her, so he didn't.

Because they were here, and she was beside him, naked and soft and the epitome of every desire he'd ever had.

"What I want has been trivial for years. No one asked me if I wanted to lose a sister. No one asked if I wanted my brother to go through what he did. And most of all, since the moment I met you, Wendy, what I wanted hasn't meant a damned thing."

She looked down and then back up, a sheen of tears glimmering there, and he hated that he'd put them there. And he loved it.

Because it mattered, this thing between them. It mattered now and it always would.

"I don't like that, Boone."

"You know it's true. We had to do the right thing."

"We did the right thing," she said. She scooted closer to him and put her hand on his shoulder, then leaned in, her breast pressing against him. "And this is our reward."

She felt hollow and sad after her exchange with Boone earlier.

This is our reward.

Was it? Was this all?

Was this it?

This furtive, intense sex that was trying to compensate for all their years of pent-up desire? Maybe that was all. Boone wasn't offering more. But Boone was also…

He was stoic and strong. He was commanding and he was so damned good.

All things that were beginning to indicate to her he was a champion martyr.

What I want is trivial.

He claimed he didn't blame himself for Buck leaving, but he clearly did. He seemed to almost relish things being hard.

He was good at being uncomfortable.

She would have said a bull rider had to be, but in the grand scheme of things, she didn't think Daniel did discomfort. Ever.

Eight seconds of physical pain, and then alcohol to numb

the aftereffects. Sex when he wanted it with who he wanted it with, while his wife kept house and peace at home.

Not Boone.

He rode bulls, not because he wanted to—though he claimed he'd found passion for it—but because he was fulfilling the destiny of his older brother, who was gone now.

He took care of his parents and worked to fill a space his dad wanted him in because he felt like he had to. Because of their losses, she assumed. It had started with his sister, that much was clear.

Even wanting her was an extension of just how happy Boone was to sit in discomfort.

He seemed happy enough to indulge with her, but there was a ticking clock on that indulgence. Wendy was starting to feel wounded by that. Crushed by it.

She was starting to question it.

Boone seemed to have made his peace with the pain in life. She wondered if he had any idea how to have joy.

Do you?

Ouch.

That was a dark question from her psyche she didn't really care to answer.

But then she picked the girls up from school and she knew the answer was a definitive yes. She knew how to have joy.

She had it in spades, even while she had something less than joy, and that might be one of the greatest tricks in life.

To be able to feel this immense pure joy while in the middle of such a massive shift. While in the middle of questioning everything she knew about herself and her life, and where she was headed.

"How was school?" she asked, once Sadie was buckled in and Mikey had finished a monologue about art class.

"Great," said Sadie.

Which was what Sadie would say no matter what.

"What was especially great?"

"Oh nothing." She sounded vacant, and guilt made Wendy's heart squeeze.

Had there been something going on at school that she'd missed while she was busy being consumed by thoughts of torrid sex?

"What's wrong?"

"Nothing, Mom."

"I don't believe you."

"Well, I don't want to talk about it."

"Talking will make you feel better," Mikey said from the back.

"Shut up, Mikey, I'm not you!"

"Okay, that's enough. You don't need to tell Mikey to shut up. She's trying to be nice."

"She's being pushy, you both are. If Dad were here, he would know not to push me."

Because your dad doesn't care as much as I do.

Wow. Thank God she'd managed to hold back those words, because that wasn't fair at all. Daniel had been a dick to her, but when he was home, he was a good dad. The girls were mad at him right now, but they wouldn't always be.

Well, Mikey always would be a little. She had a pure soul that was rooted in honesty, and in some ways, Wendy thought her daughter was a little too like her. Like she wanted maybe a little bit too much from a world that was never going to give it. That made her unforgiving and rigid sometimes, and also made her say things to her grumpy older sister like *talking will make you feel better*, because she only ever said what she believed.

Sadie, though, would forgive him. Because Sadie wanted things not to hurt so much, and forgiving her dad would make that relationship hurt less.

Wendy needed her girls to be able to forgive him.

She needed to keep some of the spite to herself.

You have Boone for your spite.

Well, that was almost a worse thought. Boone wasn't her human crutch, and he sure as hell wasn't there to just listen to her endlessly complain about her marriage.

He would say he was happy to do that, she knew.

Because that was Boone entirely.

What did his feelings matter?

What did his desires matter?

She thought of him ordering her down onto her knees. With a cushion firmly in place for her comfort.

She turned her car down the driveway to the ranch, and had the sudden image of one of her first dates with Daniel, at a pizza parlor that had pinball machines. She'd watched him play for a couple of hours, and she'd thought then that she was so dizzy with her infatuation for him she might as well be one of the balls in the machine.

She felt like a pinball now.

Worried about her kids. Worried about their relationship with their dad.

Flashbacks to giving a blowjob to the hottest man she knew.

Ping. Ping.

And right into the hole.

"We're having dinner at Boone's tonight."

"I'm not in the mood!" Sadie wailed. "I don't want to be social. I just want to have a plate of food and go to my room."

Well, this was wonderful.

"You can have a plate of food at Boone's and then leave, no one is asking you to stay and chat all night."

"You can't just dump this on me."

"I can't just dump you eating dinner next door to the house we're staying in, with someone you like a lot, who has generously given us a place to stay?"

"Yes!" She said that as if it was obvious, and also as if Wendy was an actual monster.

"Fine, Sadie, I'll leave you a plate at home, then."

"You're leaving me by myself?"

She said that tremulously and angrily, and if Wendy weren't also overwrought, she might have laughed. "Unsolvable problem, Sadie," she said. She was often reminding her daughter that she loved to present her mother with a problem, then when given solutions, she had a ready spate of reasons they wouldn't work.

Which was fifteen and fair, she guessed, but why did everything have to be a struggle?

"I just don't know why we have to go to Boone's."

"Because he is my friend and I wanted to spend the evening with him, and he wanted to see you both because he hasn't."

"I want to go to Boone's," said Mikey. "I haven't even been inside the house and we've been here for four days."

That earned a growl from Sadie, and Wendy accepted that there would be no consensus. Which was just life and parenting sometimes, but she didn't like it especially.

She knew she could be a hard-ass about Sadie's attitude if she wanted to be. But the thing was, Wendy had an attitude about things a lot of the time too. She'd smashed Daniel's headlights in after all. And yes, it had felt deserved.

But she knew all of this felt real and deserved to Sadie.

Maybe also you feel a lot of guilt over the whole thing.

Maybe.

Which wasn't fair, it wasn't her fault.

Not the divorce...you wanting to spend time with Boone.

Yeah. Okay fine.

They got home and Sadie went straight to her room while Wendy started dinner with Mikey sitting at the kitchen table. She could have cooked at Boone's, but she would rather be here talking to Mikey while she worked, and in close proximity to the melting down teenager.

"I don't know what her deal is," Mikey said.

"She's fifteen."

"I won't act that way when I'm fifteen."

Her heart squeezed tight. *Oh, Mikey. You will.*

"Thanks, honey."

"What are you making?"

"Lasagna."

"Yum."

At least she was doing something right in Mikey's world. Right now, she'd take it.

And after she was done with dinner and it was time to head to Boone's, Sadie appeared in a hoodie, with her hands stuffed in her kangaroo pouch pockets and the hood firmly over her head. But she appeared.

"Lasagna?" she asked.

"Yes. I can dish you a plate and you can go back to your cave, or you can come over for a little while."

She shrugged. "I'll come over."

So they made their way over to Boone's with a big bowl of salad, a pan of lasagna and no small amount of resentment from Sadie, like a parade. If only a very small one.

Boone opened the door and grinned. "Thanks for the dinner party."

And she noticed Sadie was charmed by him, even if reluctantly.

The house was better organized now, even though they'd spent the last two days having sex, which had taken up a good portion of her cleaning time. Apparently when she was motivated she could get a lot done.

But to his credit, Boone had set the table nicely for them, and he had an array of soft drinks in the fridge, which she knew was for the girls.

"Thank you," she said softly, as the girls dished their plates and took their seats.

"How is everything?" Boone asked.

Thankfully Sadie didn't implode and Mikey took the lead, talking about her art classes and her new friends with a lot of enthusiasm.

It made Wendy feel conflicted because Mikey was clearly finding a group she enjoyed here, even after four days, and Wendy was planning on going somewhere else after the month ended.

You were planning on getting away from Boone's charity, it doesn't mean you have to leave.

No, it didn't.

But how could she live near him without…

Why was she so afraid of that? Why couldn't she entertain the idea of a future with him?

She knew why. She knew all the logical reasons why. You shouldn't go from being married to being with someone new, and the stakes were so high. Her daughters had been through enough and she didn't want to drag them through any extra instability. And it was possible she felt pressure to be the most perfect parent so they would always stay on her side.

Well. She wasn't going to win that game. She was the parent most actively parenting, so she was going to be the bad one sometimes and there was nothing she could do about that.

She looked across the table and met Boone's gaze.

And resisted the feeling of rightness that washed through her.

This had been a weird mistake.

A form of torture.

She hadn't thought it through.

Sitting around a family dinner table with him and eating all together. Seeing where he could fit into her life. Into the most important spaces of it.

"And how was your day?" he asked, now looking directly at Wendy.

She blushed. She could feel it. Her whole face went hot and she hoped—she really hoped—her children would continue to be the preteen/teenage narcissists she could generally count on them to be and not notice subtle shifts in their mother.

"It was good, thank you. And yours?" She nearly coughed as she took a bite of her salad.

"Best I've had in a while."

She almost kicked him under the table.

True to her word, Sadie melted away as soon as dinner was over, but Mikey lingered, and Boone and Wendy ended up at the sink doing dishes while she chattered about the drawing techniques she was experimenting with, and how her favorite YouTubers did certain kinds of animation styles.

Wendy looked sideways at Boone, who looked down at her and smiled. Her shoulder touched his, and it was her turn to feel like she was in middle school.

Her stomach fluttered.

And without thinking she leaned in and brushed her arm against his very deliberately, which earned her a grin.

And another stomach flutter for good measure.

"But I really need to get some alcohol markers, because I think it would help with making the lines on my art crisper."

That jolted Wendy back into the moment. "Oh. Okay."

They finished up the dishes and she walked back to the house with Mikey.

"I really like Boone," Mikey said. "He's cool."

"Yeah. He is. I like him too." An understatement, but the most she was going to say to her twelve-year-old, who blessedly hadn't noticed any of the subtext happening all night.

Unfortunately, Wendy felt steeped in subtext.

And in the aching window into another life tonight had given her.

What would it be like if she stopped worrying about what

she thought was smart, or right—in the context of what other people would say—and just went for what she wanted?

If she closed her eyes and thought of her perfect life, Boone was in it.

So why was she fighting that so hard?

To try and protect herself.

But that ship had sailed, along with her inhibitions, right about the time she'd first kissed him.

The only real question was if she was going to keep on letting her childhood, the pain in her past, Daniel, the pain of his betrayal and the years' worth of lies decide what she got to have.

Yes, it was fast. But it also wasn't.

Boone had been there all along, and so had her feelings for him.

She had kept them in the most appropriate place possible. She had been a good wife. She'd honored her vows.

But the feelings had been there all the same. Daniel had been a great reason not to act on them then. He didn't get to be her reason anymore.

She was her reason.

And because of how she loved she could trust everything to flow from there.

Because she loved her girls, and their happiness would feed hers. She could trust herself.

To make the best decisions she was capable of making— not perfect ones, but not wholly selfish ones either.

She just had to hope that in the end, Boone wanted the same things she did.

But if not...

She was strong. And she had a lot of things to live for, and smile for.

She knew how to hold happiness and sadness in her hands at the same time.

So, if she had to, she'd just hold it all, and keep living.

Chapter Nine

When his phone rang, he half expected it to be Daniel because he had heard from the disgruntled asshole more times in the last few days than he would like to. Actually just twice, but that was more than he would like, and he especially didn't want to speak to him after having incredible transformative sex with the guy's soon-to-be ex-wife. Not because Boone was ashamed, and not because he found it weird. It was because, as angry as he had been before, he was even angrier now. Wendy deserved better. She deserved a whole lot better, and he wasn't going to be able to restrain himself from saying that. Because she was everything.

It wasn't Daniel, however, it was Flint.

"Hey. Calling from your private jet?"

"She doesn't travel by private jet. She thinks that's problematic for the environment."

"Wow. Not because you can't afford to."

"She's very famous," said Flint.

"You don't find that threatening to your masculinity?"

His brother laughed. The sound deep and rolling across the phone line. "No. My masculinity is good. Anyway. Tansey and I are coming into town tomorrow, and I was hoping we could get together for a family barbecue."

"Yeah. Sounds good."

That would be time spent away from Wendy, though. He

could bring her, of course, but that would be integrating her into the family in a way that…

Hell.

"I hear your hesitation. I'm wondering if it's because of your houseguest."

"I don't have a houseguest," he said, mentally trying to determine which person might have told Flint what was going on.

"I talked to Jace," he said. "He mentioned you had Wendy Stevens staying with you."

"Not with me. Wendy and her daughters are staying in the cottage on my property, and Wendy is doing some work for me. I'm paying her, and I'm giving her a place to stay while she works on extricating herself from that situation with her cheating husband."

"Got it. And it has no connection whatsoever with your personal feelings for her?"

"Of course it does. I don't just go offering a place to any random woman."

There was no point lying about it.

"Yeah. Well. Maybe you should bring her."

"Yeah, I was thinking…"

"I know you were thinking. I could practically hear you thinking. But you might as well bring her. And the kids."

"That might be weird."

"It's only weird if you make it weird, Boone. Maybe you should figure yourself out."

"There's nothing to figure out. I'm not in any way confused about what's happening right now."

"Well. Good for you. You're the only one of us who's managed to get entangled with somebody and not be confused."

"It's not an entanglement. I've known her for a long time, and she's a friend. She needs somebody right now. And I'm not going to lie and say there's nothing more happening. But, you know, I would never put pressure on her to make it too much. And that's the problem," he said. "Yeah. That's the problem. If I go inviting her to a family thing she might think I'm pushing her for too much too soon."

"Or she might be grateful. You should leave it up to her."

That was the second time he'd had that feedback from one of his brothers. The second time they had pointed out he was making the decisions for Wendy, and maybe he shouldn't do that.

He could understand. And he even agreed. Because he didn't think it was right to make decisions on a woman's behalf. But he was just... He could foresee issues here, and again, he didn't hold out blind hope something wouldn't be awkward when it was clear it would be.

Except not inviting her...

Dammit.

"Fine. I'll invite her. I'm looking forward to seeing you."

"You too."

He got off the phone, and decided to walk straight back to his place. And there she was. In all her glory. He'd already been back to see her today, already made love to her. And she was looking at him with wide eyes. "I have to go get the girls in, like, ten minutes."

"I could get it done in ten minutes."

Her cheeks turned pink. "I'm sure you could..."

"That isn't why I'm here. My brother Flint and his fiancée, Tansey, are coming into town tomorrow. We're having a barbecue and I thought maybe you and the girls might come."

"As in... Tansey Martin."

"Yes. Tansey Martin. I know she and their breakup are very famous. As is their reconciliation, since there are now songs about that, too, and about to be a whole album."

"My girls are going to freak out." She shook her head. "We probably shouldn't go. Because it's a family thing, and they're just going to be starstruck."

"Oh, they are. Not you."

She laughed. "Okay. I will be a little bit, but I'll be able to control it. Because I'm an adult."

"It's okay. She brings that out in people. You can be starstruck. But also if…if it seems weird to you to come to a thing with my whole family…"

She frowned. "It's weird for you, isn't it?"

"I didn't say that."

"Your face said it. You don't want me to go."

"Wendy," he said, regret tugging at his chest. "I do want you to go. I'm honest, right? I'm being honest. I was just a little bit worried about some of the…"

"You're worried about getting too involved."

"Yes. Because everything feels great right now, but it isn't going to last."

"Why not?"

She looked at him, so open and trusting, and it killed him.

"You know why. I've still got some time in the rodeo left. You and Dan aren't even divorced…"

"That sounds like a lot."

"We don't need to get ahead of ourselves," he said.

"Don't pull away from me just because of all that."

He let out a hard breath. "I'm not. You're the one who said you wanted to leave at the end of the month."

"I might not leave town."

"Great. I'd love it if you didn't leave town."

Except that felt like something clawing at his chest, and he couldn't quite say why.

"Maybe we both just settle down a little bit. And I will come to the family thing, as long as you're good with it."

"I'm very good with it. Perfectly happy."

"If the girls found out Tansey Martin was going to be a thing at your parents' house and they weren't allowed to go…"

"You're welcome to be there. I'm sorry."

He looked at her, and he felt… Wounded. It was the strangest thing. He had messed that up. He hadn't handled it well, and he just had to wonder if in the end he was going to do more harm than good to her. It was the last thing he wanted.

Of all the things, he knew that. But she was just asking those questions. Why couldn't they be together? Why not?

There weren't simple words for why not. That was the problem. Maybe he'd been avoiding thinking about whether or not his plan was to end up by himself because he hadn't planned on finding somebody or because that was the way it was going to be.

The fact was, the one woman he'd been able to imagine himself being with was Wendy. And it had been one thing when she was with another man. One thing when she was married. That had been destiny. She was safe from him when they'd met.

And now, everything else was due to Daniel's shortcoming. It didn't count.

It wasn't a thing.

It meant he got to have her now. It didn't mean he had anything different up ahead of him.

He had to keep clearheaded about it.

"I'll see you later."

"Yeah. I… I probably won't make the girls come over and have dinner tonight."

"Hey. Fair."

"But they'll enjoy the family thing on Saturday. So. And I'll see you before then. I…"

"Yeah. I know."

"Okay, I'll see you."

He didn't move. She did, though, headed past him and out to her car. And somehow, he felt like he'd made a mistake. He just didn't know what it was.

Chapter Ten

She had underestimated how awkward it would be to load everyone up into Boone's truck again with the amount of tension she felt just looking at him.

She was sure even her narcissistic teenagers would feel the tension.

Surely.

They didn't seem to, though. It was only Wendy who was sweaty and nervous and far too hot as they drove from Boone's ranch at one end of Lone Rock, to his family ranch all the way on the other end and out the other side of town.

She was never half so grateful for how absorbed teenagers were in their own issues than she had been these last few days. Or maybe that was simply because she was so absorbed in her own issues. Maybe it wasn't a teenage thing. Maybe it had to do with life being exciting. New.

It was always like that for her kids. Bless them. It was like that right now for her. Bless Boone.

She looked at his strong profile as he pulled the car up into the front of his parents' massive home. Yes, things were definitely exciting with him. But somehow, not easy. And you would think that if you had wanted a man for fifteen years, the coming together would be the easy part.

But maybe that was the problem. Something was holding him back. And she could understand there were logical things. There were things that had been holding her back.

But maybe that was the problem. Maybe she had to go all in. *You've done that before.*

Yes. She had. She had gone all in with Daniel. But it wasn't the same.

It just wasn't.

Boone…

Maybe calling it love now, this early, was a little bit foolish.

But maybe she felt a little bit foolish.

Maybe she was foolish. Certainly jumping into bed with a man on the rebound was somewhat typical behavior, but falling for the idea that it might be something more? There was almost no chance of anybody making that mistake unless they were doing it willingly.

Willfully even.

But what if it wasn't a mistake? What if it was him? What if it was always supposed to be him? Or maybe, even more beautifully, it was supposed to be him now, and the way she had felt about him up until this point was essential to being brought here to this moment.

Maybe.

But as she stared at his profile, intently, she just knew something.

She wasn't entirely sure what. But it was certain and settled in her soul. And the one thing she couldn't do in response was hold herself back.

She had to be all in. She had to be his.

"Let's go in," she said.

"Yeah," he said, looking at her and forcing a smile.

Wendy felt heavy, but she got out of the truck, and the girls followed suit.

"Is Tansey Martin really going to be here?" Mikey asked her mom, her eyes large.

"Yes. Why would I say that if it wasn't true?"

"To try and beat Sadie out of her room."

"I would never try and beat Sadie with something as basic as a pop-country crossover star. Sadie is not that basic."

"I'm basic," said Mikey.

"Mom," said Sadie. "You make me sound like a snob."

"I'm not making you sound like a snob. You are a snob. But it's okay. You're fifteen. It's your right."

"Tansey is very nearly my sister-in-law. I assume you know about the song," said Boone.

"Yes," said Mikey seriously. "We watched the short film."

"You should make sure to tell Flint that. He loves it. He's a huge fan. It did great things for his life."

Wendy looked at him in warning. "Don't tell teenagers things like that. They'll do it."

"I'm counting on it."

"What are you supposed to do when there's just, like, a famous person there?" Sadie asked.

"You just, like, eat your hamburger," Boone said, grinning at her.

Sadie smiled, which was glorious for Wendy to see.

Boone was so good with them.

They had a dad. But Boone would make a great masculine figure to have in their lives. He was protective. He was fun.

She wanted him.

He would make her happy.

Or at least contribute quite a bit to her happiness. That would help everybody.

Just jump in feetfirst. You're already there.

The Carson family home was massive, and beautiful, with floor-to-ceiling windows overlooking the craggy mountains and rustic decor throughout.

It was filled with all the siblings—even Boone's sister Callie, who Wendy knew vaguely from the rodeo. That was the great thing. It wasn't a room full of strangers. She knew Boone's parents, and she knew all his brothers, even if only in passing.

She had spent enough time at the circuit to feel like they were family in many ways.

"And how are you finding the single life?" This question came from Abe Carson.

"I'm not technically single," she said, grateful her daughters were occupied across the room. Talking to Tansey, who was warm and wonderful and actually not at all intimidating.

"Philosophically," said Abe.

"Thanks, Dad," said Boone.

"I see," said Abe. "Well, hurry up and get that divorce finalized so my son can make an honest woman out of you."

Her scalp prickled. "Well, I am happy to move it quickly."

She didn't see the point in protesting. Because hell, she kind of wanted Boone to make an honest woman out of her. Or a dishonest one. She just wanted to be with him. And her parameters for what that could look like were becoming quite elastic. At first, she had been a bit concerned about her girls knowing she was sleeping with a man she wasn't married to. But if they had a relationship... She was willing to have a serious and grown-up talk about it. Because this was life, and it was messy. She was in a situation she hadn't chosen, but she didn't have to be miserable.

"Actually, Wendy is looking for some new work. You know she managed Daniel."

"She could manage you," said Abe. "And there are some other guys I know who would love to have competent representation."

"I'm not sure I'm going to be anybody's favorite, considering I just kicked their buddy to the curb."

"If they have half a brain then *he's* not their favorite. I've never had patience for a man who would go out for cheap ground beef when he had filet mignon at home."

"Seems to me," Flint said from across the room, "that it's the man with quality issues, not the woman."

"Sorry, son," said Abe. "I know I'm not woke."

"I don't think I'm woke," said Flint. "I just like women."

Wendy couldn't help but smile at the exchange.

They were a good family. Everybody involved was just… They cared about each other. And it didn't matter if they disagreed about things or saw things differently, they cared about each other. It felt different than what she'd imagined family might be. It had just been her and her mother after all.

And now it was her and the girls.

But even though she had a good relationship with Sadie and Mikey, it hadn't quite been this. Or at least, it had never quite been this between herself and Daniel. Because one thing she noticed was the way Abe and his wife interacted with each other.

There was an ease to them. And she didn't think she and Daniel had ever had that ease.

She looked at Boone. She wanted to feel it with him.

But she had a feeling if she put her hand on his, he would pull away, and she didn't want that.

She felt like they could have something easy and wonderful. If only they were brave enough to take the chance.

So she got up from her position on the couch and moved over to him, sitting next to him. It was a fairly unambiguous move.

No one said anything, but they all looked.

The other reason she couldn't go putting her hand on him just yet was the girls.

She needed to talk to them. At least, it felt like she should.

Not to get their permission, just to give them a warning. A heads-up. Her mother had never dated when Wendy was growing up, because her father had done such a number on her she had never wanted a man in her life again. It made Wendy sad, in hindsight.

And maybe the only way Sadie and Mikey would ever

be able to understand Wendy wanting to be with somebody else was going to be in hindsight. Or maybe that assumption wasn't fair to them.

"We should go shooting," said Jace.

"What in the redneck?" Cara asked.

"It's a Carson family tradition. We love a good target practice."

Callie looked at her husband. "Will you stay with the baby?"

"Sure," he said.

"I'll stay with the baby," said Callie's mother. "You can all go shoot. I don't mind."

"Can I watch?" Mikey asked.

"Sure," said Wendy.

She had a feeling they were all going out for target practice.

"I guess I'll go," said Sadie, keeping an eye on Tansey, obviously curious about whether or not her new best friend was going.

"Sounds great," said Tansey brightly.

And so with that, they all trooped outside.

"We like to shoot up this way near this big gravel pit. It's got good secure backings so the bullets don't go drifting off anywhere they shouldn't."

"Good to know."

"My dad has extra ear protection in the shed."

"Oh good. So as far as adventurous activities go…"

"This one is occurring in a well-controlled fashion. No worries."

"I wasn't actually worried. I know you would never do anything to put yourself or the girls in danger."

He looked down at her, the exchange between them feeling weighty. Significant.

"I wouldn't," he said.

The girls were behind them, and so she didn't take his hand.

But she did bump her shoulder against his, and he looked down, smiling. She smiled back.

"I like you."

He looked a little bit like she had hit him in the side of the head. "I like you too."

It felt pale in comparison to what she was actually feeling, but she didn't know how to say the other things. She didn't know what else to say.

It felt sharp and dangerous still. And this was the problem with never having been good at math. Order of operations was something she struggled with. She wanted to kiss him now. In front of everybody. Because there was a significant part of her that had already realized she had to go all in. That had already realized there was no going back. That had already realized she would never be able to quit him, never be able to forget him.

And there would be no protecting herself from any manner of heartbreak.

She would be heartbroken to lose him. Whether she told him she was in love with him or not. Whether she said she wanted everything or not.

Whether she did the important work of extricating herself from her marriage, and then tried to do some healing on her own, she was always going to come back to him. So she might as well... She just might as well.

Put herself out there. But there were ways that she needed to go about it. She knew that.

So she just smiled, and she kept *like* as the word, even though it wasn't enough. Not even close.

When they got up to the gravel pit, she and the girls put on ear protection and hung back while they took turns shooting things. Targets, yes, some kind of jelly target that healed itself. And also water jugs. Which did not heal themselves, but exploded grandly.

Mikey was very invested in the spectacle, and Sadie pretended to be just a little bit too cool. But ended up enjoying it all the same. Wendy could tell by the small smile on her face.

She felt a rush of euphoria right then. This could be their family.

Don't rush ahead of yourself and start glorifying all of this. They're just people. And they're not going to fix the difficult situation you're in.

No. That was what she had to be extra careful about.

Boone wasn't a crutch. He never would be. He was more than that.

And she felt…scared. It reminded her of old times.

She didn't like it.

But she really did want him and all these things that he came with. That wasn't so bad, was it?

She knew all these things he could do for her. All these things he had done for her.

And yes, she was working for him, but it wasn't the same.

She wanted to think of something she could do for him.

He felt so much responsibility toward everybody in his life.

And she didn't want to be just another responsibility to him. She wanted to be something more.

She watched as he shouldered the rifle, and she squeezed her thighs together, because whether she should or not, she was always going to find that hot.

Or maybe it was just him. And he could breathe and she would experience a pulse of arousal. Entirely possible. The man had an extreme effect on her.

He blew up the water jug with one shot, and she laughed and clapped. She couldn't help herself.

Maybe it was a little juvenile. But she felt juvenile, she'd already admitted that. This felt new. Wonderful. Terrifying.

And she wanted it. All of it.

They had target practice contests, and in the end it was their sister Callie who bested everybody. Afterward, they hoisted her up on their shoulders, while she screeched in protest, and Tansey, Wendy and the girls clapped. Cara pretended to be furious, while Shelby and Juniper made grand shows out of being gracious losers, since they had competed as well.

When they started the walk back, Flint was up with his sister, and Wendy lagged behind with her girls.

"I want to tell you something," said Wendy.

"What?" asked Sadie.

This was dangerous. Because the girls could make a big scene right here. But…she didn't really care.

Mostly because she just wasn't ashamed of any of it. If they had a bad reaction to it, they were going to have to deal with it.

"I just wanted to let you know that I…that I like Boone."

"Of course you do," said Mikey. "He's cool."

"No, Mikey. I…I *like* like Boone."

Both the girls stopped walking. "You're not serious?" Sadie asked.

"I am. And I wanted to tell you before…"

"Before what?" Sadie asked.

"Just before. That's all. Before anyone else."

"You're not even divorced yet," said Sadie.

"I know. I'm just being honest. And maybe it's premature. I don't know what's going to happen, if anything. Entirely possible *nothing*. But I just like him."

It wasn't Sadie who reacted. It wasn't Sadie who had an explosion. To Mikey's credit, it wasn't an explosion. But she put her head down, and she ran ahead. She wasn't quite in a group with anyone, but she held herself with her head down, and walked, and Wendy was too stunned to catch up with her. She felt frozen, and kept walking at the pace she'd been walking at before, uncertain of what to do. She really hated all the uncertainty.

"It's weird," said Sadie.

"I know," said Wendy.

"She'll get over it."

She looked at Sadie. "Are you over it?"

"I don't know. I think it's weird because… Because it hasn't been that long. But he's been really nice to us, and I know he makes you happy. You haven't been happy. And really, you shouldn't be. You left just a few weeks ago, and everything's been crazy, and you were not happy until we got here."

"But you're not especially happy here, are you?"

"I don't know. I do know that I wasn't happy back home either. I'm trying to be. But this is all weird, and it's a change."

"I want you girls to be happy. And I would never do anything to compromise that."

"That's the thing. I'm not sure there's anything you can do one way or the other. Sometimes we're just unhappy."

It was clarity from her oldest daughter that she hadn't really expected. But she could understand the truth there. They were teenagers. And she wasn't going to be able to make them happy. Not all the time.

"Okay. I accept that. But I do want you to know that I love you," she said. "No matter what. And all this stuff… I don't want it to make you afraid."

"What?"

"We haven't talked that much about what it was like for me growing up. But for good reasons, my mom was afraid of some things. And she made me afraid of them too. And I don't want my issues to become yours. I have them. Of course I do. And you can have your own. Like you said, you can't be happy all the time. Because you have your own life. I'm not in charge of that. But I love you, and I'm here for you. And to the best of my ability, I don't want the stuff I'm going through to mess with you. If you're miserable here, I want you to tell me. But I think I want to try to make a life with Boone. I don't know if he's going to want that with me."

"Okay. I guess that's…fair."

She could tell Sadie wasn't exactly overjoyed, but she didn't look upset or outraged either.

"I'll talk to Mikey."

"Maybe you should talk to Boone first," said Sadie.

"Well, what if Mikey can't deal?" She hated all this fear. This fear that made up her life. She'd been so certain that marrying Daniel had gotten rid of it, but it hadn't. She was stitched together by fear, her whole life a patchwork quilt. Hunger, fear, then family, love. But the thread was fear either way.

She'd been so scared of losing Daniel, of losing her stability, and now she had. She was afraid of messing things up with her kids, afraid of losing Boone…

There was just so much to be afraid of. And it was what she'd known from the time she was a kid.

"Mikey is twelve," said Sadie. "I don't think you should go making decisions based on her moods."

"I could apply the same thing to you."

"I know. You shouldn't make decisions because of me. You're the adult."

She *was* the adult. But she was a freaked-out adult.

Still, she had to act like the adult.

And maybe as much as she wanted to be gentle with her kids right now, there was a merit in setting boundaries too. And in that, she supposed Sadie was right. Maybe she had to figure herself out first. She had a little bit of that epiphany earlier. But there was a certain amount of happiness she had to find before she could be the best parent.

This conversation with Sadie was confirming it. Removing barriers and obstacles she had put in her own way.

"Okay. I'll sort it out with Boone."

"He is nice. It'll be weird for you to be with someone that isn't Dad. But…"

"Yeah, life is weird. I guess if you've learned one thing

from me, I don't want this to scar you, but it's not the worst thing to learn, it's that life changes. And sometimes the best thing you can do is just go with it."

So she was going to go with it. Whether it was smart or advised or not anything of the kind. She was going to go with it because it was her life. And it didn't matter what best practices were. She was living. And it was messy. Real. One of her kids understood, and one of them didn't. She wasn't going to get a one hundred percent buy-in here. She was just going to have to love them.

And herself.

And Boone.

And in the end she was going to have to hope it was enough.

Because fate might've put her in his path all those years ago, but fate wasn't going to make the right decisions for her now. Only she could do that.

She had resisted for a while. But what she wanted was going to require some work. So she was going to have to get busy.

Chapter Eleven

When Boone woke up the next morning, coffee was on in the kitchen.

And he could smell bacon.

It was Sunday, but he still had ranch work to do. He wondered if Wendy...

Yesterday with his family had been a whole trip. He had been so close to pulling her into his arms on multiple occasions, and yet he had known he couldn't. Because what was the point of it? But she was here today.

He walked downstairs, and there she was in the kitchen.

"Good morning."

"What are you doing over here?"

"I decided to make you breakfast."

"Thank you."

"You're welcome."

"Do the girls think you're having an early shift?"

"You're hilarious. It's the weekend. The girls aren't going to know anything until sometime after 10 a.m. But, anyway, I'm not worried about it. I told them."

"You told them?"

"Yes."

"What did you tell them?"

"Not that we were banging on every surface in the house, but that I liked you."

"That you liked me."

"Yes. That I *like you* like you."

"And how did that go?"

"Fifty-fifty. But I wasn't asking anybody's permission."

"Okay…"

She held up a hand. "You don't have to say anything."

"I figure I probably should."

"There's not much to say."

"Well. The thing is… I thought you were leaving in a month." He'd reminded himself of it every day. The reality of it. Of the situation.

She was still married.

She had kids.

She was leaving.

"I keep telling you, I'm not necessarily leaving. I appreciate everything you've done for me. What do you need?"

He looked at her dumbfounded. "What?"

"Boone, what do you need? You're retiring, you're starting this ranch. Do you want to take over the commission?"

"I told you, it doesn't really matter what I want—"

"Why not? Why do other people get all the consideration? Your father doesn't need you to take over the rodeo commission. That's about want. His. So why does it outweigh yours? Or why do your wants not even get to be up for consideration? I don't understand that. It doesn't make any sense to me."

"Because what the hell else am I going to do with my life, Wendy?"

"I was thinking about that the other day. And I was thinking about what your dad said. That I could represent the other cowboys. I know we didn't talk about that for very long yesterday, but I could do that. He's right. It's just a matter of going out and making the most of my connections. I'm really good at this. Representing people. I could do you too. But the thing is, opportunities don't just come to you. And I've understood that when it comes to agenting. But I haven't always been great about that in my personal life. And you're great. You're wonderful with the rodeo, you've got this property, all of that. But do you know... Do you understand that you can't just let life carry you down a current? You have to—"

"Yes I know that," he said. "I'm not just drifting. And I resent the hell out of the suggestion that I am."

"That isn't what I meant. I just meant you can't wait for things to fall into place. You have to get them. And you have to care."

"I care. I care so much that I have shoved everything I've ever wanted to the side. For my mother. For my father. For my friendship with your idiot husband."

"Well, Daniel isn't our problem anymore."

"He's the father of your kids. He is still our problem."

She shook her head. "I don't love him. I haven't for a long time. I don't love him, and I don't want that life back. I don't. It costs so much. And I didn't even realize it. It was so expensive to stay in that marriage. I thought it would be too expensive to leave it. But that isn't it at all. The real expense was in staying there. I wasn't happy. I liked being in that house by myself. I didn't like being in it with him. I didn't like *him*. I like being alone more. I convinced myself that I liked him, but what I felt was a holdover from what we used to have. What I liked, I think, was the part-time nature of it. I don't love him. And I was going to just...let duty or honor or the fear of change hold me there.

"I'm not sorry that I didn't do something disreputable. I'm not sorry that we didn't... I'm not sorry that I was faithful to him. I'm not. But I am a little bit sorry that I convinced myself somehow that doing the right thing would be what made me the happiest. When I say the right thing, what I mean was this idea of the right thing, this idea of what marriage vows were, this idea my husband didn't even agree with. I convinced myself it had to be the best thing, it had to be fate. It's not about fate. It was about fear. Fear of change. Fear of finding out if I left him, I'd have nothing, but that's a terrible reason to stay married. We get to make choices. And we get to demand more. We get to demand better. Anyway, I'm just… I'm deciding. And I'm here to have breakfast."

"Breakfast and demands. That's a whole thing."

"Well, *I'm* a whole thing. But I don't actually want to make demands."

"Except you want to know what I want."

"Let me care about that. Please. If you won't."

But he didn't have words. He didn't have anything. Nothing but a weird, pounding sense of panic moving through his chest, so he leaned in and he kissed her. Because it was better than talking. Because it was better than just about anything. Because when she asked what he wanted all he could think of was her, and everything else felt like details. Everything else felt like it might not matter.

He kissed her because she was what he wanted. Because she was everything.

Because she always had been.

He kissed her because it was like breathing.

It didn't much matter if it made sense. It had never made sense. He held her against his body, and growled.

"There's bacon," she said weakly.

"Fuck the bacon."

She blinked. "Okay."

He backed her up against the wall, kissing her, consuming her.

"I want you, Wendy. And none of it matters. None of it matters."

"Yes," she said.

Except that was wrong. It was wrong that he just… It was terrifying. Because it couldn't last. Nothing ever could.

He could already feel himself losing her. He could feel it

in the dissatisfaction she was expressing this morning. In her asking for things he didn't know how to give.

He could feel it in the way his heart pounded when he tried to imagine forever, but could only picture his house empty.

He was losing her.

By inches.

Because that was what happened when someone was close to you. As close as a person could be. They had to start moving away at some point.

It was the natural order of things. An inevitability.

It was inevitable and he knew it.

He *knew* it.

It was just the way of the world. But right now, he was holding her. Firm against his body, and he was holding her so tight he was shaking.

And it would never be enough.

That was the other problem. When you cared about people, no amount of time could ever be enough.

There was no good cut-off point to a relationship. There just wasn't.

But sometimes things were terminal. And you had to accept it.

It would never feel like quite enough. And he was so unbearably, horribly aware of that as he pressed her soft body against the hard wall of his body and poured every ounce of his need into the kiss.

It was somewhere beyond need. It was desperation.

He stripped her shirt up over her head, but it got hung up on the apron because he couldn't think. Because he couldn't do things in the right order.

Hell. That seemed like a metaphor.

He untied the apron and threw it down onto the floor, taking the shirt with it.

She had on a sexy, lacy bra, not the normal kind of thing she wore.

And it was for him. And that mattered more than the bra itself. That she was wearing it for him, and he knew it.

All of this was for him. The coffee, the bacon, the sex. It was his.

And why did that feel terrifying?

Why did this feel like the beginning of the end? He didn't have an answer for that.

All he had was need.

So he kissed her like he was dying, because he thought he might be.

Because the idea of having to answer the question of what he wanted beyond what he'd already said seemed like a gallows.

And when he had her naked against the wall, he freed himself from his jeans and lifted her leg up over his hip and slid deep inside of her.

He watched her face as he began to move, as he moved deep inside of her, he wanted her. Wanted this. He wanted it to go on forever. But nothing ever did. Nothing ever did. His climax came on too hot, too strong, too fast.

He resented it.

And so he held back, bit the inside of his cheek so he could keep on going. Until she cried out, until her internal muscles pulsed around him. Until she was coming apart all over him, because he needed her to be as shattered as he was.

He needed to gain some control.

He put his hand between them, stroked her, brought her to climax again. He withdrew from her body, and sank to his knees, burying his face between her thighs and licking her until she shattered again.

He would do whatever he had to, to keep this going. Until he couldn't bear it anymore. Until he was so hard it hurt. Until the memory of what it had been like to be buried inside of her became too much, and he pulled her down onto the floor and over top of him, down onto his length, letting her ride him for two easy movements until he couldn't stand it anymore. Until he reversed their positions and pounded hard into her. Losing himself in this. In her.

Losing himself entirely.

And that moment felt endless. And over all too quickly.

And when she shattered again, he lost his own control.

He growled, letting go. Of everything. Absolutely everything.

And it felt like a loss when it was done.

And all she'd asked him was what he wanted.

But it had broken something inside of him.

"I love you."

And that was it. That was the beginning of the end.

Because this bright, white light tried to ignite in his chest and it was the one thing he could never accept. Not ever.

"Wendy…"

"No," she said. "Don't."

"Don't what?"

"Don't argue with me. Don't disagree with me. Don't make this harder than it has to be. You don't need to answer me right now, you don't. We can take our time. I'm sorry, I'm jumping ahead. But I don't know how else to let you know that I don't want to have a time limit on this."

"But everything has a time limit," he said. "Nothing lasts forever. It's better this way. If we can just decide on an end-point and—"

"It's been sixteen years. It's been sixteen years and I want you more today than I ever have. It has been sixteen years since you walked into that bar right after I married my husband and ruined my life, Boone. You ruined me. I have not wanted another man since. I haven't even entertained the idea."

"Except the man you were married to."

"That's different. It should have gone away, and it would've gone away. With time. You know, with the fact that I had children with somebody else. That I was supposed to love him and honor and cherish him for the rest of our lives."

"The only reason you didn't is because of him."

"I know that. I know that. You don't need to tell me why my marriage ended. You don't need to tell me what happened. I am well aware."

"I'm just saying, you were with somebody else and now you're not. And I'm an itch."

"Don't do that. Don't cheapen what we have. If you have to run away from this, then at least take it like a man. Don't belittle what we have. It's not fair. I deserve more than that, and so do you. Just be honest. Be honest about the fact that you can't cope, or that something's holding you back, or that you just don't feel the same as I do, but don't make it about me. I spent my whole life afraid, Boone. I'm just tired of it. I'm done. I don't want to leave a legacy of fear for my daughters. I don't want to be small and reduced because of something somebody else did to me. I want to live. I want to live, and I really, preferably would like to live with you. Yes, I came into this thinking there was no way it could be more now. How could it be? How could it be when you and I both know what a stupid idea it is to jump into a relationship at this point in my life? But I actually think it was stupid for us not to be together the whole time. Or maybe it wasn't. Maybe it had to be this. Maybe this is our timing. Whether it makes sense or not, maybe this is what's right for us. We didn't get here by betraying anybody, or by hurting anybody. We got here because it was where the road led us, and maybe that's okay. Maybe it's enough. Maybe that's what fate is. And now we have to grab hold of it."

"I love you," he said. "I do. I have. But it can't look the way that you want it to. It just can't. I'm not the right man to be in your daughters' lives. I don't want the responsibility. I have too much already, you know that. Because the thing is, I could never be Daniel. I could never go halfway. I can never mess up like that. I—"

"No. That's a lie, Boone. I know you. You can't love me and want to walk away."

"But I do. Because there isn't another choice. Not for me."

"Why?"

"Because everything ends. Everything. I can't live that way. If you're out there, and I love you, that doesn't end. But if you're here, if you're with me…you have to be realistic about these things."

She nodded. Slowly.

"I get it. Because I know what it is to be afraid. You're afraid. And you have every right to be. Life is crazy. And hard. You never know what's coming. But you can cling to what you want. You can fight for it. It doesn't have to be…" Suddenly something in her softened, even as she broke. "It's easier to want what other people want. To try and do it for them, because if you want something then you're the one that's going to get hurt. If you want me and you can't have me, you can love me but… You don't want me to love you. Because that's what you can't trust."

"That isn't it."

"It is. You don't trust me. You don't trust the world. Because it took a lot from you. You trusted your brother, and he left you. You were just a kid, and your sister died. Of course you don't trust in things to last. Of course you don't trust in people not to leave. Boone, I married a man because I felt passion for the first time, and then I was pregnant. And I didn't want to be alone. I entered my first relationship out of fear. Now I'm not afraid. And I'm not afraid to be alone."

"I thought she wouldn't die," he gritted out. "My parents told us she would. They said…they said the kind of cancer she had there was no chance. I didn't believe it. They were honest, but I couldn't deal with it. When she was gone I… I fell apart.

I hoped. I hoped and I believed…past reality, and it damned near killed me and I knew I could never do that again."

She wanted to weep. For the boy he'd been. The boy that was still in him now. Who was afraid to hope. Afraid to love.

"Boone, it took bravery to decide to be with you. I wasn't running from something. I was running to it. It's different. And I know it is. And no, I can't promise you that the world won't continue to be harsh and hard. But I can promise you that I am in this forever. Because if my love was so easily destroyed, then I would've gotten rid of it a long time ago. But I can't. I can't. I love you. And it's only right now, standing here, that it feels like a clear sky filled with stars. It was always cloudy until now. My love was there, but it couldn't shine bright. I couldn't see it clearly. But now I can. Now I do. It's been love all along."

She could see in his eyes that he knew it too. It was the thing that terrified him. Knowing he was afraid didn't help this hurt less, but it did make her feel resolved. She wasn't going to be afraid. She wasn't going to flinch, not now. Because she could see the fabric of her whole life, stitched together by this fear. Fear of scarcity. Fear that there just wasn't going to be enough love to go around. That there wasn't going to be enough of anything. It had driven her into her relationship with Daniel, and it had kept her there. It had made her cling to the companionable, the unobjectionable. It had made her ignore any red flags that might've been there, because she didn't think she deserved to see them. Didn't think she could afford to. She wasn't going to do that now.

"We've both been given a lot of bad things," she said. "We have both been given a lot of bullshit. But we have a chance to have each other. We have a chance to have something new, something different, and I'd like to take that chance."

"I want you to be happy," he said, his voice rough. "More than I want anything in the whole world, I want that. But I can't…"

She looked at him, and she felt pity. "I can be happy without you."

Something flashed through his eyes, and she saw the contrary nature, the complexity of it all. He wanted her to leave him be because he was afraid. He wanted her to be happy, but he also didn't. Maybe he wanted them both to be a little bit sad all the time because they couldn't have each other, but they could have the possibility of it. Maybe that was the problem. If she was out there, away from him, he would be able to think about what might've been. Instead of trying and failing and knowing what couldn't be.

But he didn't understand that her love would cover all the failure.

"Sorry," she said. "But it's true. Because I have Mikey and Sadie. And that means I'll be happy. Because I have a life. Because I have skills. Because I am going to move forward in this work that I've enjoyed doing. Because I'm happy enough with myself. That doesn't mean a part of my heart won't be broken. My life would be better for having you in it. But I won't be miserable. I'll never love another man the way that I love you. I don't even have any interest in it. My life is full enough without a man. It will never be full enough without you, though. But life is complicated. In the same way I was able to be committed to my marriage while knowing the possibility of you and I existed in the world, I will be able to be happy if you can't get yourself together. You're not going to hold my heart hostage. Not all of it. A piece of it. Yes. You might hold my body hostage too. I think I'm set for sex. Unless it's you. So yes. Part of me will be crushed. Part of me will be devastated. Part of me will never get over you. But you can rest in the knowledge that I'm out there happy in the world. You can rest in that. And you can love me from a distance. We can have half. We'll be fine. We did it for all these years." She swallowed hard. "But why? Life breaks us enough, why should we break ourselves? Why, when all we need is a little hope?"

"I can't believe in impossible things anymore. I have to believe in reality."

"Why is a sad ending more believable than a happy one?"

He said nothing.

She dressed, slowly and methodically, and she began to prepare to go.

"Wendy…"

"Don't say anything else. Because you can't say anything true. And I'm done with lies. I get that the lies are to yourself. But I just… I can't."

And when she walked out, she did cry. Real tears, falling hard and fast. And she felt like something in her chest was irrevocably cracked.

She stood there for a long moment, examining the difference. Between losing Daniel and losing Boone. Between knowing that it was over with him, and knowing it was over with Daniel.

The problem with Boone was he'd been there, a possibility, a distant fantasy, for fifteen years.

He had been the other part of her marriage. A piece of herself that she held back. Reserved for him. And now she'd given everything.

It was horrendous. And it hurt.

And she wouldn't trade it.

Wouldn't trade going all out. Wouldn't trade taking the risk.

She only hoped that in the end it was a lesson. If not for her, then for Mikey and Sadie.

That even if it was improbable, and even if it would hurt you, even if other people did not understand, you had to try for everything.

Because you were worth it.

Chapter Twelve

He didn't know what to do with himself. He had just done the dumbest thing he'd ever done in his whole life. And he rode bulls for a living.

He let her go.

You had to.

Why?

These were the rules he had set out for himself all these years ago, this embargo on hope, and now what were the rules doing for him? What had they gotten him?

He'd hurt the woman he cared for most.

And he'd devastated himself.

It hadn't protected him.

He felt like that boy, crumpled outside a hospital after being told his little sister was dead. He hadn't tried to hope and he still felt that way.

Because it won't last. It won't last.

And nobody understood that half as well as he did.

Screw Buck. Honestly. And cancer and everything else. Everything that had ever taken something from him.

He couldn't breathe.

He walked out of the main house, and stood there in the middle of the driveway, considering going to the cottage. To what end? Because what the hell was he going to do about any of it?

She was right. He was afraid. But he didn't know how not

to be. And why did somebody like Daniel—heedless, reckless—get to have her? Treat her lightly, hold their love loosely and shatter it almost intentionally?

How are you any different?

Dammit.

And how was he any different than Buck for that matter? Who had run away rather than trying to sort it all out. Who had shut his family out, shut out everyone who cared about him.

How was Boone any different?

He wasn't different.

He'd just built a different wall around himself. He called it responsibility. He let himself believe it made him different than those he didn't respect.

It hit all the ways that he was the same.

He texted his brothers.

Because he had to fix this. He had to fix himself. And one thing he knew was that he couldn't do it alone.

But the biggest difference between himself and those men was that he was going to fix this.

He was going to fix himself.

Because otherwise, it was only hurting other people to protect yourself.

He wouldn't do that to Wendy.

Because he loved her. And if there was one thing he knew, it was that.

She agreed to meet with him. Finally.

This was the last little pocket of fear. The last foothold. She was done with it.

Because what did she have to lose? She went back to the house that night, and she texted Daniel, and told him she wanted to meet in the middle. So the next morning, she took the girls to school, and then got onto the road, headed a few hours west to where he was stationed—not their house, somewhere out on the rodeo circuit—and walked into the diner that he suggested, feeling oddly calm.

There he was. Her husband of all those years. She was still mad at him. It was impossible not to be. He'd lied to her. Nobody felt good about that. Ever. Nobody liked to be tricked.

But she wasn't in love with him, and she was clear on that. She wasn't in love with him, so it felt…it felt not painful in that specific way.

He looked up from the mug of coffee in front of him and half waved.

"Hey, Wendy."

"Hi. Looks like you got your truck fixed."

"I just got a new one. I mean I traded it in."

That sounded like Daniel. Why fix what you had when you could just trade it for something new?

They were different that way. It was sobering to realize. All the ways in which she had ignored this.

"I want to see the girls," he said.

"I'm not keeping them from you. I realize it might feel that way because I left. But you go this long without seeing them all the time."

"I know that. I know I've been a pretty shitty partner and dad. I mean, there's not even anything to say about what kind of husband I was. I don't know how to explain… But it was like I had two lives. And it just felt easy. To go from one to the other."

She almost laughed. "The sad thing is, I understand what you mean. It's just that I had a different life than you. But I pretty much felt like a single mom while you were away, and I kind of enjoyed the time to myself. I didn't think about you much when you were gone. And I thought that was healthy. To not miss you. To not be clingy. I realize now that maybe there was just something missing." She chewed on the next couple of words for a long moment. "I did want to be with someone else. I just didn't do it. I let that make me feel superior to you. But the truth is, my heart wasn't with you the whole time. And I'm not saying that to be hurtful or cruel."

"I know," he said.

"You know what? That I'm not trying to be hurtful?"

"I know you want someone else. I know you and Boone… I know there's something between you. There always has been."

And then she felt ashamed. He'd known that the whole time, and they never talked about it. All the things she and Daniel had never talked about. They hadn't had a marriage. They were roommates with kids.

"I'm not accepting responsibility for your behavior, and I want to make that really clear. But we were not good together. We didn't fight. We weren't ever toxic. The most toxic thing that happened was me breaking your headlights. But we shouldn't have been married. I thought because we didn't fight, because you weren't cruel to me, that there was no reason to leave you. But we weren't in love, Daniel."

"I loved what we had," he said, and he did sound miserable.

"I believe you. I did too. In a lot of ways. But there was something… We can have more. You'll find somebody someday that makes it unthinkable for you to be with anyone else. Someone you feel passion for."

"I guess I don't understand what that means. I wanted you. And that was real. It always has been."

"Just not enough to not want other people."

It didn't hurt her feelings; it didn't make her feel insecure. She had a man who wanted her in that deep, all-consuming, specific way. She didn't need Daniel to want her that way. Not now. It would've been nice if he had when they were married. More than nice. It would've been right. But that ship had sailed. And she'd moved on.

"I'm not with Boone, I would like to make that clear. It's not happening right now."

"You want it to."

"I do. I'm in love with him, Daniel. And I have been. I mean, I guess not really, because I didn't let myself know him well enough to have called it that when you and I were married. I tried very hard to protect our marriage."

"I didn't," said Daniel. "I'm sorry about that."

"You didn't. But I can't be mad, not about that specifically. I'm mad that you tricked me. I'm mad that I had to find out the way I did. But we were never much for honest conversations. So it had to get to a place where it came to that, I guess. I'm sorry. I don't think you were all that smooth. I just let you get away with it, because I wasn't paying attention."

"You were a good wife, though. I just didn't want to be a full-time husband. It's as simple as that, and I convinced myself I didn't have to be because what you didn't know wouldn't hurt you."

"I know you didn't want to hurt me. I actually know you're not a malicious man."

"I don't know if I feel all right about you being with Boone."

"Well, it doesn't matter what you feel. I have slept with him. Just so you know." A part of her, a small, mean part, enjoyed the bit of shock and hurt in his eyes. "He doesn't want to be with me, though. So don't worry about it."

"So you're just going to leave it at that? It's hard for me to believe he doesn't want to be with you after… He cut all ties with me over this."

"Boone has his own issues. And I'm not going to talk about them to you. I'm just letting you know the status of the situation. If it changes, and I hope to God it does, I'll let you know. But you and I need to be very clear with each other. And we have to figure out how to parent the girls. Because if Boone and I do end up together, there doesn't need to be a story from them or from you about how I tried to replace you. Not in their lives. You're their father. I want them to forgive you. I want them to have a relationship with you. Because the one good thing we did was them."

"It was. It is. I promise you, I'm going to do a better job. And I'm going to prove to them they can trust me as a dad."

"Good. For now, I'm staying in Lone Rock. I'm happy there. I need to find another place to live, but the girls are doing well at the school."

"I'm all the way in Bakersfield…"

"Not all year. And maybe you'll see fit to move, I don't know. Houses are cheaper up here anyway. You can get something big."

"I'll think about it."

"Okay. Well, I need to go because I have to drive back, and I have to get the girls from school. But I'm glad we could talk, Daniel."

"Me too."

"Maybe now that we aren't together anymore we'll be able to do that."

She said goodbye to him, and she didn't feel any pull to go back.

She hadn't thought she would, but it felt healing and clarifying to face him.

It was the right thing. She'd done what she needed to do for her daughters.

For herself.

When she got into her car and started back to Lone Rock, she cried. Because she still didn't have Boone, and she wanted him.

This was heartbreak. It was a strange thing. Her marriage had dissolved only a month earlier, and her heart hadn't been broken at all. It was losing the possibility of Boone that had done it. But at least she knew she could survive that.

She didn't have to be afraid of anything. And maybe in that small way, Daniel had done her a favor. He'd set her free from fear. And it was like that thread that had held her together—that thread she *thought* had held her together—all these years had suddenly vanished. And she didn't feel so much like a patchwork quilt now. She just felt whole. And like herself.

She knew that every choice she made from here on out wouldn't be because of fear.

It would be because of love.

That was a gift. And if it was all she took away…it would have to be enough.

Chapter Thirteen

"I need an intervention," Boone said.

He looked at Kit and Jace and Chance and Flint, sitting in chairs in a half circle, and folded his hands.

"Okay. For what?" Kit asked.

"Dumb emotional shit. Go. Fix me. How are you all in love? Tell me."

"Because there was no choice," said Chance.

"None whatsoever," said Kit. "I wanted Shelby for years, and once I could ever—"

"I convinced myself that I didn't want Cara," said Jace. "But I was lying to myself."

"Great. How did you not lie to yourself? I'm familiar with wanting somebody for years. And not having them. Shelby was the same as Wendy. She was married to somebody else, so tell me how you fix it. Because you need to help me fix it."

"Wendy?"

"She loves me," he said. "I love her. I love her and I just... I imagine... What if I lose her? What if I mess it up?"

"Yeah. That's scary," said Kit. "It's damned scary. I got Shelby pregnant, so I kind of had to figure it out, didn't I?"

"But now you aren't scared."

"Shit, dude, I have a baby. I'm scared all the time."

"All the time," said Jace. "We don't even have kids."

"What?"

"Why do you think I broke up with Tansey? The first time.

The last time. I'm never breaking up with her again, but it was because I was terrified," said Flint. "We had it hard."

"So hard," said Chance. "You never get over having someone in your family die like we did. Not really."

"Hell, I closed off all my feelings. My hope of anything. I didn't believe in miracles of any kind. Because that belief failed me when Sophia died," said Jace. "Which was why I didn't see that Cara was a miracle. She was another chance to find that kind of hope again."

"Shelby and I have both been through loss," said Kit. "She loved her husband. Chuck was a great guy. I know she would've loved him for the rest of her life. I also know that life is just… It can be merciless sometimes. But she got to love him for the amount of time she had him. Just like I got to love Sophia while she was here. And I will love Shelby, I'll love our son. No matter what. No matter the cost. Because it's worth it. It just is. Loving people has only ever made us better. So even though it hurts, we cling to that."

"But you're not…afraid?"

His brothers laughed. "Hell no. When you care about things life feels high stakes," said Chance. "I love Juniper more than anything else in the world. I'm not worried I'm going to mess it up, because it drives me. No, I can't guarantee anything. But she's the reason I wake up every day. My life changed because of her. And I don't regret a damned thing about it. I never could. I would never live a life where I didn't love her."

"But I just thought that if I loved her, and made her life better…"

"I would never live a life where she didn't love *me*," said Chance. "It's hard. When you've been through the kinds of things we have, it's really hard to accept the fact that you can't protect yourself. Because if you do, you're just living half a life. You gotta let her love you. You could have her, you could have stepkids, and kids. You can have a house full of love."

"It's just…it's so much easier to be a martyr about it." As he said it, he knew it was true. "To just tell myself I have all these responsibilities to people. To call it that is not love. To call it that and not… I don't know what to do about how unfair the world is. I don't know what to do with Buck leaving. With Sophia dying. I used to have hope, and it didn't get me anything so now I do things instead of feel them. I'm just trying not to grieve the losses I've already had. And trying not to ever earn any more grief."

"It's okay to grieve." That came from Flint. "It's another expression of love."

"It just feels risky."

"It is. But you have to ask yourself, what's life without risk? We are bull riders. We're a fucking metaphor. Accept it."

He laughed. "I don't think I'm actually all that brave. I'd rather throw myself on the back of a bull than… Than let myself hope. And have that hope get destroyed."

It was too vivid in his mind even now.

That burning bright certainty he'd had that Sophia would get better because the world couldn't be that cruel.

And then it was.

"But hope is what it's all about. I read that somewhere. Faith, hope and love. Without them, what's the point?"

He couldn't answer that. He didn't know what the point was without Wendy.

He needed her.

He needed her, and that was the truth.

And maybe that was the miracle. Nothing else seemed as terrifying now. Nothing but not having her. After living that way for all these years, he'd thought it was the safe thing. The easy thing.

But he wanted more now.

Looking around at his brothers, he thought more just might be possible. Maybe everything was.

Maybe that was healing. Maybe that was the miracle of love.

To live in a world, a broken, pain-filled world, and be able to want love, no matter the cost.

Suddenly it was like all the walls were gone. Torn down. Suddenly it was like he could see clearly.

This was life.

And it *did* matter what he wanted. What he wanted might hurt him. Might kill them.

But he wanted it all the same. And actually, maybe he would be the rodeo commissioner. Maybe not. He realized that none of it had mattered because all he really wanted this whole time was Wendy.

So he was going to have to win her back.

Wendy was just getting out of the car with the girls when Boone pulled up to the cottage in his truck.

"Wendy," he said, looking wild-eyed. "I love you."

She blinked. "Okay."

"I love you and I want to be with you. Fuck everything else. Sorry. Screw everything else."

The girls exchanged a look.

"Boone…"

"I love you." And then he pulled her into his arms and kissed her. Then she lost herself a little bit, it was impossible not to.

"Boone," she said, looking at Mikey and Sadie, who were staring at them both.

"Sorry," he said. "I'm sorry, and there's another part of this conversation," he said. "And it includes the two of you."

She had just been talking to the girls about how she'd seen Daniel, and how he wanted to see them. This was all very inconvenient timing.

But it was life. And it was happening. A lot of feelings, a lot of un-ideal sorts of moments clashing with each other.

"I'm not trying to take your dad's spot, because he's your

dad. But I've known you since you were born, and I care about you. And I love your mom. And I'd be happy if you were all right with that."

"Everything is changing," Mikey said sadly.

"I know," said Boone. "And I don't like it, either, quite frankly. I just about messed everything up so I could keep some things the same. Because nobody likes change. I can't say that I've been happy all these years by myself. But it seemed pretty safe. And I was happy with that. So when your mom said she wanted to be with me, I said no. But I realized that I'm more afraid of not having her in my life. More afraid of not sharing a house with all three of you. More afraid of what the future looks like if you're not my family. I want you to be." He cleared his throat. "I... I have hope, Mikey. Even if I'm not certain. And I'm tired of living without hope."

And it was like Mikey realized for the first time that adults had feelings. Feelings and fears and all of this scared them too.

"Oh."

"I care about both you girls a lot," he reiterated, his voice hoarse. "I care about whether or not you're happy."

"I want my mom to be happy," Sadie said. "And you should be happy too."

"We should be happy," Boone said, looking at Wendy.

"Boone," she said, wrapping her arms around him and just hugging him. Because the connection between them had been more than sex. And she wanted to show him that now.

And also not make out with him in front of her kids. Because they were asking a whole lot of the girls, and she didn't need to traumatize them on top of it.

"What changed?" she asked.

"I accepted that there was always going to be some level of risk. I accepted that I had to let love be bigger than my fear. And you know what? I just don't feel afraid anymore."

And neither did she. Because the love inside of her was too big for that.

This was fate. Nothing less than waiting, stumbling through the darkness blind, fighting through all the issues they were beset by.

Grabbing hold of each other and refusing to let go.

It was that simple.

"I dreamed that at my brother's wedding, I crossed the room and kissed you," he said, keeping his voice low. "I dreamed it every night for weeks. And it's funny, I thought because you were off-limits there wasn't anything to learn from that except that I wanted you and couldn't have you. But there was. It was up to me to cross the room."

"And now it's up to us to hold on."

"I'm never letting go now. You know…you're the most beautiful woman I've ever seen."

"What's for dinner?" Mikey asked.

"Meatloaf," she said.

And it hadn't even broken the moment. Both girls went in the house and Wendy just stood there in Boone's arms.

Finally.

"I think this is going to work," he said. "I have hope. In you."

She smiled. "Good. Because I love you."

"That's all I need."

Epilogue

Welcome to Lone Rock...

He hadn't seen that sign in years. He wasn't sure if he felt nostalgic, or just plain pissed off.

He supposed it didn't matter. Because he was here.

For the first time in twenty years, Buck Carson was home.

And he aimed to make it a homecoming to remember.

* * * * *

THE RANCHER

JOANNE ROCK

To the Rockettes, for keeping me company
while I write.

One

Chiara Campagna slipped into her host's office and silently closed the heavy oak door, leaving the raucous party behind. Breathing in the scents of good bourbon and leather, she held herself very still in the darkened room while she listened for noise outside in the hallway to indicate if anyone had followed her.

When no sounds came through besides the pop song people danced to in the living room of Miles Rivera's spacious Montana vacation home, Chiara released a pent-up breath and debated whether or not to switch on a lamp. On the one hand, a light showing under the door might signal to someone passing by that the room was occupied when it shouldn't be. On the other, if someone found her by herself snooping around in the dark, she'd be raising significant suspicions that wouldn't be easy to talk her way around.

As a prominent Los Angeles-based social media influencer, Chiara had a legitimate reason to be at the party given by the Mesa Falls Ranch owners to publicize their environmental good works. But she had no legitimate reason to be *here*—in Miles Rivera's private office—snooping for secrets about his past.

She twisted the knob on the wall by the door, and recessed lighting cast a warm glow over the heavy, masculine furnishings. Dialing back the wattage with the dimmer, she left it just bright enough to see her way around the gray leather sofa and glass-topped coffee table to the midcentury modern desk. Her silver metallic dress, a gorgeous gown with an asymmetrical hem and thigh-high slit to show off her legs, moved around her with a soft rustle as she headed toward the sideboard with its decanter full of amber-colored liquid. She set aside her tiny silver handbag, then poured two fingers' worth into one of the glasses beside the decanter. If anyone discovered her, the drink would help explain why she'd lingered where she most definitely did not belong.

"What secrets are you hiding, Miles?" she asked a framed photo of her host, a flattering image of an already handsome man. In the picture, he stood in front of the guest lodge with the five other owners of Mesa Falls Ranch. It was one of the few photos she'd seen of all six of them together.

Each successful in his own right, the owners were former classmates from a West Coast boarding school close to the all-girls' academy Chiara had attended. At least until her junior year, when her father lost his fortune and she'd been booted into public school. It would have been no big deal, really, if not for the fact that the public school had no art program. Her dreams of attending a prestigious art university to foster her skills with collage and acrylic paint faltered and died. Sure, she'd parlayed her limited resources into fame and fortune as a beauty influencer thanks to social media savvy and—in part—to her artistic sensibilities. But being an Instagram star wasn't the same as being an artist.

Not that it mattered now, she reminded herself, lingering on the photograph of Miles's too-handsome face. He stood flanked by casino resort owner Desmond Pierce and game developer Alec Jacobsen. Miles's golden, surfer looks were a contrast to Desmond's European sophistication and Alec's stubbled, devil-may-care style. All six men were wealthy and successful in their own right. Mesa Falls was the only business concern they shared.

A project that had something to do with the ties forged back in their boarding school days. A project that should have included Zach Eldridge, the seventh member of the group, who'd died under mysterious circumstances. The boy she'd secretly loved.

A cheer from the party in the living room reminded Chiara she needed to get a move on if she wanted to accomplish her mission. Steeling herself with a sip of the aged bourbon, she turned away from the built-in shelves toward the desk, then tapped the power button on the desktop computer. Any twinge of guilt she felt over invading Miles's privacy was mitigated by her certainty the Mesa Falls Ranch owners knew more than they were telling about Zach's death fourteen years ago. She hadn't been sure of it until last Christmas, when a celebrity guest of the ranch had revealed a former mentor to the ranch owners had anonymously authored a book that brought the men of Mesa Falls into the public spotlight.

And rekindled Chiara's need to learn the truth about what had happened to Zach while they were all at school together.

When the desktop computer prompted her to type in a passcode, Chiara crossed her fingers, then keyed in the same four numbers she'd seen Miles Rivera code into his phone screen earlier in the evening while ostensibly reaching past him for a glass of champagne. The generic photo of a mountain view on the screen faded into the more businesslike background of Miles's desktop with its neatly organized ranch files.

"Bingo." She quietly celebrated his lack of high tech cyber security on his personal device since she'd just exhausted the extent of her code-cracking abilities.

"Z-A-C-H." She spoke the letters aloud as she typed them into the search function.

A page full of results filled the screen. Her gaze roved over them. Speed-reading file names, she realized most of the files were spreadsheets; they seemed to be earnings reports. None used Zach's name in the title, indicating the references to him were within the files themselves.

Her finger hovered over a promising entry when the doorknob turned on the office door. Scared of getting caught, she jammed the power button off on the computer.

Just in time to look up and see Miles Rivera standing framed in the doorway.

Dressed in a custom-cut tuxedo that suited his lean runner's build perfectly, he held his phone in one hand before silently tucking it back in his jacket pocket. In the low light, his hair looked more brown than dark blond, the groomed bristles around his jaw and upper lip de-

cidedly sexy. He might be a rancher, normally oversee-
ing Rivera Ranch, a huge spread in central California,
yet he was always well-dressed anytime the Mesa Falls
owners were in the news cycle for their efforts to bring
awareness to sustainable ranching practices. His suits
were always tailored and masculine at the same time.
Her blog followers would approve. She certainly ap-
proved of his blatant sexiness and comfort in his own
skin, even though she was scared he was about to have
her tossed out of his vacation home on the Mesa Falls
property for snooping.

His blue eyes zeroed in on her with laser focus. Missing nothing.

Guilty heart racing, Chiara reached for her bourbon
and lifted it to her lips slowly, hoping her host couldn't
spot the way her hand shook from his position across
the room.

"You caught me red-handed." She sipped too much
of the drink, the strong spirit burning her throat the
whole way down while she struggled to maintain her
composure.

"At what, exactly?" Miles quirked an eyebrow, his
expression impossible to read.

Had he seen her shut off the computer? She only had
an instant to decide how to play this.

"Helping myself to your private reserves." She lifted
the cut-crystal tumbler, as if to admire the amber contents in the light. "I only slipped in here to escape the
noise for a few minutes, but when I saw the decanter, I
hoped you wouldn't mind if I helped myself."

She waited for him to call her out for the lie. To ac-
cuse her of spying on him. Her heartbeat sounded so
loud in her ears she thought for sure he must hear it, too.

He inclined his head briefly before shutting the door behind him, then striding closer. "You're my guest. You're welcome to whatever you like, Ms. *Campagna*."

She sensed an undercurrent in the words. Something off in the slight emphasis on her name. Because he knew she was lying? Because he remembered a time when that hadn't been her name? Or maybe due to the simple fact that he didn't seem to like her. She had enough of an empath's sensibilities to recognize when someone looked down on her career. She suspected Miles Rivera was the kind of man to pigeonhole her as frivolous because she posted beauty content online.

As if making women feel good about themselves was a waste of time.

"You're not a fan of mine," she observed lightly, sidling from behind his desk to pace the length of the room, pretending to be interested in the titles of books on the built-in shelves lining the back wall. "Is it because of my profession? Or does it have more to do with me invading your private domain and stealing some bourbon? It's excellent, by the way."

"It's a limited edition." He unbuttoned his jacket as he reached the wet bar, then picked up the decanter to pour a second glass, his diamond cuff-link winking in the overhead lights as he poured. "Twenty-five years old. Single barrel. But I meant what I said. You're welcome to my hospitality. Including my bourbon."

Pivoting on his heel, he took two steps in her direction, then paused in front of his desk to lean against it. For a moment, she panicked that he would be able to feel that the computer was still warm. Or that the internal fan of the machine still spun after she'd shut it off.

But he merely sipped his drink while he observed

her. He watched her so intently that she almost wondered if he recognized her from a long-ago past. In the few times they'd met socially, Miles had never made the connection between Chiara Campagna, social media star, and Kara Marsh, the teenager who'd been in love with Miles's roommate at school, Zach Eldridge. The old sense of loss flared inside her, spurring her to turn the conversation in a safer direction.

"I noticed you neatly sidestepped the matter of my profession." She set her tumbler on a granite-topped cabinet beside a heavy wire sculpture of a horse with a golden-yellow eye.

He paused, taking his time to answer. The sounds of the party filtered through to the dim home office. One dance tune blended seamlessly into another thanks to the famous DJ of the moment, and voices were raised to be heard over the music. When Miles met her gaze again, there was something calculating in his expression.

"Maybe I envy you a job that allows you to travel the globe and spend your nights at one party after another." He lifted his glass in a mock salute. "Clearly, you're doing something right."

Irritation flared.

"You wouldn't be the first person to assume I lead a charmed life of leisure, full of yachts and champagne, because of what I choose to show the world on social media." She bristled at his easy dismissal of all the hard work it had taken to carve herself a place in a crowded market.

"And yet, here you are." He gestured expansively, as if to indicate his second home on the exclusive Mesa Falls property. "Spending another evening with Hollywood celebrities, world-class athletes and a few heavy-weights from the music industry. Life can't be all bad, can it?"

In her agitation, she took another drink of the bourbon, though she still hadn't learned her lesson to sip carefully. The fire down her throat should have warned her that she was letting this arrogant man get under her skin.

Considering her earlier fears about being caught spying, maybe she should have just laughed off his assumption that she had a shallow lifestyle and excused herself from the room. But resentment burned fast and hot.

"And yet, you're at the same party as me." She took a step closer to him before realizing it. Before acknowledging her own desire to confront him. To somehow douse the smug look in his blue eyes. "Don't you consider attendance part of your job, not just something you do for fun?"

"I'm the host representing Mesa Falls." His broad shoulders straightened at her approach, though he didn't move from his position leaning his hip against the desk. "Of course it's a work obligation. If I didn't have to take a turn being the face of Mesa Falls tonight, I would be back at my own place, Rivera Ranch."

His voice had a raspy quality to it that teased along her nerve endings in a way that wasn't at all unpleasant. He was nothing like the men who normally populated her world—men who understood the beauty and entertainment industries. There was something earthy and real about Miles Rivera underneath the tailored garments, something that compelled her to get closer to all those masculine, rough edges.

"And I'm representing my brand as well. It's no less a work obligation for me."

"Right." He shook his head, an amused smile playing at his lips, his blue eyes darkening a few shades. "More power to you for creating a brand that revolves around long-wearing lipstick and international fashion shows."

This view of her work seemed so unnecessarily dismissive that she had to wonder if he took potshots as a way to pay her back for invading his office. She couldn't imagine how he could rationalize his behavior any other way, but she forced herself to keep her cool in spite of his obvious desire to get a rise from her.

"I'm surprised a man of your business acumen would hold views so narrow-minded and superficial." She shrugged with deliberate carelessness, though she couldn't stop herself from glaring daggers at him. Or taking another step closer to hammer home her point. "Especially since I'm sure you recognize that work like mine requires me to be a one-woman content creator, marketing manager, finance director and admin. Not to mention committing endless hours to build a brand you write off as fluff."

Maybe what she'd said resonated for him, because the condescension in his expression gave way to something else. Something hotter and more complex. At the same moment, she realized that she'd arrived a foot away from him. Closer than she'd meant to come.

She couldn't have said which was more unnerving: the sudden lifting of a mental barrier between them that made Miles Rivera seem more human, or her physical proximity to a man who…stirred something inside her. Good or bad, she couldn't say, but she most definitely didn't want to deal with magnified emotions right now. Let alone the sudden burst of heat she felt just being near him.

Telling herself the jittery feelings were a combination of justified anger and residual anxiety from her snooping mission, Chiara reached for her silver purse on the desk. Her hand came close to his thigh for an instant before she snatched up the handbag.

She didn't look back as she stalked out the office door.

Still shaken by his unexpected encounter with Chiara Campagna, Miles made a dismal effort to mingle with his guests despite the loud music, the crowd that struck him as too young and entitled, and the text messages from the other Mesa Falls Ranch owners that kept distracting him. Trapped in his oversize great room that took "open concept" to a new level of monstrosity, he leaned against the curved granite-topped cabinetry that provided a low boundary between the dining area and seating around a stone fireplace that took up one entire wall. Open trusswork in the cathedral ceilings added to the sense of space, while the hardwood floor made for easy dancing as the crowd enjoyed the selections of the DJ set up near the open staircase.

Miles nodded absently at whatever the blonde pop singer standing next to him was saying about her reluctance to go back on tour, his thoughts preoccupied by another woman.

A certain raven-haired social media star who seemed to captivate every man in the room.

Miles's gaze followed Chiara as she posed for a photo with two members of a boy band in front of a wall of red flowers brought into the great room for the party. He couldn't take his eyes off her feminine curves draped in that outrageous liquid silver dress she wore. Hugged between the two young men, her gown reflected the flashes of multiple camera phones as several other guests took surreptitious photos. And while the guys around her only touched her in polite and socially acceptable ways, Miles still fought an urge to wrest her away from them. A ludicrous reaction, and totally out of character for him.

Then again, *everything* about his reaction to the wildly sexy Chiara was out of character. Since when was he the kind of guy to disparage what someone else did for a living? He'd regretted his flippant dismissal of her work as soon as he'd said the words, recognizing them as a defense mechanism he had no business articulating. There was something about her blatant appeal that slid past his reserve. The woman was like fingernails down his back, inciting response. Desire, yes. But there was more to it than that. He didn't trust the femme fatale face she presented to the world, or the way she used her femininity in an almost mercenary way to build her name. She reminded him of a woman from his past that he'd rather forget. But that wasn't fair, since Chiara wasn't Brianna. Without a doubt, he owed Chiara an apology before she left tonight.

Even though she'd definitely been on his computer when he'd entered his office earlier. He'd seen the blue glow of the screen reflected on her face before she'd scrambled to shut it down.

"How do you know Chiara Campagna?" the woman beside him asked, inclining her head so he could hear her over the music.

He hadn't been following the conversation, but Chiara's name snagged his focus, and he tore his gaze away from the beauty influencer who'd become a household name to stare down at the earnest young pop singer beside him.

He was only on site at Mesa Falls Ranch to oversee things for the owners for a few weeks. His real life back at Rivera Ranch in central California never brought him into contact with the kind of people on the guest list tonight, but the purpose of this party—to promote the green ranching mission of Mesa Falls by spreading the word among celebrities who could use their platforms to highlight the environmental effort—was a far cry from the routine cattle raising and grain production he was used to. Just like his modern marvel of a home in Mesa Falls bore little resemblance to the historic Spanish-style main house on Rivera Ranch.

"I don't know her at all," Miles returned after a moment. He tried to remember the pop singer's name. She had a powerful voice despite her petite size, her latest single landing in the top ten according to the notes the ranch's publicist had given him about the guests. "But I assume she cares about Mesa Falls's environmental mission. No doubt she has a powerful social media platform that could help our outreach."

The singer laughed as she lifted her phone to take a picture of her own, framing Chiara and the two boy band members in her view screen. "Is that why we're all here tonight? Because of the environment?"

Frowning, he remembered the real reason for this particular party. While the green ranching practices they used were touted every time they hosted an event, tonight's party had a more important agenda. Public interest in Mesa Falls had spiked since the revelations that the owners' high school teacher and friend, Alonzo Salazar, had been the author behind the career-ending tell-all *Hollywood Newlyweds*. In fact, the news story broke at a gala here over Christmas. It had also been revealed that Alonzo had spent a lot of time at Mesa Falls before his death, his association with the ranch owners drawing speculation about his involvement with the business.

Tonight, the partners hoped to put an end to the rumors and tabloid interest by revealing the profits from *Hollywood Newlyweds* had gone toward Alonzo Salazar's humanitarian work around the globe. They'd hoped the announcement would put an end to the media interest in the Mesa Falls owners and discourage newshounds from showing up at the ranch. There'd been a coordinated press release of the news at the start of the party, a toast to the clearing of Alonzo's good name early in the evening, and a media room had been set up off the foyer with information about Alonzo's charitable efforts for reporters.

But there was something the owners weren't saying. While it was true a share of the book profits had benefited a lot of well-deserving people, a larger portion had gone to a secret beneficiary, and no one could figure out why.

"So the threat of global warming didn't bring you here tonight," Miles responded with a self-deprecating smile, trying to get back on track in his host duties. He watched as Chiara left behind the band members for one of the Mesa Falls partners—game developer Alec Jacobsen—who wanted a photo with her. "What did? A need to escape to Montana for a long weekend?"

He ground his teeth together at the friendly way Alec placed his hand on the small of Chiara's back. Miles remembered the generous cutout in her dress that left her completely bare in that spot. Her hair shimmered in the overhead lights as she brushed the long waves over one shoulder.

"Honestly? I hoped to meet Chiara," the singer gushed enthusiastically. "Will you excuse me? Maybe I can get a photo with her, too."

Miles gladly released her from the conversation, chagrined to learn that his companion had been as preoccupied with Chiara as he was. What must life be like for the influencer, who'd achieved a different level of fame from the rest of the crowd—all people who were highly accomplished in their own right?

Pulling out his phone, Miles checked to see if his friend and fellow ranch owner, Gage Striker, had responded to a text he'd sent an hour ago. Gage should have been at the party long ago.

Miles had sent him a text earlier:

How well do you know Chiara Campagna? Found her in my study and I would swear she was riffling through my notes. Looking for something.

Gage had finally answered:

Astrid and Jonah have known her forever. She's cool.

Miles knew fellow partner Jonah Norlander had made an early exit from the party with his wife, Astrid, so Miles would have to wait to check with him. Shoving the phone back in the pocket of his tuxedo, Miles bided his time until he could speak to Chiara again. He would apologize, first and foremost. But then, he needed to learn more about her.

Because she hadn't just been snooping around his computer in his office earlier. She'd been there on a mission. And she hadn't covered her trail when she'd rushed to close down his screen.

Somehow, Chiara Campagna knew about Zach. And Miles wasn't letting her leave Mesa Falls until he figured out how.

Two

Chiara grooved on the dance floor to an old disco tune, surrounded by a dozen other guests and yet—thankfully—all by herself. She'd spent time snapping photos with people earlier, so no one entered her personal dance space while she took a last glance around the party she should have left an hour ago.

Normally, she kept a strict schedule at events like this, making only brief appearances at all but the biggest of social engagements. The Met Gala might get a whole evening, or an Oscar after-party. But a gathering hosted by a Montana rancher in a thinly disguised PR effort to turn attention away from the Alonzo Salazar book scandal?

She should have been in and out in fifty minutes once her spying mission in Miles Rivera's office had proven a bust. Finding out something about Zach had been her real motive for attending, yet she'd lingered long after she'd failed in that regard. And she knew the reason had something to do with her host. She knew because she found herself searching him out in the crowd, her eyes scanning the darkened corners of the huge great room hoping for a glimpse of him.

Entirely foolish of her.

Annoyed with herself for the curiosity about a man who, at best, was keeping secrets about Zach and at worst thought her work shallow and superficial, she was just about to walk off the dance floor when he reentered the room. His sudden presence seemed to rearrange the atoms in the air, making it more charged. Electrified.

For a moment, he didn't notice her as he read something on his phone, and she took the opportunity to look her fill while unobserved. She was curious what it was about him that held her attention. His incredibly fit physique? Certainly with his broad shoulders he cut through the guests easily enough, his size making him visible despite the crowd around him. Or maybe it was the way he held himself, with an enviable confidence and authority that implied he was a man who solved problems and took care of business. But before she could explore other facets of his appeal, his gaze lifted from his device to land squarely on her.

Almost as if he'd known the whole time she'd been watching him.

A keen awareness took hold as she flushed all over. Grateful for the dim lighting in the great room, she took some comfort in the fact that at least he wouldn't see how he affected her. Even if he had caught her staring.

Abruptly, she stepped out of the throng of dancers with brisk efficiency, determined to make her exit. Heels clicking purposefully on the hardwood, she moved toward the foyer, texting her assistant that she was ready to leave. But just as the other woman appeared at her side to gather their entourage, Miles intercepted Chiara.

"Don't go." His words, his serious tone, were almost as much of a surprise as his hand catching hers lightly in his own. "Can we speak privately?"

It might have been satisfying to say something cutting now in return for the way he'd behaved with her earlier. To hold her head high and march out his front door into the night. She looked back and forth between Miles and her assistant, Jules Santor, who was busy on her phone assembling vehicles for the return to their nearby hotel. But the reason Chiara had come here tonight was more important than her pride, and if there was any chance she could still wrest some clue about Zach's death from Miles after all this time, she couldn't afford to indulge the impulse.

"On second thought," she told Jules, a very tall former volleyball player who turned heads everywhere she went, "feel free to take the rest of the evening off. I'm going to stay a bit longer."

Jules bit her lip, her thumbs paused midtext as she glanced around the party. "Are you sure you'll be okay? Do you want me to leave a car for you?"

"I'll be fine. I'll text if I need a ride," Chiara assured her before returning her attention to whatever Miles had in mind.

At her nod, he guided her toward the staircase behind the dining area, one set of steps leading to an upper floor and another to a lower. He took her downstairs, never relinquishing her hand. A social nicety, maybe, because of her sky-high heels, long gown and the open stairs. Yet his touch made her pulse quicken.

When they reached the bottom floor, there was a small bar and a mahogany billiards table with a few guys engaged in a game. He led her past a smaller living area that was dark except for a fire in the hearth, through a set of double doors into a huge room with a pool and floor-to-ceiling windows on three sides. Natural stonework surrounded the entire pool deck, making it look like a grotto complete with a small waterfall from a raised hot tub. The water was illuminated from within, and landscape lights showcased a handful of plantings and small trees.

"This is beautiful." She paused as they reached two easy chairs flanking a cocktail table by the windows that overlooked the backyard and the Bitterroot River beyond.

Withdrawing her hand from his, she took the seat he gestured toward while he made himself comfortable in the other.

"Thank you." He pulled his gaze from her long enough to look over the pool area. "I keep meaning to come here during the summer when I could actually open all the doors and windows and feel the fresh air circulating."

"You've never visited this house during the summer?" She wondered if she misunderstood him. The house where he was hosting tonight's party was at least fourteen thousand square feet.

"I'm rarely ever in Montana." His blue eyes found hers again as he leaned forward in the wingback, elbows propped on his knees. "Normally, my brother oversees Mesa Falls while I maintain Rivera Ranch, but Weston had his hands full this year, so I'm helping out here for the month." His jaw flexed. "I realize I did a poor job in my hosting duties earlier this evening, however."

Surprised he would admit it, she felt her brows lift but waited for him to continue. The sounds of the game at the billiards table drifted through the room now and then, but for the most part, the soft gurgle of the waterfall drowned out the noise of the party. The evening was winding down anyhow.

"I had no right to speak disparagingly of your work, and I apologize." He hung his head for a moment as he shook it, appearing genuinely regretful. "I don't know what I was thinking, but it was completely inappropriate."

"Agreed." She folded her fingers together, hands in her lap, as she watched him. "Apology accepted."

He lifted his head, that amused smile she remembered from earlier flitting around his lips again. "You're an unusual woman, Chiara Campagna."

"How so?" Crossing her legs, she wished she didn't feel a flutter inside at the sound of her name on his lips. She couldn't have walked away from this conversation if she tried.

She was curious why he'd sought her out for a private audience again. Had she been in his thoughts as much as he'd been in hers over the last hour? Not that it should matter. She hadn't decided to stay longer at the party because he made her entire body flush hot with a single look. No, she was here now because Miles knew something about Zach's death, and getting to know Miles might help her find out what had really happened.

"Your candor, for one thing." He slid a finger beneath his bow tie, expertly loosening it a fraction.

Her gaze tracked to his throat, imagining the taste of his skin at the spot just above his collar. It was easier to indulge in a little fantasy about Miles than it was to reply to his opinion of her, which was so very wrong. She'd been anything but truthful with him this evening.

"I appreciated the way you explained your job to me when I made a crack about it," he continued, unbuttoning his tuxedo jacket and giving her a better view of the white shirt stretching taut across his chest and abs. He looked very…fit. "I had no idea how much work was involved."

Her gaze lingered on his chest as she wondered how much more unbuttoning he might do in her presence tonight. She didn't know where all this physical attraction was coming from, but she wished she could put the lid back on it. Normally, she didn't think twice about pursuing relationships, preferring to focus on her work. But then, men didn't usually tempt her to this degree. The awareness was beyond distracting when she needed to be smart about her interaction with him. With an effort, she tried to focus on their conversation.

"I'm sure plenty of jobs look easier from the outside. You're a rancher, for example, and I'm sure that amounts to more than moving cattle from one field to the next, but that's really all I know about it."

"Yet whereas you have the good sense to simply admit that, I made presumptuous wisecracks because I didn't understand your work." He studied her for a long moment before he spoke again. "I appreciate you being here tonight. I do recognize that our ranch party probably wouldn't be on your list of social engagements if not for your friendship with Jonah Norlander's wife, Astrid."

"Astrid is one of my closest friends," she said, wary of going into too much detail about her connections to the Mesa Falls partners and their spouses. But at least she was telling the truth about Astrid. The Finnish former supermodel had caused Chiara's career to skyrocket, simply by posting enthusiastic comments on Chiara's social media content. Because of her friend, she'd gone from an unknown to a full-blown influencer practically overnight. "As someone who doesn't have much family, I don't take for granted the few good friends I have in my life."

Another reason she planned to honor Zach's memory. She counted him among the people who'd given her the creative and emotional boost she'd needed to find her professional passion.

"Wise woman." Miles nodded his agreement. "I guess you could say I'm here tonight because of my good friends, too. I do have family, but I don't mind admitting I like my friends better."

His grin was unrepentant, giving his blue eyes a wicked light.

"What about Weston?" She wondered what he thought of his younger brother, who held a stake in Mesa Falls with him.

"We have our moments," he told her cryptically, his lips compressing into a thin line as some dark thought raced across his expression.

"Does owning the ranch together make you closer with him?"

One eyebrow arched. "It does."

His clipped answer made her hesitate to probe further. But she couldn't stop herself from asking, "If you're close to the other Mesa Falls owners, why don't you spend more time here? I know you said you run Rivera Ranch, but why build this huge, beautiful house if you didn't ever plan on making time to be in Montana?"

She wondered what kept him away. Yes, she was curious if it had anything to do with Zach. But she couldn't deny she wanted to know more about Miles. With luck, that knowledge would help her keep her distance from this far-too-sexy man.

He took so long to answer that she thought maybe he'd tell her it was none of her business. He watched the spillover from the hot tub where it splashed into the pool below, and she realized the sounds had faded from the other room; the billiard game had ended.

"Maybe I was feeling more optimistic when we bought the land." He met her gaze. "Like having this place would bring us together more. But for the most part, it's just another asset we manage."

Puzzled why that would be, she drew in a breath to tease out the reason, but he surprised her into silence when his hand landed on her wrist.

"Isn't it my turn to ask you something?" Mild amusement glinted in his eyes again.

Her belly tightened at his attention, his touch. There was a potent chemistry lurking between them, and she wanted to exercise extreme caution not to stir it any further. But it was incredibly tempting to see what would happen if she acted on those feelings. Too late, she realized that her pulse leaped right underneath the place where his hand rested. His thumb skated over the spot with what might pass for idleness to anyone observing them, but that slow caress felt deliberate to her.

As if he wanted to assess the results of his touch.

"What?" she prodded him, since the suspense of the moment was killing her.

Or maybe it was the awareness. She was nearly brought to her knees by physical attraction.

"I saw you dancing alone upstairs." His voice took on that low, raspy quality that sent her thoughts to sexy places.

She remembered exactly what she'd been thinking about when he'd caught her eye earlier. She would not lick her lips, even though they suddenly felt dry.

"That's not a question," she managed, willing her pulse to slow down under the stroke of his thumb.

"It made me wonder," he continued as if she hadn't spoken. "Would you like to dance with me instead?"

The question, like his touch, seemed innocuous on the surface. But she knew he wasn't just asking her to dance. She *knew*.

That should have given her pause before she answered. But she gave him the only possible response.

"I'd like that." She pushed the words past the sudden lump in her throat. "Very much."

Even before he'd asked her to be his dance partner, Miles knew the party upstairs had ended and that this would be a private dance.

The Mesa Falls PR team excelled at keeping events on schedule, and the plan had been to move the late-night guests into the media room to distribute gift bags at midnight. His public hosting duties were officially done.

His private guest was now his only concern.

Which was a good thing, since he couldn't have taken his eyes off her if he tried. He needed to figure out what she was up to, after all. What would it hurt to act on the attraction since he had to keep track of what she was doing anyway? Keep your friends close and your enemies closer. Wherever Chiara ended up on the spectrum, he'd have his bases covered.

Helping her to her feet, he kept hold of her hand as

he steered her toward the billiards room, now empty. Stopping there, he flipped on the speaker system tucked behind the bar, then dimmed the lights and pressed the switch for the gas fireplace at the opposite end of the room. Her green eyes took in the changes before her gaze returned to him.

"Aren't we going upstairs?" she asked while the opening refrain of a country love song filled the air.

Miles shrugged off his tuxedo jacket and laid it over one of the chairs at the bar. If he was fortunate enough to get to feel her hands on him tonight, he didn't want extraneous layers of clothes between them.

"The DJ is done for the night." He led her to the open floor near the pool table and pulled her closer to him, so they faced one another, still holding hands. He waited to take her into his arms until he was certain she wanted this. "I thought if we stayed down here we'd be out of the way of the catering staff while they clean up."

"I didn't realize the party was over." She didn't seem deterred, however, because she laid her free hand on his shoulder, the soft weight of her touch stirring awareness that grew by the minute. He was glad he'd ditched his jacket, especially when her fingers flexed against the cotton of his shirt, her fingernails lightly scratching the fabric.

"It's just us now." He couldn't help the way his voice lowered, maybe because he wanted to whisper the words into her ear. But he still didn't draw her to him. "Are you sure you want to stay?"

"It's too late to retract your offer, Miles Rivera." She lifted their joined hands, positioning them. "I'll have that dance, please."

Damn, but she fascinated him.

With far more pleasure than a dance had ever inspired in him, he slid his free hand around Chiara's waist. He took his time to savor the feel of her beneath his palm, the temperature of her skin making her dress's lightweight metallic fabric surprisingly warm. Sketching a touch from her hip to her spine, he settled his hand in the small of her back where the skin was bare, then used his palm to draw her within an inch of him.

Her pupils dilated until there was only a dark green ring around them.

"That's what I hoped you'd say." He swayed with her to the mournful, longing sound of steel guitars, breathing in her bright, citrusy scent.

Counting down the seconds until he kissed her.

Because he had to taste her soon.

Not just for the obvious reasons, like that she was the sexiest woman he'd ever seen. But because Chiara had gotten to the heart of the loneliness he felt in this big Montana mansion every time he set foot in the state. With her questions and her perceptive gaze, she'd reminded him that Mesa Falls might be a testament to Zach Eldridge's life, but it remained a hollow tribute without their dead friend among them.

He'd hoped that ache would subside after they'd owned the property for a while. That Mesa Falls could somehow heal the emptiness, the pervasive sense of failure, that remained in him and his partners after they'd lost one of their own. But for Miles, who'd defined his whole life by trying to do the right thing, the consequences of not saving his friend were as jagged and painful as ever.

"Is everything okay?" Chiara asked him, her hand

leaving his shoulder to land on his cheek, her words as gentle as her expression.

And damned if that didn't hurt, too.

He didn't want her sympathy. Not when her kiss would feel so much better.

With an effort, he shoved his demons off his back and refocused on this woman's lush mouth. Her petal-soft fingertips skimming along his jaw. Her hips hovering close enough to his to tantalize him with what he wanted most.

"Just wondering how long I can make this dance last without violating social conventions." He let his gaze dip to her lips before meeting her gaze again.

She hesitated, her fingers going still against his cheek. He could tell she didn't buy it. Then her hand drifted from his face to his chest.

"You're worried what I'll think about you?" she asked lightly, her forefinger circling below his collarbone.

The touch was a barely there caress, but it told him she wasn't in any hurry to leave. The knowledge made his heart slug harder.

"A host has certain obligations to the people he invites under his roof." He stopped swaying to the song and looked into her eyes.

He kept one hand on the small of her back, the other still entwined with hers.

"In that case—" Her voice was breathless, but her gaze was steady. Certain. "I think you're obligated to make sure I don't dance alone again tonight."

Three

She needed his kiss.

Craved it.

Chiara watched Miles as he seemed to debate the merits of continuing what he'd started. He was a deliberate, thoughtful man. But she couldn't wait much longer, not when she felt this edgy hunger unlike anything she'd felt before.

She simply knew she wanted him. Even if what was happening between them probably shouldn't.

Maybe the impatience was because she'd had very little romantic experience. In her late teens, she'd mourned Zach and wrestled with the mix of anxiety and depression that had come with his death. Her lifestyle had shifted, too, after her father went bankrupt and she'd been forced to change schools. Giving up her dream of going to an art school had changed her, forging her into a woman of relentless ambition with no time for romance.

Not that it had really mattered to her before, since she hadn't been impressed with the few relationships she'd had in the past. The explosive chemistry other women raved about had been more of a simmer for her, making her feel like she'd only been going through the motions with guys. But tonight, dancing with Miles in this huge, empty house now that all the party guests had gone home, she felt something much different.

Something had shifted between them this evening, taking them from cautiously circling enemies to charged magnets that couldn't stay apart. At least, that's how she felt. Like she was inexorably drawn to him.

Especially with his broad palm splayed across her back, his thumb and forefinger resting on her bare skin through the cutout in the fabric of her gown, the other fingers straying onto the curve of her ass. A touch that made her very aware of his hands and how much she wanted them all over her without the barrier of clothes.

Determined to overcome his scruples, or host obligations, or whatever it was that made him hesitate, Chiara lifted up on her toes. She was going to take this kiss, and whatever else he was offering, because she needed it. She'd worry about the repercussions in the morning. For now, she grazed her mouth over his. Gently. Experimentally.

Hopefully.

She breathed him in, a hint of smoky bourbon enticing her tongue to taste his lower lip.

The contact sparked through her in unexpected ways, leaping from one pulse point to the next until something hot flamed to life. Something new and exciting. And as much as she wanted to explore that, she hesitated, worried about compounding her subterfuge with this man by adding seduction into the mix. Or maybe she just feared she didn't have the necessary skills. Either way, she needed to be sure he wanted this, too.

Just when she was about to pull back, his fingers tangled in her hair, anchoring her to him and deepening the kiss. And every cell in her body cried out a resounding *yes*.

The heat erupted into a full-blown blaze as he took over. With one hand he drew her body against his, sealing them together, while he used the other to angle her face in a way that changed the trajectory of the kiss from sensual to fierce and hungry. She pressed her thighs together against the sudden ache there.

From just a kiss.

Her body thrilled to the new sensations even as her brain struggled to keep up with the onslaught. Her scalp tingled when he ran his fingers through her hair. Her nipples beaded, skin tightening everywhere. A soft, needy sound emanated from the back of her throat, and the noise seemed to spur him on. His arm banded her tighter, creating delicious friction between their bodies as he backed her into the pool table. She wanted to peel off her gown and climb all over him. She simply *wanted*.

Her hands went to his shirt, ready to strip away the barriers between them, her fingers taking in the warm strength of all that delectable male muscle as she worked the fastenings. He lifted her up, seating her on the pool table as he stepped between her knees, never breaking the kiss. The long slit in her silver gown parted, making the fabric slide away as it ceased to cover her. The feel of him against her *there*, his hips pressing into the cradle of her thighs, made her forget everything else. Her fingers fell away from the shirt fastenings as she raked in a gasp, sensation rocking her.

Miles edged back, his blue eyes now a deep, dark ultramarine as his gaze smoked over her, checking in with her.

"I need to be sure you want to stay." His breathing was harsh as he tipped his forehead to hers, his grip going slack so that his palms simply rested on her hips. "Tell me, Chiara."

She respected his restraint. His concern for her. Things had spiraled out of control in a hurry, but she didn't want to stop now, no matter how it might complicate things down the road. She wanted to know real passion. What it was like to be carried away on that wave of hot, twitchy, need-it-now hunger.

"I've never felt the way you're making me feel tonight," she confided in a low voice, her hands gripping the side rails of the table, her nails sinking into the felt nap. "But I've always wanted to. So yes, I'm staying. I have to see what I've been missing all the years I chose work over...fun."

His lips quirked at that last bit. He straightened enough to look into her eyes again. The flames from the fireplace cast his face half in shadow.

"It's going to be more than fun." His thumbs rubbed lightly where they rested on her hips, the certainty in his tone assuring her he knew how to give her everything she craved.

She resisted the urge to squeeze his hips between her thighs and lock her ankles so he couldn't leave her. "Promise?"

His fingers clenched reflexively, which made her

think that she affected him as thoroughly as he was affecting her.

"If you make me a promise in return."

"What is it?" She would have agreed to almost anything to put his hands in motion again. To experience another mind-drugging kiss with the power to set her on fire. How did he do that?

"I get a date after this." He pressed his finger to her lips when she'd been about to agree, silencing her for a moment while she battled the urge to lick him there. "One where you'll tell me why you've chosen work over fun for far too long," he continued, removing his finger from her mouth so she could speak.

Her conscience stabbed her as Zach's face floated through her mind. She had no idea how she'd appeal to Miles for information about Zach in the aftermath of this. He'd probably hate her when he found out why she'd come to Montana in the first place. He'd never look at her the same way again—with heat and hunger in his eyes. Was it so wrong to chase the feelings Miles stirred inside her?

"Deal," she told him simply, knowing he'd never follow through on the request once he understood what had brought her here in the first place. Her fingers returned to the studs in his shirt, wanting the barriers between them gone.

He tipped her chin up to meet his gaze before he breathed his agreement over her lips. "Deal."

His kiss seemed to seal the pact, and her fingers forgot how to work. All her thoughts scattered until there was only his tongue stroking hers, teasing wicked sensations that echoed over her skin, dialing up the heat. She shifted closer to him, wanting to be near the source of that warmth. He answered by bracketing her hips and tugging her forward to the edge of the table, pressing her against the rigid length beneath his fly.

She couldn't stifle the needy sound she made at the feel of him, the proof of his hunger pleasing her almost as much as having him right where she wanted him. Almost, anyway. A shiver rippled through her while he tugged the straps of her gown off her shoulders.

"I need to see you," he said as he broke the kiss, watching the metallic silver gown slide down her body.

The material teased her sensitive nipples as it fell, since she hadn't bothered to wear a bra. Miles's eyes locked on her body, and the peaks tightened almost painfully, her breath coming faster.

"And I need to *feel* you." She might not have a ton of romance experience, but she believed in voicing her needs. And damn it, she knew what she wanted. "Your hands, your body, your mouth. You pick."

His blue eyes were full of heat as they lifted to hers again. "Let's find a bed. Now."

He plucked her off the table and set her on her feet while she clutched enough of her gown to keep it from falling off. Holding her hand, Miles tugged her through the bar area and past an office to a bedroom with high wooden ceilings and lots of windows. She guessed it wasn't the master suite in a home like this, given its modest size and single closet, yet she glimpsed a pair of boots near the door and toiletries on the granite vanity of the attached bath.

Miles closed the door behind her, toed off his shoes, then made quick work of his shirt, tossing it on a built-in window seat.

She was about to ask why he was staying in a guest

bedroom of his own home when he came toward her. The words dried up on her tongue at the sight of his purposeful stride.

When he reached her, he took the bodice she was clutching and let it fall to the floor, the heavy liquid silver pooling at her feet. Cool air touched her skin now that she was almost naked except for an ice-blue silk thong.

She didn't have long to feel the chill, however, as Miles pressed her body to his. Her breasts molded to his hard chest as his body radiated heat. He took his time wrapping her hair around his hand, lifting the heavy mass off her shoulders and watching it spill down his forearm.

"My hands, my body, my mouth." He parroted the words back to her, the rough sound of his voice letting her know how they'd affected him. "I pick all three."

Oh.

He kissed her throat and the crook behind her ear, then trailed his lips down to her shoulder, letting her feel his tongue and his teeth until she twined her limbs around him, wanting to be closer. He drew her with him to the bed, his hands tracing light touches up her arms, down her sides, under her breasts. When her calf bumped into the mattress, she dropped onto the gray duvet, pulling him down with her into the thick, downy embrace. She wanted to feel the weight of him against her, but he sat beside her on the edge of the bed instead, leaning down to unfasten the strap of her sequined sandal with methodical care.

A shiver went through her that had nothing to do with room temperature. When the first shoe fell away, he slid a warm palm down her other leg, lifting it to undo the tiny buckle on her other ankle. Once that shoe dropped onto the floor, he skimmed his hand back up her leg, circling a light touch behind her knee, then following the line of muscle in her thigh. Higher.

Higher.

She was on fire, desperate for more, by the time he pressed her back onto the bed. He followed her down, combing his fingers through her dark hair and kissing her neck, bracketing her body between his elbows where he propped himself over her. He kissed her jaw and down her neck, tracing a touch down the center of her breastbone, slowing but not stopping as he tracked lower. Lower.

Her pulse rushed as she inhaled sharply. She noticed he was breathing faster, too, his eyes watching the movement of his fingers as he reached the low waist of the ice-blue silk thong that still clung to her hips. As he slipped his fingers beneath the fabric, the brush of his knuckles made her stomach muscles clench, tension tightening as he stroked a touch right where she needed it. His gaze returned to her face as a ripple of pleasure trembled through her. She was already so close, on edge from wondering what would happen between them. Her release hovered as she held her breath.

He must have known. She didn't know how he could tell, but he leaned down to speak into her ear.

"You don't need to hold back." That deep, suggestive voice vibrated along her skin, evaporating any restraint. "There's no limit on how many times you can come."

His fingers stroked harder, and she flew apart. She gripped his wrist, whether to push him away or keep him there, she didn't know, but he didn't let go. Expertly, he coaxed every last shudder from her while waves of pleasure rocked through her. Only when she went still, her breathing slowing a fraction, did he slide off the bed.

She would have mourned the loss, but he shoved off his pants and boxers, reminding her how much more she had to look forward to. He disappeared into the bathroom for a moment but returned a moment later in all his delectable naked glory, condom in hand. Yet even as she tried to memorize the way he looked, to take in all the ways his muscles moved together so that she'd never forget it, she experienced a moment's trepidation. Just because he'd known how to touch her in a way that had made the earth move for her didn't mean she could return the favor.

But when he joined her on the bed, handing her the condom and letting her roll it in place, the worries faded. Having him next to her, covering her with all that warm male muscle as he kneed her legs apart to make room for himself, made it impossible to think about anything but this.

Him.

The most tantalizing encounter she'd ever had with a man.

He kissed her as he eased his way inside her, moving with her as easily as if they'd done this a thousand times before. Closing her eyes, she breathed in his cedarwood scent, letting the heat build between them again, hotter and stronger this time. The connection between them felt so real to her, even though she knew it could only be passion or chemistry, or whatever that nameless X-factor was that made for amazing sex.

Still, when she opened her eyes and found his intense gaze zeroed in on her, she could have sworn he'd seen deep inside her, past all the artifice that was her whole life and right down to the woman underneath. The thought robbed her of breath, stirring a hint of panic until he kissed her again, shifting on top of her in a way that created heart-stopping friction between their bodies.

He thrust again. Once. Twice.

And she lost all her bearings, soaring mindlessly into another release. This time, she brought him with her. She could feel him going still, his shout echoing hers, their bodies utterly in sync. For long moments, all she could do was breathe, dragging in long gulps of air while her heart galloped faster.

Eventually, everything slowed down again. Her skin cooled as Miles rolled away, but he dragged a cashmere throw up from the base of the bed, covering them both. He pulled her against him, her back tucked against his chest, as he stroked her hair in the darkened room. Words failed her, and she was grateful that he didn't say anything, either. She was out of her depth tonight, but she wasn't ready to leave. The only solace she took was that he didn't seem to want her to go.

In the morning, she'd have to come clean about what she was doing here. She hoped he wouldn't hate her for sleeping with him after she'd tried spying on him. Chances seemed slim that he'd understand the truth—that the two things were entirely unrelated.

Who was she kidding? He'd never believe that.

Guilt and worry tightened in her belly.

"Whatever you're thinking about, stop," came Miles's advice in her ear, a warm reassurance she didn't deserve. "Just enjoy it while we can."

How had he known? Maybe he'd felt her tense. Either

way, she didn't feel compelled to wreck what they'd just shared, so she let out a long breath and tucked closer to his warmth.

The morning—and all the consequences of her decision to stay—would come soon enough.

Miles awoke twice in the night.

The first time, he'd reached for the woman in his bed on instinct, losing himself in her all over again. She'd been right there with him, touching him with the urgency of someone who didn't want to waste a second of this time together, as if she knew as well as he did that it wouldn't be repeated. The knowledge gave every kiss, every sigh a desperate need that only heightened how damned good it all felt.

The second time he'd opened his eyes, he'd felt her stirring beside him, her head tipping to his chest as if she belonged there. For some reason, that trust she would have never given him while awake seemed as much a gift as her body had been.

Another moment that he wouldn't be able to repeat.

So when daylight crept over the bed, he couldn't pretend that he felt no regrets. Not about what they'd shared, because Chiara cast a long shadow over every other woman he'd ever been with. No, he didn't regret what had happened. Only that the night was a memory now.

And that's what it had to remain.

He guessed Chiara knew as much, since the pillow next to his was empty. He heard the shower running and left some clothes for her in the dressing room outside the bathroom. The T-shirt and sweats with a drawstring would be huge on her, but a better alternative than her evening gown.

He grabbed cargoes and a Henley for himself before retreating to the pool to swim some laps and hit the shower there. Afterward he retreated to the kitchen to work on breakfast, making good use of the fresh tortillas from a local source his brother, Weston, had mentioned to him. While he and Wes had never been close, they shared a love for the food from growing up with their *abuela* Rosa's incredible cooking on Rivera Ranch. Miles scrambled eggs and browned the sausage, then chopped tomatoes and avocadoes. By the time Chiara appeared in the kitchen to help herself to coffee, the breakfast enchiladas were ready.

"Morning." She pulled down a mug from a hook over the coffee bar and set it on the granite. "I didn't mean to wake you."

At first look, there was something soft and vulnerable about her in the clothes he'd left for her. She'd rolled up the gray sweats to keep them from dragging on the floor; he saw she was wearing his gym socks. The dark blue T-shirt gaped around her shoulders, but she'd tucked a corner of the hem into the cinched waist of the sweats. Memories of their night together blindsided him, the need to pull her to him rising up again as inevitably as high tide.

Then she met his gaze, and any illusion of her vulnerability vanished. Her green eyes reflected a defensiveness that went beyond normal morning-after wariness. She appeared ready to sprint out of there at the first opportunity. Had her spying mission been a success the night before, so that she could afford to walk away from him now? He hadn't been aware that at least a part of him—and yeah, he knew which part—had hoped she'd stick around if she wanted to learn more about Mesa Falls.

Damn it. He needed to be smarter about this if he wanted to remain a step ahead of her.

"You didn't wake me," he finally replied as he grappled with how to put her at ease long enough to have a conversation about where things stood between them. "At home, I'm usually up before now." Gesturing toward the coffee station, he took the skillet off the burner. "Grab your cup and join me for breakfast."

He carried the dishes over to their place settings at the table for eight. The table felt big for two people, but he arranged things so he'd be sitting diagonally from her and could easily gauge her reaction to what he had to say.

Chiara bypassed the single-cup maker for the espresso machine, brewing a double shot. When she finished, she carried her mug over and lowered herself into one of the chairs.

"You didn't have to go to all this trouble." She held herself straight in the chair, her posture as tense as her voice.

What he couldn't figure out was why she was so nervous. Whatever preyed on her mind seemed weightier than next-day second thoughts. Was she thinking about whatever information she'd gleaned from his study during the party?

"It was no trouble." He lifted the top of the skillet to serve her. "Can I interest you in any?" At her hesitation, he continued, "I won't be offended either way."

Her eyes darted to his before she picked up her fork and slid an enchilada onto her plate. "It smells really good. Thank you."

He served himself afterward and dug in, debating how best to convince her to spend more time in Montana. He didn't want to leverage what happened between them unfairly—or twist her arm into keeping that date she'd promised him—but questions remained about what she was doing in his office the night before. If she knew about Zach, he needed to know how and why.

While he puzzled that out, however, Chiara set her fork down after a few bites.

"Miles, I can't in good conscience eat your food— which is delicious, by the way—when I haven't been honest with you." She blurted the words as if they'd been on the tip of her tongue for hours.

He slowly set aside his fork, wondering what she meant. Would she confess what she'd been doing in his office last night? Something else?

"I'm listening." He took in her ramrod-straight posture, the way she flicked a red-painted fingernail along the handle of the mug.

A breath whooshed from her lungs before she spoke again.

"I'm an old friend of Zach Eldridge's." The name of his dead friend on her lips sent a chill through him. "I came here last night to learn the truth about what happened to him."

Four

Miles didn't remember standing up from the table, but he must have after Chiara's startling announcement. Because the next thing he knew, he was staring out the kitchen window into a side yard and the Bitterroot River meandering in a bed of slushy ice. He felt ice on the inside, too, since numbing his feelings about his dead friend had always been a hell of a lot easier than letting them burn away inside him.

Snow blanketed the property, coating everything in white. Spring might be around the corner, but western Montana didn't know it today. Staring at the unbroken field of white helped him collect his thoughts enough to face her again.

"You knew Zach?" It had never crossed his mind that she could have had a personal relationship with Zach even though he'd seen the search history on his computer. He'd assumed she'd heard an old rumor. If she'd known him, wouldn't she have come forward before now?

Zachary Eldridge had never talked about his life before his stint in a foster home near Dowdon School on the edge of the Ventana Wilderness in central California where the ranch owners had met. The way Zach had avoided the topic had broadcast all too clearly the subject was off-limits, and Miles had respected that. So he didn't think Chiara could have known him from that time. And he'd never heard rumors of her being in the foster system, making it doubtful she'd met him that way. Zach had been on a scholarship at their all-boys boarding school, a place she obviously hadn't attended.

"Dowdon School did events with Brookfield Academy." She clutched the espresso cup tighter, her gaze sliding toward the river-stone fireplace in the front room, though her expression had the blankness of someone seeing another place and time. Miles was familiar with the prestigious all-girls institution in close proximity to his alma mater. "I met Zach through the art program the summer before my sophomore year."

"You were at Brookfield?" Miles moved back toward the table, struggling to focus on the conversation—on her—no matter how much it hurt to remember the most painful time of his life. And yes, he was drawn to the sound of her voice and a desire to know her better.

He dropped back into his seat, needing to figure out how much she knew about Zach's death and the real motives behind her being in Mesa Falls all these years later.

"Briefly." She nodded her acknowledgment, her green eyes refocusing on him as he returned to the table. "I only attended for two years before my father lost everything in a bad investment and I had to leave Brookfield to go to public school."

Miles wondered why he hadn't heard of her connection to Zach or even to Brookfield. While he'd never sought out information about her, he would have thought her school affiliation would have been noted by the ranch's PR department when she was invited to Mesa Falls events.

Questions raced through his mind. How close had she been to Zach? Close enough to understand his mind-set the weekend he'd died?

A hollow ache formed in his chest.

"How well did you know him?" He regretted the demanding sound of the question as soon as it left his lips, unsure how it would come across. "That is, I'm interested how you could make friends during a summer program. The school staff was strict about prohibiting visits between campuses."

Her lips quirked unexpectedly, her eyes lifting to meet his. "Zach wasn't afraid to bend rules when it suited him, though, was he?"

Miles couldn't help a short bark of laughter as the truth of that statement hit home. "'Rules are for people with conventional minds,' he once told me."

Chiara sat back in her chair, some of her rigid tension loosening as warmth and fondness lit her gaze. "He painted over an entire project once, just an hour before a showing, even though I was a wreck about him ruining the beautiful painting he'd done. He just kept slapping oils on the canvas, explaining that an uncommon life demanded an uncommon approach, and that he had all-new inspiration for his work."

The shared reminiscence brought Zach to life in full

color for a moment, an experience Miles hadn't had in a long time. The action—and the words—were so completely in keeping with how he remembered his friend.

"He was a bright light," Miles agreed, remembering how often they'd looked up to his fearlessness and, later, stood beside him whenever he got into scrapes with schoolmates who weren't ready for the Zach Eldridges of the world.

"I never met anyone like him," Chiara continued, turning her mug in a slow circle on the table. "Not before, and not since." Halting the distracted movement, she took a sip from her cup before continuing. "I knew him well enough to have a crush on him, to the point that I thought I loved him. And maybe I did. Youthful romances can have a profound impact on us."

Miles searched her face, wondering if Chiara had been aware of Zach's sexual orientation; he'd come out to his friends the summer before sophomore year. Had that been why things hadn't worked out between them?

But another thought quickly crowded that one out. A long-buried memory from the aftermath of that dark time in Miles's life.

"There was a girl who came to Dowdon after Zach's death. Around Christmastime." He remembered her telling Miles the same story. She loved Zach and needed the truth about what had happened to him. But Miles had been in the depths of his own grief, shell-shocked and still in denial about the cliff-jumping accident that had killed his friend.

Chiara studied him now, the long pause drawing his awareness to a clock ticking somewhere in the house.

"So you remember me?" she asked, her words jarring him.

He looked at her face more closely as slow recognition dawned. He couldn't have stopped the soft oath he breathed before he spoke again.

"That was you?"

Chiara watched the subtle play of emotions over Miles's face before he reined them in, regretting the way she'd handled things even more than when she'd first awoken.

But she couldn't back down on her mission. She would have answers about Zach's death.

"Yes." Her stomach clenched at the memory of sneaking onto the Dowdon campus that winter to question Zach's friends. "I spoke to you and to Gage Striker fourteen years ago, but both of you were clearly upset. Gage was openly hostile. You seemed…detached."

"That girl couldn't have been you." Miles's jaw flexed, his broad shoulders tensing as he straightened in his chair. "I would have remembered the name."

Defensiveness flared at the hard look in his blue eyes.

"I was born Kara Marsh, but it was too common for Instagram, so I made up Chiara Campagna when I launched my career." Perhaps it made her sound like she'd hidden something from him, but her brand had taken off years ago, and she no longer thought of herself as Kara. Her family certainly hadn't cared, taking more of an interest in her now that she was famous with a big bank account than they ever had when she was under their roof saving her babysitting money to pay for her own clothes. "I use the name everywhere for consistency's sake. While I don't try to conceal my identity, I also don't promote it."

"Yet you kissed me. Spent the night."

Her gaze lingered on the black Henley he was wearing with a pair of dark brown cargo pants, the fitted shirt calling to mind the feel of his body under her hands.

"That wasn't supposed to happen," she admitted, guilt pinching harder at the accusation in his voice. "What took place between us was completely unexpected."

The defense sounded weak even to her ears. But he'd been there. He had to know how the passion had come out of nowhere, a force of nature.

The furrow in his brow deepened. "So you'll admit you were in my study last night, looking up Zach's name on my computer."

A chill crept through her. "You knew?" She bristled at the realization. "Yet you kissed me. Invited me to spend the night."

She parroted his words, reminding him he'd played a role in their charged encounter.

"You didn't clear the search history. A page of files with Zach's name on them was still open." He didn't address the fact that he'd slept with her anyway.

Because it hadn't mattered to him? Because *she* didn't matter? She stuffed down the hurt she had no business feeling, shoving aside the memories of how good things had been between them. She'd known even then that it couldn't last. She'd told herself as much when Miles had wrested a promise from her that he could have a date afterward. He wouldn't hold her to that now.

Steeling herself, she returned to her agenda. Her real priority.

"Then you know I'm desperate for answers." Regret burned right through all the steeliness. "I'm sorry I invaded your privacy. That was a mistake. But I've been digging for clues about Zach's death for fourteen years. Now that the media spotlight has turned to the Mesa Falls owners thanks to your connection to Alonzo Salazar, I saw a chance to finally learn the truth."

"By using your invitation into my home to spy on me," he clarified.

"Why wasn't Zach's death in the papers? Why didn't the school acknowledge it?" She'd searched for years. His death notice had been a line item weeks after the fact, with nothing about the person he'd been or how he'd died.

"You say you were friends with him, but I only have your word on that." Miles watched her suspiciously. Judging her? She wondered what had happened to the man she'd been with the night before. The lover who'd been so generous. This cold stranger bore him no resemblance. "How do I know this isn't another attempt by the media to unearth a story?"

"Who else even knows about him but me?" she asked, affronted. Indignant. "There was never a public outcry about his death. No demand for answers from the media. Maybe because he was just some foster kid that—"

Her throat was suddenly burning and so were her eyes, the old emotions coming back to surprise her with their force while Miles studied her from across the breakfast table. With an effort, she regained control of herself and backed her chair away from the table.

"I'd better go," she murmured, embarrassed for the ill-timed display of feelings. But damn it, Zach had deserved a better send-off. She'd never even known where to attend a service for him, because as far as she'd known, there hadn't been one.

That broke her heart.

Miles rose with her, covering her hand briefly with his.

"It was a simple question. I meant no offense." He shifted his hand away, but the warmth remained where his fingers had been. "We've safeguarded our friend's memory for a long time, and I won't relax my protection of him now. Not for anyone."

She tilted her chin at him, trying her damnedest to see some hint of warmth in that chilly facade.

"What memory?" she pressed. "He vanished without a trace. Without an opportunity for his friends to mourn him."

"His friends *did* mourn him. They still do." His expression was fierce. "We won't allow his name to be drawn into the public spectacle that Alonzo Salazar brought to the ranch because of that damned tell-all book."

"I would never do that to Zach." She hugged her arms around herself, recalling too late that she wore Miles's clothes. Her fingers rested on the cotton of his sweats. The scent of him. As if she wasn't feeling vulnerable already. "As for his friends mourning him, you weren't the only ones. There were a lot of other people who cared about Zach. People who never got to say goodbye."

For a long minute, they regarded each other warily in the quiet room, the scents of their forgotten breakfast still savory even though no food could possibly tempt her. Her stomach was in knots.

But even now, in the aftermath of the unhappy exchange, awareness of him lingered. Warmth prickled along her skin as they stood facing each other in silent challenge, reminding her of the heat that had propelled her into his arms the night before.

The chime of her cell phone intruded on the charged moment, a welcome distraction from whatever it was that kept pulling her toward a man who was determined to keep his secrets. He was as quick to seize on the reprieve from their exchange as she was. He turned toward the table to begin clearing away their half-finished meal.

She retrieved the device from where it lay on the table, checking the text while she carried her coffee cup to the sink. The message was from her assistant, Jules.

All your platforms hacked. On phone with IG now. Sent help notices to the rest. Some joker who didn't like a post? I'm on it, but knew you'd want heads-up.

She didn't realize she'd gone still until she heard Miles asking, "What's wrong?"

Her brain couldn't quite compute what was wrong. The timing of the attack on all her platforms at once seemed strange. Suddenly feeling a little shaky, she dropped into the closest seat, a bar stool at the island.

"Someone hijacked my social media accounts," she whispered, stunned and not buying that it was the work of a disgruntled commenter. "All of the platforms at once, which seems really unusual."

"Does that happen often?" Miles jammed the food in the huge refrigerator, working quickly to clean up.

"It's never happened before." She gulped back a sick

feeling, tapping the tab for Instagram on her phone to see for herself. "I have friends who have had one platform hijacked here or there, but not all at once."

Miles dumped the remaining dishes in the sink and toweled off his hands before tossing the dishcloth aside. He rejoined her, gripping the back of her chair. "That feels like someone has an ax to grind."

The warmth of his nearness was a distraction she couldn't afford. She scooted forward in her seat.

"Someone with enough tech savvy to take over all my properties at once." She checked one profile after another, finding the photos changed, but still of her.

Less flattering images. Older images. But they weren't anything to be embarrassed about. She'd had friends whose profiles were hacked and replaced with digitally altered pictures that were highly compromising.

"Any idea who'd do something like that?" Miles asked, the concern in his voice replacing some of the animosity that had been there before. "Any enemies?"

"I can't think of anyone." She'd had her fair share of trolls on her account, but they tended to stir up trouble with other commenters as opposed to targeting her.

Her phone chimed again. She swiped the screen in a hurry, hopeful Jules had resolved the problem. But the text in her inbox was from a private number. Maybe one of the social media platforms' customer service used that kind of anonymous messaging?

She clicked open the text.

Today's takeover is a warning. Stay out of Zach's business or your accounts will be seriously compromised.

Her grip on the phone tightened. She blinked twice as the threat chilled her inside and out.

"Are you okay?" Miles touched her shoulder, the warmth of his fingers anchoring her as fear trickled through her.

"I've got to go." Shaky with the newfound realization that someone was keeping close tabs on her, she wondered who else could possibly know she was investigating Zach's death besides Miles.

She slid off the bar stool to her feet, needing to get back to her laptop and her assistant to figure out the extent of her cybersecurity problem. This felt like someone was watching her. Or tracking her online activity.

"You're pale as the snow." Miles steadied her by the elbow when she wobbled unsteadily. "What's going on?"

She didn't want to share what she'd just read with him when he mistrusted her. When she mistrusted him. But his touch overrode everything else, anchoring her in spite of the hollow feeling inside.

"Look." She handed him her phone, unable to articulate all the facets of the new worries wriggling to life. "I just received this." Pausing until he'd had time to absorb the news, she continued, "Who else even knows about Zach, let alone what I came here for?"

His jaw flexed as he stared at the screen, stubble giving his face a texture she remembered well from when he'd kissed her during the night. She fisted her hands in the pockets of the sweatpants to keep herself from doing something foolish, like running an exploratory finger along his chin.

"I didn't think anyone else remembered him outside of my partners and me." He laid her phone on the kitchen island behind her. "As for who else knows why you came here, I can't answer that, as I only found out moments ago."

She hesitated. "You saw my attempt to check your computer last night. So you knew then that I had an interest. Did you share that information with anyone?"

A scowl darkened his expression.

"I texted Gage Striker about an hour into the party to ask how well he knew you, since I thought you'd been going through my files."

She shouldn't be surprised that Miles had as much reason to suspect her of hiding something as she'd had to suspect him. She'd recognized that they'd been circling one another warily the previous night before the heat between them burned everything else away. If anything, maybe it soothed her grated nerves just a little to know he hadn't been any more able to resist the temptation than she had.

"And Gage could have told any one of your other partners. They, in turn, could have confided in friends or significant others." Reaching back to the counter, she retrieved the cell and shoved it in the pocket of Miles's sweats. "So word could have spread to quite a few people by this morning."

"In theory," he acknowledged, though his voice held a begrudging tone. "But Gage didn't even put in an appearance at the party. So he wouldn't have been around anyone else to share the news, and I'm guessing he had something big going on in his personal life that kept him from attending."

"Maybe he needed to hire someone to hack all my accounts." She couldn't rule it out, despite Miles's scoff. Anger ramped up inside her along with a hint of mistrust. "But for now, I need to return to my hotel and do everything I can to protect my brand."

"Wait." He stepped in front of her. Not too close, but definitely in her path.

Her pulse quickened at his nearness. Her gaze dipped to the way the fitted shirt with the Rivera Ranch logo skimmed his broad shoulders and arms. Her mouth dried up.

Maybe he felt the same jolt that she did, because he looked away from her, spearing a hand through his hair.

"Let me drive you back," he told her finally. "Someone might be watching you. And until you know what you're dealing with, you should take extra precautions for your safety."

The thought of spending more time alone with this man was too tempting. Which was why she absolutely had to decline. Things were confused enough between them already.

"I'll be fine. My assistant will send a car and extra security." She withdrew her phone again—a good enough excuse to take her eyes off him—and sent the request. "I just need to get my dress and I'll be on my way."

Still Miles didn't move.

"Where are you staying?" he pressed. "You can't ghost me. You owe me a date."

"I think we both know that's not a good idea in light of how much things have gone awry between us." She couldn't believe he'd even brought it up. But perhaps he only wanted to use that time with her as a way to keep tabs on her while she sought the information he was determined to keep private.

"I still want to see you." He didn't explain why. "Where will you be?"

"I've been in a local hotel, but today I've got a flight to Tahoe to spend time with Astrid. I haven't seen her since she had the baby."

Jonah and Astrid had a house on the lake near a casino resort owned by Desmond Pierce, another Mesa Falls partner. Spending time with Astrid would be a way to keep an eye on two of the ranch owners while removing herself from the temptation that Miles presented just by being in the same town.

Even now, looking into Miles's blue eyes, she couldn't help recalling the ways he'd kissed and touched her. Made her fly apart in his arms.

For now, she needed to regroup. Protect her business until she figured out her next move in the search for answers about Zach.

"I don't suppose it's a coincidence that half of the Mesa Falls partners live around Tahoe," Miles observed drily. "Maybe I should go with you. No doubt we'll be convening soon to figure out who could be threatening you. Zach's legacy is important to us."

She shrugged, averting her eyes because she knew they'd betray her desire for him. "You can look into it your way. I'll keep looking into it mine. But I don't think it's a good idea for us to spend more time alone together after what happened last night."

Just talking about it sent a small, pleasurable shiver up her spine. She had to hold herself very still to hide it. The least movement from him and she would cave to temptation.

"I disagree. And if we both want answers, maybe we should be working together instead of apart." His voice gentled, taking on that low rasp that had slid right past her defenses last night. "You wouldn't have checked my computer files if you didn't think I had information that could help you. Why not go straight to the source?"

For a moment, the idea of spending another day with him—another night—rolled over her like a seductive wave. But then she forced herself to shake it off.

"If you wanted to share information with me, you could tell me now." She put it out there like a dare, knowing he wouldn't spill any secrets.

He and his friends had never revealed anything about Zach. Not then. And not now. Because Miles was silent. Watchful. Wary.

Her phone chimed again, and she didn't need to check it to know her ride was out front.

"In that case, I'd better be going." She turned on her heel. "Maybe I'll see you in Tahoe."

"Chiara." He called her name before she reached the stairs leading back to the bedroom suite.

Gripping the wood rail in a white-knuckled grip, she looked over her shoulder at him.

"Be careful. We don't know who you're dealing with, but it could be someone dangerous."

The reminder brought the anxiety from earlier churning back. She tightened her hold on the rail to keep from swaying.

"I'll be careful," she conceded before stiffening her spine with resolve. "But I'm not backing down."

Five

Miles began making phone calls as soon as Chiara left. He poured himself a drink and paced circles around the indoor pool, leaving voice messages for Gage and Jonah. Then he tapped the contact button for Desmond Pierce, his friend who owned the casino resort on Lake Tahoe.

For fourteen years, the friends who'd been with Zach Eldridge when he died had kept the circumstances a secret. At first, they'd done so because they were in shock and grieving. Later, they'd remained silent to protect his memory, as a way to honor him in death even though they'd been unable to save him.

But if someone outside the six friends who owned Mesa Falls knew about Zach—about the circumstances that had pushed him over the edge that fateful day—then his secrets weren't safe any longer. They needed to figure out their next steps.

A voice on the other end of the phone pulled him from his thoughts, and he paused his pacing around the pool to listen.

"Hey, Miles," Desmond answered smoothly, the slot machine chirps and muted conversation of the casino floor sounding in the background. "What's up?"

"Problems." As succinctly as possible, he summarized the situation with Chiara and the threat against her if she kept looking for answers about Zach's death.

When Miles was done, Desmond let out a low whistle. The sounds of the casino in the background had faded, meaning he must have sought privacy for the conversation.

"Who else knows about Zach but us?" Desmond asked. "Moreover, who the hell would have known Chiara was asking questions within hours of her showing up at Mesa Falls?"

Miles stared out the glass walls around the enclosed pool, watching the snow fall as he let the question hang there for a moment. He was certain Desmond must have come to the same conclusion as him.

"You know it points to one of us," Miles answered, rattling the last of the ice in his drink. "I texted Gage last night when I thought she was snooping in my office."

He didn't want to think Gage would go to the length of hacking her accounts to protect their secrets, but every one of the partners had his own reasons for not wanting the truth to come to light. Gage, in particular, bore a weight of guilt because his influential politician father had kept the truth of the accident out of the media. Nigel Striker had made a substantial grant to the Dowdon School to ensure the incident was handled the way he chose.

Quietly. Without any reference to Zach's connection to the school. Which explained why Chiara hadn't been able to learn anything about it.

Desmond cleared his throat. "Gage could have shared that information with any one of us."

"I can't believe we're even discussing the possibility of a leak within our group." The idea made everything inside him protest. They'd spent fourteen years trying to protect the truth.

Who would go rogue now and break that trust?

"Just because we're discussing it doesn't prove anything," Desmond pointed out reasonably. "Chiara could have confided her intentions to someone else. Or someone could have tracked her searches online."

"Right. But we need to meet. And this time, no videoconferencing." He remembered the way the last couple of meetings had gone among the partners—once with only four of them showing up in person, and another time with half of them participating remotely. "We need all six of us in the same room."

"You really think it's one of us?" Desmond asked. Despite Desmond's normally controlled facade, Miles could hear the surprise in his friend's tone.

"I'm not sure. But if it's not, we can rule it out faster if we're together in the same room. If one of us is lying, we'll know." Miles might not have spent much time in person with his school friends in the last fourteen years, but their bond ran deep.

They'd all agreed to run the ranch together in the hope of honoring Zach's life. Zach had loved the outdoors and the Ventana Wilderness close to their school.

He would have appreciated Mesa Falls's green ranching mission to protect the environment and help native species flourish.

"Do you need help coordinating it?" Desmond asked, the sounds of the casino again intruding from his end of the call.

"No. I think we should meet in Tahoe this time. But I wanted to warn you that Chiara is on her way there even now. She says she's going to see Astrid, but I have the feeling she'll be questioning Jonah, too. She might even show up at your office." Miles couldn't forget the look in her eyes when she'd said she wouldn't back down from her search for answers about Zach.

There'd been a gravity that hinted at the strong stuff she was made of. He understood that kind of commitment. He felt it for Rivera Ranch, the family property he'd inherited and would protect at any cost.

Of course, he felt that way about Zach and Mesa Falls, too. Unfortunately, their strong loyalties to the same person were bound to keep putting them at odds. Unless they worked together. The idea made him uneasy. But did he really have a choice?

The thought of seeing her again—even though she'd only walked out his door an hour ago—sent anticipation shooting through him. He'd never forget the night they'd shared.

"I'll keep an eye out for her," Desmond assured him. "Thanks for the heads-up."

Miles disconnected the call and pocketed his phone. He would hand off the task of scheduling the owners' meeting to his assistant, since coordinating times could be a logistical nightmare. But no matter how busy they were, this had to take priority.

Things were coming to a head for Mesa Falls. And Zach.

And no matter how much Miles didn't trust Chiara Campagna, he was worried for her safety with someone threatening her. Which would have been reason enough for him to fly to Tahoe at the first opportunity. But he also couldn't deny he wanted to see her again.

She'd promised him a date. And he would hold her to her word.

That night, in her rented villa overlooking Lake Tahoe, Chiara tucked her feet underneath her in the window seat as she opened her tablet. The nine-bedroom home and guesthouse were situated next door to Desmond Pierce's casino resort, assuring her easy access to him. The separate guesthouse allowed her to have her assistant and photo team members nearby while giving all of them enough space. Astrid and Jonah lived just a few miles away, and Chiara would see them as soon as she could. She'd already made plans to meet Astrid for a spin class in the morning.

This was the first moment she'd had to herself all day. First there'd been the morning with Miles, then the flight to Truckee and drive to Tahoe Vista, with most of the travel time spent on efforts to stabilize her social media platforms.

She should probably be researching cybersecurity experts to ensure her social media properties were more secure in the future, even though she'd gotten all of her platforms corrected by dinnertime. It only made good business sense to protect her online presence. But she'd spent so many years making the right decisions for her public image, relentlessly driving her empire to keep growing that she couldn't devote one more minute to work today. Didn't she deserve a few hours to herself now and then? To be a woman instead of a brand?

So instead of working, she thumbed the remote button to turn on the gas fireplace and dimmed the spotlights in the exposed trusswork of the cathedral ceiling. Settling back against the yellow cushions of the window seat, Chiara returned her attention to the tablet and found herself scrolling through a web search about Miles Rivera.

She'd like to think it was all part of her effort to find out more about Zach. Maybe if she could piece together clues from the lives of his friends during the year of Zach's death, she would find something she'd overlooked. But as she swiped through images of Miles at the historic Rivera Ranch property in the Red Clover Valley of the Sierra Nevada foothills, pausing on a few of him at galas in Mesa Falls and at the casino on Lake Tahoe, she realized she had ulterior motives. Even on the screen he took her breath away.

He looked as at home in his jeans and boots as he did in black tie, and not just because he was a supremely attractive man. There was a comfort in his own skin, a certainty of his place in the world that Chiara envied. She'd been born to privilege as the daughter of wealthy parents, but she'd always been keenly aware she didn't belong. Her mother had never known what to do with her; she'd been awkward and gangly until she grew into her looks. As a girl, she'd been antisocial, preferring books to people. She'd lacked charm and social graces, a failure that confirmed her mother's opinion of her as a hopeless child. So she'd been packed off to boarding school on the opposite coast, where she'd retreated into her art until she met Zach, her lone friend.

Then Zach died, and her parents lost their fortune.

Chiara transferred to public school and made even fewer friends there than she had at Brookfield. She fit in nowhere until she founded her fictional world online. Her Instagram account had started as a way to take photos of beautiful things. That other people liked her view of the world had shocked her, but eventually she'd come to see that she was good at being social on the other side of a keyboard. By the time she gained real traction and popularity, her awkwardness in person didn't matter anymore. Her followers liked her work, so they didn't care if she said very little at public events. Fans seemed to equate her reticence with the aloofness they expected in a star. But inside, Chiara felt like a fraud, wrestling with impostor syndrome that she'd somehow forged an extravagant, envied life she didn't really deserve.

Her finger hovered over an image of Miles with an arm slung around his friend Alec Jacobsen and another around Desmond Pierce. It was an old photo, similar to the one she'd seen in Miles's office at his house. She thought it was taken around the time the six friends had bought Mesa Falls. She'd known even before she'd restarted her search for answers that the men who'd bought the ranch had been Zach's closest friends at Dowdon. One of them knew something. Possibly all of them. What reason would they have to hide the circumstances of his death?

She'd contacted his foster home afterward, and years later, she'd visited the department of social services for information about Zach. The state hadn't been under any legal obligation to release details of his death other than to say it was accidental and that issues of neglect in foster care hadn't been a concern. She'd had no luck tracking down his birth parents. But Miles knew something, or else he wouldn't have been so emphatic about protecting Zach's privacy.

Staring into Miles's eyes in the photograph didn't yield any answers. Just twenty-four hours ago, she'd been convinced he was her enemy in her search. Sleeping with Miles had shown her a different side of him. And reminiscing with him about Zach for those few moments over breakfast had reinforced the idea that he'd shared a powerful bond with their shared friend. What reason did Miles have to push her away?

When she found herself tracing the angles of his face on the tablet screen, Chiara closed the page in a hurry. She couldn't afford the tenderness of feeling that had crept up on her with regard to Miles Rivera. It clouded her mission. Distorted her perspective when she needed to be clearheaded.

Tomorrow, she'd find a way to talk to Desmond Pierce. Then she'd see if Alec Jacobsen was in town. If she kept pushing, someone would divulge something. Even if they didn't mean to.

Turning her gaze to the moon rising over the lake through the window, she squinted, trying to see beyond her reflection in the glass. She needed to learn something before her anonymous blackmailer discovered she was still asking questions. Because while she was prepared to risk everything—the fame, the following, the income that came from it—to find out the truth of Zach's death, she couldn't help hoping Miles didn't have anything to do with it.

* * *

"Dig deep for the next hill!" The spin class instructor kept up her running stream of motivational commentary from a stationary bike at the center of the casino resort's fitness studio. "If you want the reward, you've got to put in the work!"

Chiara hated exercise class in general, and early-morning ones even more, but her friend Astrid had insisted the spin class was the best one her gym offered. So Chiara had pulled herself out of bed at the crack of dawn for the last two mornings. She'd dragged Jules with her, and Astrid met them there to work out in a room that looked more like a dance club than a gym. With neon and black lights, the atmosphere was high energy and the hip-hop music intense. Sweating out her restlessness wasn't fun, but it felt like a way to excise some of the intense emotions being with Miles had stirred up.

"I can't do another hill," Astrid huffed from the cycle to Chiara's right, her blond braid sliding over her shoulder as she turned to talk. A former model from Finland, Astrid had happily traded in her magazine covers for making organic baby food since becoming a mother shortly before Christmas. "You know I love Katja, but being pregnant left me with no muscle tone."

"I would have chosen the yoga class," Chiara managed as she gulped air, her hamstrings burning and her butt numb from the uncomfortable seat. "So I blame this hell on you."

"I would be *sleeping*." Jules leaned over her handlebars from the bike on Chiara's left, her pink tank top clinging to her sweaty shoulders. "So I blame both of you."

"Please," Chiara scoffed, running a skeptical eye over Jules's toned legs. "You were a competitive volleyball player. I've seen you play for hours."

Chiara's family had lived next door to Jules's once upon a time, and the Santors were more like family to her than her own had ever been. When her business had taken off, she'd made it her mission to employ as many of the family members as she could, enjoying the pleasure of having people she genuinely liked close to her. Even now, back in Los Angeles, Jules's mom was in charge of Chiara's house.

"Spiking balls and attacking the net do not require this level of cardio," Jules grumbled, although she dutifully kicked up her speed at their instructor's shouted command to "go hard."

Chiara felt light-headed from the exercise, skipping breakfast, and the swirl of flashing lights as they pedaled.

"We owe ourselves lunch out at least, don't we?" Astrid pleaded, letting go of her handlebars long enough to take a drink from her water bottle. "Jonah got us a sitter tomorrow for the first time since I had Katja, so I've got a couple of hours free."

"This is the first time?" Chiara asked, smiling in spite of the sweat, the aches and the gasping for air.

Astrid had been nervous about being a mom before her daughter was born, but she'd been adorably committed to every aspect of parenting. Chiara couldn't help but compare her friend's efforts with her own mother's role in her life. Kristina Marsh had handed her daughter off to nannies whenever possible, which might not have been a problem if there'd been a good one in the mix. But she tended to hire the cheapest possible household help in order to add to her budget for things like clothes and jewelry.

"I hate leaving her with anyone but Jonah," Astrid admitted, slowing her pedaling in spite of their coach's motivational exhortation to "grind it out."

"But I think it's important to have someone trained in Katja's routine in case something comes up and I need help in a hurry."

"Definitely." Chiara wasn't about to let her friend hover around the babysitter when she could get her out of the house for a little while. "Plus you deserve a break. It's been two months."

"That's what Jonah says." Astrid's soft smile at the thought of her husband gave Chiara an unexpected pang in her chest.

She hadn't realized until that moment how much she envied Astrid's rock-solid relationship with a man she loved and trusted. Chiara hadn't even given a second thought to her single status in years, content to pursue her work instead of romance when she had difficulty trusting people anyhow. And for good reason. Her family was so good at keeping secrets from her she hadn't known they'd lost everything until the headmistress at Brookfield told her they were sending her home because her tuition hadn't been paid in months.

Chiara shoved that thought from her head along with any romance envy. She cheered along with the rest of the class as the instructor blew her whistle to signal the session's end. Jules slumped over her handlebars as she recovered, clicking through the diagnostics to check her stats.

Chiara closed her eyes for a long moment to rest them from the blinking red and green lights. And, no surprise, an image of Miles Rivera appeared on the backs of her eyelids, tantalizing her with memories of their night together.

She could live to be a hundred and still not be able to account for how fast she'd ended up in his bed. The draw between them was like nothing she'd ever experienced.

Astrid's softly accented words broke into Chiara's sensual reverie.

"So where should we meet for lunch tomorrow?" The hint of Finland in Astrid's words folded "where" to sound like "vere," the lilt as attractive as every other thing about her. "Des's casino has a bunch of places."

Chiara's eyes shot open at the mention of Desmond Pierce, one of Miles's partners. She needed to question him and Astrid's husband, Jonah, too. Subtly. And, ideally, close to the same time so neither one had a chance to warn the others about Chiara's interest in the details of Zach's final days.

"The casino is perfect." Chiara slid off her cycle and picked up her towel and water bottle off the floor, locking eyes with another woman who lingered near the cycles—a pretty redhead with freckles she hadn't noticed earlier. Why did she look vaguely familiar? Distracted, she told Astrid, "Pick your favorite place and we'll meet there."

The redhead scurried away, and Chiara guessed she didn't know the woman after all.

"There's an Indo-Mexican fusion spot called Spice Pavilion. I'm addicted to the tikka tacos." Astrid checked her phone as the regular house lights came up and the spin class attendees shuffled out of the room. "Can you do one o'clock? Jonah has a meeting that starts at noon, so I can shop first and then meet you."

A meeting? Chiara's brain chased the possibilities of what that might mean while she followed Jules toward the locker room, with Astrid behind them.

"Perfect," Chiara assured her friend as they reached the lockers and retrieved their bags. "Is Jonah's meeting at the casino, too?"

"Yes. More Mesa Falls business," Astrid answered as she hefted her quilted designer bag onto one shoulder and shut the locker with her knee. "Things have been heating up for the ranch ever since that tell-all book came out."

Didn't she know it. Chiara had plenty of questions of her own about the ranch and its owners, but she'd tried not to involve Astrid in her hunt for answers since she wouldn't use a valued friendship for leverage.

But knowing that Zach's friends would be congregating at the resort tomorrow was welcome information.

"Then you can leave Jonah to his meeting and we'll gorge ourselves on tikka tacos," Chiara promised her, calling the details over her shoulder to Jules, who had a locker on the next row. "Today I'm going to finish my posts for the week, so I can clear the whole day tomorrow. Text me if you're done shopping early or if you want company."

If all the men of Mesa Falls were in town, there was a chance she'd run into one of them at the casino anyhow. Desmond Pierce had been avoiding her calls, so she hadn't even gotten a chance to meet him. But she needed to speak to all of them.

Although there was one in particular she couldn't wait to see, even though she already knew he had nothing else to say to her on the subject of Zach's death.

Miles might be keeping secrets from her. And he

might be the last man she'd ever trust with her heart because of that. But that didn't mean that she'd stopped thinking about his hands, his mouth or his body on hers for more than a few seconds at a time since she'd left Montana.

No doubt about it—she was in deep with this man, and they'd only just met.

Six

Steering his borrowed SUV around a hairpin turn, Miles pulled up to the massive lakefront villa where Chiara was staying for the week. He'd been in town for all of a few hours before seeking her out, but ever since he'd heard from Jonah that the place she'd rented was close to the casino where Miles was staying, he'd needed to see her for himself.

The property was brightly lit even though the sun had just set, the stone turrets and walkways illuminated to highlight the architectural details. Huge pine trees flanked the building, while a second stone guesthouse sat at an angle to the villa with a path linking them.

Stepping out of the casino's Land Rover that he'd commissioned for the evening, Miles hoped all the lights meant that Chiara was taking her security seriously. He'd kept an eye on her social media sites since she'd left Mesa Falls to make sure no one hacked them again, but that hadn't done nearly enough to soothe his anxiety where she was concerned. Someone was threatening her for reasons related to Zach, and that did not sit well with him. He'd messaged her earlier in the day to let her know he would be in town tonight, but she hadn't replied.

Now, walking up the stone path into the central turret that housed the front entrance, he tucked his chin into the collar of his leather jacket against the chill in the wind. He could see into one of the large windows. A fire burned in the stone hearth of a great room, but he didn't notice any movement inside.

He shot a text to Chiara to warn her he was outside, then rang the bell. No sense adding to her unease during a week that had already upset her.

An instant later, he heard a digital chime and the bolt sliding open, then the door swung wide. Chiara stood on the threshold, her long dark hair held off her face with a white cable-knit headband. She wore flannel pajama bottoms in pink-and-white plaid. A V-neck cashmere sweater grazed her hips, the pink hue matching her fuzzy socks.

She looked sweetly delicious, in fact. But his overriding thought was that she shouldn't be answering her own door while someone was watching her movements and threatening her. Fear for her safety made him brusque.

"What happened to taking extra precautions with your safety?" He didn't see anyone else in the house with her. No bodyguard. No assistant.

Tension banded his chest.

"Hello to you, too." She arched a brow at him. "And to answer your question, the door was locked, and the alarm system was activated." She stepped to one side, silently inviting him in. "I gave my head of security the evening off since I had no plans to go out."

Relieved she'd at least thought about her safety, he entered the foyer, which opened into the great room with its incredible views of the lake. He took in the vaulted ceilings and dark wood accents along the pale walls. The scent of popcorn wafted from deeper in the house, the sound of popping ongoing.

"Right. I realize the level of security you use is your own business, I've just been concerned." He noticed a throw blanket on the floor in front of the leather sofa. A nest of pillows had been piled by the fireplace, and there was a glass of red wine on the hearth. "Early night?"

"My job isn't always a party every evening, contrary to popular opinion." She hurried toward the kitchen, a huge light-filled space separated from the great room by a marble-topped island. "Have a seat. I don't want my popcorn to burn."

He followed more slowly, taking in the honey-colored floors and pale cabinets, the row of pendant lamps casting a golden glow over the island counter, where a popcorn popper quickly filled with fluffy white kernels. The excessive size and grandeur of the space reminded him they moved in very different circles. For all of his wealth, Miles spent most of his time on his ranch. His life was quiet. Solitary. Hers was public. Extravagant.

But at least for now, they were alone.

"I didn't mean to intrude on your evening." He had to admit she looked at home in her sprawling rented villa, her down-to-earth pj's and sweater a far cry from the metallic dress she'd worn to the ranch party. She seemed more approachable. "I'm in town to meet with my partners, and I wanted to make sure there have been no new incidents."

He lowered himself onto a backless counter stool, gladder than he should be to see her again. She'd been in his thoughts often enough since their night together, and not just because he'd been concerned about her safety. Her kiss, her touch, the sound of her sighs of pleasure had distracted him day and night.

"Nothing since I left your house. Can I get you a glass of wine?" she asked, turning the bottle on the counter. "It's nothing special, but it's my preferred pairing with popcorn."

Her light tone hinted she wanted to change the subject from the threat she'd received, but he was unwilling to let it go.

"No, thank you. I won't keep you long." He stood again, if only to get closer to her while she leaned a hip on the island.

The urge to pull her against him was so strong he forced himself to plant a palm on the marble countertop instead of reaching for her.

"Well, you don't need to fear for my safety. My assistant's boyfriend is also my bodyguard, and they're both staying in the guesthouse right on the property." She pointed out the window in the direction of the smaller lodge he'd seen close by. "I'm in good hands."

He'd prefer she was in *his* hands. But he ignored the need to touch her; he was just glad to hear she hadn't taken the threat lightly.

"Did you report the incident to the police?" His gaze tracked her emerald eyes before taking in her scrubbed-clean skin and high cheekbones. She smelled like orange blossoms.

"I didn't reach out to them." She frowned, folding her arms. "I was so busy that day trying to get all my social media accounts secured that I never gave it any thought."

He hated to upset her unnecessarily, but her safety was important to him. "You should let the authorities know you're being harassed. Even if they can't do anything to help, it would be good to have the episode on the record in case things escalate."

She mattered to him. Even when he knew that was problematic. She didn't trust him, and he had plenty of reason not to trust her. Yet that didn't stop him from wanting to see her again. He could tell himself all day it was because staying close to her would help him protect Zach's memory. But he wasn't that naive. The truth was far simpler. Their one night together wasn't nearly enough to satisfy his hunger for this woman.

"I'll report it tomorrow," she conceded with a nod, her dark hair shifting along her sweater. "I can head to the local station in the morning, before I have lunch with Astrid."

"Would you like me to go with you?" he offered, his hand leaving the marble counter to rest on top of hers. Briefly. Because if he touched her any longer, it would be damn near impossible to keep his head on straight. "Spending hours at the cop shop is no one's idea of fun."

A hint of a smile curved her lips. "I'll be fine," she insisted.

Refusing his offer, but not moving her fingers out from under his. He shifted fractionally closer.

Her head came up, her gaze wary. Still, he thought there might have been a flash of hot awareness in those beautiful eyes.

"What about the date you promised me?" He tipped up her chin to better see her face, read her expression.

She sucked in a quick breath. Then, as if to hide the reaction, she bit her lip.

He imagined the soft nip of those white teeth on his own flesh, a phantom touch.

"Name the day," he coaxed her as the moment drew out, the desire to taste her getting stronger with each passing breath.

"I told you that it's a bad idea for us to spend more time together," she said finally, not sounding the least bit sure of herself. "Considering how things spiraled out of control after the party at your house."

He skimmed a touch along her jaw, thinking about all the ways he hadn't touched her yet. All the ways he wanted to.

"I've spent so much time thinking about that night, I'm not sure I can regret it." His gaze dipped to the lush softness of her mouth. He trailed his thumb along the seam. "Can you?"

Her lips parted, a soft huff of her breath grazing his knuckle.

"Maybe not." She blinked fast. "But just because you successfully run into and escape from a burning building once doesn't mean you should keep tempting fate with return trips."

"Is that what this is?" He released her, knowing he needed to make his case with his words and not their combustible connection. "A burning building?"

"You know what I mean. We seem destined to be at odds while I search for answers about Zach. There's no point blurring the battle lines." She spoke quickly, as if eager to brush the whole notion aside so she could move on.

He hoped the hectic color in her cheeks was evidence that he affected her even a fraction of how much she tempted him. But he didn't want to press her more tonight for fear she'd run again. For now, he would have to content himself that she'd agreed to speak to the police tomorrow.

"Then we'll have to disagree on that point." He shoved his hands in the pockets of the leather jacket he'd never removed. "The fact is, you owe me a date, and I'm not letting you off the hook."

Still, he backed up a step, wanting to give her space to think it over.

"You're leaving?" She twisted a dark strand of hair around one finger.

He would not think about how that silky hair had felt wrapped around his hand the night they'd been together. "You deserve an evening to yourself. And while I hope you'll change your mind about a date, I'm not going to twist your arm. I have the feeling we'll run across each other again this week since we have a common interest in Zach's story."

"Maybe we will." Her bottle-green eyes slid over him before she squared her shoulders and picked up her bowl of popcorn. "Good night, Miles."

He would have liked to end the night very differently, but he would settle for her roaming gaze and the memory of her biting her lip when they touched. Those things might not keep him warm tonight, but they suggested the odds were good of her landing in his bed again.

For now, that was enough.

* * *

So much for her relaxing evening in front of the fire with popcorn and a book.

Chiara couldn't sit still after Miles left. Unsatisfied desires made her twitchy and restless. After half an hour of reading the same page over and over again in her book, never once making sense of it, she gave up. She replaced the throw blanket and pillows on the sofa, then took her wine and empty popcorn bowl into the kitchen.

Even now, as she opened her laptop and took a seat at the island countertop, she swore she could feel the place where Miles's thumb had grazed her lip. That, in turn, had her reliving his kisses and the way their bodies had sought one another's that night in Mesa Falls.

Could that kind of electrifying chemistry be wrong? She guessed *yes*, because she and Miles were going to be at odds over Zach. All the sizzling attraction in the world was only going to confuse her real goal—to honor Zach's memory by clearing away the mystery of his death.

But denying that she felt it in the first place, when she wasn't deceiving anyone with her protests, seemed foolish. Miles had surely recognized the attraction she felt for him. And yet he'd walked away tonight, letting her make the next move.

Instead of losing herself in his arms, she opted to search her files on Zach one more time. Checking her inbox, she noticed a retired administrator from Dowdon School had gotten back to her on an email inquiry she'd made long ago. Or, more accurately, the administrator's former assistant had responded to Chiara. She hadn't asked directly about Zach; instead, she'd asked for information about the school year when he'd died under the guise of writing a general retrospective for a class reunion.

Apparently, the assistant hadn't cared that she wasn't a former student. She had simply attached a few files, including some flyers for events around campus, including one for the art fair where Chiara had last seen Zach. There was also a digital version of the small Dowdon yearbook.

After saving all the files, she opened them one by one. The art fair poster brought a sad, nostalgic smile to her face but yielded no clues. Seeing it reminded her how much of an influence Zach had on her life, though, his eye for artistic composition inspiring her long afterward. Other pamphlets advertised an author visit, a homecoming dance in conjunction with Brookfield and a football game. She wrote down the email contact information for the dance and sent a message to the address, using the same pretext as before.

Pausing to sip her wine, Chiara swiped through the yearbook even though she'd seen it twice before. Once, as soon as it came out; she'd made an excuse to visit the Brookfield library to examine a copy since the school kept all the Dowdon yearbooks in a special collection. She only paged through it enough to know Zach hadn't been in there. No photo. No mention.

Like he'd never existed.

Then, a year ago, she'd seen Jonah's copy at Astrid's house and had flipped through. Now, she examined the content more carefully in the hope of finding anything she'd overlooked.

First, however, she searched for Miles's photo. He was there, alphabetized in his class year next to his brother, Weston Rivera. They weren't twins, but they were as close in age as nontwin siblings could be.

The Rivera men had been swoonworthy even then. Wes's hair had been longer and unruly, his hazel eyes mischievous, and his look more surfer than rancher. Miles appeared little changed since the photo was taken, beyond the obvious maturing of his face and the filling out of the very male body she remembered from their night together. But his serious aspect and set jaw were the same even then, his blue eyes hinting at the old soul inside.

Before she could stop herself, her finger ran over his image on the screen.

Catching herself in the midst of fanciful thinking, she dismissed the unfamiliar romantic notions that had somehow attached themselves to Miles. She navigated away from the student photos section to browse the rest of the yearbook while she nibbled a few pieces of cold popcorn.

Half an hour later, a figure caught her eye in the background of one of the candid group shots taken outdoors on the Dowdon soccer field. It was a young woman in a knee-length navy blue skirt and sensible flats, her blond hair in a side part and low ponytail.

An old memory bubbled to the surface of seeing the woman. And she was a woman, not a girl, among the students, looking more mature than those around her.

Chiara had seen her before. Just once. Long ago.

With Zach.

The thrill of discovery buoyed her, sending her mind twirling in twenty directions about what to do with the new information. Funny that the first person who came to mind to share it with was Miles.

Would he know the woman? She picked up her phone, seeing his contact information still on the screen since the last message she'd received had been from him, letting her know he was at her door. The desire to share this with him was strong. Or was it only her desire to see him again? The ache of seeing him walk out her door was still fresh.

With an effort, she set the phone aside.

As much as she wanted to see if Miles recognized the mystery woman, she acknowledged that he might not answer her truthfully. He'd made it clear he planned to keep Zach's secrets. That she couldn't trust someone who could turn her inside out with a look was unsettling.

Tonight, she would research all she could on her own. Tomorrow, she would meet Astrid for lunch and—with a little good luck in the timing department—maybe she could waylay Astrid's husband before he went into his meeting with the Mesa Falls partners.

All she wanted was a real, unfiltered reaction to the image of the woman she'd seen with Zach. Miles was too guarded, and he knew her motives too well. Perhaps Jonah wouldn't be as careful.

Intercepting one of the Mesa Falls partners before the meeting Astrid had mentioned proved challenging. Chiara arrived at the Excelsior early, but with multiple parking areas and valet service, the casino resort didn't have a central location where she could monitor everyone who entered the building. For that matter, having her bodyguard with her made it difficult to blend in, so she'd asked Stefan to remain well behind her while she scoped out the scene.

Chiara decided to surveil the floor with the prominent high-roller suite the group had used for a meeting a month ago when she had first started keeping tabs on them. She hurried up the escalator near a courtyard fountain among the high-end shops. Water bubbled and splashed from the mouth of a sea dragon into a marble pool at the base of the fountain, the sound a soothing murmur when her nerves were wound tight. The resort was already busy with tourists window-shopping and taking photos.

As she reached the second-floor gallery, she spotted Gage Striker entering the suite. The huge, tattooed New Zealander was too far ahead for her to flag his attention, but at least she knew she was in the right place. Maybe Jonah and Astrid would come this way soon. As she darted around a pair of older ladies wearing matching red hats, Chiara pulled her phone from her handbag shaped like a rose, wanting the device ready with the right screen to show Jonah the photo of the mystery woman.

A voice from over her right shoulder startled her.

"Looking for someone?"

The deep rasp that could only belong to Miles skittered along her nerve endings.

Her body responded instantly, thrilled at the prospect of this man's nearness. But she battled back those feelings to turn toward him coolly.

"You're not much for traditional greetings, are you?" She eyed his perfectly tailored blue suit, the jacket unbuttoned over a subtly pinstriped gray shirt with the collar undone. Her attention snagged on the hint of skin visible at the base of his neck before she remembered what she was saying. "Most people open with something like *hello*. Or *nice to see you, Chiara*."

A hint of a smile lifted his lips on one side as he stopped just inches from her. With any other man getting this close, Stefan might have come to her side, but her security guard had been at the party in Mesa Falls the night Chiara stayed with Miles. Stefan didn't intervene now.

"Maybe other people can't appreciate the pleasure I find in catching you off guard." Miles lingered on the word *pleasure*.

Or else she did. She couldn't be certain. She was too distracted by the hint of his aftershave hovering between them.

"I'm joining Astrid for lunch while Jonah attends another super-secret Mesa Falls meeting." She glanced at her nails and pretended to inspect her manicure. She'd far rather he think her superficial than affected by his nearness.

Miles studied her. Keeping her focus on her hands, she felt his gaze more than saw it. She wouldn't have a chance to speak to Jonah now. Not without Miles being present, anyway. While she considered her plan B, a group of women in tiaras and feather boas strolled past, with the one in the center wearing a pink sash that said, "Birthday Girl."

"How did it go at the police station?" Miles asked, his fingers alighting on her forearm to draw her farther from the thoroughfare that led to the second-floor shops.

There were two couches in front of the high-roller suite and a low, clear cocktail table between them. Miles guided her to the area between the couches and the door to the suite, affording them a little more privacy.

"I had some other things to take care of this morning, but I'll call after lunch." She'd been so consumed with finding out the identity of the woman in the yearbook photo, she'd forgotten all about reporting the harassment.

Miles frowned. "I can't in good conscience let you put it off. After the meeting, I'll take you myself."

She bristled at his air of command. "I don't need an escort. I'll take care of it."

He pressed his lips together, as if reining in his emotions for a moment before he spoke. "Remember when you told me you had to be a one-woman content creator, marketing manager and finance director?" He clearly recalled how she'd defended her hard work when he'd been dismissive of her job. "Why don't you let someone else give you a hand?"

His thoughtfulness, underscored by how well he'd listened to her, made her relax a little. "It does sound better when you say it like that," she admitted.

"Good. And this way, you can ask me all the questions you want about the meeting." He nodded as if the matter was settled.

"Any chance you'll actually answer them?" She wasn't sure it was wise for them to spend more time alone together, but maybe she could find a way to ask him about the photo of the unidentified woman without putting his guard up.

"I've said all along we should be working together." He took her hand in his, holding it between them while he stroked her palm with his thumb. "Where should I look for you after I finish up here?"

Her breath caught from just that smallest of touches. Her heart pounded harder.

"Spice Pavilion," she answered, seeing Astrid and Jonah heading toward them out of the corner of her eye.

"I'll look forward to it." Miles lifted the back of her hand to his lips and kissed it before releasing her.

Skin tingling pleasantly, she watched him disappear into the high-roller suite and wondered what she'd just gotten herself into. She noticed his brother followed him a moment later, while Astrid and Jonah gave each other a lingering goodbye kiss nearby. The blatant public display of affection seemed all the more romantic considering the couple were new parents.

What would it be like to have that kind of closeness with someone day in and day out?

Not that she would be finding out. Although her recent night with Miles reminded her how rewarding it was to share passion, she owed it to Zach not to let the connection distract her from her goal. She would spend time with Miles because he was still her most promising resource for information. And despite the coincidental timing of the threats against her, she'd had time to realize Miles was too honorable a man to resort to those tactics. She was safe with him.

She just had to find a way to get him talking.

Seven

Restless as hell, Miles prowled the perimeter of the high-roller suite, waiting for the meeting to get underway. Weston and Desmond were deep in conversation on a curved leather sofa in the center of the room, while a server passed through the living area with a tray of top-shelf bottles. Gage stared down into the fire burning in a sleek, modern hearth, a glass of his preferred bourbon already in hand. A massive flat-screen television was mounted over the fireplace, but the display was dark. In the past, the group had used the screens to teleconference in the missing Mesa Falls owners, but today all were present in person. Even Jonah, the new father, and Alec Jacobsen, the game developer who spent most of his time globe-hopping to get inspiration for the complex world-building required for his games. The two of them lounged near the pool table.

On either side of the fireplace, windows overlooked Lake Tahoe, the clear sky making the water look impossibly blue. Miles paused by one of them, waving off the offer of a beverage from the bow-tied server. He'd need his wits sharp for his meeting with Chiara afterward.

Hell, maybe he needed to worry more about having his instincts honed for the meeting with his friends. The possibility of a traitor to their shared cause had kept him up at night ever since Chiara had been threatened. He'd never doubted the men in this room before. But who else even knew about Zach to make a threat like the one Chiara had received?

"Are we ready?" Miles stopped pacing to ask the question, his back to a mahogany bookcase. He wasn't usually the one to spearhead discussions like this, but today the need for answers burned hot. "I know you're all busy. The sooner we figure out a plan, the sooner we can all go home."

Desmond gave a nod to the server, who left the room quickly, closing the door to the multilevel suite behind her. As the owner of Excelsior, Desmond commanded the operations of the resort and served as their host when they met on the property.

Weston cleared his throat. "Can you bring us up to speed on what's happening?"

The fact that his brother was the first to respond to him surprised Miles given the enmity between him and Wes that had started when they'd been pitted against one another at an early age by their parents. The tension had escalated years ago when they'd briefly dated the same woman. But they'd made strides to put that behind them over the last year. Miles suspected Wes had mellowed since finding love with April Stephens, the financial investigator who'd discovered where the profits of Alonzo's book were going.

"Chiara Campagna has been digging around to find out how Zach died. She knew him in school," he told them bluntly, fisting his hands in the pockets of his pants as he tried to gauge the reactions of his friends. "She attended Brookfield before she became an internet sensation, and she met Zach through the school's art program."

There were no murmurs of reaction. The only sound in the room was the clink of ice cubes in a glass as a drink shifted. But then, they'd known the meeting was called to discuss this issue before walking in the door. So Miles continued.

"She wants to know the circumstances of Zach's death, suspecting some kind of cover-up since there was no news released about it." As he explained it, he understood her frustration. And yes, pain.

Just because she'd been a fifteen-year-old with a crush on a friend didn't diminish their connection. He recognized the power and influence those early relationships could hold over someone.

Near the fireplace, Gage swore and finished his drink. His influential father had been the one to insist the story of Zach's accident remain private. The gag order surrounding the trauma had been one more complication in an already thorny situation.

"But why now?" Alec asked, spinning a cue ball like a top under one finger while he slouched against the billiard table. He wore a T-shirt printed with shaded outlines of his most iconic game characters, layered under a custom suit jacket. "Zach's been dead for fourteen years. Doesn't it seem strange that she's taken a renewed interest now?"

"No." Gage stalked over to the tray the server had left on the glass-topped cocktail table and helped himself to another shot of bourbon, tattoos flashing from the cuffs of his shirtsleeves as he poured the drink. "Chiara told Elena that she'd given up searching for answers about Zach until the Alonzo Salazar story broke at Christmas. With Mesa Falls and all of us in the spotlight, Chiara saw an opportunity to press harder for the truth."

Miles mulled over the new information about Chiara, interested in anything he could gather about the woman who dominated his thoughts. Elena Rollins was a lifestyle blogger who'd visited Mesa Falls to chase a story on Alonzo, but she'd ended up falling for Gage and had backed off. The two women had developed a friendship when Chiara had lent the power of her social media platform to bolster Elena's following.

"But that opportunity is going away now that we've given the public a story about where the profits from Alonzo's book went," Alec chimed in again, using his fingers to shoot the eight ball into a side pocket with a backspin. "Media interest will die out, and we'll go back to living in peace. No one needs to find out anything about Zach."

Even now, it was difficult to talk about the weekend that Zachary Eldridge had jumped to his death off a cliff into the Arroyo Seco River. The men in this room had once argued to the point of violence over whether Zach had planned to take his own life or it had truly been an accident. Eventually, they'd agreed to disagree about that, but they'd made a pact to keep their friend's memory away from public speculation. It had been tough enough for them to deal with the possibility that Zach had jumped to his death on purpose. The thought of dredging all that up again was…unbearable.

"Maybe. Maybe not," Miles returned slowly, turning it over in his head, trying to see what they knew from another angle. "But just because the public doesn't know about the mystery benefactor of the book profits doesn't mean we should just forget about him. We know the boy is thirteen years old puts his conception around the time of the accident. The last time we met, we were going to have a detective track the boy and his guardian."

He didn't remind them of the rest of what they needed to know—if there was a chance any of them had fathered the child.

Around the holidays, a woman had worked briefly at the ranch under the alias Nicole Smith and had claimed that Alonzo's book profits were supporting her dead sister's son—a boy born in a hospital close to Dowdon School seven and a half months after Zach's death. But before any of the ranch owners could speak to her directly, Nicole was abruptly fired. When they'd tried to track down the supervisor responsible for dismissing her, they learned the guy had quit the next day and didn't leave a forwarding address.

All of which raised uncomfortable questions about the integrity of the group in this room. Had one of them ordered the woman's dismissal? Had Nicole been too close to the truth—that Alonzo Salazar had been helping to support Nicole's nephew because he knew who'd fathered the boy? They'd learned that the woman's real name was Nicole Cruz, and they'd obtained some basic information about the boy, Matthew. But they were trying to find her to meet with her in person.

"I'm handling that." Weston sat forward on the couch to flick on the huge wall-mounted television screen controlled by a tablet in front of him. "A detective is following a lead to Nicole and Matthew Cruz in Prince Edward Island. He's supposed to land tonight to check out the address."

Wes flicked through a series of photos on his tablet that then appeared on the TV screen, images of Nicole and Matthew—neither of whom they recognized—followed by grainy security system footage from when Nicole had worked at the ranch, as well as some shots of the boy from his former school. The different angles didn't do anything to help Miles recognize the boy.

"With any luck, the detective finds them." Miles turned his attention back to his colleagues. "And brings them to Mesa Falls so we can speak to the guardian at length and request permission to run a DNA test on the boy."

"Right." Wes clicked to another slide labeled "instructions for obtaining DNA."

"In the meantime, I've sent you all the file and collection kits by courier service. Most of you have already submitted yours, but we still need samples from Gage and Jonah. I've got a shipper ready to take them before you leave the meeting today. Alonzo's sons have already provided samples."

The silence in the room was thick. Did Jonah or Gage have reasons for dragging their feet? It had taken Miles two seconds to put a hair in a vial and ship the thing out.

Jonah blew out a sigh as he shoved away from the pool table and wandered over to a piano in the far corner of the room. He plunked out a few chords while he spoke. "That's fine. But none of us is going to be the father. Alonzo would have never stood by idly and paid for the boy's education if any of us were the dad. He would have demanded we own up to our responsibility once we were old enough to assume that duty."

"Maybe he was a mentor to the boy's mother, and not the father," Gage mused aloud, not sounding convinced. "This kid might not have anything to do with us."

"Possibly," Wes agreed. "But the kid was important to Alonzo, and that makes him important to us. Let's rule out the more obvious connection first."

"Agreed." Miles met his brother's hazel eyes, trying to remember the last time they'd been on the same page about anything. "But the more pressing issue today is that Chiara's social media accounts were hacked and she received an anonymous text threatening more attacks if she kept pursuing answers about Zach's death."

Recalling that morning at his house, Miles felt anger return and redouble that someone had threatened her, a woman who'd gotten under his skin so fast he hasn't seen it coming. That it had happened while she was in his home, as his guest, only added to his sense of responsibility. That it could be one of his friends, or someone close to them, chilled him.

"Anyone remember her from when she attended Brookfield?" Gage asked as Wes switched the image on the screen to show a school yearbook photo of Chiara. "When she was known as Kara Marsh?"

Wariness mingled with suspicion as Miles swung around to face Gage. "You knew?"

He'd texted Gage that night to ask him what he knew about Chiara, and he'd never mentioned it.

"Not until two days ago." Gage held both hands up in a sign of his innocence. "Elena told me. She and Chiara have gotten close in the last month. Apparently Chiara mentioned she used to go by a different name and that none of us remembered her even though she attended a school near Dowdon. If she confided in Elena, she obviously wasn't trying to hide it. And Astrid must be aware."

Miles studied Gage's face but couldn't see any hint of falseness there. Of all of them, Gage was the most plainspoken and direct. The least guarded. So it was tough to envision the big, bluff New Zealander keeping secrets.

From across the room, Alec's voice sliced through his thoughts.

"I remember Kara Marsh." Alec's eyes were on the television screen. "She came to Dowdon that Christmas asking questions about Zach."

Of all the friends, Alec had been closest to Zach. After the accident, he had retreated the most. To the point that Miles had sometimes feared the guy would follow in Zach's footsteps. He'd wondered if they'd wake up one morning to find out Alec had stepped off a cliff's edge in the middle of the night. Alonzo Salazar had shared the concern, speaking privately to all of them about signs to look for when people contemplated suicide. Alec came through it, as they all had. They were good now. Solid. But it had been a rough year.

"Did you talk to her?" Miles asked, needing to learn everything he could about Chiara.

He'd called this meeting out of a need to protect Zach's memory. And yet he felt a need to protect Chiara, too. To find out if any of his partners were the source of the leak that led to Chiara's getting hacked. He'd been watching them all carefully, studying their faces, but he hadn't seen any hint of uneasiness in any one of them.

"No." Alec shook his head as he stroked his jaw, looking lost in thought before his gaze came up to fix on Miles. "But you did. She spoke to you, and then she went to Gage. I was hanging out under the bleachers near the football field with—" he hesitated, a small smile flashing before it disappeared again "—with a girl I knew. Anyway, I was there when I saw Kara sneak onto the campus through the back fence."

"You followed her?" Jonah asked, dropping onto the bench in front of the piano.

Alec shrugged, flicking a white cue ball away from him where he still leaned against the pool table. "I did. The girl I was with was in a snit about it, but I wanted to see what Kara was up to. Besides, in those days, I was more than happy to look for diversions wherever I could find them."

They had all been emotionally wrecked during those weeks, not sleeping, barely eating, unable to even talk to each other since being together stirred up painful memories. Miles had thrown himself into work, taking a part-time job in the nearest town to get away from school as much as possible.

"Did Chiara see you?" Miles wished like hell he remembered that day more clearly.

"I don't think so." He spun the ball under one fingertip, seeming more engaged in the activity than the conversation. But that had always been his way. He had frequently disappeared for days in online realms as a kid and had used that skill as a successful game developer. "She looked nervous. Upset. I had the impression she was afraid of getting caught, because she kept glancing over her shoulder."

Miles tried to conjure up a better picture of her from that day when she'd cornered him outside the library. Mostly he remembered that her voice had startled him because it was a girl's, forcing him to look at her more closely since she'd been dressed the same as any of his classmates—jeans, loafers, dark jacket. The clothes must have been borrowed, because they were big on her. Shapeless. Which was probably the point if she wanted to roam freely among them.

Even her hair had been tucked half under a ball cap and half under her coat.

The memory of Chiara's pale face the morning she'd received the threat returned to his brain, reminding him he needed to figure out who would threaten her. Clenching his fist, he pounded it lightly against the window sash before he spoke.

"Who else even knows about Zach?" he asked the group around him, the friends he thought he knew so well. "Let alone would feel threatened if his story came to light?"

For a long moment, the only sounds were the billiard balls Alec knocked against the rails and the sound of ice rattling in Gage's glass. The silence grated Miles's nerves, so he shared his last piece of important news to see if it got his friends talking.

"I'm taking Chiara to the police station after this to let them know about the threats she's receiving, so there's a chance we'll have to answer questions from the authorities about Zach." He knew it went against their longtime promise to protect their friend's memory. But her safety had to come first.

"You would do that?" Alec shook his head and pushed away from the pool table.

Desmond spoke at the same time. "The negative publicity around Mesa Falls is going to have consequences."

From his seat on the leather sofa, Wes shut down the television screen on the wall before he spoke.

"In answer to your question about who else would remember Zach, he was well-known at Dowdon. Teachers and other students all liked him. As for why someone wouldn't want his story to come out..." Wes hesitated, his hazel eyes flicking from one face to the next. "He had a past. And secrets of his own. Maybe we didn't know Zach as well as we thought we did."

That left the suite even quieter than before. Desmond broke the silence with a soft oath before he leaned over and poured himself a drink from the tray in front of the couch.

The meeting ended with a resolution to convene the next day in the hope they got word from their investigator about Matthew and Nicole Cruz by then. As they began filing out of the suite, Alec and Jonah were still arguing about the idea that they didn't know Zach after all. Miles didn't stick around, not sure what he thought about the possibility.

For now, he needed to see Chiara.

Stalking out of the meeting room, he ran into a young woman hovering around the door. Dressed in leggings and high-top sneakers paired with a blazer, she didn't have the look of a typical casino guest. A red curl fell in her face as she flushed.

"Sorry. Is the meeting over?" she asked, pushing the curl away from her lightly freckled face. As she shifted, her blazer opened to reveal a T-shirt with the characters from Alec's video game. "I'm waiting for Alec—" She glanced over Miles's shoulder. "Is he here?"

Miles nodded but didn't open the door for her since his partners were still discussing Zach. "Just finishing up. He should be out in a minute. Do you work with Alec?"

She hesitated for the briefest moment, a scowl darkening her features, before she thrust out her hand. "I'm his assistant, Vivian Fraser."

Miles shook it, surprised they hadn't met before. "Miles Rivera. Nice to meet you, Vivian."

Politely, he moved past her, writing off the awkward encounter as his thoughts turned to Chiara.

He'd promised her a date, yes. And the drive to see her was stronger than ever after a meeting that had shaken his foundations. But more importantly, he had questions for her. Questions that couldn't afford to get sidelined by their attraction, no matter how much he wanted to touch her again.

Chiara sent her bodyguard home for the day when she saw Miles approaching the restaurant. Astrid had departed five minutes before, after seeing Jonah's text to meet him in a private suite he'd taken for the rest of their afternoon together.

The new mother had seemed surprised, flustered and adorably excited to have her husband all to herself for a few hours. Chiara had felt a sharp pang of loneliness once she'd left, recognizing that she'd never felt that way about a man. The lack had never bothered her much. Yet between the incredible night she'd spent with Miles and seeing Astrid's happiness transform her, the universe seemed to be conspiring to make her crave romance.

So when Miles slowed his step near the hostess stand of Spice Pavilion, Chiara bristled with defensiveness before he'd even spoken. It didn't help that he was absurdly handsome, impeccably dressed and only had eyes for her, even though he attracted plenty of feminine attention.

"Hello, Chiara." He spoke the greeting with careful deliberation, no doubt emphasizing his good manners after she'd mentioned his habit of skipping the social niceties. "Did you enjoy your lunch?"

She'd been too preoccupied—and maybe a little nervous—about spending more time with him to eat much of anything, but she didn't share that. She rose from the bench where she'd been waiting, restless and needing to move.

"It's always a treat to see Astrid," she told him instead, her slim-cut skirt hugging her thighs as she moved, her body more keenly aware whenever he was near her. "But what about you? Have you eaten?"

She didn't know what went on behind closed doors during a Mesa Falls owners' meeting, but she couldn't envision some of the country's wealthiest men ordering takeout over a conference table. As they walked through the wide corridor that connected the shops to the casino, Chiara dug in her handbag for a pair of sunglasses and slid them into place, hoping to remain unrecognized. The casino crowd was a bit older than her traditional fan base, but she didn't want to risk getting sidetracked from her goal.

"I'm too keyed up to be hungry." Miles took her hand in his, the warmth of his touch encircling her fingers. "Let's take care of reporting the threats against you, and then we need to talk."

She glanced over at him, but his face revealed nothing of his thoughts.

"We're on the same page then." She kept close to him as he increased his pace, cutting through the crowd of tourists, gamblers and locals who visited the Excelsior for a day of entertainment. "Because I hardly touched my lunch for thinking about how much we needed to speak."

He slowed his step just long enough to slant her a sideways glance. "Good. After we take care of the errand at the police station, we can go to your house or my suite. Whichever you prefer for privacy's sake."

The mention of that kind of privacy made her remember what happened when they'd been alone behind closed doors at his home in Mesa Falls. But she agreed. They needed that kind of security for this conversation.

"You have a suite here?" she asked, her heartbeat picking up speed even though they were already heading toward the parking lot, where she guessed Miles had a car waiting.

She suddenly remembered Astrid's face when Jonah had texted her to meet him in a suite for the afternoon. Her friend had lit up from the inside. Chiara had the feeling she looked the exact same way even though her meeting behind closed doors with Miles had a very different purpose.

"I do." His blue gaze was steady as he stopped in the middle of the corridor to let a small troop of feather-clad dancers in matching costumes and sky-high heels glide past them. "Should we go there afterward?"

A whirlwind of questions circled beneath that deceptively simple one. Would she end up in his bed again? Did he want her there? But first and foremost, she needed to know what had happened at the meeting and if Miles had any ideas about who was threatening her.

So she hoped for the best and gave him the only possible response.

"Yes, please."

Eight

Filing a formal complaint with the proper authorities took more time than Chiara would have guessed, which left her more than a little frustrated and exhausted. She hitched her purse up on her shoulder as she charged through the sliding door of the local police station and into a swirl of late-afternoon snow flurries. The whole process had stretched out as Miles spoke to multiple officers at length, eliciting information on possible precautions to take to protect her.

Each cop they'd spoken to had been courteous and professional but not very encouraging that they would be able to help. With the rise of cybercrime, law enforcement was tapped more and more often for infractions committed online, but most local agencies weren't equipped to provide the necessary investigative work. The FBI handled major cases, but at the local level, the best they could do was point her in the direction of the appropriate federal agency, especially considering the threat had targeted Chiara's livelihood and not her person. Still, the importance of the case was increased by the fact that she was a public figure. She'd worked with the local police to file the complaints with the proper federal agencies, and they'd suggested she keep careful records of any problems in the future.

Bottom line, someone would look into it, but chances were good nothing more would come of it unless the threats against her escalated. And thanks to Miles, she wasn't handling this alone.

Chiara glanced back over her shoulder at him as he rebuttoned his suit jacket on their way out the door.

"Thank you for going with me." Chiara held the handrail as she descended the steps outside the municipal building almost three hours after they'd arrived. Her breath huffed visibly in the chilly mountain air as flurries circled them on a gust of wind. "I know it wasn't as satisfying as we might have hoped, but at least we've laid the groundwork if the hacker follows through on his threats."

"Or *her* threats," Miles added, sliding a hand under her elbow and steering her around a patch of ice as they reached the parking lot. "We haven't ruled out a woman's hand in this."

She pulled her coat tighter around her, glad for Miles's support on the slick pavement. The temperature had dropped while they were inside. Then again, thinking about someone threatening her business empire might have been part of the chill she felt. She'd given up her dream of becoming an artist to build the social media presence that had become a formidable brand. That brand was worth all the more to her considering the sacrifices she'd made for it along the way.

"Did you speculate about who might be behind the threats in your meeting today?" she asked, unwilling to delay her questions any longer as they reached his big black Land Rover with snow dusting the hood. "You said you'd share with me what you discussed. And I know Zach's legacy is a concern for you and your friends."

Miles opened the passenger door for her, but before he could reply, a woman's voice called from the next row over in the parking lot.

"Chiara Campagna?"

Distracted, Chiara looked up before thinking the better of it. A young woman dressed in black leggings and a bright pink puffer jacket rushed toward them, her phone lifted as if she was taking a video or a picture.

Miles urged Chiara into the SUV with a nudge, his body blocking anyone from reaching her.

"We should have kept your bodyguard with us," he muttered under his breath as other people on the street outside the municipal building turned toward them.

"Can I get a picture with you?" the woman asked her, already stepping into Miles's personal space and thrusting her phone toward him as she levered between the vehicle and the open door. "I'm such a huge fan."

Chiara put a hand on Miles's arm to let him know it was okay, and he took the phone from the stranger. Chiara knew it might be wiser to leave now before the crowd around them grew, but she'd never been good at disappointing fans. She owed them too much. Yet, in her peripheral vision, she could see a few other people heading toward the vehicle. Impromptu interactions like this could be fun, but they could quickly turn un-comfortable and borderline dangerous.

"Sure," Chiara replied, hoping for the best as she tilted her head toward the other woman's, posing with her and looking into the lens of the camera phone. "But I can only do one," she added, as much for Miles's ben-efit as the fan's.

Miles took the shot and lowered the phone, appear-ing to understand her meaning as he met her gaze with those steady blue eyes of his. Without ever looking away from her, he passed the woman in the puffer jacket her phone.

"Ms. Campagna is late for a meeting," he explained, inserting himself between Chiara and the fan before shifting his focus to the other woman. "She appreci-ates your support, but I need to deliver her to her next appointment now."

He backed the other woman away, closing and lock-ing the SUV's passenger door just in time, as two teen-aged boys clambered over to bang on the vehicle's hood and shout her name, their phones raised.

The noise made her tense, but Chiara slid her sun-glasses onto her nose and kept her head down. She dug in her bag for her own phone, hoping she wouldn't need to call Stefan for assistance. She'd been in situations with crowds that had turned aggressive before, and the experiences had terrified her. She knew all too well how fast things could escalate.

But a moment later, the clamor outside the SUV eased enough for Miles to open the driver's door and slide into his own seat. She peered through the wind-shield then, spotting a uniformed police officer disband-ing the gathering onlookers who had quickly multiplied in number. The teenaged boys were legging it down the street. The woman in the puffer jacket was showing her phone to a group of other ladies, gesturing excitedly with her other hand. People had gathered to see what was happening, stepping out of businesses in a strip mall across the parking lot.

"I'm sorry about that." Miles turned on the engine and backed out of the parking space. He gave a wave to the officer through the windshield. "Does that happen often?"

"Not lately," she admitted, shaken at the close call. "I've gotten better in the last year about wearing hats and sunglasses, keeping security near me, and having my outings really scripted so that I'm never in public for long."

She'd been so distracted ever since spending the night with Miles that she was forgetting to take precautions. She pressed farther back in her seat, ready to retreat from the world.

"That doesn't sound like a fun way to live." He steered the vehicle out of the parking lot and started driving away from town. "And now that news of your presence here has no doubt been plastered all over the web, I'd like to take you to the villa you rented instead of the resort. It will be quieter there."

"That's fine." She appreciated the suggestion as the snow began falling faster. "I'll message Stefan—he's my head of security—and ask him to bring in some more help for the rest of my stay."

"Good." Miles nodded his approval of the plan, his square jaw flexing. "Until we find out who's been threatening you, it pays to take extra safety measures."

She drew a deep breath, needing to find a way to

reroute this conversation. To return to her goal for this time with Miles, which was to learn more about what happened to Zach. But she hadn't quite recovered from the near miss with fans who could turn from warm-hearted supporters to angry detractors with little to no warning. It only took a few people in a crowd to change the mood or to start shoving.

"Or…" Miles seemed to muse aloud as he drove, the quiet in the car all the more pronounced as they left the more populated part of the lakeshore behind them.

When he didn't seem inclined to finish his thought, Chiara turned to look at him again, but she couldn't read his expression, which veered between a frown and thoughtful contemplation.

"Or what?" she prodded him, curious what was on his mind.

"I was just going to say that if you decide at any time you would prefer more seclusion, my ranch in the Sierra Nevada foothills is open to you." He glanced her way as he said it.

"Rivera Ranch?" She knew it was his family seat, the property he invested the majority of his time in running.

The invitation surprised her. First of all, because Miles seemed like an intensely private man, the most reserved of the Mesa Falls owners. He didn't strike her as the kind of person to open his home to many people. Secondly, she wouldn't have guessed that she would rank on the short list of people he would welcome.

"Yes." His thumbs drummed softly against the steering wheel. "It's remote. The property is gated and secure. You'd be safe there."

"Alone?" The word slipped out before she could catch it.

"Only if you chose to be. I'm happy to escort you. At least until you got settled in."

The offer was thoughtful, if completely unexpected. Still, it bore consideration if the threats against her kept escalating.

"I hope it doesn't come to that," she told him truthfully. "But thank you."

"Just remember you have options." He turned on the long private drive that led to her villa on the lake. "You're not in this alone."

She was tempted to argue that point. To tell him she felt very much alone in her quest to learn more about Zach since Miles refused to talk about their mutual friend. But he was here with her now. And he'd said they needed to help each other. Maybe he was ready to break his long silence at last.

Yet somehow that seemed less important than the prospect of spending time alone with this man who tempted her far too much.

Miles recognized the couple waiting in front of Chiara's villa as he parked the vehicle. The tall, athletic-looking brunette was Chiara's assistant, and the burly dude dressed all in black had been Chiara's bodyguard the night of the party at Mesa Falls Ranch. The two held hands, wearing matching tense expressions. They broke apart when Miles halted the vehicle but still approached the passenger door as a team.

"They must have seen photos from the police department parking lot online." Chiara sighed in frustration as she unbuckled her seat belt and clutched her handbag. "I'll just need a minute to bring them up to speed."

"Of course." Miles nodded at the muscle-bound man

who opened Chiara's door for her. "Take your time. I'll check out your lake view to give you some privacy."

"That's not necessary," she protested, allowing her bodyguard to help her down from the vehicle.

Opening his own door, Miles discovered the tall assistant was waiting on his side of the Land Rover. Meeting her brown eyes, he remembered her name from the party at Mesa Falls.

"Hi, Jules," he greeted the woman, who had to be six feet tall even in her flat-soled running shoes. She wore a sweater and track pants, seemingly unconcerned with the cold. "Nice to see you again."

"You, too." She gave him a quick smile, but it was plain she had other things on her mind. A furrow between her brows deepened before she lowered her voice to speak to him quietly. "I wanted to warn you that while you were out with Chiara today, you attracted the interest of some of her fans."

"Should I be concerned?" He stepped down to the pavement beside her while, near the rear of the SUV, Chiara related the story of what happened at the police department to her security guard.

"Not necessarily." Jules hugged her arms around her waist, breathing a white cloud into the cold air. "But since Chiara's fan base can be vocal and occasionally unpredictable, you should probably alert your PR team to keep an eye on the situation."

"I'm a rancher," he clarified, amused. He stuffed his hands in his pockets to ward off the chill of the day. "I don't have a PR team."

"Mesa Falls has a dedicated staffer," she reminded him, switching on the tablet she was holding. A gust of wind caught her long ponytail and blew it all around her. "I remember because I dealt with her directly about the party at your place. Would you like me to contact her about this instead?"

Puzzled, Miles watched the woman swipe through several screens before pausing on an avatar of the Montana ranch.

"Just what do you think could happen?" he asked her, curious about the potential risks of dating someone famous.

If, in fact, what they were doing together could even be called dating. His gaze slanted over to Chiara, who was heading toward the front door of the villa, flashes of her long legs visible from the opening of her coat. He realized he wanted more with her. At very least, he wanted a repeat of their incredible night together. Preferably, he wanted many repeats of that night.

Beside him, Chiara's assistant huffed out a sigh that pulled him back to their conversation.

"Anything could happen," Jules told him flatly as she frowned. "You could become a target for harassment or worse. Your home address could be made public, and you could find yourself or your family surrounded in your own home. Your business could be boycotted if Chiara's fans decide they don't like you. People have no idea how brutal it can be in the public eye."

She sounded upset. Miles wondered what kinds of things Chiara had weathered in the past because of her fame.

He felt his eyebrows rise even as the idea worried him more for Chiara's sake than his own. "I appreciate the warning. If you don't mind sending a message to the Mesa Falls publicity person, I'd appreciate it."

"Of course." She nodded, tapping out some notes

on her tablet even as snowflakes fell and melted on the screen. "And you should consider security for yourself once you leave the villa. At least for the next week or so until we know how the story plays out."

"I'll consider it," he assured her, sensing it would be better to placate her for now, or until he had a better handle on the situation for himself. He didn't want to rile Chiara's assistant when the woman already seemed upset. "Did today's incident cause problems for you?"

Jules shoved her tablet under her arm again. "For me personally? Not yet. But having her photographed in front of a police station is already causing speculation that we'll have to figure out how to address."

He nodded, beginning to understand how small missteps like today could have a big impact on Chiara's carefully planned public image. "I should have taken steps to ensure she wasn't recognized."

A wry smile curved the woman's lips. "Bingo."

"I can't fix what already happened today, but I can promise I'll take better care of her in the future," he assured the woman, gesturing her toward the house.

Jules pivoted on the heel of her tennis shoe and walked with him toward the stone steps at the side entrance. "If she keeps you around, I would appreciate that."

Miles chucked softly as he opened the front door for her. "Do you think my days are numbered with her after this?"

"No. Well, not because of today. But Chiara is notoriously choosy when it comes to the men in her life." She lowered her voice as they crossed the threshold of the huge lakefront house.

From the foyer, Miles could see Chiara standing with

her bodyguard in the kitchen. Behind her, the setting sun glittered on the lake outside the floor-to-ceiling windows.

"That's a good thing." Miles was damned choosy himself. Until Chiara, he hadn't let any woman close to him for more than a night ever since he'd accidentally ended up dating the same woman as his brother. "I admire a woman with discriminating taste."

Jules laughed. "Then maybe you two have more in common than I would have guessed. I've worked with Chiara for three years, and you're the first man she's ever changed her schedule for."

He wanted to ask her what she meant by that, but as soon as the words were out, Chiara entered the foyer alone. Something about the way she carried herself told him she was upset. Or maybe it was the expression on her face, the worry in her eyes. And damned if he hadn't spent enough time studying her to recognize the subtle shift of her moods.

"Jules." Chiara still wore her long coat, her arms wrapped around herself as if she was chilled. "Stefan went out the back to the guesthouse, but he said he'll meet you out front if you still want to head into town."

Jules looked back and forth between them, but then her attention locked in on Chiara, perhaps seeing the same stress that Miles had noted. Jules stroked her friend's hair where it rested on her shoulder. "I don't want to go anywhere if you need me."

Miles wondered if he'd missed something. If the photos online were a bigger deal than he was understanding. Or was it his presence causing the added stress?

"I can take off if this is a bad time," he offered,

unwilling to stay if they needed to take care of other things. He'd come a long way from the guy who'd written off Chiara's job as glorified partying, but no doubt he still didn't understand the nuances of her work, let alone the ramifications of the day's unexpected encounter with her fans.

Chiara's green eyes lifted to his. "No. I'd like to talk." Then she turned to her assistant and squeezed Jules's hand. "I'm fine. But thank you. I want you to have fun tonight. You work too hard."

"It never feels like work for me when we're hanging out," the other woman insisted before she gave a nod. "But if you're sure you don't mind—"

"I insist." Chiara walked toward the oversize door with her. "Stefan already has two guards watching the house tonight, and Miles will be here with me for a few more hours."

He couldn't help but hope that boded well for their evening together. Although maybe Chiara was just trying to soothe her friend's anxiety about leaving her.

In another moment, Jules departed, and the house was vacant except for the two of them. The sound of the door shutting echoed from the cathedral ceiling in the foyer. Chiara took a moment to check that the alarm reset before she turned toward him again.

"May I take your coat?" he asked, moving closer to her.

Wanting to touch her, yes. But wanting to comfort her, too.

She looked down at what she was wearing and shook her head, clearly having forgotten that she'd left her coat on.

"Oh. Thank you." She sucked in a breath as he

stepped behind her and rested his hands on her shoulders for a moment. "I think I got a chill while we were out."

"Or maybe it's the combination of dealing with the threats, the police and the work crisis that seems to have snowballed from having our photo taken today." He took hold of the soft wool and cashmere cloak and helped her slide it from her arms.

The movement shifted her dark waves of hair and stirred her citrusy scent. He breathed it in, everything about her affecting him. As much as he wanted to turn her toward him and kiss her, he realized he wanted to ease her worries even more. So after hanging the coat on a wooden peg just inside the mudroom off the foyer, he returned to her side, resting his hand lightly on her spine to steer her toward the living room.

"You're probably right. The police station visit would have been daunting enough without the drama afterward." She shivered and hugged her arms tighter around herself.

Miles led her to the sofa, moving aside a throw pillow to give her the comfortable corner seat. Then he pulled a plush blanket off the sofa back and draped it around her before finding the fireplace remote and switching on the flames. The blinds in the front room were already drawn, but he pulled the heavy curtains over them, too.

Then he took a seat on the wide ottoman, shoving aside a tray full of design books and coasters to make more room.

"May I take these off for you?" He gestured toward the high leather boots she was still wearing.

Her lips lifted on one side. "Really?" A sparkle re-

turned to her green eyes, a flare of interest or anticipation. At least, he hoped that's what it was. "If you
don't mind."

"I want to make you comfortable. And I don't want
you to regret sending away your friends tonight." He
lowered the zipper on the first boot, reminding himself he was only doing this to help her relax. Not to seduce her.

Although skimming his hand lightly over the back
of her calf as he removed the boot was doing a hell of
a job of seducing *him*.

"I won't." Her gaze locked on his hands where he
touched her. "I've been anxious to talk to you all day."

The reminder that this wasn't a real date came just
in time as Miles eased off the second boot. Because
he'd been tempted to stroke back up her leg to her knee.

And linger there.

Even now, the hem of her skirt just above her knee
was calling to him. But first, they needed to address
the topic he'd avoided for fourteen years.

Damn it.

With an effort, he set aside her footwear and released
her leg. Then he took the seat next to her on the couch.

"Okay." He braced himself, remembering that his
friends hadn't been any help today. It was time to break
the silence. "Let's talk."

"I have a question I've been wanting to ask you."
Reaching beneath the blanket, Chiara shifted to gain
access to a pocket on the front of her houndstooth skirt.
She withdrew a piece of paper and smoothed it out to
show him a grainy photo. "Do you know who this is,
Miles?"

He glanced down at the photo, and passion faded

as suspicion iced everything he'd been feeling. Apparently Chiara wasn't stopping her quest for answers about Zach. Because the face staring back at Miles from the image was someone he and Zach had both known well. And he couldn't begin to guess why Chiara wanted to know about her.

Nine

Chiara didn't miss the flare of recognition in Miles's eyes as he looked at the yearbook photo.

"You're pointing at this woman in the background?" he asked, stabbing the paper with his index finger.

"The one with the side part and the navy blue skirt," she clarified. "She doesn't look like a student."

"She wasn't. That's Miss Allen, one of the student teachers at Dowdon." He met her gaze as he smiled. "Lana Allen. We were all a little in love with her."

"A teacher?" Shock rippled through her, followed by cold, hard dread. "Are you sure? She's not in the year-book anywhere else. How old do you think she was?"

Miles must have read some of her dismay, because his expression went wary. He tensed beside her on the sofa.

"There was major backlash about her being at our

school since she was just nineteen herself. She didn't stay the full year at Dowdon after one of the administrators complained she was a distraction. She worked with Alonzo Salazar briefly during the fall semester and then she was gone—" His jaw flexed as if mulling over how much to say. "Before Christmas break. Why?"

Her stomach knotted at the implications of what this new revelation meant. She hoped it wasn't a mistake to confide in him. But if one of them didn't take the leap and start sharing information, they'd never figure out who was harassing her or what it had to do with Zach.

Taking a deep breath, she sat up straighter and told him. "I saw Zach kissing her. As in a real, no-holds-barred, passionate kiss."

Miles shook his head then gripped his temples between his thumb and forefinger, squeezing. "Impossible. It must have been someone else."

"No." She was certain. How many times had she relived that moment in her mind over the years? "Miles, I had the biggest crush on him. I followed him around like the lovesick teenager I was, just hoping for the chance to talk to him alone. I never would have mistaken him for someone else."

"Then you're confused about her," he insisted. "It was a long time ago, Chiara, how can you be sure—"

"I picked her face out of the background crowd in this photo just like that." She snapped her fingers. "The memory has been burned into my brain for fourteen years, because it broke my heart to see that Zach already had a girlfriend."

"She couldn't have been his girlfriend—"

"His romantic interest, then," she amended, staring into the flames flickering in the fireplace as she tucked her feet beneath her and pulled the plush throw blanket tighter around her legs. "Or hers, I guess, since she was a legal adult by then and he was still technically a kid." The woman had no business touching a student, damn it. The idea made her ill.

"Zach was older than us—seventeen when he died. But obviously that doesn't excuse her. If anything, the relationship gives a probable cause for Zach's unhappiness before he died." His scowl deepened.

A fresh wave of regret wrenched her insides at the thought of Zach hurting that much. "I saw them together at the art show where Zach and I were both exhibiting work. I couldn't find him anywhere, so I finally went outside looking for them, and they were hidden in one of the gardens, arms wound around each other—"

She broke off, the memory still stinging. Not because of the romantic heartbreak—she'd gotten over that in time. But she'd left the art show after that, turning her back on Zach when he'd called after her. Little did she know she'd never see him again. Remembering that part still filled her with guilt.

Miles studied her face, seeming content to wait for her to finish, even as he saw too much. When she didn't speak, he reached between them to thread his fingers through hers. The warmth of his touch—the kindness of it—stole her breath. He'd been an anchor for her on a hard day, and she didn't have a chance of refusing the steadiness he offered.

"Okay. Assuming you're correct, why would Zach tell us he was gay if he wasn't?"

"He might have been confused. Fourteen years ago there wasn't as much discussion about sexuality, so he could have misidentified himself." Although he'd always seemed so sure of himself in other ways... She remembered how mature Zach had been. "Or maybe he thought he was protecting her—misdirecting people so no one suspected their relationship."

Miles seemed to consider this for a moment.

"But he told us over the summer," Miles argued. "We had a group video call before the semester even started, and he told us then."

"Zach and I were both at school all summer," she reminded him. "For our art program. Lana Allen could have been around Dowdon during the summer months, too."

Miles swore softly under his breath, and she wondered if that meant he was conceding her point. He dragged a hand over his face and exhaled as he turned to look her in the eye. His thigh grazed her knee where her legs were folded beneath her, the contact sizzling its way up her hip.

"This is huge." He squeezed her palm, his thumb rubbing lightly over the back of her hand. "It changes everything."

"How so?" She went still, hoping he was finally going to trust her enough to share the truth about Zach's death.

He looked uneasy. Then, taking a deep breath, he said, "For starters, I think Zach might have a son."

The news was so unexpected it took her a moment to absorb what he was saying.

"By this woman?" she wondered aloud, doing the math in her head. Zach had been seventeen at the time, and he'd died fourteen years ago. His son would be at least thirteen by now. "Why? Have you seen her?"

"No." Releasing her hand, Miles rose to his feet as

if seized by a new restless energy. He massaged the back of his neck while he paced the great room. When he reached the windows overlooking the mountains, he pivoted hard on the rug and stalked toward her again. "A woman came to Mesa Falls a few months ago claiming to have custody of her sister's child—a thirteen-year-old boy of unknown paternity. The mother died suddenly of an aneurysm and had never told anyone who the father was."

Chiara hugged herself as she focused on his words. "And that's the child you think could be Zach's son?"

He nodded. "The woman claimed the kid's upbringing was being funded by profits from *Hollywood Newlyweds*. At the time, we wondered if the child could have been one of ours, since Alonzo had helped us all through the aftermath of Zach's death. He was a mentor for all of us."

She covered her lips to smother a gasp of surprise as new pieces fell into place. The news that a private school English teacher had been the pseudonymous author behind *Hollywood Newlyweds* had been splashed everywhere over Christmas, sending tabloid journalists scrambling to piece together why the author had never taken credit for the book before his death. It made sense to her that he would keep it a secret if he was using the profits to help Zach's son.

Aloud, she mused, "You think Salazar knew about Zach's son and was trying to funnel some funds to the mother to help raise the baby?"

"Since Lana Allen was his student teacher, maybe he discovered the affair at some point. Although if he knew and didn't report her to the authorities—*hell*. Maybe he felt guilty for not intervening sooner." Miles stopped at the other end of the great room, where Chiara had left her sketchbook. He traced a finger over the open page. "It's all speculation, but you can see where I'm going with this."

Her mind was spinning with the repercussions of the news, and she wasn't sure what it meant for the friends Zach had left behind. For her. For Miles. And all the other owners of Mesa Falls Ranch. Was this the secret her hacker was trying to steer her away from finding? And if so, why?

Needing a break from the revelations coming too fast to process, she slid off her throw blanket and rose to join Miles near the table that held her sketchbook. For the moment, it felt easier to think about something else than to wade through what she'd just learned.

So instead, she wondered what he thought of her drawings. She couldn't seem to give up her love of art even though she'd ended up working in a field that didn't call for many of the skills she wished she was using.

Yet another question about Zach's son bubbled to the surface, and she found herself asking, "Where is the boy now? And the woman who is guarding him—his aunt? She might have the answers we need."

Miles spoke absently as he continued to peruse the sketches. "We have a private detective following a lead on them now. We discussed this at yesterday's meeting, but I don't know if the lead panned out yet." He pulled his attention away from her drawings to meet her gaze. "These are yours?"

She suspected he needed a break from the thoughts about Zach as much as she did.

"Yes." Her gaze followed the familiar lines of pencil

drawings from long ago. She'd been carrying around the sketchbook ever since her days at Brookfield, hoping that seeing the drawings now and then would keep her focused on her quest to find out what happened to Zach. Seeing them now helped her to say to Miles, "You're welcome to look at them, but I wish you'd tell me about the day Zach died. I know you were with him."

She'd learned long ago that the Mesa Falls Ranch owners had all been on a horseback riding trip that weekend. She knew seven riders had left Dowdon but only six had returned.

The firelight cast flickering shadows on Miles's face as he flipped a page in the sketchbook, revealing a cartoonish horse in muted charcoals. He must have recognized the image, because his expression changed when he saw it.

"This horse looks like the one in Alec's video game," he noted, the comment so off-topic from what she'd asked that she could only think Miles wasn't ready to talk about it.

Frustrated, she shook her head but let him lead her back to the discussion of the drawings.

"No." She pointed at the image over his shoulder, the warmth of his body making her wish she could lean into him. "That's a favorite image of Zach's. The horse motif was really prevalent in his work over the four months before he died." She thought she'd done a faithful job of copying the sort of figure Zach had sketched so often. He'd inspired her in so many ways. "Why? What does it have to do with a video game?"

Miles's brow furrowed. "Alec Jacobsen—one of my partners—is a game developer. The series he created using this horse as a character is his most popular."

How had she missed that? She made a mental note to look for the game.

"Then Zach's work must have inspired him," she said firmly, knowing that her friend had worked similar images into most of his dreamlike paintings.

"No doubt. Those two were close friends. I think Alec credited Zach somewhere on his debut game." He flipped another page in the book while a grandfather clock in the foyer struck the hour with resonant chimes. "As for how Zach died, it's still disputed among us."

Her nerve endings tingled to hear the words. To realize she was close to finally learning the truth after all this time. She held her breath. Waiting. Hoping he would confide in her.

Miles never took his gaze from the sketchbook as he spoke again. Quietly.

"He jumped off one of the cliffs into the Arroyo Seco River on a day after heavy rainstorms that raised the water level significantly." He dragged in a slow breath for a moment before he continued. "But we were never sure if he jumped for fun, because he was a daredevil who lived on the edge, or if he made that leap with the intent to end his life."

Chiara closed her eyes, picturing the scene. Zach has been a boy of boundless energy. Big dreams. Big emotions. She could see him doing something so reckless, and she hurt all over again to imagine him throwing everything away in one poor decision.

"He drowned?" Her words were so soft, they felt like they'd been spoken by someone else.

"He never surfaced. They found the body later downstream." Miles paused a moment, setting down the sketchbook and dragging in a breath. "Since there were no suspicious circumstances, they didn't do an autopsy. His death certificate lists drowning as the cause of death."

"How could it not be suspicious?" she asked, her heart rate kicking up. She felt incensed that no one had investigated further. "Even now, you don't know what happened for sure."

"The accident was kept quiet since suicide was a possibility. And Zach had no family."

"Meaning there was no one to fight for justice for him," she remarked bitterly, knowing from personal experience how difficult it had been to find out anything. "So the school ensured no one found out that a fatal incident occurred involving Dowdon students."

The bleakness in his eyes was impossible to miss. "That's right." His nod was stiff. Unhappy. "On the flip side, there was concern about the rest of us. We were all shell-shocked."

Something in his voice, the smallest hesitation from a man normally so confident, forced her to step back. To really listen to what he was saying and remember that this wasn't just about Zach. What happened on that trip had left its mark on Miles and all of his friends.

"I'm sorry," she offered quietly, threading her fingers through his the way he had earlier. "It must have been awful for you."

"We all went in the water to look for him," he continued, his blue gaze fixed on a moment in the past she couldn't see. "Wes could have died—he jumped right in after him. The rest of us climbed down to the rocks below to see if we could find him."

For a long moment, they didn't speak. She stepped

closer, tipping her head to his shoulder in wordless comfort.

"Time gets fuzzy after that. I don't know how we decided to quit looking, but it took a long time. We were all frozen—inside and out. Eventually, we rode back to get help, but by then we knew no one was going to find him. At least—" his chin dropped to rest on the top of her head "—not alive."

Her chest ached at the thought of sixteen-year-old Miles searching a dangerously churning river for his friend and not finding him. She couldn't imagine how harrowing the aftermath had been. She'd grappled with Zach's loss on her own, not knowing the circumstances of his death. But for Miles to witness his friend's last moments like that, feeling guilt about it no matter how misplaced, had to be an unbearable burden. A lifelong sorrow.

Helpless to know what to say, she stepped into him, wrapping her arms around his waist. She tucked her forehead against his chest, feeling the rhythmic beat of his heart against her ear. She breathed in the scent of him—clean laundry and a hint of spice from his aftershave. Her hands traced the contours of his strong arms, the hard plane of his chest and ridged abs.

At his quick intake of breath, she glanced up in time to see his eyes darken. Her heart rate sped faster.

Miles cupped her chin, bringing her mouth closer to his.

"I never talk about this because it hurts too damned much." His words sounded torn out of him.

"Thank you for trusting me enough to tell me." She'd waited half her life to hear what had happened to her friend. "At least he wasn't alone."

"No. He wasn't." Miles stroked his fingers through her hair, sifting through the strands to cup the back of her head and draw her closer still. "Any one of us would have died to save him. That's how close we were."

She'd never had friendships like that when she was a teen. Only later, once she met Astrid and then Jules, did she feel like she had people in her life who would have her back no matter what. Could she trust what Miles said about his love for Zach? She still wondered at his motives for keeping the details of Zach's death private. But as she drew a breath to ask about that, Miles gently pressed his finger against her mouth.

"I promise we can talk about this more," he told her, dragging the digit along her lower lip. "But first, I need a minute." He wrapped his other arm around her waist, his palm settling into the small of her back to seal their bodies together. "Or maybe I just need you."

Miles tipped his forehead to Chiara's, letting the sensation of having her in his arms override the dark churn of emotions that came from talking about the most traumatic day of his life. He felt on edge. Guilt-ridden. Defensive as hell.

He should have been at Zach's side when he jumped. He knew the guy was on edge that weekend. They'd stayed up half the night talking, and he'd known that something was off. Of course, they'd *all* known something was off since Zach had initiated the unsanctioned horseback riding trip precisely because he was pissed off and wanted to get away from school.

But he'd hinted at something bigger than the usual problems while they'd talked and drank late into the night. Miles had never been able to remember the conversation clearly, since they'd been drinking. The night only came back to him in jumbled bits that left him feeling even guiltier that he hadn't realized Zach was battling big demons.

Miles had still been hungover the morning of the cliff-jumping accident. He hadn't wanted to go in the first place because of that, and he sure as hell hadn't been as clearheaded as he should have been while they'd trekked up the trail. He'd lagged behind the whole way, and by the time he realized that Zach had jumped despite the dangerous conditions, Miles's brother was already throwing himself off the precipice to find him.

His brain stuttered on that image—the very real fear his brother wouldn't surface, either. And it stuck there.

Until Chiara shifted in his arms, her hips swaying against him in a way that recalibrated everything. His thoughts. His mood. His body. All of his focus narrowed to her. This sexy siren of a woman who fascinated him on every level.

Possessiveness surged through him along with hunger. Need.

A need for her. A need to forget.

He edged back to see her, taking in the spill of dark hair and mossy-green eyes full of empathy and fire, too. When her gaze dipped to his mouth, it was all he could do not to taste her. Lose himself in her.

But damn it, he needed her to acknowledge that she wanted this, too.

"I could kiss you all night long." He stroked along her jaw, fingers straying to the delicate underside of her chin where her skin was impossibly soft.

He trailed a touch down the long column of her throat and felt the gratifying thrum of her pulse racing there.

He circled the spot with his thumb and then traced it with his tongue.

"Then why don't you?" she asked, her breathless words sounding dry and choked.

"I can't even talk you into the date you owe me." He angled her head so he could read her expression better in the light of the fire. Her silky hair brushed the back of his hand. "It seems presumptuous of me to seduce you."

"Not really." She tilted her face so that her cheek rubbed against the inside of his wrist, her eyelids falling to half-mast as she did it, as if just that innocent touch brought her pleasure.

Hell, it brought him pleasure, too. But then his brain caught up to her words.

"It wouldn't be presumptuous?" he asked, wanting her to take ownership of this attraction flaring so hot between them he could feel the flames licking up his legs.

"No." Her breath tickled against his forearm before she kissed him there then nipped his skin lightly between her teeth. "Not when being with you is all I think about every night."

The admission slayed him, torching his reservations, because *damn*. He thought about her that much, too. More.

"Good." He arched her neck back even farther, ready to claim her mouth. "That's…good."

His lips covered hers, and she was even softer than he remembered, sweetly yielding. Her arms slid around him, her body melting into his, breasts molding to his chest. He could feel the tight points of her nipples right through her blouse and the thin fabric of her bra. It felt like forever since he'd seen her. Held her. Stripped off her clothes and buried himself inside her.

He couldn't wait to do all those things, but he wouldn't do them here in the middle of the living room. With someone tracking her activities, he wanted as many locked doors between them and the rest of the world as possible. He needed her safe. Naked and sighing his name as he pleasured her, yes.

But above all, safe.

Breaking the kiss, he spoke into her ear. "Take me to your bedroom. Our night is about to get a whole lot better."

Ten

Chiara didn't hesitate.

She wanted Miles with a fierceness she didn't begin to understand, but ever since their one incredible night together, she'd been longing for a repeat. Maybe a part of her hoped that she'd embellished it in her mind, and that the sizzling passion had been a result of other factors at work that night. That it was a result of her nervousness at being caught in his office. Or her fascination with meeting one of Zach's closest friends.

But based on the way she was already trembling for want of Miles, she knew her memory of their night together was as amazing as she remembered. Wordlessly, she pulled him by the hand through the sprawling villa. At the top of the split staircase, she veered to the right, where the master suite dominated the back of the house.

She drew him into the spacious room, where he paused to close the door and lock it, a gesture that felt symbolic more than anything, since they were the only ones home. The soft *snick* of the lock sent a shiver through her as she flipped on the light switch and dimmed the overhead fixture. A gas fire burned in the stone hearth in the wall opposite the bed, and even though the flames lit the room, she liked to have the overhead light on to see Miles better. She watched him wander deeper into the room to the doors overlooking the lake. He shrugged off his blue suit jacket and laid it over the back of a leather wingback by the French doors. Picking up the control for the blinds, he closed them all and turned to look at her.

With his fitted shirt skimming his shoulders, it was easy to appreciate his very male physique. Her gaze dropped lower, sidetracked by the sight of still *more* maleness. All for her.

She wanted him, but it felt good to know he wanted her every bit as much. She dragged in breath like she'd just run a race. Heat crawled up her spine while desire pooled in her belly.

After a moment, Miles beckoned to her. "You're too far away for us to have as much fun as I was hoping."

The rasp of his voice smoked through her. Anticipation spiked, making her aware of her heartbeat pulsing in unexpected erogenous zones. But she didn't move closer. She lifted her gaze, though, meeting his blue eyes over the king-size bed.

"Give me a moment to take it all in. The first time we were together, I didn't get to appreciate all the details." In her dreams, she'd feverishly recreated every second with him, but there were too many gaps in her memories. How his hair felt in her fingers, for example. Or the texture of his very capable hands. "Tonight, I'm savoring everything."

As soon as she said it, she realized it made her sound like she was falling for him. She wanted to recant the words. To say what she meant another way. But if Miles noticed, he didn't comment. Instead he turned his attention to unbuttoning his shirt.

"I like the way you think." His lips curved in a half smile. "But if I'm going to show you all my *details* to savor, I hope you plan to do the same."

She knew she should just be grateful for the out— he hadn't taken her words to mean anything serious. And she hadn't meant them that way. But now that the idea was out there in the ether, she had to acknowledge that it rattled her. Worried her. She couldn't fall for Miles.

Could she?

A swish of material jolted her attention back to Miles's shirt falling to the floor. His chest and abs were burnished gold by the firelight, the ripples of muscle highlighted by the shadowed ridges in between them. She wanted to focus on him. On them.

"Chiara." He said her name as he charged toward her. "What's wrong?"

His hands slid around her waist. Bracketed her hips. The warmth of his body rekindled her heat despite her spiraling thoughts.

"Is it crazy for us to indulge this?" She steadied herself by gripping his upper arms, and he felt so good. Solid. Warm.

Like he was hers.

For tonight, at least.

"Why would it be?" He frowned as he planted his feet wider to bring himself closer to her eye level. "What could possibly be wrong with finding pleasure together after the day you've had? Your business has been threatened, but the cops won't help. I'm scared as hell that you could be vulnerable, and yet you don't want to let me get too close to you or take care of you."

The urge to lean into him, to let him do just that, was almost overwhelming. But she had to be honest, even if it doused the flame for him. "Trust comes hard for me."

Her parents hadn't bothered to tell her when they lost their fortune. Zach had kept secrets from her. Miles kept secrets, too. Although he *had* confided more to her tonight.

"Which is why I haven't pushed you to stay with me so I can protect you. But you told me yourself that you thought about being with me every night." His hands flexed against her where he held her hips, a subtle pressure that stirred sweet sensations. "So maybe you could at least trust me to make you feel good."

"I do." She swayed closer, telling herself she could have one more night with him without losing her heart. "I have absolute faith in that."

He gripped the silk of her blouse at her waist and slowly gathered the fabric, untucking the shirttail from her skirt.

"I'm glad. Remember when you told me you chose work over fun for a long time?" he asked, leaning closer to speak into her ear. And to nip her ear with his teeth.

A shiver coursed through her along with surprise that he recalled her words. "Y-yes."

"That ends now."

* * *

Miles kissed his way down her neck, smoothing aside her thick, dark hair to taste more of her. She needed this as much as he did. Maybe even more.

It stunned him to think he read her so clearly when they'd spent so little time together, but he recognized how hard she pushed herself. How much she demanded of herself even when her world was caving in around her. The devotion of her staff—all personal friends, apparently—spoke volumes about who she was, and it made him want to take care of her, if only for tonight. He was going to help her forget all about her burdens until she lost herself in this.

In him.

Not that he was being unselfish. Far from it. He craved this woman.

Flicking open the buttons on her blouse, he nudged the thin fabric off her shoulders and let it flutter to the floor before he lifted his head to study her in the glow of the firelight.

"Are you still with me?" He followed the strap of her ivory lace bra with his fingertip.

The dark fringe of her eyelashes wavered before she glanced up at him, green eyes filled with heat. "Definitely."

The answer cranked him higher. He raked the straps from her shoulders and unhooked the lace to free her. The soft swells of her breasts spilled into his waiting hands, stirring the citrus fragrance he'd come to associate with her.

Hauling her into his arms, he lifted her, taking his time so that her body inched slowly up the length of his. He walked her to the bed and settled her in the space between the rows of pillows at the head and the down comforter folded at the foot, her hair spread out behind her like a silky halo. She followed his movements with watchful green eyes as he unfastened the side zipper of her skirt and eased it down her hips, leaving her in nothing but a scrap of ivory lace.

She made an enticing picture on the bed while he removed the rest of his own clothes. When he paused in undressing to find a condom and place it on the bed near her, she kinked a finger into the waistband of his boxers and tugged lightly.

"You're not naked enough." She grazed a touch along his abs, making his muscles jump with the featherlight caress.

"I'm working on it," he assured her, stilling her questing hand before she distracted him from his goal. "But we're taking care of you first."

"We are?" Her breath caught as he leaned over her and kneed her thighs apart to make room for himself.

The mattress dipped beneath them, their bodies swaying together.

"Ladies first." He kissed her hip, and she arched beneath him. "Call me old-fashioned."

He slid his hand beneath the ivory lace and stroked the slick heat waiting for him there. Her only reply was a soft gasp, followed by a needy whimper that told him she was already close.

She sifted her fingers through his hair, wriggling beneath him as he kissed and teased her, taking her higher and then easing back until they were both hot and edgy. The third time he felt her breathing shift, her thighs tensing, he didn't stop. He fastened his lips to her as she arched against him, and with a hard shudder, she flew apart.

He helped her ride out the sensations, relishing every buck of her hips, every soft shiver of her damp flesh. When he kissed his way back up her torso, he stopped at her breasts to pay homage to each in turn. Chiara patted around the bed for the condom and, finding it, rolled it into place. The feel of her hands on him, that efficient stroke of her fingers, nearly cost him his restraint. He closed his eyes against the heat jolting through him.

"Your turn," she whispered huskily in his ear before she gently bit his shoulder. "I'm in charge."

She pushed against his shoulder until he flipped onto his back. When she straddled him, her dark hair trailed along his chest while she made herself comfortable. Her green eyes seemed to dare him to argue as she arched an eyebrow at him.

But Miles couldn't have denied her a damn thing she wanted. Not now, when her cheeks were flushed with color, her nipples dark and thrusting from his touch. The glow of the chandelier brought out the copper highlights in her raven-colored hair. He caught her hips in his hands, steadying her as she poised herself above him.

Their eyes met, held, as he lowered her onto him. Everything inside him stilled, the sensation of being inside her better than any feeling he'd ever known.

Damn.

He cranked his eyes closed long enough to get command of himself. To grind his teeth against the way this woman was stealing into his life and rewiring his brain. When he opened his eyes again, he sat up, wrapping his arms around her waist to take her to the edge of the bed so she was seated on his lap.

They were even this way. Face-to-face. They had equal amounts of control.

He told himself that with every thrust. Every breath. Every heartbeat. They moved together in sweet, sensual harmony. Their bodies anticipating one another, pushing each other higher. She held on to his shoulders. He gripped her gorgeous round hips.

By the time he saw her head tilt back, her lips part and felt her fingernails dig into his skin, he knew he couldn't hold back when she came this time. He let the force of her orgasm pull him over the edge. They held on to each other tight while the waves of pleasure crashed over them, leaving them wrung out and panting.

Breathless.

Miles found a corner of the folded duvet at the foot of the bed and hauled it around them as he laid them both back down. They were still sideways on the mattress, but it didn't matter. He couldn't move until the world righted. For now, he tucked her close to him, kissing the top of her head, needing her next to him.

He breathed in the scent of her skin and sex, the passion haze behind his eyelids slowly clearing. He'd wanted to make her feel good, and he was pretty sure he'd accomplished that much. What he hadn't counted on was the way being with her had called forth more than a heady release. He'd damned near forgotten his name.

And even worse? After today, he was pretty sure he'd never be able to dig this woman out of his system.

Chiara awoke some hours later, when moonlight filtered through a high transom window over the French doors in the master suite. Even now, Miles's hand rested on her hip as he slept beside her, in just the same position as they'd fallen asleep, her back to his front.

For a moment, she debated making them something to eat since they'd never had dinner, but her body was still too sated sexually to demand any other sustenance. What a decadent pleasure to awake next to this man in her bed.

And yet, no matter how fulfilled her body, her brain already stirred restlessly. After fourteen years, she now knew what had happened to Zach Eldridge. Or at least, she seemed to know as much as Miles did. Miles had insisted he wasn't sure—that none of his friends were sure—whether or not Zach had jumped to end his life or if he'd jumped in a moment of reckless thrill seeking.

Maybe it didn't matter.

But what if it did? What if one of the Mesa Falls Ranch owners knew more about Zach's motives or mindset than they let on? Was one of them more morally responsible than the others for not stopping Zach's trek up to the top of those cliffs in the first place? Was one of them responsible for Zach's death?

She burrowed deeper into her down pillow, trying to shut out the thoughts. If she didn't get some sleep, she wouldn't be able to solve the mystery. Yet her brain kept reminding her that someone knew she was looking into Zach's death, and whoever it was felt threatened enough by her search that he—or she—had tried blackmailing her into giving up.

"Everything okay?" the warm, sleep-roughened voice behind her asked.

A shiver went through her as Miles stroked his palm along her bare hip under the covers. What might it have been like to meet him under different circumstances?

Would she have been able to simply relax and enjoy the incredible chemistry?

"Just thinking about Zach. Trying to reconcile the things you told me with my own understanding of him." That was true enough, even if she had bigger concerns, too. Absently, she traced the piping on the white cotton pillowcase.

Propping himself on his elbow, he said, "If he had an affair with a teacher and she ended up pregnant, it definitely accounts for why he was stressed that weekend. She could have gone to prison for being with him, too, which would have provided another level of stress."

His other hand remained on her hip, his fingers tracing idle patterns that gave her goose bumps.

"She put him in a position no seventeen-year-old should ever be in. Who's to say how he felt about her that weekend? He could have been stressed because she ended things with him. Or because someone found out their secret." She tried to envision what would drive Zach to total despair or to feel reckless enough to make that unwise jump. "Then again, maybe he was stressed because she wanted him to commit to her."

Miles's hand stilled. "What nineteen-year-old woman would want to play house with a seventeen-year-old kid?"

"The same woman who would have had an affair with a student in the first place." Even fourteen years later, she felt angry at the woman for taking advantage of someone she should have been protecting. No matter how much more mature Zach seemed than the other students around him, he was still a kid.

"I should check my phone." Rolling away from her, Miles withdrew his hand from under her body to reach for his device on the nightstand. "I might have heard back from the PI about the stakeout around Nicole Cruz's house."

Instantly alert, Chiara sat up in the bed, dragging a sheet with her. The room was still dark except for the moonlight in the transom window, so Chiara flicked the remote button to turn on the gas fireplace. Flames appeared with a soft whoosh while Miles turned on his phone then scrolled through various screens, his muscles lit by the orange glow.

When his finger stopped swiping, she watched his expression as his blue eyes moved back and forth. Tension threaded through his body. She could see it in his jaw and compressed lips.

"What is it? Did they find her?"

For a moment, when he looked up at her blankly, she wondered if he would go back to shutting her out of news about Zach. Or news about this woman—whether or not she had a direct tie to Zach.

But then his expression cleared, and he nodded.

"According to Desmond's note, Nicole Cruz won't return to Mesa Falls with our private investigator until all the ranch owners submit DNA for paternity testing." His voice was flat. His expression inscrutable. "She's agreed to submit a sample from her sister's son."

"That's good news, right?" she asked, feeling a hunch the child wouldn't be linked to any of them. Her gut told her the mystery boy was Zach's son. "And in the meantime, maybe your detective can see if there's a link between Nicole Cruz and the teacher—Lana Allen. Were they really sisters?"

Miles's fingers hovered over his phone screen. "It would be good to have a concrete lead to give him."

He hesitated. "Are you comfortable with me sharing what you told me?"

The fact that he would ask her first said a lot about his ability to be loyal. To keep a confidence. He'd certainly maintained secrecy for Zach's sake for a long, long time. The realization comforted her now that she more clearly understood his reluctance to reveal the truth.

"Would you be sharing the information directly with the investigator, or are you asking for permission to communicate it with all your partners?" She understood that Miles trusted his friends, but her first loyalty had to be to Zach.

A veil of coolness dropped over Miles's features as a chill crept into his voice. "Until now, my partners and I have pooled our knowledge."

She waited for him to elaborate, but he didn't.

She needed to tread carefully, not wanting to alienate him now that he'd finally brought her into his confidence. And yet her feelings for him—her fear of losing him—threatened her objectivity. Hugging the sheet tighter to her chest, she felt goose bumps along her arms. If only it was the room getting cooler and not Miles's mood casting a chill. She weighed how to respond.

"I know you trust your friends." She couldn't help it if she didn't. "But you have to admit that the last time you communicated my interest in Zach to that group, the threats against me came very quickly afterward."

If she'd thought his face was cool before, his blue gaze went glacial now.

"Coincidence," he returned sharply. "I'm not in the habit of keeping secrets from the men I trust most."

A pain shot through her as she realized that the last few hours with Miles hadn't shifted his opinion of her or brought them closer together. If anything, she felt further apart from him than ever. The hurt made her lash out, a safer reaction than revealing vulnerability.

"You realize my entire livelihood rests in the balance?" She couldn't help but draw a second blanket over her shoulders like armor, a barrier, feeling the need to shore up her defenses that had dissolved too fast where he was concerned. "And possibly my safety?"

She thought she spied a thaw in his frosty gaze. He set his phone aside and palmed her shoulder, his fingers a warm, welcome weight.

"I've already told you that I will do everything in my power to keep you safe." The rasp in his voice reminded her of other conversations, other confidences he'd shared with her. She wanted to believe in him.

"I want to find out what drove Zach over that cliff as much as anyone." She swallowed back her anxiety and hoped she wasn't making a huge mistake. "If you think it's best to share what I told you with his other friends in addition to the PI, then you're welcome to tell them what I knew about Zach and the teacher—Miss Allen."

Miles's gaze held hers for a moment before he gave a nod and picked up his phone again to type a text. For a long time afterward, Chiara couldn't help but think his expression showed the same uneasiness she felt inside. But once Miles hit the send button, she knew it was too late to turn back from the course they'd already set.

Eleven

Snow blanketed the Tahoe vacation villa, the world of white momentarily distracting Miles from the tension hanging over his head ever since he'd shared Chiara's insights about Zach with his friends two days ago. A storm had taken the power out the day before, giving them a grace period to watch the weather blow in, make love in every room of that huge villa and not think about their time together coming to an end as they got closer to learning the truth about Zach's death.

Miles had continued to shove his concerns to the back burner this morning, managing to talk Chiara into taking a walk through the woods with him after breakfast. They'd ridden a snowmobile to the casino the day before to retrieve some clothes from his suite.

Now, he held her gloved hand in his as they trudged between sugar pines and white fir trees, the accumulation up to their knees in most places. A dusting clung to her jeans and the fringe of her long red wool jacket. Her cheeks were flushed from the cold and the effort of forging a path through the drifts. Her dark hair was braided in a long tail over one shoulder, a white knitted beanie framing her face as she smiled up at a red-tailed hawk who screeched down at them with its distinctive cry.

For a moment, he saw a different side of her. With no makeup and no fans surrounding her, no couture gown or A-list celebrities clamoring for a photo with her, Chiara looked like a woman who might enjoy the same kind of quiet life he did.

But he knew that was only an illusion. She circulated in a glamorous world of nightlife and parties, far from the ranch where he spent his time.

"I'm glad we got out of the house." She leaned against the rough bark of a Jeffrey pine as they reached an overlook of the lake, where the water reflected the dull gray of the snow clouds. "While having a snow day was fun yesterday, it only delayed the stress fallout from visiting the police station and having it posted online. I feel like I'm still waiting for the other shoe to drop."

Miles leaned back against the trunk near her, still holding her hand. The reminder of those things hanging over them still made him uneasy, and he wished he could distract her. How she felt mattered to him more than it should, considering the very lives they led. And how fast she'd be out of his life again.

He knew her time in Tahoe was bound to her search for answers about Zach, which was why Miles hadn't found a way to tell her yet about the DNA test results he'd received from Desmond earlier that morning. All the Mesa Falls owners had been ruled out, as had Alonzo Salazar through DNA provided by his sons.

Which meant there was a strong chance Zach was the father. But Miles hadn't shared that yet, knowing damn well Chiara might leave once she knew. The possibility of her going weighed him down like lead, but he was also still worried about her safety after the anonymous threats. But he ignored his own feelings to try to reassure her.

"It's been two days since the photos of us at the police station started appearing online." He'd checked his phone before driving over to the casino for his clothes, wanting to make sure there'd been no backlash from her fans. "Maybe it won't be a big deal."

Below them on the snowy hill, a few kids dragged snow tubes partway up the incline to sled down to the water, even though the conditions seemed too powdery for a good run. A few vacation cabins dotted the coastline, and he guessed they were staying in one of them. Chiara's gaze followed the kids, too, before she looked up at him.

"Maybe not." She didn't sound convinced. "And my social media accounts are still working." She held up her phone with the other hand. "I successfully posted a photo of the snow-covered trees a moment ago."

While he was glad to hear her accounts hadn't been hacked, he was caught off guard by the idea of her posting nature photos to her profile that was full of fashion. And he was grateful to think about something besides the guilt gnawing at him for not confiding in her about the DNA news.

"Just trees?" He gave her a sideways glance, studying her lovely profile.

Her lips pursed in thought. "I've been posting more artistic images." She shifted against the tree trunk so she faced him, her breath huffing between them in a drift of white in the cold air. "Thinking more about Zach this week has made me question how I could have gotten so far afield from the mixed media art that I used to love making."

Regret rose as he remembered how he'd dismissed her work when they'd first met. "I hope it didn't have anything to do with what I said that night about your job. I had no right—"

She shook her head, laying a hand on his arm. "Absolutely not. I know why I launched my brand and created the blog since I couldn't afford art school. But there's nothing stopping me from doing something different now. From reimagining my future."

While the kids on the hill below them laughed and shouted over their next sled run, Miles shifted toward Chiara, the tree bark scraping his sheepskin jacket as he wondered if she could reimagine a future with him in it. Did he want that? Gazing into her green eyes, he still wrestled with how much they could trust each other. He felt her wariness about his friends. And for his part, he knew she was only here now because of her loyalty to Zach.

So he kept his response carefully focused on her even when he was tempted as hell to ask for more.

"No doubt, you could do anything you wanted now." He brushed a snowflake from her cheek, the feel of her reminding him of all the best highlights from their past two nights together.

Funny that despite seeing stars many times thanks to her, the moments he remembered best were how she'd felt wrapped around him as he fell asleep the last two nights, resulting in the best slumber he'd had in a long time. He'd been totally relaxed, like she was supposed to be right there with him.

She closed her eyes for a moment as he touched her. He'd like to think she relished the feel of him as much he did her. Her long lashes fluttered against her cheeks for a moment before she raised her gaze to meet his again.

"For a long time, I worried that any artistic talent I once had was only because of the inspiration from the year I knew Zach," she confided quietly. "Like I was somehow a fraud without him."

The statement stunned him, coming from someone so obviously talented. "You built your success because of your artistic eye. And hell yes, I know that because I read up on you after we met."

He wasn't about to hide that from her if he could leverage what he'd learned to reassure her. He lifted her chin so she could see his sincerity.

"Thank you." Her gloved fingers wrapped around his wrist where he touched her, the leather creaking softly with the cold. "Oddly, I've been more reassured as I've reconnected with my old sketchbooks. There is a lot more original work in there than I remembered. I think I let Zach's influence magnify in my mind over the years because of the huge hole he left in my life in other ways. I spent at least a year just redrawing old works of his from memory, trying to keep him in my heart."

Tenderness for her loss swamped him. He recognized it. He'd lived it. "I know what you mean. All of us tried to fill the void he left in different ways. Weston took up search and rescue work. Gage disappeared into numbers and investing."

He mused over the way his friends had grown an unbreakable bond, while at the same time venturing decidedly away from the experience they'd shared. Zach's death had brought them together and kept them all isolated at the same time.

"What about you?" Chiara asked as his hand fell from her chin. "What did you do afterward?"

He couldn't help a bitter smile. "I became the model son. I threw myself into ranching work to help my father and prepare for taking over Rivera Ranch."

"That sounds like a good thing, right?" She tipped her head sideways as if not sure what she was hearing. "Very practical."

"Maybe it was. But it only increased the divide between my brother and me." He hated that time in his life for so many reasons. The fact that it had alienated him from the person who knew him best had been a pain that lasted long after. "I could do no wrong in my parents' eyes after that, and it was the beginning of the end for my relationship with Wes."

Her brows knit in confusion as the snow started falling faster. A flake clung briefly to her eyelash before melting.

"Why would your brother resent your efforts to help your family?" she asked with a clarity he could never muster for the situation.

The fact that she saw his life—him—so clearly had him struggling to maintain his distance. The intimacy of the last two days was threatening to pull him under. Needing a breather, he stirred from where he stood.

"He didn't." Miles shrugged as he straightened, gesturing toward the path back to her villa. "But our parents treated us so differently it got uncomfortable for Wes to even come home for holidays. I hated how they treated him, too, but since I spent every second away from school working on Rivera Ranch, I let that take over my life."

For a few minutes, they shuffled back along the paths they'd made through the deep snow on their way out. He, for one, was grateful for the reprieve from a painful topic. But then again, if there was a chance he would be spending more time with Chiara in the future, he owed her an explanation of his family dynamics.

He held his hand out for her to help her over an icy log in the path.

"It seems like the blame rests on your parents' shoulders. Not yours or Weston's," she observed, jumping down from the log to land beside him with a soft thud of her heavy boots.

The sounds from the sledders retreated as they continued through the woods.

"Maybe so. But then, on one of Wes's rare trips home, we ended up dating the same woman without knowing. That didn't help things." It had been a misguided idea to date Brianna in the first place, but Miles had been on the ranch and isolated for too long. So even though Brianna was a rebel and a risk taker, he'd told himself his life needed more adventure.

He'd gotten far more than he'd bargained for when he'd seen Wes in a lip lock with her at a local bar a few weeks later. That betrayal had burned deep.

"That sounds like her fault. Because you may not have known, but she must have." She scowled as she spoke.

Miles couldn't help a laugh. "I appreciate your defense of me. Thank you."

He could see Chiara's villa ahead through the trees

and the snow, and his steps slowed. He wasn't ready to return to the real world yet. Didn't want to know what had happened with Nicole Cruz, or with Chiara's anonymous hacker. He wanted more time with her before he lost her to her work and her world where he didn't belong.

Chiara slowed, too, coming to a halt beside him. They still held hands. And for some reason stepping out of the trees felt like it was bringing them that much closer to the end of their time together.

"I like you, Miles," she admitted, dropping her forehead to rest on his shoulder as if she didn't want to return to the real world yet, either. "In case you haven't guessed."

Her simple words plucked at something inside him. Made him want to take a chance again for the first time in a long time. Or confide in her, at the very least. But long-ingrained habit kept him silent about the deeper things he was feeling. Instead, he focused on the way they connected best.

"I like you a whole lot, too," he growled, winding an arm around her waist to press her more tightly to him. "I'll remind you how much if you take me home with you."

She lifted her eyes to his, and for the briefest of seconds, he thought he saw her hesitate. But then her lids fell shut and she grazed her lips over his, meeting his kiss with a sexy sigh and more than a little heat.

Chiara was half dazed by the time Miles broke the kiss. Heat rose inside her despite the snow, her body responding to everything about him. His scent. His touch. His wicked, wonderful tongue.

Heartbeat skipping, she gladly followed him as he led her back toward the huge stone-and-wood structure, her thoughts racing ahead to where they'd take the next kiss. Her bed? The sauna? In front of the massive fireplace? Sensual thoughts helped keep her worries at bay after the way Miles seemed to pull back from her earlier. Or had that been her imagination?

Sometimes she sensed that he avoided real conversation in favor of touching and kissing. But when his every touch and kiss set her aflame, could she really argue? She'd let her guard down around him in a big way, showing him a side of herself that felt new. Vulnerable. Raw.

Breathless with anticipation, she tripped into the side door behind him, peeling off her snowy boots on the mat. Her hat and gloves followed. He shook off his coat and boots before stripping off her jacket and hanging it on an antique rack for her. He didn't wait to fold her in his arms and kiss her again. He gripped her hips, steadying her as he sealed their bodies together. Heat scrambled her thoughts again, her fingers tunneling impatiently under his cashmere sweater where she warmed them against his back before walking them around to his front, tucking them in the waistband of his jeans.

The ragged sound in his throat expressed the same need she felt, and he pulled away long enough to grip her by the hand and guide her across the polished planked floor toward the stairs.

Her feet were on the first wide step of the formal divided staircase when a knock sounded on the back door.

Miles stopped. His blue gaze swung around to look at her.

Her belly tightened.

"Maybe it's just Jules checking to see how we're faring after the storm." At least, she hoped that was all it was.

Still, her feet didn't move until the knock sounded again. More urgently.

"We'd better check," Miles muttered, frustration punctuating every word. He kept holding her hand as he walked with her through the kitchen.

She sensed the tension in him—something about the way he held himself. Or maybe the way he looked like he was grinding his teeth. But she guessed that was the same sexual frustration she was feeling right now.

Still, her nerves wound tight as she padded through the room in her socks. Through a side window, she could see Jules and Stefan—together—on the back step. Vaguely, she felt Miles give her hand a reassuring squeeze before she pulled open the door.

"What's up?" she started to ask, only to have Jules thrust her phone under Chiara's nose as she stepped into the kitchen, Stefan right behind her.

Miles closed the door.

"Your page is down." Jules's face was white, her expression grim as she waggled the phone in front of Chiara with more emphasis. "We've been hacked."

She could have sworn the floor dropped out from under her feet. Miles's arm wrapped around her. Steadying her.

Chiara stared at Jules's device, afraid to look. Closing her eyes for a moment, she took a deep breath before she accepted the phone. Then, sinking onto the closest counter stool, she tapped the screen back to life.

Miles peered over her shoulder, his warmth not giving her the usual comfort as a shiver racked her. His hand rubbed over her back while her eyes focused on what she was seeing.

Oddly, the image at the top of her profile page—her home screen—was of Miles. Only he wasn't alone. It was a shot of him with his face pressed cheek to cheek with a gorgeous woman—a brown-eyed beauty with dark curling hair and a mischievous smile. A banner inserted across the image read, "Kara Marsh, you'll always be second best."

Miles might have said something in her ear, but she couldn't focus on his words. If she'd thought the floor had shifted out from under her feet before, now her stomach joined the free fall. As images went, it wasn't particularly damaging to her career.

Simply to her heart.

Because the look on Miles's face in that photo was one she'd never seen before. Pressed against that ethereally gorgeous creature, Miles appeared happier than he'd ever been with Chiara. In this image, his blue eyes were unguarded. Joyous. In love.

And that hurt more than anything. In the woods this morning, when she'd tentatively tested out his feelings with a confession that she liked him—not that it was a huge overture, but still, she'd tried—he'd responded with sizzle. Not emotions.

Jules crouched down into her line of vision, making Chiara realize she'd been silent too long. With an effort, she tried to recover herself, knowing full well her hurt must have been etched all over her face in those first moments when she'd seen the picture.

"It could be worse," she managed to say, sliding the phone across the granite countertop to Jules, avoiding pieces from a jigsaw puzzle she'd worked on for a little while with Miles during the snowstorm. "That's hardly a damning shot."

"I agree," Jules said softly, her tone a careful blend of professionalism and caution. "But the banner—coupled with the fact that you were recently photographed with Miles—creates the impression that either Miles or his—" she hesitated, shooting a quick glance at Miles "—um, former girlfriend were the ones to hijack your social media properties. This same image is on your personal blog, too. I'm worried your fans will be defensive of you—"

"I'm sure we'll get it cleared up soon." She wasn't sure of any such thing as she picked up one of the puzzle pieces and traced the tabs and slots. But the need to confront Miles privately was too strong for her to think about her career. Or whatever else Jules was saying. "Could you give us a minute, Jules? And I'll come over to help you figure out our next steps in a little while?"

Her heartbeat pounded too loudly for her to even be sure what Jules said on her way out. But her friend took Stefan by the arm—even though her bodyguard looked doubtfully from Miles to Chiara and back again—and tugged him out the villa's back door.

Leaving her and Miles alone.

He put his hands on her shoulders, gently swiveling her on the counter stool so that she faced him.

"Are you all right?" He lowered himself into the seat next to her, perching on the edge of the leather cushion. "Would you like me to get you something to drink? You don't look well."

"I'm fine." That wasn't true, but a drink wouldn't help the tumultuous feelings inside her. The hurt deeper than she had a right to feel over a man she'd vowed could only be a fling.

"You don't look fine." His blue eyes were full of concern. Though, she reminded herself, not love. "You can't think for a second I had anything to do with posting that."

"Of course not." That hadn't even occurred to her. She hadn't roused the energy to think about who was behind the post because she was too busy having her heart stepped on. Too consumed with feelings she'd assured herself she wasn't going to develop for this man. But judging by the jealousy and hurt gnawing away at her insides, she couldn't deny she'd been harboring plenty of emotions for this man.

Still, she needed to pull herself together.

"For what it's worth, that's obviously not a recent photo," Miles offered, his hands trailing down her arms to her hands where he found the puzzle piece she was still holding. He set it back on the counter. "I'm not sure where someone would have gotten ahold of it, but—"

"Social media," she supplied, thinking she really needed to get back online and start scouring her pages to see what was happening. Jules had to be wondering why Chiara had only wanted to talk to Miles. "It looks like a selfie. My guess is your old girlfriend has it stored on one of her profiles."

"Makes sense." He nodded, straightening, his touch falling away from her. "But I was going to say that I haven't seen Brianna Billings in years, so I'm sure she wouldn't be sending you anonymous threats."

Not wanting to discuss the woman in the photo, or the feelings it stirred, Chiara stared out the window behind Miles's head and watched the snowfall as she turned the conversation in another direction.

"So if we rule out you and your ex for suspects in hacking the page," she continued, knowing she sounded stiff. Brusque. "Who else should we look at? I'll call the police again, of course, but they'll ask us who we think might be responsible. And personally, I think it's got to be one of your partners at Mesa Falls. One of Zach's former friends."

"No." He shook his head resolutely and stood, then walked over to the double refrigerator doors and pulled out a bottle of water. He set it on the island before retrieving two glasses. "It can't be."

She didn't appreciate how quickly he wrote off her idea. Especially when her feelings were already stirred up disproportionately at seeing a different side of Miles in that photo. She felt Miles pulling away. Sensed it was all plummeting downhill between them, but she didn't have a clue how to stop things from going off the rails.

"Who else would be tracking my efforts to find out what happened to Zach, and would know about your past, too?" she asked him sharply. "I'm not the common denominator in that equation. It's the Mesa Falls group."

"It's someone trying to scare you away from looking into Zach's past. Maybe Nicole Cruz?" he mused aloud as he filled the two glasses of water. Although as soon as he said it, he glanced up at her, and she could have sworn she saw a shadow cross through his eyes.

Then again, she was feeling prickly. She tried to let go of the hurt feelings while he returned the water bottle to the stainless steel refrigerator. Frustration and hurt were going to help her get to the bottom of this.

"It could be whoever fathered the mystery child," she pressed, wondering about the DNA evidence. "Once we know who the father is—"

"It's none of us," Miles answered with a slow shake of his head. He set a glass of water in front of her as he returned to the seat beside her.

His answer sounded certain. As if he knew it for a fact. But she guessed that was just his way of willing it to be the truth.

"We'll only know that for sure once the test results come in," she reminded him before taking a sip of her drink.

"They already have. All of the Mesa Falls partners have been cleared of paternity, along with Alonzo Salazar, courtesy of DNA provided by his sons." Miles's fingers tightened around his glass.

Surprised, Chiara set hers back down with a thud, sloshing some over the rim.

"How long have you known?" she asked, her nerve endings tingling belatedly with uneasiness.

"Desmond texted me early this morning."

"And just when were you going to tell me?" She knew logically that not much time had passed. But she'd been waiting half of a lifetime for answers about Zach. And damn it, she'd spent her whole life being in the dark because of other people's secrets. Her family's. Zach's friends'. Even, she had to admit, Zach's.

Indignation burned. Her heart pounded faster, her body recognizing the physical symptoms of betrayal. Of secrets hidden.

"Soon," Miles started vaguely, not meeting her eyes. "I just didn't want—"

"You know what? It doesn't matter what you did or

didn't want." She stood up in a hurry, needing to put distance between herself and this man who'd slid past her defenses without her knowing. She didn't have the resources to argue with him when her heart hurt, and she'd be damned if she'd let him crush more of the feelings she'd never meant to have for him.

She needed to get her coat so she could go talk to Jules and focus on her career instead of a man who would never trust her. More than that, she needed to get out of the same town as him. Out of the same state.

There was no reason to linger here any longer. The time had come to return home, back to her own life in Los Angeles.

"Chiara, wait." Miles cut her off, inserting himself in her path, though he didn't touch her.

"I can't do secrets, Miles," she said tightly, betrayal stinging. And disillusionment. And anger at herself. "I'm sure that sounds hypocritical after the way I searched your computer that night—"

"It doesn't." He looked so damned good in his jeans and soft gray sweater, his jaw bristly and unshaven. "I know trust comes hard for you."

"For you, too, it seems." She folded her arms to keep herself from touching him. If only the want could be so easily held at bay.

"Yes. For me, too," he acknowledged.

She waited for a long moment. Waited. And heaven help her, even hoped. Just a little. But he said nothing more.

Tears burning her eyes, she sidestepped him to reach for her coat.

"I'm going to be working the rest of the day," she informed him, holding herself very straight in an effort to keep herself together. Her heart ached. "I'll head back to LA tomorrow. But for tonight, I think it would be best if you weren't here when I return."

Miles didn't argue. He only nodded. He didn't even bother to fight for her.

Once she had her boots and coat on, she shoved through the door and stepped out into the snow. Some wistful part of her thought she heard a softly spoken, "Don't go" from behind her. But she knew it was just the foolish wish of a heart broken before she'd even realized she'd fallen in love.

Twelve

Three days later, gritty-eyed despite rising late, Miles prowled Desmond's casino floor at noon. Navigating the path to Desmond's office through a maze of roulette wheels, blackjack tables and slot machines, he cursed the marketing wisdom that demanded casino guests walk through the games every time they wanted to access hotel amenities.

No doubt the setup netted Desmond big profits, but the last thing Miles wanted to see after Chiara's defection was a tower of lights blinking "jackpot!" accompanied by a chorus of electronic enthusiasm. A herd of touristy-looking players gathered around the machine to celebrate their good fortune, while Miles suspected he'd never feel lucky again.

Not after losing the most incredible woman he'd ever met just two weeks after finding her. He'd surely set a record for squandering everything in so little time.

He hadn't been able to sleep for thinking about the expression on her face when she'd discovered he hadn't told her about the DNA test results. He'd known—absolutely known—that she would be hurt by that given the trust issues she'd freely admitted. And yet he'd withheld it anyhow, unwilling to share the news that would send her out of his life.

So instead of letting her choose when she should return to her California home once she'd found out all she could about Zach, he'd selfishly clung to the information in the hope of stretching out their time together. And for his selfishness, he'd hurt her. Sure, he'd like to think he would have told her that afternoon. He couldn't possibly have gone to bed by her side that night without sharing the news. But it didn't matter how long he'd kept that secret.

What mattered was that she'd told him how hard it was for her to trust. Something he—of all people—understood only too well. Yeah, he recognized the pain he'd caused when he'd crossed the one line she'd drawn with him about keeping secrets.

When he finally reached the locked door of the back room, a uniformed casino employee entered a code and admitted him. At least the maze of halls here was quiet. The corridors with their unadorned light gray walls led to a variety of offices and maintenance rooms. Miles bypassed all of them until he reached stately double doors in the back.

Another uniformed guard stood outside them. This one rapped his knuckles twice on the oak barrier before admitting Miles.

A stunning view of Lake Tahoe dominated one side of the owner's work suite, with glass walls separating a private office, small conference room and a more intimate meeting space. All were spare and modern in shades of gray and white, with industrial touches like stainless steel work lamps and hammered metal artwork. Desmond sat on a low sofa in front of the windows overlooking Lake Tahoe in the more casual meeting space.

Sunlight reflecting off the water burned right into Miles's eyes until he moved closer to the window, the angle of built-in blinds effectively shading the glare as he reached his friend. Dressed in a sharp gray suit and white collared shirt with no tie, Desmond drank a cup of espresso as he read an honest-to-God newspaper— no electronic devices in sight. The guy had an easy luxury about him that belied a packed professional life.

As far as Miles knew, he did nothing but work 24/7, the same way Gage Striker had when he'd been an investment banker. Gage's wealth had convinced him to start taking it easier as an angel investor the last couple of years, but Desmond still burned the candle at both ends, working constantly.

"Look what the cat dragged in," Desmond greeted him, folding his paper and setting it on a low glass table in front of him. With his posh manners and charm, Desmond looked every inch the worldly sophisticate. And it wasn't just an act, either, as he held dual citizenship in the United States and the UK thanks to a Brit mother.

But Miles remembered him from darker days, when Desmond's father had been a ham-fisted brute, teaching his son to be quick with a punch out of necessity, to protect himself and his mother. It was a skill set Desmond hid well, but Miles knew that a lot of his work efforts still benefited battered women and kids. And he'd channeled his own grief about Zach into something positive, whereas Miles still felt like the old wounds just ate away at his insides. What did he have to show for the past beyond Rivera Ranch? All his toil had gone into the family property. And he hadn't really done anything altruistic.

"I only came to let you know I'm returning to Mesa Falls." Miles dropped onto a leather chair near the sofa, eager to leave the place where his brief relationship with Chiara had imploded. "I'm meeting the pilot this afternoon."

"Coffee?" Desmond offered as he picked up a black espresso cup.

Miles shook his head, knowing caffeine wouldn't make a dent in the wrung-out feeling plaguing his head. He'd barely slept last night for thinking about Chiara's parting words that had been so polite and still so damned cutting.

I think it would be best if you weren't here when I return.

"It's just as well you came in." Desmond set aside his empty cup and leaned back into the sofa cushions. "I was going to message you anyhow to let you know you don't need to return to Mesa Falls."

Miles frowned as he rubbed his eyes to take away some of the gritty feeling. "What do you mean? Someone's got to oversee things."

"Nicole Cruz is flying to Montana tonight," Desmond informed him, brushing some invisible item from the perfectly clean cushion by his thigh. "I assured her I would be there to meet her. Them."

Miles edged forward in his seat, trying to follow.

"You want to be there to meet the guardian of the kid who's most likely Zach's son?" he clarified, knowing something was off about the way Desmond was talking about her.

Was it suspicion?

He'd like to think they were all suspicious of her, though. This seemed like something different.

"I've been her only point of contact so far," Desmond explained, giving up on the invisible dust. He gave Miles a level gaze. "The only one of us she's communicated with. We can't afford to scare her off when it took us this long to find her."

"Right. Agreed." Miles nodded, needing to rouse himself out of his own misery to focus on their latest discovery about Zach. "If Matthew is Zach's son, we don't want to lose our chance of being a part of his life."

Regret stung as he considered how much Chiara would want to meet the boy. He didn't want to stand in her way, especially when they might not have come this far figuring out Zach's secrets without her help.

Desmond's phone vibrated, and he picked it up briefly.

"I've asked the PI to back off investigating Nicole and Matthew," Desmond continued as he read something and then set the device back on the table. Sun glinted off the sleek black case.

"Why?" Miles picked up his own phone, checking for the thousandth time if there were any developments on who had targeted Chiara's sites. Or, if he was honest, to see if she had messaged him. Disappointment to find nothing stung all over again.

He missed her more than if she'd been out of his life for years and not days. He'd only stuck around Lake Tahoe this long in hopes he'd be able to help the local police, or maybe in the hope she'd return to town to see Astrid. Or him.

But there was only a group message from Alec telling any of the Mesa Falls partners still on site at the casino to meet him at Desmond's office as soon as possible. Miles wondered what that was about.

"Nicole has been dodging our investigators to protect Matthew for weeks. She's exhausted and mistrustful. She asked me to 'call off the dogs' if she agreed to return to Montana, and I have given her my word that I would." Desmond straightened in his seat, appearing ready to move on as he checked his watch. "And, actually, I have a lot to do today to prepare my staff for my absence. Alec agreed to watch over things here, but he's late."

As he spoke, however, a knock sounded at the outer double doors before they opened, and Alec appeared.

Miles only had a second to take in his friend's disheveled clothes that looked slept in—a wrinkled jacket and T-shirt and rumpled jeans. His hair stood up in a few directions, and his face had a look of grim determination as he wound through the office suite to the glassed-in room where Desmond and Miles sat.

"Sorry I'm late." Alec juggled a foam coffee cup in his hand as he plowed through the last door. "I've been at the police station giving my statement. They arrested my personal assistant, Vivian, for threatening Chiara Campagna."

"You're kidding." Miles tensed, half rising to his feet. Then, realizing the woman in question was already in custody, he lowered himself into the chair again. "How did they find out?"

Miles had checked with the local police just the night

before but hadn't learned anything other than that they were still looking into the complaint Chiara filed after the second incident.

Alec lowered himself into the chair opposite Miles at the other end of the coffee table. He set his coffee cup on a marble coaster.

"Apparently it wasn't tough to track her once they got a cybercrimes expert to look into it. Vivian and I were working late last night when she got a call from the police asking her to come in so they could ask her some questions." Alec shrugged and then swiped his hand through the hair that was already standing straight up. "I drove her over there, never thinking they already had evidence on her. They arrested her shortly afterward."

"Does Chiara know?" Miles wanted to call her. Check on her. Let her know that the police had done their job.

Hell. What he really wanted was to fold her into his arms.

But holding her wasn't his right anymore.

"I'm not sure if they've contacted her yet." Alec retrieved his coffee cup, a thick silver band around his middle finger catching the light and refracting it all over the room. "I'm still trying to process the news myself."

Before Miles could ask more about it, a knock sounded again on the outer door, and his brother, Weston, ambled in wearing jeans and a T-shirt. With his too-long hair and hazel eyes, he and Miles couldn't be less alike.

"What's up? April and I were going to hit the slopes today. Conditions are incredible." He stopped himself as he looked around at his friends. "What happened?"

As he sank to a seat on the other end of the couch

from Desmond, Alec repeated the news about Vivian before adding, "I had no idea Vivian was imagining we had a much deeper relationship than we do, but sometime in the last few years she started crossing the line as my assistant to make sure things went my way— bribing contacts into taking meetings with me, padding the numbers on our financial statements to make the gaming company look stronger for investors, a whole bunch of stuff unrelated to what happened with Chiara."

Miles recalled meeting Vivian lurking outside the high-roller suite that day after the meeting of the Mesa Falls partners. "So why would she hassle Chiara?"

"I guess she intercepted a text on my phone about Chiara's interest in Zach." Alec glanced upward, as if trying to gather his thoughts, or maybe to remember something. "Vivian never liked her. She was a student at Brookfield, too, and I was with her that day at Dowdon that Kara—Chiara—came to school to talk to Miles and Gage."

Miles remembered Alec saying he'd been with a girl under the bleachers that day. Still, fourteen years seemed like a long time to hold a grudge against Chiara. Once again his protective instincts kicked into gear. If he couldn't be with Chiara or make her happy, he owed it to her to at least keep her safe. Which meant getting full disclosure on everything related to Zach's death.

Desmond spoke before Miles had a chance to ask about that.

"So Vivian must have known about Zach if you've been friends that long." Desmond seemed to put the pieces together faster, but maybe it was easier to have more clarity on the situation than Miles, who'd lost objectivity where Chiara was concerned a long time ago.

"Maybe she figured it was somehow helping you to keep Chiara from asking too many questions."

Weston whistled softly under his breath. "She sounds like a piece of work."

Alec bristled. "She's smart as hell, actually. Just highly unethical."

The conversation continued, but Miles couldn't focus on it with the urge to see Chiara, to make sure she knew that her hacker was in custody, so strong. He wanted to share the news with her, to give her this much even though he'd failed their fledgling relationship.

"Why did she feel the need to post a picture of me with an old girlfriend on Chiara's page?" he found himself asking, curious not so much for himself, but for Chiara's sake. He'd known that image had bothered her.

And if he was able to see her again—or even just speak to her—he wanted to share answers with her. Answers he owed her after the way he'd withheld information from her before.

Alec took another drink of his coffee before responding. "I wondered about that, too. I guess Vivian was upset about a photo of me with Chiara from that night at your party, Miles. Then, when she saw the pictures of you at the police station with Chiara—looking like a couple—she figured the best way to hurt Chiara would be with an image of you and someone else."

Miles remembered the jealousy that had gone through him when he saw Alec's hand on the small of Chiara's back that night, touching her bare skin through the cutout of her silver gown.

Weston spoke up. "For a smart woman, she definitely made some stupid mistakes. But lucky for us, right? Because now she's behind bars." He stood as if to leave. "I've got to get back to April to meet the car taking us to the mountain."

Miles rose as well, edgy to be out of Tahoe. Now that he'd been relieved of his duties at Mesa Falls, he was free to use the afternoon's flight to see Chiara. To share what he'd learned, at least. "Desmond, if you've got things covered at Mesa Falls, I'm going to head back home."

"You're returning to Rivera Ranch?" Desmond stood and walked to the door with them, though his question was for Miles.

"Eventually." Miles could only think about one destination today, however. "I need to make a stop in Los Angeles first."

After a quick exchange of pleasantries, Miles and Weston left the owner's suite together.

"Los Angeles?" Weston wasted no time in posing the question.

Slowing his step in the long, empty corridor between the casino floor and the offices, Miles couldn't deny the rare impulse to unburden himself. His brother, after all, owed him a listening ear after the way Miles had helped him patch up his relationship with April Stephens, the woman Wes loved beyond reason.

"I messed up with Chiara," he admitted, done with trying to label what happened as anything other than his fault. "I was selfish. Stupid. Shortsighted—"

Weston halted in the middle of the echoing hall, clamping a hand on Miles's shoulder. "What happened?"

Miles explained the way he'd withheld the news about the DNA evidence to give himself more time with her, to try to think of a way to make her stay, even though he'd known about her past and the way her own family had kept secrets from her. Even though she'd told him how hard it was for her to trust. When he finished, Weston looked thoughtful.

"You remember when I screwed up with April, you told me that I needed to be the one to take a risk. To put myself on the line?"

"Yes." Miles remembered that conversation. Of course, taking chances was like breathing to his brother, so it hadn't seemed like too much to ask of him to be the one to tell April he loved her. "I also told you that not everyone can be such a romantic."

Miles knew himself too well. He had two feet on the ground at all times. He was a practical man. Salt of the earth. A rancher. He didn't jump first and ask questions later. That had always been Wes's role. But maybe it was time to take a page from his brother's book, to step up and take a risk when the moment called for it. His gut burned to think he hadn't already done so.

"News flash. What you're feeling doesn't have a thing to do with romance. It has everything to do with love, and you're going to lose it, without question, if you can't get your head on straight and see that." Weston's expression was dire.

Grave.

And Miles wasn't too proud to admit it scared the hell of out of him. Especially if what he'd walked away from was love. But by the way the word encapsulated every single aspect of his feelings for Chiara, he knew Weston was right.

"You think I already blew it for good?" He wondered how fast his plane could get to LA.

"It's been three days and you haven't even called?

Haven't gone there to tell her how wrong you were?" Weston shook his head. "Why didn't you call me sooner to help you figure this out? I owed you, man. Maybe, with more time, I could have—"

Miles cut his brother off, panic welling up in his chest.

"I've got a plane to catch." He didn't wait to hear any more about how much he'd screwed up. If time was of the essence, he wasn't wasting another second of it to see Chiara and tell her how he felt about her.

That he loved her.

Thirteen

Seated in a low, rolled-arm chair close to her balcony, Chiara sniffed a small vial of fragrance, knowing she'd have a headache soon if she kept testing the samples from her perfumer. Although maybe the impending headache had more to do with all the tears she'd shed for Miles this week. Still, she needed the distraction from her hurt, so she sniffed the floral fumes again, trying to pinpoint what she didn't like about the scent.

The setting sun smudged the western sky with lavender and pink as lights glowed in the valley below her Hollywood Hills home. The glass wall was retracted between her living room and the balcony so that the night air circulated around the seating area where she tested the samples. She'd adored this property once, so modern and elegant, but it felt incredibly lonely to her since she'd returned to it earlier in the week. As for the

fragrance vial in her hand, the hint of honeysuckle—
so pleasing in nature—was too heavy in the mixture.
She handed it back to Mrs. Santor, her housekeeper. In
addition to her regular duties, she was giving her input
on developing a signature fragrance for Chiara's brand.

"I didn't like that one, either," Mrs. Santor said from
the seat beside her, packing away the vial in a kit Chiara had received from a perfumer. "You should call it
a night, honey. You look spent."

Amy Santor was Jules's mother and a former next-
door neighbor in Chiara's old life. Mrs. Santor had
cleaned houses all her life, and when Chiara's business had taken off, she would have gladly given Mrs.
Santor any job she wanted in her company to repay her
for kindnesses she'd shown Chiara in her youth. But
Jules's mom insisted that she enjoyed keeping house,
and Chiara felt fortunate to have a maternal figure in
her home a few times a week.

"I shouldn't be. It's still early." She checked her
watch, irritated with herself for not being more focused.

She'd given Jules a much-needed night off but hadn't
taken one herself, preferring to lose herself in work ever
since the heartbreak of leaving Lake Tahoe.

She'd heard from a detective today about arresting
the woman who'd hijacked her social media, so it should
have felt like she had closure. But that conversation had
only made her realize how much more losing Miles had
hurt her than any damage a hacker could wreak.

At any rate, she'd *tried* to lose herself in work since
that had always been her escape. Her purpose. Her calling. She'd built it up in spite of the grief she'd had for
Zach, trusting the job to keep her grounded. But it didn't
provide a refuge for her now.

"I'll make you some tea before I go," Mrs. Santor continued, putting away the paperwork from the fragrance kit. "I know you don't want to talk about whatever happened on your travels, but trust me when I tell you that you need to take care of yourself."

And with a gentle squeeze to Chiara's shoulder, Mrs. Santor started the kettle to boil in the kitchen while Chiara tried to pull herself together. Maybe she should have confided in her longtime friend. She hadn't talked to Jules, either, refusing to give the people she loved the chance to comfort her.

For so many years she'd been an island—isolated, independent, and no doubt taking too much pride in the fact. But what good was pride when she felt so empty inside now?

Walking away from Miles was the hardest thing she'd ever done. Second only to the restraint it took every day—every hour—not to call or text him. She wondered if he'd returned to Mesa Falls by now or if he'd gone back to Rivera Ranch. Mostly, she wondered if he ever missed her or regretted the way they'd parted.

A moment later, Mrs. Santor returned with a steaming cup and set it before her. "I'm heading out now, hon. I'll see you Saturday, okay?"

Grateful for the woman's thoughtfulness, Chiara rose and hugged her. "Thank you."

Jules's mother hugged her back with the same warmth she gave her own daughter. "Of course. And don't work too hard."

When Mrs. Santor left, Chiara settled in for the evening. But just as she took a sip of her tea to ward off the loneliness of her empty house, the guard buzzed her phone from the gate downstairs. She picked up her device.

"Ms. Campagna, there's a Miles Rivera to see you."
Everything inside her stilled.

There'd been a time he could have had security toss her out of his home for invading his privacy, but instead, he'd listened to her explanation. For that alone, he deserved an audience now. But more than that, she couldn't resist the chance to see him again. She'd missed him so much.

"You can let him in," she answered, feelings tumbling over each other too fast for her to pick through them.

She'd been thinking about him and wishing she could see him. Now that he was here, was she brave enough to take a chance with him? She didn't want to let Miles go, either. What good did her pride do her if it left her feeling heartbroken and lonely?

Chiara resisted the urge to peek in a mirror, although she may have fluffed her hair a little and smoothed her dress. Who didn't want to look their best in front of the one who got away?

She rose from the seat to stand out on the balcony. Even though she was staring out at the spectacular view with her back to the house, Chiara could tell when Miles was close. The hairs on the back of her neck stood, a shiver of awareness passing over her. She pressed her lips together to ward off the feelings, reminding herself of what had happened to drive them apart.

"I've never seen such a beautiful view." The familiar rasp in his voice warmed her. Stirred her.

Turning on her heel, she faced him as he paced through the living area and out onto the balcony. With his chiseled features and deep blue eyes, his black custom suit that hinted at sculpted muscles and the lightly tanned skin visible at the open collar of his white shirt, he was handsome to behold.

But she remembered so many other things about him that were even more appealing. His thoughtfulness in watching out for her. His insistence she go to the police. His touch.

"Hello to you, too," she greeted him, remembering his fondness for launching right into conversation. "I'm surprised to see you here."

"I wanted to be sure you heard the news." He stepped closer until he leaned against the balcony rail with her. "That your harasser is behind bars."

She shouldn't be disappointed that this practical man would be here for such a pragmatic purpose, yet she couldn't deny she'd hoped for more than that. Should she tell him how much she'd missed him? How many times she'd thought about calling?

Absently, she drummed her fingernails against the polished railing, trying not to notice how close Miles's hands were to hers. "Yes. A detective called me this morning with some questions about Vivian Fraser from our time together at Brookfield. I didn't realize she worked for Alec now."

"Were you aware she was jealous of you?"

"No. I don't remember her well from Brookfield other than recalling she was a popular girl with a lot of friends. Our paths never crossed much, as she favored chess club and science over the art activities that I liked." She'd been stunned to hear that Alec's personal assistant had intercepted his messages and decided to "protect" Zach's memory for him by attempting to scare Chiara away from her search for answers.

But apparently there was a clear digital trail that led

to Vivian's personal computer, and she'd admitted as much to the police. The woman was in love with Alec and would do anything to protect him. She'd also done her best to keep other women away from him since they'd had an on-again, off-again relationship dating all the way back to high school. It was sad to think a promising young woman had gotten so caught up in wanting attention from a man that she'd given up her own dreams and identity in an effort to capture his notice.

"I breathed a whole lot easier once I heard the news," Miles said as he looked over the lights spread out below them now that the pink hues of sunset had faded. "I'm sure you did, too."

She couldn't help but glance over at his profile. The strong jaw and chin. The slash of his cheekbone. His lips that could kiss her with infinite tenderness.

"I guess." She spoke quickly once she realized she'd stared too long. "But the whole business with my blog and Vivian were distractions from my real purpose. I really went there to find out about Zach's final days."

She felt more than saw Miles turn toward her now. His eyes looking over her the way she'd studied him just a moment ago. Her heat beat faster as a soft breeze blew her white dress's hem against her legs, the silk teasing her already too-aware skin.

"I know you did, Chiara. And I'm sorry that I got in the way of what you were doing by not sharing what I knew as soon as I knew it." The regret and sincerity in his voice were unmistakable. "You deserved my full help and attention. And so did Zach."

Drawn by his words, she turned toward him now, and they faced one another eye to eye for the first time tonight. He seemed even closer to her now. Near enough to touch.

"I recognize that I probably should have been more understanding. Especially after the way you overlooked me trying to get into your personal files. I crossed a line more than you did." She hadn't forgotten that, and the unfairness of her response compared to his seemed disproportionate. "But I didn't know you when I sneaked into your office. Whereas—"

"The situations were completely different." He shook his head, not letting her finish her sentence. "You had every right to think I might have been a bad friend to Zach or even an enemy. But I knew you had his best interests at heart that day I kept quiet about the DNA. My only defense was that I wanted one more day with you."

Startled, she rewound the words in her mind, barely daring to hope she'd heard him right. "You—what?"

"I knew that once I told you the DNA results you'd have no reason to stay in Tahoe any longer." He touched her forearm. "And our time together had been so incredible, Chiara, I couldn't bear for it to end. I told myself that keeping quiet about it for a few more hours wouldn't hurt. I just wanted—" He shook his head. "It was selfish of me. And I'm sorry."

The admission wasn't at all what she'd expected. "I thought you were keeping secrets to hold me at arm's length. It felt like you didn't want to confide in me."

But this? His reason was far more compelling. And it shot right into the tender recesses of her heart.

"Far from it." A breeze ruffled Miles's hair the way she longed to with her fingers. His hand stroked up her arm to her shoulder. "Talking to you was the highlight of my week. And considering everything else that happened, you have to know how much it meant to me."

She melted inside. Absolutely, positively melted.

"Really?" She'd hoped so, until he'd walked away. But she could see the regret in his eyes now, and it gave her renewed hope.

"Yes, really." He stepped closer to her, one hand sliding around her waist while the other skimmed a few wind-tossed strands of hair from her eyes. "Chiara, I got burned so badly the last time I cared about someone that I planned to be a lot more cautious in the future. I figured if I took my time to build a safe, smart relationship, maybe then I could fall in love."

Her pulse skipped a couple of beats. She blinked up at him, hanging on his words. Trying not to sink into the feeling of his hands on her after so many days of missing him. Missing what they'd shared. Aching for more. For a future.

"I don't understand. Are you suggesting we didn't build a safe relationship?"

"I'm suggesting that whatever my intentions were, they didn't matter at all, because you showed up and we had the most amazing connection I've ever felt with anyone." His hold on her tightened, and she might have stepped a tiny bit closer because the hint of his aftershave lured her.

"I felt that, too," she admitted, remembering how that first night she'd felt like the whole world disappeared except for them. "The amazing connection."

"Right. Good." His lips curved upward just a hint at her words. "Because I came here tonight—why I *really* came here tonight—to tell you that I fell in love with you, Chiara. And if there's any way you can give me another chance, I'm going to do everything in my power to make you fall in love with me, too."

Her heart hitched at his words, which were so much more than she'd dared hope for—but everything she wanted. Touched beyond measure, she couldn't find her voice for a moment. And then, even when she did, she bit her lip, wanting to say the right thing.

"Miles, I knew when we were in the woods that day that I loved you." She laid her hand on his chest beside his jacket lapel, just over his heart. She remembered every minute of their time together. "I didn't even want to go back to the house afterward because it felt like our time together was ending, and I didn't want to lose you."

He wrapped her tight in his arms and kissed her. Slowly. Thoroughly. Until she felt a little weak-kneed from it and the promise it held of even more. When he eased back, she was breathing fast and clinging to him.

"You're not going to lose me. Not now. Not ever." His blue eyes were dark as midnight, the promise one she'd never forget.

It filled her with certainty about the future. Their future.

"You won't lose me, either," she vowed before freeing a hand to gesture to the view. "Not even if I have to leave all this behind to live on Rivera Ranch with you."

"You don't have to do that." He tipped his forehead to hers. "We can take all the time you want to talk about what makes most sense. Or hell, just what we want. I know you want to go back to art school one day, so we can always look at living close to a good program for you."

No one had ever put her first before, and it felt incredibly special to have Miles do just that. The possibilities expanded.

"You don't need to be at the ranch?" she asked, curious about his life beyond Mesa Falls. She wanted to learn everything about him.

"I've worked hard to make it a successful operation that runs smoothly. I've hired good people to maintain that, so even if I'm not there, the ranch will continue to prosper." He traced her cheek with his fingers, then followed the line of her mouth.

She sucked in a breath, wanting to seal the promise of their future with a kiss, and much, much more. Lifting her eyes to his, she read the same steamy thoughts in his expression.

"I'll be able to weigh the possibilities more after I show you how much I've missed you," she told him, capturing his thumb between her teeth.

With a growl that thrilled her, he lifted her in his arms and walked her inside the house.

She had a last glimpse of the glittering lights of the Hollywood Hills, but the best view of all was wherever this man was. Miles Rivera, her rancher hero, right here in her arms.

* * * * *

RICH, RUGGED RANCHER

JOSS WOOD

One

"So, have you bagged your cowboy yet?"

Seraphina Martinez whipped the rented convertible onto the open road leading to Blackwood Hollow Ranch and punched the accelerator, ignoring Lulu's squeal of surprise at the sudden burst of speed.

"Slow down, Fee. I don't want to die on a lonely road in East Texas," Lulu grumbled.

"Relax, it's an empty road, Lu," Fee replied, glad she'd wrangled her thick hair into two fat braids—as opposed to Lulu who was fighting, and losing, the war with the wind.

Lulu held her hair back from her face and glared at Fee. "I'm going to look like I've been dragged through a bush when we get there."

Fee shrugged.

Perfect makeup, perfect clothes, perfect hair…being a reality TV star took work, dammit.

"Well, have you?" Fee demanded.

"Found a cowboy? No, not yet," Lulu replied.

"What about the lawyer guy who seems to be everywhere we are lately?" Fee asked. While scouting filming locations for *Secret Lives of NYC Ex-Wives*, the attorney for the Blackwood estate had been everywhere they looked, keeping his lawyerly eye on Miranda Blackwood and the rest of the cast and crew.

"Kace LeBlanc?" Lu asked, aiming for super casual and missing by a mile.

Fee darted a look at her best friend, amused. Of course she had noticed the looks Lulu sent Kace when she didn't think anyone was looking. Lu thought the attorney was hot. And, with his unruly brown hair and those gorgeous brown eyes, he was…until he opened his mouth. Then he acted like she and her costars and the crew were going to break his precious town of Royal or something.

"The guy is a pill," Lulu said before sighing. "God, he's hot but he's so annoying."

Fee agreed but she also admired Kace's determination to look after the late Buck Blackwood's interests and to ensure the terms of his will were followed to the letter. And the terms of the will were, from the little she'd gleaned, astonishing. She couldn't blame his kids for being pissed off at Buck for leaving everything he owned to Fee's costar Miranda, who was his ex and as New York as she and Lulu were. It had to be a hard slap to their born-and-bred Texas faces.

If they'd scripted this story for *Secret Lives*, their viewers would think they were making it up—aging billionaire leaves much, much younger second wife everything at the expense of his children. Buck also, so she'd heard, had an illegitimate son and this news didn't seem to surprise anyone. Buck, apparently, had liked the ladies.

This plot twist was ratings gold, pure made-for-TV drama.

Lulu looked to her right, her attention captured by a herd of Longhorn cows.

"Did you ever live in Texas?" Lulu asked her, still holding her hair back with two hands.

Fee took some time to answer, trawling through her memories. Being an army brat and having a father who jumped at any chance to move, she'd lived all over the country and attended fourteen schools in twelve years. But she couldn't recall living in Texas.

"I think we did a stint in New Mexico," Fee replied. "But I was young. I don't remember much of it."

Lulu turned in her seat and Fee felt her eyes on her. "I'm still amazed at your excitement over visiting a new place. We've been doing this for years, Fee. Aren't you sick of all the traveling? Don't you miss your own bed?"

Fee sent her a quick smile. "I rent my apartment furnished, Lu. You know that I don't get attached to things or places." She might live in Manhattan but she wasn't as attached to the city as her co-stars were.

"Because you moved so often when you were a child."

"I learned that if you get attached, it hurts like hell when you have to leave." Fee shrugged. "So, it makes sense not to get attached."

"Do you think you'll ever settle down?"

That was a hell of a question. Maybe, possibly, she might one day find a town or city she didn't want to leave. But, because she was a realist, she knew that, while she might stay in a place a couple of months or a few years, she would probably end up moving on. It was what she did.

The grass was always greener around the next corner...

And if you didn't get attached, you couldn't get hurt, especially by people. Her nomadic parents and her own brief marriage to the philandering son of one of NYC's most famous families had taught her that.

She loved people, she did, but underneath her exuberant personality still resided a little girl who knew that relationships (and places) were temporary and believing that any commitment would last was crazy.

She was currently living in Manhattan, in a gorgeous but expensive fully furnished rental in Chelsea. Her practical streak hated the idea of renting when she could easily afford to buy an apartment but Manhattan wasn't a place where she could put down roots. When *Secret Lives* ended, she'd move on, but for now she was comfortable. Not settled but, yeah, temporarily okay with where she laid her head.

She was the captain of her own ship, the author of her own book. And if she was using *Secret Lives* to feather her own nest, to make bank, that was her business. She might be loud, frequently over-the-top, but she was also pragmatic and fully understood how quickly things could change. And if her situation did change—*Secret Lives* was popular now but that could change tomorrow—she wanted her nest to be well feathered.

Because, as she knew, moving from place to place, town to town, wasn't cheap.

And that was why she took every opportunity to maximize her little taste of fame: first with the line of accessories she'd created using her husband's famous last name. Her *Not Your Mama's Cookbook*, written last year, was still on the bestseller lists. Maybe she should think about doing another cookbook…or something else entirely.

It was something to think about.

"Have you decided on your Royal project yet?" Lulu asked her, breaking her train of thought.

"I have no idea what you are talking about," Fee answered, injecting a healthy amount of prim into her tone.

Lulu rolled her eyes. "You can't BS me, Fee. I know it

was you who organized giving last season's intern a make-over. Who set Pete, our lighting director, up with Dave, the sound guy. Who read the scriptwriter's—what was his name?—screenplay? Miranda might be our Mama Bear but you are our Little Miss Fix-It."

Fee wrinkled her nose. Little Miss Fix-It? She opened her mouth to speak then realized she couldn't argue the point. She did tend to identify a need and try to meet it.

"I don't know if I'll find anyone to fix in Royal. I think I'll take a break from meddling while I'm there."

Lulu's laughter danced on the wind. "Yeah, right. That's not going to happen."

Fee frowned at her. "What? I can back off!"

"You cannot!" Lulu retorted. "Honey, we're always getting into trouble because you can't leave a situation alone! We nearly got arrested when you jumped between those two guys fighting in Nero's, and we did get arrested when you—" Lulu bent her fingers to make air quotes "—*confiscated* that abused horse in Kentucky. You are constantly getting trolled on social media because you stand up for LGBT rights, women's rights, immigrants' rights. That's not a criticism, I admire your outspokenness, but you don't have to fight every fight, babe."

Fee knew that. But she also knew what it was like to have no one fighting in her corner, no one to rely on. She knew how it felt to feel invisible and when she stepped out of the shadows, how it felt to be mocked and bullied.

God, she'd come a long way.

"I guarantee you will find a project and you won't be able to resist meddling," Lulu told her, blue eyes laughing.

"Want to bet?" Fee asked her as they approached the enormous gates to what was Buck Blackwood's—now Miranda's—ranch. The gates to Blackwood Hollow appeared and she flung the car to the right and sped down the long driveway. Lu hissed and Fee grinned.

"What's the bet?" Lulu asked, gripping the armrest with white fingers. "And you drive like a maniac."

"You give me your recipe for Miss Annie's fried chicken for my next cookbook, if I decide to do another one." She'd been trying to pry Lulu's grandma's recipe from her since the first time Lulu fed her the delicious extra-crispy chicken at a small dinner five years earlier.

"She'll come back and haunt me." Lulu gasped, placing her hand on her chest. "I can't. Just like you can't stop yourself from meddling…"

"I can. And you know I can or else you wouldn't be hesitating…"

Lu narrowed her eyes at Fee as they approached a cluster of buildings that looked like a Hollywood vision of a working ranch. A sprawling mansion, guest cottages, massive barns. Despite visiting the spread days before, it was still breathtaking.

"There's the crew's van." Lulu pointed toward the far barn and Fee tapped the accelerator as she drove past the main house that went on and on and on.

"What could be so interesting down by the barns?" Fee wondered.

"That."

Fee looked where Lulu pointed and…holy crispy fried chicken. A man riding a horse at a gallop around a ring shouldn't be a surprise, but what a man and what a horse. Fee didn't know horses—she thought the speckled black-and-white horse might be a stallion—but she did know men.

And the cowboy was one hell of a man. Broad shoulders, muscled thighs, big biceps straining the sleeves of his faded T-shirt. She couldn't see the color of his hair or the lines on his face, the Stetson prevented her from making out the details, but his body was, like the horse, all sleek muscles and contained strength.

Hot, hot, hot…

He also looked familiar. Where did she know him from?

Fee took her foot off the accelerator and allowed the car to roll toward to where the other vehicles—the crew's van, a battered work truck and a spiffy SUV—were parked. All her attention was focused on the horse and rider, perfectly in sync. He seemed oblivious to his audience: a couple of cowboys sitting on the top railing of the fence and Miranda, Rafaela and Zooey standing with their arms on the white pole fence, their attention completely captured by the rider hurtling around the ring in a blur of hooves and dust.

God, he was heading straight for the fence. They'd either crash through it or he'd have to jump it because there was no way he'd be able to stop the horse in time.

Fee released the wheel and slapped her hands over her mouth, her attention completely caught by the drama in the paddock. She wanted to scream out a warning and was on the point of doing so when the rider yanked on the reins and the stallion braked instantly, stopping when his nose was just an inch from the fence.

That collision didn't happen, but another did when Fee's very expensive rented Audi convertible slammed into the bumper of the battered farm truck.

Lulu released a small shriek and Fee flung her arm out in a futile effort to keep Lulu from lurching forward. Their seat belts kept them in place but metal scraped against metal and steam erupted from her car as the hood got up close and personal with the back of the rust-covered truck.

"Are you okay?" Fee demanded, looking at Lulu.

"Fine," Lulu replied, then winced at the carnage in front of her. "Your car is toast, though—the hood is crumpled."

"I can see that." Fee nodded, releasing her seat belt. "How come it's always the crap cars that sustain the least damage?"

"That crap car is a seventy-two Chevy pickup I am in the process of restoring."

Fee yanked her eyes off Lulu and turned her head to the right, looking straight into faded denim covering strong thighs and a very nice package.

Strong, broad hands rested on his hips, the veins rising on his tanned forearms lightly covered with blond hair. The red T-shirt had faded to orange in places but the chest underneath it was broad and those biceps were big and bitable. His horse—had they jumped the fence to get to her so quickly?—laid its chin on the cowboy's shoulder but neither she, nor the cowboy, were distracted by the animal's interference in their conversation.

Fee kept her focus on him, utterly entranced by his strong face, the blond stubble covering his chiseled jaw, the thin lips, the long, straight nose. The feeling of familiarity coalesced into certainty, she'd seen him before, this cowboy—here at Blackwood Hollow a few days before—but she couldn't recall his name. Probably because he'd just fried most of her brain cells.

She wanted to see his eyes; no, she needed to see his eyes. On impulse, Fee clambered up to stand on her car seat.

God he was tall. Fee pushed the rim of his Stetson up with her finger, her eyes clashing with the deepest, saddest, green-gold-gray eyes.

Hard eyes, angry eyes, sad, sad eyes.

Fee couldn't decide what she wanted to do more, hug him or jump him.

Save the horse and ride the cowboy, indeed.

* * *

Clint Rockwell was a guy of few words but if Buck Blackwood were magically resurrected, he'd have had more than a few to hurl at his friend and mentor's head. What the hell had he been thinking to ask Clint to mind the property during his long illness and after his death?

Since Buck's funeral, Clint had been coming over to Blackwood Hollow a few times a week, to check on the hands and to exercise Buck's demon horse, Jack.

He and Jack were finally starting to bond and their skills were improving. Clint lifted his hand to hold Jack's cheek, enjoying the puffs of horse breath against his neck.

Animals were cool; people were not.

People hurt people—and sometimes things, his pickup being a case in point. Ignoring Jack, Clint walked over to the hood of the Audi convertible and dropped to his haunches to inspect the damage to his pickup. He didn't much care about the damage to the convertible, they were dime a dozen, but his truck was vintage and worth a pretty penny.

Hey, Rock, if I don't make it, finish my truck for me. Only original parts, man, gold and cream.

You are going to make it because if you don't, I'm going to paint it pink and white, Clint had told him, his hand in the hole in Tim's chest, trying to stem the river of blood soaking his hand, Tim's clothing and the dirt road beneath them.

They'd both known Clint's optimism was a lie, that Tim needed blood and a surgeon and that he was out of time.

I'll haunt you if you do anything stupid to my baby, Tim had muttered.

This accident probably qualified as a haunting.

Hell, Clint didn't sleep anyway, so Tim was welcome to pop in for a chat. His army ranger buddies were the only people Clint liked being around for any length of time, the only people on the planet who understood. They'd seen what he had, had watched men they loved be blown apart, women and children die, buildings being ravaged and lives destroyed.

They got him.

Civilians didn't.

Oh, the people in this town tried, sure. No man with his money and property ever had to be lonely if he didn't want to be. He wanted to be. His army days were behind him and he was now a rancher and oilman—more rancher than oilman, truth be told. His land and animals were what mattered.

Shaking off his thoughts, Clint stood up, automatically using his good leg to take his weight. He had to stop doing that; he had to start treating his prosthetic as another leg but, shit, it was hard. Leaving the force had been hard, losing a limb had nearly killed him and being forced to deal with people, civilians, was the cherry on his crap sundae.

Clint turned and cursed when he saw he was the focus of much attention and quickly, and automatically, took in all the salient details. Since he was still ignoring the driver of the convertible—he wasn't ready to deal with her yet—he turned his attention to the passenger. Sporting glossy black hair with dark eyes, she'd left the car and was standing with Miranda Blackwood, Buck's ex-wife. With them was also a fresh-faced beauty and an Italian bombshell who reminded him of one of Grandpa's favorite actresses, Sophia Loren.

The four women, Buck's ex-wife and her reality TV co-stars, watched him with avid interest. They looked as out of place as he would on a catwalk, their spiked heels digging into the grass, designer sunglasses covering their eyes.

The Blackwood ranch hands couldn't keep their eyes off them…

He uttered a low, sharp order for them to get back to work and they hopped off the fence with alacrity, tossing admiring looks at the New Yorkers as they ambled off.

The next problem was to get the cars untangled so he could accurately assess the damage to Tim's truck. But first he had to take care of Jack: animals first, things later.

Clint called out to a hand and when he jogged back to where Clint was standing, Clint passed him Jack's reins. "Can you cool him down, then brush him for me?"

"Sure, boss."

Clint didn't correct him since he was, by Buck's decree, the temporary boss. And ordering people around wasn't something new to him; he'd been the owner–operator of Rockwell Ranch since he was eighteen and a lieutenant in Delta Force. Despite their enormous wealth, thanks to ranching and business acumen and large deposits of oil, serving was family tradition: his great grandfather saw action in France in 1917, his grandfather fought the Japanese in the Philippines. His father did two years in the military but never saw any action. His dad didn't see much of anything, having died shortly before Clint's fifth birthday.

Anyway, it felt natural to join the army, and then it felt natural to become one of the best of the best.

Excellence was what he did.

Jack stepped on his foot as he walked away—bastard horse—and Clint didn't react. If he'd been alone, he'd have told Jack he'd lost his leg above the knee and having his foot stood on barely registered on his pain-o-meter but there were people about. He never discussed his prosthetic leg, ever.

Mostly because he was allergic to pity and he was terrified of people thinking he was weak. He might be half the man he'd once been but he'd rather die than allow people to coddle him.

He didn't need anybody or anything…not anymore.

But he did need this damn car moved.

"Look, I'm sorry, I lost focus."

She sounded more defensive than sorry, Clint decided as he walked back to the driver's door of the Audi. The driver was now sitting on the top of the front seat, brand-new cowboy boots on the white leather. Clint started there, at those feet, and slowly made his way upward. Now that the red haze had lifted from his vision—he was still mad as hell but he was in control—he could take in the details.

Holy crap…

Slim legs in skin-tight blue jeans, curvy hips and a teeny waist he was sure he could span with his hands. She wore a lacy, button-down shirt and a heap of funky necklaces. Two thick braids, deep brown at the top and lighter at the ends, rested on a fantastic pair of breasts.

He lifted his eyes to her face, his mouth dry. Yep, she had a rocking body but her face was 100 percent gorgeous. A stubborn chin, a mouth made for kissing, high cheekbones and merry, mischievous, naughty eyes—deep brown—framed by long, long lashes and a cocky pair of eyebrows.

A straw Stetson covered her head.

She might be pint-sized but Clint just knew every inch of her was trouble

He jerked his head sharply. "Move."

She cocked her head and sent him a slow smile. "No."

Okay, admittedly he hadn't had a lot of interaction with people lately but when he used his don't-mess-with-me voice, people generally hustled. "What?"

"Say please."

Clint stared at her, not sure he'd heard her correctly. Shaking his head, he tried again. "Lady, move."

The smile grew sweeter. And deadlier. "No."

What the everlasting…

"Have you heard of the phrases *please* and *thank you*?" she asked, cocking her head.

She was lecturing him on manners? She'd dinged his truck, probably putting back his restoration by months and months, had barely apologized herself and then had the balls to throw his manners in his face?

Red haze descending again, he didn't trust himself to speak so Clint took the next easiest option. Stepping up to the car, he swiftly slid one arm under her knees, the other around her slim back and swung her off her perch.

But instead of placing her feet on the ground, he held her to his chest, fighting the wave of lust running through him. There was something about the soft, fragrant give of a woman, the curve of her hip beneath his fingers, the softness of her breast pushing into his chest. Her minty breath, the surprise in those deep dark eyes.

Soft, sexy lips he desperately wanted to taste…

God, he needed sex. It had been a while…another thing that changed when he lost his leg. He hated pity, from others and loathed a woe-is-me attitude but experience had taught him that normal women, women who weren't loons and gold diggers, weren't crazy about one one-legged guys with too many scars to count. His girlfriend sure as hell hadn't.

"So, this is comfortable," she purred, looking as relaxed as if she was stretched out on a lounger by a sparkling pool, margarita in her hand.

Did anything faze her?

Wanting to find out, Clint loosened his grip on her and she fell a few inches before he caught her again. Instead of squealing she just tightened her arms around his neck and those eyes, the color of his favorite dark chocolate, met his. "You wouldn't drop me."

"Watch me." Knowing there was a half decimated, now loosely packed hay bale behind him, he whipped her around and released her. Her face reflected her horror and anger as she braced to hit the hard ground. When her pretty butt landed on the hay, her eyes widened and her comical what-just-happened expression almost made him smile.

But he didn't. Because smiling wasn't something he did anymore.

Pulling his eyes off his faux cowgirl, he hopped into the convertible, cranked the engine and released the brake. Slapping the car into Reverse, he pulled away from his truck and stared down at the dashboard, noticing the flashing warning lights. Water, oil, temperature were all going nuts. Yep, she wasn't going anywhere, anytime soon.

Not his problem…

Clint cut the engine and exited the car. Ignoring the tiny woman who was trying to extract herself from the inside of the hay bale, he walked over to his truck and slapped his hand on his hip. It wasn't as bad as he'd feared. The tailgate was damaged but he was pretty sure he could find another. The lights were broken but he knew a guy who had spares. It would cost him but he could afford to pay for the damage.

Actually, he should just get the peanut to pay. Judging by the rocking diamond ring on her right hand and the fat diamond studs she wore in her ears, she could afford to pay the bill out of pocket rather than forcing him to haggle with an insurance agency.

He tossed a look over his shoulder at her. "I expect you to pay for the repairs. Twenty grand should cover it." Twenty thousand was ten times more than he needed but he figured she should pay for inconveniencing him. "I don't want to wait for the insurance company, so you can pay me and fight with them."

Her head jerked up and she pushed up the brim of her cowboy hat to glare at him. "What?"

"I want twenty K. Preferably in cash."

Those eyes hardened. "Are you off your meds? I'm not paying you twenty grand! You could buy a new truck for less than that."

Sure, but could he buy a 1972 Chevy pickup with an original, hardly used engine, original seats and fixtures? Not damn likely.

"You can find me at Rockwell Ranch. Don't make me come looking for you," Clint warned her as he walked around the hood of his truck to the driver's door. He climbed in, grabbing the steering wheel and pulling himself up, his upper body strength compensating for his missing limb. Slamming the door closed, he rested his arm on the window, surprised to see she was still glaring at him, utterly unintimidated.

Now that was a surprise because Clint knew his hard face, gruff voice and taciturn attitude scared most people off.

Instead of being frightened, she stomped over to him, pieces of hay stuck in her braid. Intrigued to see what she would do, or say, he held her hot gaze.

"You need a lesson in manners."

"Probably. I also need sex. Are you offering that too?"

Instead of blushing or throwing her hands up in the air, insulted, she narrowed her eyes. "In your dreams, cowboy. Who do you think—"

"Who are you?" he interrupted her, purely to be ornery.

"Fee… Seraphina Martinez."

Fee suited her. Seraphina didn't.

And that mouth. It was sassy and sensuous and made for sex. Talking? Not so much.

"Bring the money to my ranch—don't make me come looking for you," Clint told her, thinking he'd better leave before he did something stupid, like using his own mouth to cut off the tirade that was, obviously, coming.

Shit, he was losing it.

"I'm ten miles down the road. You'll see the gates." Clint cranked the engine and placed his hand on the gear stick. He tapped his Stetson with two fingers.

"Ma'am," he said, purely to irritate her.

Annoyance and frustration jumped into her eyes. "Don't you 'ma'am' me! I *will* get you to learn some manners."

Hell, if she was under him, naked, he'd learn anything she wanted him to. *Enough now, Rock, drive off.*

"Honey, I don't do people so I don't do manners. I just need my twenty K."

"When pigs fly," Fee muttered, her hands on those curvy hips. Clint looked at her mouth again and fought the urge to leave the car, haul her into his arms and taste it. To inhale her sweet scent and pull her into his—he looked down—rock-hard erection.

Over the roar of his engine, he heard one of the women shout across to the fake cowgirl. "Is he going to be your next project, Fee?"

Fee looked at him and her smile chilled him to his core. "You know what? I rather think he is."

What the hell did she mean by that?

Time to go.

Clint slammed his pickup into Reverse, conscious that all the New Yorkers were still staring at him. But he only wanted to see the brunette with the smart mouth and tempting curves in his rearview mirror. She was sexy as hell and, because he wasn't a total idiot, he'd noticed her attraction to him.

Clint barreled down the driveway and tossed his Stetson onto the empty seat next to him. He'd seen her checking him out and suspected she liked what she'd seen, up to a point. He'd worked hella hard to build his core, chest and back muscles. Women liked his top half but, these days, his bottom half caused him problems.

Hell, both the women—his mom and his girlfriend—he'd ever loved had been unable to come to terms with his disability...

The memories rolled back and Clint forced himself to face them. On returning from Afghanistan, he'd spent a couple of months in hospital recovering after his amputation and when he got back to the ranch, he'd spent a few more months in bed, sleeping and smoking and drinking.

Carla, his long-time girlfriend, had immediately moved in to take care of him and she'd run around, waiting on him hand and foot. It didn't matter to her that he could afford to hire teams of nurses, doctors and physiotherapists. Family money, lots and lots of money, gave him access to the best health care on the planet but Carla only allowed the bare minimum of people to have access to him.

She'd insisted on fussing over him herself, coddling and mothering him. But, as his depression lifted, he realized that he didn't like the flabby, bloated, unhealthy man he saw in the mirror. He'd always been a fitness fanatic and because he was sick of feeling sick and miserable, he turned two rooms of his ranch house into a state-of-the-art gym.

As he got fitter, and more adept with his prosthetic, he became more independent and Carla had mentally, and physically, retreated. And when his sex drive finally returned, she'd retreated some more. When he'd finally convinced her that he was well enough, strong enough, for sex and taken his prosthetic off, she bolted.

Never to be seen again.

Thanks to his frequent absences due to his career in the military, they'd drifted apart and his accident pulled them back together again. She adored his dependence on her, loved being so very needed and had he stayed that way, she might've stuck around. But being weak wasn't something Clint did. Weakness wasn't part of his DNA.

His sex life didn't improve after she left. He'd tried a couple of one-night stands and neither were successful. One woman left when she saw his leg, another, the next morning, acted like she'd done him the biggest favor by sleeping with him and Clint decided that climaxes with strangers weren't worth the humiliation.

It had been two years since he got laid and, yeah, he missed sex. And when he met someone he was instantly, ridiculously attracted to, as he'd been to that brunette back there, he missed it more than ever.

But sex was just sex; he wouldn't die from not getting any.

He didn't think.

Clint felt his phone vibrating in the back pocket of his jeans and lifted his butt cheek to pull it out. Glancing down at the screen, he saw the Dallas area code and recognized the number as one of his mother's.

The mother he no longer spoke to.

Clint briefly wondered why she, or more likely her PA or another lackey, was calling. It had been years since they'd last spoken but he didn't answer the call. He had nothing to say to his mom. Not anymore…

Mila had blown into the hospital to visit with him before his operation and he'd been cynically surprised by her show of support as she'd never been an attentive, involved mother.

Back in his room after the operation that took his leg, he'd hadn't felt strong enough to deal with his intense news-anchor mother and he'd pretended to still be under the anesthetic, hoping she'd go away. He'd just wanted the world to leave him alone but his hearing hadn't disappeared along with his leg and Mila's softly spoken words drifted over to him.

So, I'm here, he's still out so what now?

I've arranged for the press to photograph you leaving the hospital after visiting your war-hero son. Clint had recognized the voice as Greg's, Mila's business manager, whom he'd met a few times over the years. He was, so Mila said, the power behind Mila's rise to being one of the most famous, powerful and respected women in Dallas.

So, try to look worried, distressed. And proud.

I'm going to have to act my ass off, Mila had moaned. *He's, like...repulsive.*

Jesus, Mila, he's your son, Greg had said, sounding, to his credit, horrified.

I like pretty and I like perfect. He's never been perfect but before he went off to play at war, he was at least pretty, Mila had retorted. *Thank God he has that girlfriend because I'm certainly not prepared to be his nurse.*

Wow. Her words laid down just another hot layer of pain.

With her words bouncing off his brain, Clint had slipped into sleep and a six-month depression. Carla and his mother were the reasons he'd worked his butt off to become, as much as possible, the person he was before the surgery. He never wanted to be dependent on anyone ever again, not for help, sex or even company. Carla had wanted to help him too much, his mother not at all, but Clint was happy to be shot of them both.

All he wanted was for the few people he chose to interact with to see past his injury to the man he was. And he couldn't do that if he flaunted his prosthetic so he never, ever allowed anyone to see his bionic leg.

And if giving up sex was the price he paid for his independence then he'd happily live with the lack of below-the-belt action. Nothing was more important to him than his independence. And his pride.

But some days, like today, a woman came along who made him wonder, who made him burn. But he was nothing if not single-minded, and like the others he'd felt a fleeting attraction to, he wouldn't act on it.

No woman was ever worth the hassle.

Two

Fee slid into a booth in Royal's diner and nodded her appreciation. Every time she walked through the doors, she had the same thought: that this was what a diner should look like: 1950s-style decor, red fake-leather booths, black-and-white checkerboard linoleum floor and the suggestion that gossip flowed through here like a river.

She rather liked Royal, Texas. It was, obviously, everything New York City wasn't—a slow-paced small town with space to breathe.

From being yanked from town to town with her parents, Fee had honed the ability to immediately discern whether a town would, temporarily, suit her or not. She'd hated Honolulu—weird, right?—and loved Pensacola, tolerated Tacoma and loved Charleston. But something about Royal called to her; she felt at ease here.

She would never belong anywhere—Manhattan was where she'd chosen to work and socialize but it still wasn't home, she didn't think any place would be—but Royal was intriguing.

Strange that this small town with its wide, clean streets and eclectic mix of people and shops was where she felt more relaxed than she had in a long, long time.

Fee grinned. If she kept on this mental train, soon she would be thinking she could live on a ranch and raise cows. She snorted and looked down at her manicured fingers and soft hands. This from a girl who believed meat came from the supermarket and eggs from cardboard cartons?

Now, crotchety Clint Rockwell looked like he was born to ride the range. The man was one sexy cowboy. Pity he had the personality of a rabid raccoon. Fee put her hand on the box lying on the table and grinned.

Twenty thousand to fix a heap of rust? Ok, that wasn't fair, it was vintage truck and probably rare but the repair, from her research, wouldn't cost that much! She knew she was being hustled; she wasn't the village idiot.

Well, she might be a reality TV star but she was a pragmatic reality TV star and she didn't hand out money like it was M&M's.

If he hadn't been such a snot she might've tossed in a few extra grand to compensate him for the inconvenience but the guy had taken jerk to a whole new level…

He needed to be brought down a peg or six.

Fee heard the door to the diner swing open and watched as Lulu threaded her way through the tables to fall into the seat opposite her. Like her, Lulu had also dressed down in jeans. In her case, they were topped with a simple white, thigh-length jersey, a brightly colored scarf in a complicated knot around her neck. Lu slapped a paper folder on the table between them and frowned at the board game Fee had purchased from the toy shop down the road. It was a game to teach kids about money and, importantly, the notes inside looked remarkably real.

"I'm sure we can find something to do in Royal that doesn't include board games," Lulu stated.

Fee grinned. "I'm not playing with you. I'm going to play with someone else."

"You're going to pay him in toy money?" Lulu caught on instantly. That was one of the many reasons they were best friends. "Oh, clever."

Fee put her hands together as if to pray and bowed her head. "Thank you. Did the *Secret Lives* researcher dig up any information on Clint Rockwell?" she demanded, pulling the folder to her. "I mean, I don't think he's one of Royal's leading lights—not with a personality like his— but maybe he made the papers because he did something stupid. I can see him busting up a bar or racking up speeding tickets, maybe breaking and entering…"

"You have a hell of an imagination," Lulu commented, thanking the waitress when she offered coffee.

Fee was certain that Clint Rockwell was not the boy next door, not someone who was part of the Chamber of Commerce or a member of the illustrious Texas Cattleman's Club.

He was an outsider, a loner, someone who didn't do group events. Someone mysterious, possibly dangerous…

Fee flipped open the folder and looked down to see a photograph of Rockwell looking very un-farmy. In this photograph, his short dark-blond hair was covered by a tan beret immediately identifying him as an army ranger. He wore a dark blue dress uniform with about a million medals on his chest, including a Purple Heart.

Well, she'd gotten one thing right—as part of that elite regiment, he was definitely dangerous.

Fee was about to move the photograph to the side when

she heard the waitress sigh. Fee looked up to find the young girl's eyes firmly on the photograph. Fee couldn't blame her for taking a moment. Rockwell, looking like Captain America in his dress blues, was definitely sigh worthy.

"It's so sad."

Fee exchanged a look with Lulu and frowned. "What's so sad?" Lulu asked the waitress, whose name tag stated she was Julie.

Julie gestured to the photograph with her coffee carafe. "Clint Rockwell. Poor guy."

Ooh, gossip. Fee leaned back, her full attention on the waitress. "Why? What happened to him?"

"He's a Rockwell, so obviously there's no shortage of cash. Like his daddy, his granddaddy and his granddaddy before him, Clint is an oilman and a rancher. But he leases his oil fields and occupies himself with his ranch. And with coordinating Royal's volunteer fire department."

Fee's head spun with all the information. She held up a hand. "He's a fireman too?"

"Apparently, he did some firefighting course in California before he enlisted." Julie pulled her eyebrows together, looking a little confused. "Where was I? Right, his daddy died when he was young, really young, and he and his mama don't talk."

Yeah, that was sad. Her parents might have hauled her from pillar to post and back to pillar but they were now settled in Florida and she saw them occasionally. In fact, she was heading there shortly to spend Christmas with them. They weren't super close but she knew she was loved, in an abstract kind of way.

"The Rockwells are a Royal institution, a founding family and really rich."

"How rich?" Fee asked, as direct as always.

"Mega," Julie replied.

And he was stiffing her for twenty grand? The bastard!

"What else can you tell me about him?" Fee asked, her temper bubbling.

"He lost his leg in a helicopter crash. That's how he earned his Purple Heart. His leg was mangled. His whole unit was seriously injured. Apparently, the helicopter crashed in an enemy-controlled area and he, and another guy, held off the bad guys until reinforcements arrived. Half of his unit survived, but Clint lost his leg."

Fee frowned at Julie, not understanding. "He lost his leg?" She'd noticed he walked with a slight limp but never suspected he wore a prosthetic.

Julie nodded. "Yeah. That's why he left the army." Julie shrugged. "Ever since he got back, he's become a bit of a recluse and doesn't have much to do with Royal residents, except for the volunteer firefighters. And he never, ever talks about his tours, his regiment or his injury. Like, *ever*."

Someone called Julie and she sent them an apologetic smile. "Sorry, got to go."

Fee transferred her gaze to Lulu, who looked equally disbelieving. "He's disabled?"

"He looked plenty abled," Fee replied. "I would never have thought…"

"Holy crap." Lulu rested her hand on her heart. "Hot, brave and sexy—I think I might be a little in love with him."

Fee felt a surge of jealousy and did an internal eye roll. What was wrong with her? Flipping the folder closed—why had they sent the researcher to the local library when the source of good information could be pumped for details over coffee?—Fee stared out of the window and watched the activity on the street outside.

Did this information change anything? She was as much a sucker for a wounded war hero as the next person and she had a million questions. Why was he a loner? How had he managed to master his prosthetic leg to be able to ride as he did? Why was he holding her up for twenty grand if he was loaded? But mostly, she just needed to figure out whether this changed her plans.

If he hadn't lost his leg, she wouldn't have hesitated to confront him and toss the fake money in his face. But should this revelation really hold her back? Her thinking she should go easy on him because he'd lost a leg was insulting in the extreme. He'd already proven he could more than handle her, and lost leg or not, the guy needed to learn some manners.

"You're still going to confront him," Lulu stated, sounding resigned.

"Damn straight I am."

"He's pretty intimidating, Fee," Lulu said, concern in her voice. "I'm not sure whether you should go out to his ranch alone."

Fee instinctively shook her head. "He's not going to hurt me, Lu. Oh, his tongue might raise some blisters, but he'd never raise a hand to me."

"How do you know?"

Fee lifted both shoulders and ran her hand through her hair. "I have a strong gut feeling about him. He's not dangerous...sad, confused, bitter, sure. But he won't hurt me."

Lulu sighed. "And you see his lack of manners and his rudeness as a challenge."

"Sure. Someone needs to set him straight. I'm sorry he lost a leg but it doesn't give him the right to act like an ass."

Lulu pinned her to her seat with hard eyes. "Oh, I know you, Seraphina Martinez—and I know what this is really about. Yes, bad manners and rudeness annoy you, but you also see him as a challenge. You want to know if you can be the one who can break through to him, make him more sociable."

Fee avoided eye contact, waiting for Lulu to drop the topic. But her friend wasn't done.

"I don't think he's going to like being one of your projects, Fee," Lulu told her, worry coating every word. "He's not going to bend under the force of your personality and if he wanted friends, he would make his own. You don't need to rescue every stray who comes across your path, Seraphina."

Lulu's use of her full name was a solid clue to her seriousness. Fee wrinkled her nose. "Do I really do that?"

"You know you do! You have the strongest rescue gene of anyone I know! He's a veteran, you have a soft spot for soldiers because you grew up on an army base. Add hero and wounded to the mix and you want to wrap him up in a blanket and coddle him."

"I'd rather unwrap him and do him," Fee admitted. She pulled a face and forced the words out. "I'm crazy attracted to him, Lu."

"Any woman, and more than a few guys, would be," Lulu replied. "And that's okay. Although you're not big on one-night stands or brief flings, if you want to sleep with him, do. But when he puts his clothes back on, don't try to fix him, Fee. Respect his right to be alone, to choose how he interacts with the world. From the sound of it, he's gone through hell and back. If he wants to be left alone, he's earned the right." Lulu gripped her hand and continued. "Fixing him might make you feel better but it's not about you, it's about him."

Lu's words smacked her in the chest. She stared down at the folder, her breath a little ragged. She did like the feeling of accomplishment she got when she managed to solve someone else's problems. Sometimes it felt like she was filling in pieces of herself. But Lu was right, this wasn't a makeover, or a blind date, or a rescued horse. This was a man of pride, honor and discipline who'd served his country with distinction. He'd trained hard, sacrificed much, seen and experienced situations no one should have to see and she had no right to make judgments about his life. Or to presume she knew what was best for him.

Fee pulled in a deep breath and met Lulu's eyes. "Okay."

"Okay…what?"

"Okay, I won't try to fix him, to rescue him from his lonely life," Fee clarified. "But I *am* going to confront him about his rudeness and his lack of manners. You can be a hermit without being an ass."

Lulu slapped her hand against her forehead and groaned. "And are you still going to pay him off with toy money?"

Fee nodded. "Damn right I am."

"And are you going to sleep with him?"

She couldn't lie, she was very tempted. Fee lifted one shoulder and both her hands. "He's tempting, so tempting, and I shouldn't…"

"But?"

Fee didn't want to be attracted to him, and as God and Lulu knew, she wasn't in the habit of falling into bed with guys on a whim—or at all—but she didn't think she could resist the sexy, sad, rude cowboy. "But if he asks me, I just might."

Clint hated surprise visitors—he never wanted to be caught without his prosthetic or using crutches—so he'd installed cameras all over the ranch and had them wirelessly connected so they sent an alert to his phone whenever he had company. He grabbed his cell from the back pocket of his jeans, pulled up the screen connecting him to his camera feed and saw another convertible—red, this time—flying up his driveway.

Yep, she was back.

Clint, walking a mare that had colic, whistled and when Darren's head popped out from a stall, he jerked his head. "Can you carry on walking Belle for me?"

Darren's eyes widened with concern. "LT, I have no experience with horses and this one is, so I hear, one of your best."

Clint smiled at the familiar nickname for *lieutenant*. "It's just walking, Darren, and we're civilians now—you can call me Clint. If you run into trouble with her or you think something is wrong, just yell for Brad. He'll hear you and take over."

Brad, his foreman, didn't always agree with his policy of hiring out-of-work veterans instead of experienced hands but Clint insisted that learning to muck out stalls and fix fences didn't require experience. The ranch needed people who wanted to work and there were so many vets needing to find a way to support themselves and their families.

And, as he knew, open skies, fresh air and animals were a great way to deal with the memories of war.

"I'll be back as soon as I can."

Darren nodded, took the reins and led the horse to the entrance of the stable. Clint broke into a jog, heading for his dirt bike parked just outside. Gunning the accelerator, he headed back to his house, cutting around the back of the stables to arrive at the main house at the same time she did.

They both cut their engines at the same time and Clint rested his forearms on the handlebars of his bike, watching her from behind his dark glasses and the brim of his

Stetson. The sun was starting to dip and he could probably ditch both but they provided a shield he badly needed…

He couldn't let her know how attracted he was to her, how he wanted nothing more than to take her inside and get her naked and horizontal.

Actually, he just needed her naked because vertical worked too.

Clint watched as she shoved an expensive pair of designer shades into her hair, the arms raking her loose curls off her face. She wore less makeup today than she had yesterday. Her lips were a pale pink instead of bright red and her outfit consisted of a cranberry-colored jersey that worked well with her creamy skin and those brilliant dark eyes.

God, she was hot. He couldn't invite her into the house: first, because his crutches were leaning against the wall in the hallway—he'd put on his leg while sitting on the bench in the hallway early this morning—and second because he wasn't sure he could resist her.

Fee opened the door of the rental and climbed out, shapely legs in tight blue jeans tucked into low-heeled, knee-high boots. The jersey clung to her breasts and curves of her hips and Clint felt all the moisture leave his mouth.

He'd stormed houses filled with terrorists in Afghanistan, had faced down a Somalian warlord and protected his guys while they waited for an evac after the crash but he'd never experienced such a dry mouth.

But this woman, with her black-brown hair and expressive eyes, managed to achieve what a dozen treacherous situations hadn't…

And that scared the crap out of him, which added another layer to his grouch.

"Have you got my money?" he demanded, staying where he was.

"Hello, Fee, how are you? Did you find the place okay?" Fee singsonged, calling attention yet again to his lack of manners.

Tough. He didn't have the time and energy to play nice; he just wanted her to be gone before he made a stupid suggestion like, "Let's go to bed."

Because that was a disaster waiting to happen. He'd have to explain he was missing a limb and then, if she didn't rabbit, he'd have to wait and see if she could deal with his stump and scars.

Such fun...

Nope, it was a game he was better off not playing.

"You're wasting my time, Martinez," Clint warned, dismounting the bike and pocketing the keys. He waited for her at the bottom of the stairs leading up to his wraparound porch and the front door. He wouldn't invite her inside but they could, at least, get out of the sun.

Instead of following him, Fee placed her hands on her hips and tipped her head back to look at the house he still thought of as his Grandpa's—the place where he'd visited the family patriarch every summer from the time of his dad's death when Clint was five until he turned eighteen and enlisted.

At the time he hadn't cared where the army sent him, as long as it kept him away from his mother's hounding to study law or something equally boring. He couldn't have known that shortly after he enlisted, his beloved grandpa would die, and Clint would become the fifth Rockwell to own the land.

Grandpa Rockwell always said that he didn't want the land to be a burden, to be a noose around his neck. He'd been the biggest supporter of his military career so Clint hadn't felt the need to rush home when he died, comfortable to place the ranch in Brad's capable hands until his return.

He'd always preferred the ranching side of his inheritance so he'd leased his oil fields. Years later, he was still happy for someone else to deal with that side of the business.

"I like your house," Fee said, and he frowned at the note of surprise in her voice. "It's big, obviously, like everything else in Texas, but it's not ostentatious. I don't do ostentatious."

"Says the girl driving another fast, expensive convertible," he drawled.

Fee looked back at the car and her husky laughter surprised him. "Touché. But I'm a real gearhead and I don't get to drive as often as I'd like to."

"I'm sure all the residents of New York City are eternally grateful for that fact, because you have a lead foot," Clint said. "And how did you charm the rental company into trusting you with another fast car after your crash yesterday?"

"I apologized sincerely and asked them nicely," Fee retorted, her eyes flashing with irritation.

"You didn't apologize to me," Clint pointed out.

"I tried to! But then you started barking orders and tossing me into hay bales!"

Clint lifted his index finger. "One. One hay bale."

Fee rolled her eyes. "Whatever… Anyway, you should try this thing called charm or, this is a radical idea so beware, a smile. Oh, your face might crack but I think you'll survive the experience."

Clint felt the corner of his mouth twitch with amusement. He loved her sassy mouth and now rather liked the fact that he didn't intimidate her. He walked up onto the porch and gestured to a cluster of outdoor furniture to the left of the door.

"Take a seat."

Fee's winged eyebrows shot up. "Ooh, manners. There's hope for you yet."

"Don't bet on it," Clint replied, putting his hands into the back pockets of his jeans. He watched as she sat on the arm of one wicker chair, casually draping one gorgeous leg over the other and tucking her foot behind her calf. Such a female, sexy movement, full of grace and charm.

Clint waited her out, knowing silence was usually a good way to hurry the conversation along by forcing the other person to talk. But Fee confounded him again by ignoring his scowl and silence, seemingly content to watch the mares frolicking in the paddock closest to the house.

Why couldn't this woman do what he expected her to?

Clint rocked on his heels, his eyes constantly dropping to her lips, wondering whether she tasted as spicy as she sounded. He eventually broke their silence. "Why are you here, Seraphina?"

Fee flashed a smile and leaned down to tuck her hand into her very large leather bag—big enough to carry a change of clothes, a bag of groceries and a saddle or two—and pulled out a couple of rolls of cash. He saw a fifty-dollar bill under the rubber band of one and a hundred-dollar bill around the other. He sucked in his breath.

He'd been annoyed yesterday and tossed out twenty thousand as a figure, hoping to annoy her. But, judging by the cash she'd brought along, she'd taken him seriously.

He couldn't take her money, not now and not ever.

Clint was about to tell her to put it away when he noticed the rolls seemed irregular, that not all the edges of the bills lined up. If he hadn't been so distracted by her, he would've immediately noticed that something was wrong with the roll, that her sweet, innocent expression was as fake as hell.

Oh, hell no, she wouldn't dare...

He held out his hand and instead of handing the first one over, she threw it at his chest. He caught the first one, then the second and tucked it under his arm, snapping the rubber band off the first.

Yep, as he thought. A real note covering fake money. Toy money...

Clint felt a bubble of laughter rise within him, tried to swallow it and failed. When his husky-from-lack-of-use chuckle filled the space between them, he was as surprised as Fee.

He couldn't remember the last time he'd laughed...

He heard Fee's smothered laugh, a cross between a hiccup and a giggle. And because he wanted to taste his laughter on her lips, because he wanted to taste her, Clint moved quickly and, after placing his hands on either side of the arm of the chair, bent down and kissed her.

And immediately wished he hadn't.

Because, as their lips touched, as her mouth opened and her fingers came up to touch the scruff on his jaw, he knew he'd never be satisfied with just one kiss...

He wanted more. Much, much more.

He was a grouch and a grump, curmudgeonly and contrary, but hellfire, the man could kiss. Fee found herself surging to her feet, her arms looping around his neck, her breasts pushing into his chest. She felt his big hand on the top of her butt, pulling her into a very thick, concrete-hard erection, and she whimpered in delight.

He was so big, everywhere. Fee found herself on her tiptoes, straining to align their mouths, knowing they'd both have cricks in their necks at the end of this make-out session. Clint solved the problem by placing his hands on her hips and boosting her up against his body, holding her weight with ease. What else was a girl to do but wind her legs around his trim waist, hook them behind his back and slide her most sensitive spot over his impressive bulge?

Fee heard Clint's moan of appreciation and then his hand encircled the top of her leg, his fingers on the inside of her thigh, and Fee wished he had his hands on her naked flesh, that she could feel his clever mouth sucking her nipples, maybe even going lower.

His mouth, as she was coming to learn, was a weapon of mass temptation. Fee knew that if he asked, she'd eagerly follow him into his house and down the hallway to his bedroom, or whether he decided to stop. She would take whatever he'd give her, grateful to be the recipient of the profound pleasure he managed to pull to the surface.

They didn't need to talk, their bodies were better at communicating than they were. Fee felt Clint take a step and she felt the hard coolness of wood through her jeans, dimly realizing he'd planted her on the wide sill of a window.

He lifted his hands to hold her face, his thumbs caressing her cheekbones as he feathered kisses across her eyelids, down her temple. Fee closed her eyes, enjoying the moment of tenderness. Then Clint covered her right breast with his hand, and her nipple tightened, rising against the fabric of her sweater to press into his palm. Clint jerked his head back, looked at her with stormy eyes and muttered a quiet obscenity.

"Why aren't you pushing me away?" he hoarsely demanded.

"Why would I, since you kiss like a dream?" Fee responded, her voice just this side of breathy. Hearing his sharp intake of air, Fee decided to rock his boat a little more. "You are abrupt and annoying but, God, you know how to touch me."

Clint ran his knuckles up her ribcage and across her nipple. "Like this?" His fingers burrowed under her sweater and landed on her bare skin.

"Exactly like that," Fee murmured. Then Clint pulled down the lacy cup of her bra and pulled her nipple with his fingers. Fee couldn't help crying out.

Fee put her hand behind his head and shook her head. "No, don't stop! Do it again."

Clint's repeated the action and Fee arched her back, dropped her leg and banged her heel against the back of his lower thigh, just above his knee. Instead of bone and sinew, the heel of her boot bounced off metal hidden behind the fabric of his jeans.

Clint reacted like he'd been scorched. Leaping backward, he put a healthy amount of distance between them. He stared down at the floor as Fee tried to make sense of why he stopped.

The answer came to her on a quiet whisper: she'd kicked his prosthetic leg.

Well, okay then. No big deal…

"Come back here and kiss me, Rockwell," Fee suggested, wanting, no, needing his mouth on hers. She wasn't done with him, not yet.

Clint had frozen, his big arms folded across his chest, his face a blank mask. She didn't like the lack of emotion in his eyes, in his expression. She could handle pissed off and irritated, turned on and taciturn, but she didn't like this cyborg standing in front of her, acting like she was a fly he was getting ready to swat.

"I think it's time you went home," Clint said, in the blandest of bland tones. "You can take your gag money with you and start arrangements to pay me the twenty thousand we agreed upon."

They were back to this, really? "That number is just something you pulled out of your ass to piss me off, we both know it's stupidly excessive. As for leaving…"

Fee jumped down from the windowsill and walked up to Clint until her breasts brushed against his arms. She saw the flare of heat in his eyes and knew he was nowhere near as unaffected as he was pretending to be.

Good to know.

"I don't like mixed signals, Rockwell. You can't devour me one minute and ask me to leave the next."

"On my spread, I can do anything I damn well like," Clint muttered.

Fee cocked her head at his statement. "Now you're just sounding petulant. It's not a good look on you, Rockwell."

Clint rubbed his hand over his face. "Will you just go? Please?"

"No, not until we talk about why you jumped away from me like you were hit by a bolt of lightning."

Annoyance and frustration jumped into Clint's eyes and Fee didn't mind. She could deal with those emotions. She far preferred anger to his impassivity. "Let's break it down, shall we?" she continued.

"Let's not."

Fee ignored him. "You touched my boob and I banged the back of my heel against your prosthetic leg. Now, because I know that couldn't hurt you, there has to be another reason why you're overreacting."

Clint handed her a hard stare, his eyes reflecting confusion and more than a little fear. At what? What was the real problem here?

"You know I have a prosthetic leg."

Yes, she did. It was the least important thing she'd discovered about him. "I also know you are a billionaire, you were some sort of super soldier and now you are a semi-recluse, much to the dismay of the Royal residents, who've placed you somewhere between God and Friday-night football."

Finally, a hint of amusement touched his lips. "That's a huge exaggeration since I have little to do with them."

"Trust me, ten minutes dealing with your sarcasm and general orneriness would have them reevaluating your wonderfulness," Fee said, her tone tart. She slapped her hands on her hips. "But we're getting distracted from the point of this conversation."

Clint looked past her at something beyond her shoulder. "You're not going to let this go, are you?"

Damn straight. "No."

"I lost my left leg above my knee. When you kicked it, I realized I should stop this, now."

"Why?"

"To save both of us the embarrassment of you running out of here squealing when you see me, and it, fully exposed. It's not a pretty sight." Clint's smile was hard and his eyes glittered with pain-laced fury. "I don't need your sympathy or your pity. I just need sex."

Fee felt anger boil inside of her. She was angry at the people who had so obviously hurt him by making him feel less than, and angry at him for projecting those people's feelings onto her. Yes, she was a reality TV star but she wasn't shallow, dammit.

To make her point, Fee gathered a handful of Clint's T-shirt in her fist. She knew with a quick twist he could be free of her grasp, he did have a hundred pounds of muscle on her, but she was trying to make a point here.

"You just keep pissing me off, Rockwell. It's quite a talent," Fee murmured.

"Just get to the point, Seraphina. I've got work to do."

Fee pulled him over to the steps and pushed him down two of them so they were eye to eye, face to face. "That's better. Now, listen up because I'm only going to say this once…"

"Man, you're bossy."

"If I were a man, you'd call my behavior assertiveness," Fee quipped back.

"If you were a man, I would've had you in a headlock by now."

Fair point, Fee thought.

"And I certainly wouldn't have kissed you and we wouldn't be having this conversation," Clint continued.

Fee waved his words away. "I'm not going to get into an argument about semantics with you, Rockwell. Not right now anyway." Fee was surprised that Clint—a taciturn, will-only-use-one-word-when-three-are-needed man— was even arguing with her.

Fee placed her hands on either side of his face and rested her thumbs against his mouth. "Be. Quiet."

"Nothing makes me angrier than when someone who doesn't know me compares me to someone else," Fee told him, keeping her voice low but intense. "I'm lots of things—I have a hundred faults—but I am, one hundred percent, my own person. That means I make up my own mind and I get very pissed when people assume they know what's inside my head."

Clint narrowed his eyes at her and pulled his head out of her gentle grip. Fee held up her hand to silence him when he opened his mouth to speak. "Not done. I kissed you because, although you are annoying and frustrating, you're probably the best-looking guy I've stumbled across in a long, long time. You're tall, built, ripped and you kiss like you're in contention for an Olympic medal. You've got skills, Rockwell. I'm not going to deny that. And, yes, had you not behaved like a jerk—which seems to be something you specialize in—we might be naked right now. But you did, so we're not.

"I already knew you lost a leg, Rockwell, and I got the Royal diner version of how it happened. If I was turned off by your missing leg, I wouldn't have started something we couldn't finish. Again, I am lots of things, but I'm not a tease."

Fee handed him a hot look. "Fact, I want you. I wanted you the first time I saw you days ago when I first visited Blackwood Hollow. I wanted you yesterday when I saw you barreling around the ring on your demon horse, looking sweaty and hot and, God, so alive."

His eyes heated and Fee forced herself to continue, to not go with her impulse and cover his mouth with hers. She needed to say this; she had to get her point across.

"I wanted you when you castigated me about my driving. I wanted you when I was showering, and in my dreams last night. When I heard about your having lost a leg, I felt, momentarily, sorry for you." She saw him jerk at the *S* word and shrugged it off. "I felt sorry for you because that's how nice people feel when they hear about something tragic happening to a good man. But that was quickly replaced with the 'how the hell does he ride so well with one leg?' thought."

"Seraphina—"

Since he was calling her by her full name, Fee knew she hadn't broken through yet. "I'm not done, Rockwell." Fee took a deep breath. "Judge me on my own words, Clint. My own actions. Don't judge me on someone else's stupidity. It's not right and it most certainly isn't fair."

Clint rubbed the back of his neck and stared down at

the ground. It was a hell of a conversation to have after such a short acquaintance and a bruising kiss.

"And know this…" Fee concluded. "If I start something, I always finish it."

Clint raised his head, looking mystified and a little amused. "Where the hell did you come from, Seraphina Martins?"

"Martinez," she corrected. Fee stood up straight and just managed to drop a kiss on his jaw. "And I'm from everywhere. And nowhere."

She tapped her fingers lightly against the side of his jaw. "If we do this again, make sure you're prepared to let me in, to see you, to see all of you. Otherwise, don't bother."

A little bit of misery seeped into Clint's eyes. "I don't know if I can do that."

Fee rubbed her cheek against him, loving the feel of his scruff gently scratching her cheek. "That's your prerogative, Rockwell. If you can't, that's cool. But, for me, it's an all or nothing deal. You see me naked, I see you naked."

"You're whole, Fee, and I imagine you look glorious naked."

"Damn right I do." Fee dropped a small kiss onto his lips. "But beauty, as they say, is in the eye of the beholder, Clint."

She pulled back, spun around and picked up her tote bag from the floor. She looked down at the fake bundles of cash on the floor and picked up the real money and tucked the bills into the back pocket of her jeans. She tossed Clint a look over her shoulder.

"Also, while you are deciding whether you want to sleep with me or not, how about you stop messing with me about how much the repairs are going to cost and give me a figure that's in the ballpark of reasonable?"

"Of course I *want* to sleep with you, Fee," Clint said.

Fee sent him a small smile. "But not enough, Clint, not just yet."

And that was okay, she'd allow him a little time to get there. Men always needed a little extra time to get with the program.

Her program was simple—rope a cowboy, ride him hard and get him out of her system.

Really, this shouldn't be so hard.

Three

Whoever had the bright idea that the New York socialites should learn something about ranching should be shot, Clint decided. And the person who decided Clint should oversee the process should be tortured, then shot.

Back at Blackwood Hollow, Clint fought to hide his impatience as he stood outside a stall in the bigger of the two stable blocks and listened to Miranda DuPree-Blackwood and her Italian bombshell colleague bitch about the smell, the dirty hay and the smell of horse.

Well, it was a stable, and to be fair, only the brunette was bitching. Miranda just had a determined look on her face as she pitched hay into a barrow while the brunette—Rachel, Rafel… *Rafaela*—examined her nails. Clint turned around to glare at the director who was making notes on her clipboard, her iPad tucked under her arm.

Damn you, Buck, for complicating the hell out of your death.

"You do realize we have work to do and we can't hang around here all day waiting for these—" he bit back the word he really wanted to say "—*ladies* to get out of our way?" Clint demanded. He had his own ranch to look after once everything was running smoothly at Blackwood Hollow. Yet again, he cursed the day he'd agreed to keep an eye on the place after Buck got sick. He should have stuck to his role as the town hermit and said no, but while his grandfather's old friend was irascible and hard-assed, he'd had, under his prickly exterior, a heart of gold few people got to see. Buck had also kept an eye on Rockwell Ranch after Gramps died, so Clint owed him.

And he always, always, paid off his debts.

"Miranda owns this place, there's an inheritance saga, a family feud and, on top of that, the *Secret Lives* stars know nothing about ranching. I know this is frustrating but it will make fantastic TV."

Great, because that was what he cared about, making fantastic TV. He had cows to feed, fence stays to cut for repair work and he wanted to put a new wood stove in the calving barn so the calves born in late winter had a better chance of survival.

Thank God the oil side of his business was leased and the day-to-day issues associated with that business weren't his problem.

Miranda, with hay in her hair, poked her head out from the stall. "You don't need to be here, Clint. I'm sure Gabe can show us the ropes."

Gabe, Buck's longest employee, gave him a *don't leave me alone with them* look. While Miranda had inherited Blackwood Hollow and everything else from Buck, she knew diddly-squat about ranching and she couldn't afford to annoy the staff, especially Gabe.

Gabe knew the ranch inside out and Miranda, whether

she knew it or not, needed him. And the man looked frustrated and irritated and was, obviously, itching to leave.

Clint sighed. "Gabe, you carry on with the rest of your work. I'll look after this lot."

Gratitude flashed in the older man's eyes and he didn't bother to argue, he just hightailed it out of the barn as fast as he could. Clint fought the urge to run after him.

He turned back to the director, who held a clipboard to her chest. "How much more do you need?"

"Well, I thought we could film Rafaela learning to saddle a horse and taking her first riding lesson, Miranda collecting eggs from the chicken run and Lulu filling the horse nets with food."

Yeah, because that's what ranching was really about. Collecting eggs and feeding horses. What about counting the livestock, branding, checking for pregnancies, land management? Worrying about too little rain, too much rain, stock theft, beef prices, whether they had enough feed to see them through the winter after a very dry summer?

"I need to film Seraphina doing something farmy, too."

Clint held back his snort. *Farmy?* God help him.

"I can assign hands to show the ladies the ropes for the tasks you had in mind, and I can show Fee how we transport bales of hay to the pastures so the cattle have enough to eat during these winter months," Clint suggested.

"Someone mention my name?"

Clint turned and his heart kicked up when he heard her chirpy voice. He slowly turned around and he had to smile at the sight of Fee in cowgirl mode again. Her long hair was in two thick braids hanging down over her flannel shirt, which was worn over an old pair of jeans. She wore rain boots printed with—Clint leaned forward and squinted at her feet—ducks wearing rain boots.

She had a streak of dirt across her cheek and she looked

like she'd actually been doing some work instead of just playing at it.

"Lu and I are done in this stall. What's next?" Fee asked, rubbing her hands on the seat of her pants.

Clint used his height to peek over the stable door and was impressed by the full water trough and clean floor covered by fresh straw.

And they hadn't taken forever to do it.

The director consulted her clipboard. "Why don't you go with Clint and Jimmy? He can film you taking something somewhere."

Clint summoned the little patience he had left. "Hay bales to the feed stations in the pastures," Clint told her.

"Cool. How do we get the hay out there? Do we put it in wheelbarrows?"

Clint had to smile. "Since the bales are over a ton each, that would be difficult. We use a lifter…" He closed his eyes at the thought of Fee operating the lifter with its two massive forks. With her lead foot, who knew what damage she'd do?

"Yay, I get to drive." Fee bounced on her toes, looking excited.

Worst idea ever, Clint decided, as Fee bounded for the door. Clint turned to the director. "I hope your insurance and liabilities policies are up to date since Fee is a maniac behind the wheel."

"Don't break anything, Fee!" Miranda shouted from the inside the stable, obviously listening to their conversation.

"Yeah, Fee, don't break anything," Lulu said, coming to stand in the doorway of the stall. She smiled at Fee and then her expression changed and her eyes cooled. Clint looked over his shoulder to see Kace LeBlanc, standing by the sliding door at the entrance of the stable block, a dark brown Stetson throwing shadows across his face.

LeBlanc seemed to be everywhere the socialites were. Clint couldn't decide if he was taking his job as Buck's lawyer to heart by hovering around Miranda, or if his true motive was because the NYC tourists were all stunningly attractive.

But Kace only seemed to have eyes for Lulu.

Clint pulled his eyes back to Fee, who stood with her hand on her heart, her eyes full of mischief. A cameraman stood behind him, the camera pointed in Fee's direction. Clint stood aside so he wasn't in the shot. "I am truly saddened by your lack of faith in me, Miranda."

"I came by it naturally," Miranda said as she walked out of the stable, trailed by another cameraman and Rafaela who, judging by her still spotless clothes, hadn't lifted a finger to help muck out the stall.

"You did put your hand into Abby's wedding cake, and you did nearly set the kitchen on fire when we were filming in the Hamptons because you left oil on the stove. You did fall off a bar in Cancun," Miranda pointed out. "You really should stop dancing on bars."

Fee pulled a face. "That was Lulu."

"We both fell off the bar in Dublin," Lulu corrected her. "You fell off the bar in Cancun because you were flirting with the bartender and weren't looking where you were going."

Fee shook her head and her braids bounced off her shoulders. "I dispute that." She looked around and frowned. "Where's Zooey?"

"Present."

Clint turned at the faint voice drifting over to them and he saw another woman standing at the entrance to the stable, a cowboy hat tipped over her eyes, her booted foot resting against the barn wall behind her.

Clint heard Fee's huge sigh and watched as she walked

over to her friend and pushed up her hat. The cameras would pick up what he saw: a pale blonde with blue-ringed eyes, looking like she was dealing with the hangover from hell.

"Aw, honey," Fee crooned, stroking her arm from shoulder to elbow. "You look like crap, Zo."

"Feel like crap. Too many shooters with too many cowboys," Zooey replied.

That would do it.

The director turned to Clint. "I need something for Zooey to do. I have to film her doing something, preferably sitting down."

What was he, a friggin' consultant? "Get her to clean some tack." He walked up to where Fee was standing and put his hand on her back. When she looked at him with those delicious brown eyes, his heart spluttered.

Stupid thing.

"I really need to get going. You coming or not?"

"Always so gracious," Fee murmured. She looked back at the director and flashed a smile. "I'm going to feed the cows."

"Excellent. Take Jimmy with you."

Clint looked at the tall, lanky man holding a camera to his shoulder and rolled his eyes. Fabulous.

No, super fabulous.

Because, how exactly was he supposed to kiss the hell out of her when he had an audience?

Fee parked the lifter where she'd found it and slapped her hands on the steering wheel, immensely pleased with herself. She'd thought she'd be driving a tractor but could see why this machine was so effective. She shoved the prongs of the lifter into a massive bale of hay, lifted it up and transported it to a feeding trough in a nearby pasture.

She'd cut the twine off the bale—using Clint's multi-tool—
and returned the lifter to its parking spot, all without in-
juring herself, Clint, Jimmy or the machine itself.

Nothing to this ranching stuff!

Jimmy dropped his camera and held it to his side. "I'm
going to take off, Fee. Do you want to walk with me back
to the barn?"

Fee glanced at Clint, who'd hopped off the lifter. "No,
I'll catch up with you." She glanced at her watch. "Where
are we filming this afternoon?"

"We've got the afternoon off," Jimmy reminded her.

"Excellent." She glanced at Clint who was staring down
at his phone, his expression intense. "Tell Lu and the rest
that I'll see them when I see them."

"Cool."

When he was out of earshot, Fee hopped down from her
seat and walked around the back of the machine to where
Clint stood, still looking troubled. "Problem?"

"I was just checking the weather app—it's an occupa-
tional hazard." Clint looked a little distracted. "There's a
forecast for high winds."

"Winds are a problem?"

"They can be," Clint replied. "We experienced a drought
this past summer, and the grass and lands are dry. We typi-
cally start to worry about fires later in the season but even
now, because it's so dry, one spark can set off a hell of a
blaze."

Fee looked around, saw the brown grass and the cattle
in the pastures and shuddered. "That wouldn't be good."

Clint handed her one of his almost smiles. "It wouldn't."
He gestured to the lifter. "You did well. Now, you have to
do that another fifteen times today to feed all the livestock
in the paddocks closest to the house. And we haven't even
started getting feed to the livestock in the far pastures."

Fee looked aghast. "How many more times?"

Clint's slow smile caused her stomach to flip over. "Relax, I'm not going to ask you to do it. Gabe and the hands will finish up."

"Thank God," Fee said, putting her hands on her lower back and stretching. "That seat is not good for my back."

She noticed his eyes went to her breasts, and she didn't mind. In fact, she loved the flash of desire in his eyes. "Back problems?" he asked, his voice lower and huskier than before.

"Yeah. A gate fell on me when I was a kid and I've struggled with back issues ever since. Especially when I do something different and, trust me, mucking out stalls and hopping on and off machinery is very different from my normal exercise routine."

Clint walked behind her and placed his hands on her waist, his thumbs digging into two spots in her lower back. Fee groaned as sweet pain flooded her system. God, his fingers felt so good.

He moved his hands up, holding her rib cage, thumbs pushing into another set of knots and she moaned again.

"You're as tight as a drum," Clint murmured, his breath warm against her ear. She shivered, wanting to turn around and slap her mouth against his.

Hellfire, she wanted him.

Without turning around, she lifted his big hands over her breasts, arching her back to push her nipples into his broad palms. "I still want you."

Clint's thumbs swiped over her, eliciting a groan of pleasure. "Are you sure?"

Fee whipped around, instantly annoyed. "What do you need me to do, take out an ad in your local newspaper?"

Clint's mouth twitched. "Point taken." She saw him hesitate and she waited for his next excuse. Yeah, she understood his reluctance to get naked, but unless he was resigned to a celibate lifestyle, he was going to have to get over it.

Clint pulled her back into his chest, the ridge of his erection pushing into her lower back. "Come home with me."

Finally. Fee allowed her lips to curve upward. "An excellent plan. We'll take my car—it's parked out front."

"I've got a better idea."

Fee stiffened. "Not by horse, please. Firstly, it will take too long since I don't ride and also my back is already killing me.'

"Not by horseback, not today anyway," Clint told her, taking her hand and leading her to the back of the barn and then behind the stables to where a muddy dirt bike was parked.

Clint slung his leg over the seat and tipped his head. "Climb on, peanut."

Fee placed her hand on his shoulder, swung her leg over and felt herself sliding down the seat into Clint's back, her breasts pushed against his flannel shirt. When she wrapped her arms around his waist, he rested his big hand on her thigh and squeezed. "You okay?"

Fee wiggled and she smiled when Clint tensed. Yep, she was pretty sure that if she dropped her hand and allowed it to fall lower, she'd find something long and hard and ready to play. "I'm good. You?"

"My jeans are suddenly about two sizes too small," Clint admitted.

Before she could reply, he gunned the accelerator and Fee squealed as they took off. She tightened her hold on him, instinctively realizing she had to move as he did, trusting him to keep them upright.

After a few minutes, she knew Clint was as good on a bike as he was on a horse and she relaxed, spreading her fingers across his stomach, allowing one hand to drift up his chest. Instead of taking the main road, Clint cut across the ranch, using trails, skirting trees and rocks.

When they hit an open piece of land, Clint lifted one hand to cover hers with his, holding it against his heart.

It was such a small gesture but, in that instant, she felt utterly connected to this man, and to the land he knew so well.

And seemed to love as much.

They passed through a gate and Clint informed her she was now on Rockwell land, pointing out the oil derricks in the distance.

"The Rockwell wealth was built on oil and ranching," Clint told her, above the noise of the engine and the whistling wind.

"Is your father not involved in the ranch at all?"

Clint's grip on her fingers tightened. "He died when I was five. My folks separated when I was a baby and my dad, initially, had custody. When he died, I moved to Dallas with my mom but I spent every holiday here at the ranch with my grandfather. My grandfather left the ranch to me when he died."

They were getting personal and that wasn't supposed to happen. She didn't do permanent and he didn't seem to do people, so this was a one-off thing.

"So, all this land is yours?"

"Yep." Clint slowed down to allow a cow to cross the trail they were riding and sent her a mischievous look over his shoulder. "I also own a ranch close to Austin."

She loved his bad-boy look, his charming half smile, his closeness. Fee was surprised her ovaries hadn't exploded yet. "Good thing I'm only interested in your body, not your acreage," Fee lightly replied.

"Good thing," Clint quipped as he swung the bike

off one trail and onto another. Within a few minutes Fee caught glimpses of his sprawling house and she swallowed a burst of panic. What was she doing, literally riding off with a cowboy? Despite her party-hearty reputation, she didn't do one-night, or afternoon, stands; she never hopped into bed with strangers.

But there was something about Clint, something that called to her. Maybe it was the hint of vulnerability she'd heard in his voice or the sadness and loneliness she'd seen in his eyes.

She wanted him, sure, but she also wanted to make him feel a little treasured, a little cherished, even if they were only destined to spend a few hours together. Because she suspected it had been a long time, if ever, since Clint was cherished, treasured.

He probably wouldn't recognize either one if it bit him on the butt.

Clint skirted his barns and the paddock, beautiful horses with patterned coats raising their heads at the sound of the bike. He sped toward the imposing front of the house with its wrap-around veranda and stately front door.

Fee heard his low curse and saw a white SUV parked next to a quad bike and a brand-new pickup with a Rockwell Ranch logo on the door.

He parked his bike next to the SUV, hopped off and scowled. "Is today the twentieth?"

"All day," Fee answered, climbing off the bike.

Clint ran his hand through his dark blond, windblown hair. "My physiotherapist is here. I forgot she was coming today."

Ah. So, no afternoon sex then. Damn.

"You're still having physio?" Fee asked as she followed him up the stairs and through the big wooden door into a spacious hallway.

"Only once a month now. Sam comes to check up on my progress and to make sure I am not overdoing it."

"In what way?" Fee asked, looking into the luxurious great room with floor-to-ceiling windows, massive, comfortable-looking couches and a huge fireplace. Bright art adorned the walls and Fee was grateful she couldn't see any dead animal heads mounted on the walls.

She wasn't a fan of taxidermy in any shape or form.

"She's both a physio and a trainer, so she was able to get me back in shape after too long lying around, recuperating. Sam also helped me with my various prosthetics, learning how to use them, to program them."

He frowned slightly, looking a little embarrassed. "I don't know what I would've done without her these past two years so, as much as I want to whip you off to bed, I'm going to have to take a rain check, just for an hour or two."

Fee wondered what she was expected to do while she waited for him. Or if she should wait for him at all. Maybe this wasn't such a good idea.

She glanced at the front door. "Maybe I should go. But I'd have to borrow a vehicle from you."

Clint grinned and her heart sighed. "You're a maniac behind the wheel, Martinez, so that's not going to happen." Clint took her hand in his and squeezed. "Don't run off, Fee. Please?"

Before she could answer him, Clint tugged her down the long, cool hallway. Where were they going? Surely he wasn't intending to stuff her into his bedroom and expecting her to wait for him like a good little girl?

"Maybe we should table this for another day."

"Nope." Clint stopped in front of a half-open door, and he closed his eyes. "You might as well come in, meet Sam, see me. After Sam's tortured me, you can then decide if you want to stay or go."

Fee immediately knew what he was saying. If she watched his physio, she'd see him wearing his prosthetic, a prelude to seeing him naked, which was his most vulnerable state. He was giving her, and him, a gentler way to back out if she changed her mind.

Which he clearly kept expecting her to do. But he didn't know she was stubborn, and once she set her mind on something, she generally never backed down.

And, she knew with every fiber of her being, no matter how bad his leg looked, she would still want him.

Because she wasn't only attracted to his fallen angel face and his wide chest and big arms, flat stomach and thick legs, she was attracted to his soul, to his determination, to his unwillingness to stop doing what he wanted to do because he was missing a limb.

He rode horses like a crazy person, worked his ranch, rode his dirt bike. He wasn't sitting in a darkened room refusing to face life—people, maybe, but not life—and she admired his drive and persistence.

So many people would just throw their hands in the air and embrace being a victim of life's unfairly dealt cards.

Fee wouldn't change her mind about sleeping with him and the only way to prove her intention was to *not* change her mind.

She gestured to the door and bumped his shoulder with hers. "Rockwell, we're only going to get to the fun stuff if you hop to it."

The words flew out of her mouth and she only realized what she'd said when they hovered in the suddenly awkward silence between them. Fee glanced at Clint, hoping he didn't think she was mocking his disability, and she sighed in relief when she saw a flash of amusement in his eyes.

He might've lost half his leg but he hadn't, entirely, lost his ability to smile.

Thank God because she seldom thought before she spoke and she was known to be occasionally inappropriate. And irreverent.

But, hopefully, never cruel.

Four

Clint saw Sam out, and when he returned, he found Fee curled up in the easy chair in the corner of his expensive home gym, one leg dangling over an arm. Earlier he'd changed from jeans into exercise shorts and a tank for his training session with Sam, and he was conscious of his matted hair and damp chest but mostly of his matte black prosthetic.

Do or die time.

Clint pushed down the panic threatening to close his chest. Fee was one of the few women he'd allowed to see the stump tucked into his prosthetic for a long, long time. Would she bolt? She kept saying she wouldn't, but he'd learned to trust what people did, not what they said. Time for the truth, he thought as he stood in front of her, his arms folded over his chest. She'd either handle it or she wouldn't; he wouldn't allow himself to care either way.

He'd stopped caring about his mom's opinion—*I like*

pretty and I like perfect—and he shouldn't care about Fee's since she was leaving in a few weeks to go back east, so why was his heart in his mouth? Why was his stomach twisted like a pretzel?

He was so pathetic, because, dammit, when he saw female appreciation in her eyes, when she looked at him like she wanted to devour him whole, he felt like the man he used to be.

He felt strong and capable and powerful and whole... He wasn't, but she made him feel that way.

Fee swung her legs off the chair and leaned forward, examining his prosthetic. It was one of the most advanced devices on the planet and he had a full range of movement; it was just a marvel of modern technology.

But, funny thing, he'd still prefer his old leg back.

Fee rested her fingers on what should've been his knee, allowing her fingers to drift up to the suction cup. "Is it sore?"

"No. Not anymore," he answered. "It's an ugly wound but not sore."

"Phantom pains?"

Someone had done their research. He was both pleased and terrified. "Yeah, I get those but less often than I did. They are pretty annoying."

"Why do I suspect that's your way of saying they hurt like a bitch but that you would rather die than admit it?"

She was spot on. They *did* hurt like a bitch but he wasn't one for whining. Fee kept her hand on him and looked up through long, thick lashes. "I went online and read up on what you did to save your teammates, Clint. You were amazing, so focused and so brave."

There was nothing amazing about it. He'd done what he had to do to save his friends; he would not let them die in a tangle of metal in a foreign country. "Any of them would've done the same."

"Maybe, maybe not. But you were the one who did and, I know this sounds weird, considering we barely know each other but—" Fee hesitated and he saw the glint of tears in her eyes. Or a crapload of emotion. Suddenly he really wanted to know what she was about to say...no, he *needed* to know.

"But?"

Fee dropped her hand and looked at the floor, shaking her head. He cupped her jaw and tipped her face up. "What, Fee?"

She looked embarrassed. "I was just going to say I'm proud of you but that sounds weird because, you know, we don't know each other." She waved her hand in front of her eyes as if to dry the moisture. "Anyway, I'm sure your family is very proud of you."

He almost laughed at her statement. Proud? Definitely not.

He was good PR—Mila frequently mentioned her wounded war hero, Purple Heart–recipient son on her prime time news slot—but his mom hadn't want to deal with the reality of having a son who'd needed numerous operations, spent months in the hospital and who had to undergo rigorous rehabilitation to get back on one foot. Even before he was injured, he'd always been too much trouble for her, distracting her from what was important, which was making sure she was the most visible, most powerful, journalist in Dallas.

Fee was the first person he'd allowed to broach the subject, to talk about the past. And being Fee, she just looked him straight in the eye and spoke with pity and sentimentality.

"Thank you," he said, his voice husky. He felt her hand

drift onto his thigh, above his suction cup, her fingers resting lightly on his scarred skin.

"Let me see you, Clint. All of you."

It was such a big step…she was asking him to strip down, to show his most vulnerable self. With his prosthetic removed, he either needed to sit down or use his crutches, neither of which screamed rampant sex god. He would be vulnerable…

He reminded himself that she was half his size and he was trained; she couldn't hurt him if she tried. He was still a highly trained army ranger and she wasn't dangerous, not to his safety anyway. His heart maybe, but he wasn't going there…

What was the worst she could do? Laugh? Run away? Well, that had happened before and he'd survived. He'd survived his mom's lack of interest and, after losing his friends and his limb, knew he could survive anything.

But, still…

I like pretty and I like perfect…

Clint cursed, not sure if he could do this. He wasn't ready.

He didn't know if he'd ever be.

"It's okay, Clint, really," Fee said, standing up and wrapping her arms around his waist she placed her forehead on his sternum and he looked down at her mass of black curls. "I'm really pushy—it's one of my worst traits."

Clint laid his hand on her head. "I'm not pushable."

"I know," Fee said, looking up at him. "You're the most stubborn man I've ever met."

"Pot calling the kettle black, Fee?"

Fee smiled at him and his heart cracked, just a little. He'd patch it up later, before the chasm widened and he started to think of this woman in terms of tomorrow and more.

He just wanted a night, maybe a few nights, and then he would say goodbye, wave her on her way. They had today, maybe tomorrow, and he didn't intend to waste any time. But right now, he wanted to lay hands on this woman, and not in the way she thought he would.

Giving her a massage would give him some time to think, to gather his courage to let her see him, to take a chance.

"Why don't you lie on the massage table, face down?" Clint suggested.

Fee looked at the massage table in the corner of the gym, the one where Sam had worked on him earlier. "Why?"

"Trust me," Clint said, taking her hand and leading her across the room. Fee sat on the edge of the bed and he yanked off her rain boots—taking a moment to inspect the ducks. Shaking his head, he tossed them to one side and reached for the button on the band of her jeans.

Fee stopped him by frowning, placing her hand on his. He looked down and grimaced. "Sorry, I have heard about foreplay, I promise—but that's not what this is. I just wanted to loosen your pants a bit so I can massage your lower back."

"You're going to give me a massage?" Fee asked, her eyes round with surprise.

"Well, yeah." Why else did she think she was on this table? He was out of practice but he hadn't forgotten everything he knew about women. Their first time deserved a bed, not a hard table in a gym. "I've seen you grimace a few times and you keep stretching as if you are cramping."

"You really have to observe less and explain more, Rockwell," Fee said, flipping onto her stomach and pushing her jeans down to her hips. Clint's mouth dropped open when she lifted her torso and whipped off her shirt, baring the crisscross straps of her purple bra to his very appreciative gaze.

Acres of creamy skin, three freckles just below her left shoulder blade, the bumps of her spine. Clint wanted to kiss the hollow of her back, the two small dimples he could see at the top of her butt, and he would, sometime this afternoon.

But, for now, he wanted her loose and liquid. Not wanting to ruin her beautiful bra, he asked her if he could unhook it and when she nodded, he separated the hooks and eyes, allowing the purple fabric to bunch on the bed at her sides. He picked up her hair, draped it over her shoulder and lifted a few loose tendrils off her elegant neck.

He had no idea how he was going to massage her without getting distracted. Clint poured some massage oil into his hands, rubbed them together and took a deep breath as he stroked the oil onto her skin. He sucked in a hot, aroused, confused breath as he dug his fingers into her muscles. He'd had women before, lots of them and he'd never felt this turned on, this on edge.

This was life changing, important, breath stealing...

And she shouldn't be. He wouldn't let her be.

He had to stop giving her more importance in his life than she had. This was about sex, about a moment in time, about physical release.

Stop thinking, Rockwell, your head is going to explode. And that wasn't the explosion he was most looking forward to. That one would happen three feet lower...

Fifteen minutes later and he was nearly done. Clint dug his fingers into a knot beneath Fee's shoulders and heard her low groan, felt her shudder. He couldn't wait any longer, he needed her, here, now...

He couldn't deny himself any longer...

"Roll over, Seraphina," he commanded and she did,

holding her sexy bra to her breasts as she sat up. He cocked an eyebrow, amused by her reticence. She was loud and bold—he hadn't expected shyness. He hooked a finger under a cup of her bra and gently tugged. Fee sucked her bottom lip into her mouth and allowed the fabric to fall into her lap. Clint felt the punch to his heart, another to his stomach as she leaned back on her hands, allowing him to look…

And look.

She was cream and Cointreau and he knew she'd taste as good as she looked. "You are the most beautiful woman I have ever seen."

The flash of surprise in her eyes told him too few lovers had mentioned her beauty. He dragged his finger across her collarbone, down the slope of her breast and over her puckered nipple. *So responsive*, he thought. He placed his hands on her breasts, tested their weight, enjoying their fullness. Man, she was hot and yeah, he wanted her.

But not here…

Clint banded his arm around her waist and pulled her so that she sat on the edge of the massage bed and he stepped into the space between her legs. "Let's take this to the bedroom. Hook your legs around my waist."

"Okay but…first…" Fee scooted closer, draped her arms around his neck and Clint sucked in his breath when she slid her mouth across his. Her tongue traced his bottom lip and all his good intentions to take this slowly evaporated.

He needed her…now.

Clint took control of the kiss, plundering her mouth as if this were the last time he'd kiss a woman, the last time he'd have this experience. Instead of pulling back, Fee met him stroke for stroke, twisting her tongue around his and pushing her bare breasts into his chest. Frustrated at the lack of skin-on-skin contact, Clint pulled his tank over his head and then her hands were on his ribcage, sliding up and over his chest, moving around to his back. She pushed her hand under the band of his exercise shorts, growling her frustration.

"I need you, now," Fee muttered and Clint's last shred of control was obliterated.

This was going to happen in his gym, on a Tuesday afternoon a week before Christmas. Best present ever.

Clint dropped his hands to her jeans and this time she didn't stop him when he slid the zipper all the way down, pushing the opening apart so he could slide his hands inside. He sucked a nipple into his mouth and laved it while working her jeans down her hips. Fee lifted one butt cheek to help him, then the other and soon her jeans and panties were on the floor, and Fee wasted no time in making sure his exercise shorts and boxer briefs joined the pile of clothing.

He stood naked before her and, not wanting to give her time to think or pull back, reached for her, needing passion to take over, to take them away.

But Fee placed a hand on his heart, those exquisite eyes connecting with his. "Let me see you, Clint. I need to see you."

Clint knew he could distract her with a quick, hard kiss but Fee's request was powerful, sweet and not easy to deny. Tensing, he watched her face as he stepped back, feeling her eyes on his chest, his groin area and finally his leg. A part of him was relieved that he was standing, that he couldn't take off his prosthetic.

He wasn't quite ready…

"You are so beautiful, so powerful," Fee murmured, her finger running over the biceps in his left arm. "You're so ripped, so muscular but not too much. Your body is… God, spectacular."

He couldn't remember when he'd last blushed but knew he was damn close to it now. "You need your eyes tested, Martinez."

Her eyes collided with his and she shook her head. "Don't do that, okay? Don't minimize how far you've come, how hard you've worked. You took a hit, one direct to your leg, and you not only survived, you goddamn conquered. I'm in awe of you, Clint. What's happening with us might only be a ships-passing-in-the-night thing but I can still appreciate your determination, your persistence."

He felt ten feet tall, like he could take on the world. To have such a woman—gorgeous, smart and mouthy—talk this way about him, lust and admiration and appreciation in her eyes, filled his soul with something that might be happiness.

Happiness…not an emotion he was terribly familiar with. And it scared him. He didn't want to get a taste of it and have to live without it. It was better to strive for contentment, for comfort and satisfaction.

And talking about satisfaction…

"You're pretty spectacular yourself," Clint said. "Can we please stop talking now?"

Fee's eye roll was accompanied by a smile. "I like to talk, Rockwell, get used to it."

"I noticed." Clint held her face in her hands. "Now, shut up and kiss me."

"I can do that."

Still standing in front of her, Clint covered her mouth with his, pulling her legs around his waist so skin met skin, breast to chest, the V of her legs pressed into his cock. This…man.

Touching Fee was what he never knew he needed.

Clint wrenched his mouth off hers, his attention on the warmth and moisture heating his cock. "I need you, Fee. I need to be inside you but I need to protect you. And the condoms are in my bedroom."

Fee just hooked one ankle behind the other and pressed her heels into his back. "I'm on the pill and I'm clean. If you can say the same, let's not move."

Could he risk it? Should he? He knew he was clean but he never, ever placed so much control in someone else's hands. But it would also take a momentous effort to disengage, to walk away. Just this once, this one time, he would take a chance.

Clint kissed her again, his hand sliding between their bodies to test her readiness and when she bucked into his fingers, moaned in his ear, he pushed into her, keeping his thumb on her clit.

Fee's moans were incomprehensible, a mixture of English and Spanish and girl-on-the-edge groans. She scooted even closer to him and dug her fingernails into his butt.

Clint kissed her with a ferocity he took to a firefight and buried himself to the hilt, his eyes crossing at the wonder of being in her, holding her, kissing her...

She was falling apart in his arms and he loved it.

Fee's nails dug deeper, her hips lifted and he felt her inner channel clench, demanding his response. She was close, and he couldn't wait. Needing her to come, he surged into her, placing his hands under her butt to tilt her up and she gasped and...

Yeah, gushed. On him, through him, around him.

Clint felt the pressure build in his balls, at the base of his spine, and he plunged deeper into her, needing more, needing everything.

Fee released an *oh-oh-oh* in his ear, and he came with

all the force of a missile strike. Earth was destroyed, he was the conqueror...

Clint buried his face in Fee's sweet-smelling neck, the thought occurring that, by not being able to resist her, he might be the one who was vanquished, the one who was obliterated.

And right now, at this moment, he was okay with defeat.

Five

Unlike her costars who worked with personal trainers in air-conditioned gyms, Fee preferred running to keep herself in shape. So, after a meeting with the producer, director and the rest of the cast, she strapped her phone to her arm, pushed wireless buds into her ears and hit the road.

Running through Royal was a pleasure. It was a pretty town and the traffic was light at eight thirty on a Monday morning. Christmas, thank God, was over and she'd spent the holiday with her parents in Florida. Her visit had been short, less than thirty-six hours, and because her parents left for a cruise the day after Christmas, she didn't have to make excuses to return to Royal.

Her costars were also back in town and it was business as usual. The feud between the Blackwood siblings and Miranda raged on unabated, Buck's illegitimate son had yet to be found—Miranda had told her about Buck's request for him to be found and asked she not repeat that news to anyone, not even Lulu (and she hadn't)—and the director of *Secret Lives* was milking the tension for all it was worth.

And, bonus, they didn't have to write the storyline...

Trying to relax, Fee looked at the Christmas decorations still gracing the homes and lawns of Royal residents. Their yards were well tended, the Christmas decorations were picture-postcard. It was obvious the Royal residents were proud of their homes and their town. She could see why. It really did seem like the perfect place for someone looking to settle down and build not just a life but a legacy for generations to come. The sheer permanence of everything—the post office that had stood for more than a century, the diner that had been on Main Street for decades—continued to surprise her.

Fee knew nothing was permanent—her parents had taught her that lesson—and for her, putting faith in a relationship, in a town, in a friend, was asking for trouble.

She didn't belong anywhere, not even in New York City. Manhattan was just a place to temporarily lay her head and when *Secret Lives* ended—and she was a realist, it would end—she would find another city, another place to live while she wrote the next chapter of her life.

That could be in Barcelona or Bogota, Riyadh or... Royal.

Fee stopped abruptly, her expensive running shoes scraping the pavement. Where on earth had that thought come from? Yes, Royal was a pretty town but it was too small, too farmy for her. She wasn't a small-town girl, she needed the energy of the city, to be able to browse specialist bookstores, visit art galleries and museums, go to cocktail parties and to the ballet.

But when last did you go clubbing, or to an art gallery? she asked herself. *When last did you go to a party that wasn't work related? You claim to love the city but you don't avail yourself of what it offers...*

Fee started jogging again, wondering why she was so at odds with herself. She'd been feeling this way since before Christmas, since leaving Clint Rockwell's bed.

They had, after making very good use of his massage table, moved to his room where they had spent the rest of the afternoon, and a good part of the evening, in a haze of orgasmic pleasure. She, obviously, noticed that he kept his prosthetic on throughout and she hadn't asked him to remove it.

His leg, his choice.

At ten, she'd dressed and Clint had, without argument, driven her back to her hotel. They'd parted with no promises to get in touch, skipping the obligatory *I'll call you*s. Through silent but mutual agreement, they both knew one night was all they could have, was all either of them could cope with.

She because Clint was too compelling for comfort, he because...who knew?

It didn't matter. They'd slept together, it was fun and it was over. It was all good...

And a little confusing because, since that night, rogue, stupid thoughts kept jumping into her brain, causing her to falter, to question her freewheeling life. What was up with that?

Fee stopped at an intersection, looked both ways and noticed a large construction site down the road, next to a smaller building with an old fire engine parked outside. The new building looked mostly finished but what caught and held her attention was the tall figure dressed in dark blue chinos and a pale blue button-down shirt under a gray pullover. Her heart kicked up and started to thump erratically.

Clint was dressed up, looking good and spending the morning in Royal. The town's most reclusive citizen had graced the town with his presence. Why?

You're just curious, Fee told herself. *You are not excited to see him. You are not desperate to hear his deep voice, to see whether his hazel eyes are green, gold or gray today. He's just a guy you had carnal relations with...*

And Shakespeare was just a writer, and Mandela was just another activist.

Annoyed with herself, Fee debated whether to run past the fire station. If she went left instead of right, it would add another three miles to her run and she'd already run three. Running past the fire station was the shorter route and she couldn't afford to take the extra time.

She had a full schedule today. They were filming at Blackwood Hollow and she and Lulu were scheduled to do a scene where they'd discuss what they intended to wear to the Texas Cattleman's Club New Year's Eve ball. Miranda had persuaded Nigel Townsend, owner of the production company responsible for *Secret Lives of NYC Ex-Wives*, to sponsor the event, to say thank you to the good residents of Royal for allowing them to film their town and have cameras and microphones shoved in their faces.

Fee had a schedule and she was, despite what the world thought, a professional. She hated being late so she'd have to run past Clint and the men he was talking to.

It had nothing to do with the fact she really, really, desperately wanted to speak to the sexy cowboy again.

Annoyed with herself, Fee ran down the road, pretending not to have noticed Rockwell. But she knew the exact moment when he noticed her. She felt her skin prickle, then flush with heat.

What if he ignores me? What if he pretends he hasn't seen me?

"Hey, peanut."

Although she wasn't crazy about the nickname, she was grateful to hear his voice seeping past the buds in her ears. Stopping, she turned around slowly and pulled them from ears. Crossing the road, she walked up to the construction fence and brushed a curl off her cheek. "Hey."

Oh, scintillating opening line, Seraphina. Use your words, girl.

Clint's eyes traveled up her body, taking in her skin-tight exercise pants and sleeveless crop top. Her eyes connected with his and she saw passion flicker gold in all that green. Gesturing at the suits with him, Clint quickly introduced his companions, who were architects from Dallas.

"I think we're done here, Clint," the oldest of the trio said, holding out his hand for Clint to shake.

"Thanks. And I can expect the building to be fit for occupation by the middle of January?" Clint asked.

"Absolutely. If not sooner."

As they said their goodbyes, Fee walked down the fence until she found a gate and went inside the construction site, staying close to the perimeter so she wouldn't be in the way of any of the busy crew.

She placed her hands on her hips and when Clint joined her, she pulled her eyes off the building to his face. "So, this project has to be fairly important to drag you off your ranch—" she gestured to his elegant clothes "—and into a nice outfit."

Clint jammed his hands into the pockets of his blue chinos. "I'm also meeting the suits leasing my oil rich land later so I thought I'd leave the battered boots and old jeans at home."

"And your Stetson?"

Clint's eyes crinkled at the corners. "In my car." He

gestured to a fancy SUV across the road, solidly black and engineered in Germany.

Nice wheels. "Where's the beloved rust bucket?"

"In for repairs."

Fee wrinkled her nose. "Tell me what it costs and I'll pay."

"Don't worry about it."

"Clint, I damaged it, I need to pay for those damages."

Clint surprised her with his quiet okay. "It won't be twenty grand," he added.

"What a shock," Fee replied, her tone dry. She saw his mouth kick up in a half smile and her ovaries quivered.

I want him. Again. Some more. A lot more.

Calm down, Martinez, you fool. That ship has sailed. Wanting to get her mind off the fact that Clint had seen her naked, and that she wanted him to see her naked again, and vice versa, she glanced at the half-constructed building.

"What are you building here?" Fee asked, rubbing her hands on her arms, conscious that the wind had picked up and that it was on the wrong side of chilly.

Clint, being the observant soldier he was, noticed her shivers, pulled off his sweater and placed the opening over her head. Fee didn't argue, she was grateful to be warm, and threaded her arms through the sleeves, rolling back the excess material. "Thank you."

"Pleasure. This wind is picking up," Clint commented, looking at the swaying trees to the side of the building.

"Isn't that what wind does?" Fee asked, confused.

Clint looked down at her. "Farmers don't like wind, especially not when it's dry. It just takes a stray spark and the right wind and we're in trouble, fire wise."

Oh. That made sense. Fee nodded to the building. "So, this?"

Clint placed his hand on her back and Fee forced herself not to react, not to move closer so she could soak up his heat or inhale more of his aftershave.

"It's a new fire station. The old one is too small, too cramped and too outdated."

"And why are you here, having on-site meetings?"

"I spent some time in California, ages ago, doing a smoke jumping and firefighting course. Because nobody in Royal forgets anything, I ended up coordinating Roya's firefighting efforts. It's my contribution to the community," Clint told her. His small, sexy smile flickered. "I do, occasionally, interact with the folks of Royal."

But only on his terms. And he was fudging, she could tell. "I still don't understand why you were having an intense discussion with the architects."

She saw him flush, felt his hand drop away. Rockwell didn't like talking about himself, didn't like anyone seeing below the surface. But he wasn't difficult to figure out.

"Just admit it, Rockwell, you're building this fire station," Fee stated, her tone brooking no argument. "From your own pockets, I presume?"

"Yep," Clint eventually replied, lifting his shoulders in a casual shrug.

"Those are pretty deep pockets, Clint," Fee murmured, impressed. Knowing there was more to this story, she pushed. "What else are you funding?"

Clint narrowed his eyes at her. "That's none of your business."

"Fire trucks? Water tankers? New equipment?"

Clint rolled his eyes. "If I say yes, will you shut up?"

She grinned, enjoying his discomfort. "What else? New uniforms, a secretary, hmm, maybe some permanent staff since I've heard the town uses volunteers?"

"All of the above and two helicopters outfitted with the latest firefighting and crime-fighting tech—so the police can use them too," Clint admitted, sounding resigned. He stared up at the bright blue sky and shook his head. "It's something I've been working on since I returned home. How the hell do you get me to tell you stuff I don't tell anyone else?"

"It's a skill," Fee said, sounding, and feeling, smug.

"War hero, rich, sexy as hell and generous," Fee added. "You are too much, Rockwell."

"I'm not a hero. I have the money and I'm sure as hell not sexy."

He uttered those words with complete conviction. Fee shook her head in disbelief. She met his eyes and arched her eyebrows. "Did we not have this conversation? Did I not see you naked?"

Clint rubbed the back of his neck. "Holy crap, Martinez, stop."

"Why?" Fee demanded, wanting to see what he'd do, whether he was going to slam his mouth on hers, like they both were desperate for him to do. Dammit, the attraction hadn't faded; they still wanted each other as much as before.

"I want some more naked time, with you," Fee stated, holding his eye.

And her breath.

"Another one-night stand?"

Fee just nodded, unable to talk for once, since her heart sat on her tongue.

Clint looked at his watch and took forever to answer. "I have an appointment now but I can reschedule."

It was tempting—it really was. Fee was considering whether she could duck out of her commitments when Clint's phone jangled. He cursed before pulling it from the back pocket of his pants. Frowning, he quickly answered the call and his terse one-word replies gave her no hint of the subject of the conversation. Clint finished his call, told her he needed a rain check and started to walk toward his SUV across the road.

"What's the matter?" Fee demanded, walking quickly to match his long stride.

"There was a lightning strike yesterday and it set some land alight on the outskirts of town. We thought we had it under control but it sparked up again and if we don't get it under control quickly, it can become a big problem," Clint replied, sounding terse.

"Because of these winds, right?"

Clint nodded and pulled his keys from the pocket of his chinos. "I'm going to head over there, assess the situation, decide whether we need more people to fight it. So, about that rain check?"

It wasn't the right time to discuss this, he was in a hurry, but she didn't want him to think there was a possibility of anything growing between them. This was just about a passionate attraction, she was leaving soon.

She always left…

"We're still ships passing in the night, right?"

Clint cupped her jaw, ran his thumb across her lower lip. "I kind of think we're still in the harbor, on furlough, needing to have some fun before we both move on. Can I call you?"

They exchanged numbers and Fee sighed when Clint's lips met hers in a hard, passion-filled kiss. He pulled back and cursed. "I shouldn't, I don't have time but…hell."

He gathered her close, kissed her thoroughly, his tongue sliding into her mouth as if he owned it. Fee didn't mind, she was happy to stand on any pavement, anywhere being kissed by this man.

The sound of a honking car broke their kiss and Fee heard catcalls and whistles and the rich laughter of four elderly women slowly driving past. Fee, mortified, closed her eyes and wondered how long it would take for this news to hit the gossip airwaves. Ten seconds? Twenty?

"Well, that's going to cause some talk," Clint said.

Fee winced and stepped back. "Sorry."

Clint sent her a rare smile. "Worth it," he said, before climbing into his SUV and driving off.

The fire on the edge of town was under control...not extinguished but under control. Clint stamped on a burning tuft of grass as he retreated toward the road, watching the other firefighters with a critical eye. They had all worked like fiends and he was grateful for their effort since this was a volunteer gig.

As he had back in the unit, Clint felt himself taking command, keeping an eye out, feeling responsible for all the men and women who'd pulled on the safety gear he'd donated and gone out to beat back the fire threatening the houses and land on the west side of town. Somehow, because of his military training, he'd become their temporary Fire Chief. He was proud of Royal, proud of the residents and proud they were prepared to get their hands dirty.

It was nearly over and they could soon go home.

Clint turned at the beep of a horn and sighed when he saw the van pull to a stop behind the cordon. The exhale turned into a muttered curse when he saw those spectacular legs, those black curls. Fee was now dressed in black designer jeans and knee-high heeled boots and wore a thigh-length leather jacket over a white silk top. He'd give her ten minutes, tops, before the flying soot stained it beyond repair.

Clint narrowed his eyes as two men also jumped out of the van, cameras on their shoulders. Fee spoke to one cameraman, her eyes moving from the camera to the swathe of burned land beyond the cordon. She pointed to where the fire stopped on the edge of Mrs. McPherson's garden and her hands moved as fast as her mouth. He wondered what she was saying.

They started to move in his direction and Clint swallowed a curse. He glanced back at his crew, then turned to face Fee and the dreaded cameras.

"Don't have time for this, Martinez."

"Two minutes, Rockwell," Fee said, holding up her finger. "Is everything okay?"

Clint nodded "Yeah, mostly."

"Mostly?"

"There are still a couple of spots burning. We're working on them," Clint said, his tone terse. He felt a fresh gust on his cheek and frowned. The wind had died down ten minutes ago but it was picking up again. He looked around, saw wind whipping the trees and released a series of violent, army-based curses.

Fee reached across the cordon to lay her hand on the yellow sleeve of his fire jacket. "Clint? What is it?"

"The wind has changed direction and is strengthening. If we don't kill the fire now, we're going to have a helluva problem on our hands. We need more hands, and we need them quickly."

Fee handed her microphone to the cameraman—Jimmy?—and spread her hands. "Let me help."

Clint frowned at her. "What?"

Fee pointed to a firefighter who was smacking the grass with the back of a shovel. "I can do that. I want to help. And you just said you need hands."

He did. Not to mention, Fee was wearing her stubborn face and he didn't have time to argue. He wasn't about to put her to work fighting flames—hell to the no!—but there were other ways she could help. He thought for a moment. If the fire turned and started heading back in the direction of the houses, they could find themselves in a world of trouble.

"I need you to go down this street, go house to house and ask the residents to prepare to vacate their houses. I don't want to create a panic—it's a precautionary measure. Make a list of who will go, who won't and get it back to me as soon as possible. Note down any injuries, any sick people, anyone who needs special care. Basically, anybody who can't move fast."

Fee nodded. "Sure, I can do that for you. Where will you be?"

Clint gestured to a strip of flames to the east of the original fire and sighed. "There. Hang around once you've gotten your list. If I need your information, I'll find you."

"Okay." Fee grabbed his hand and squeezed. "Be safe."

Another hard kiss and she didn't seem to mind that his face was covered in grime, that he smelled of fire and smoke and burned grass. "You too. And thanks. I appreciate you pitching in."

Fee smiled. "Hey, the sooner we get this done, the sooner we can play our ships game again. Hurry the hell up."

Clint smiled and then laughed.

Fee was, at the very least, entertaining.

The small fire turned into something bigger than he'd expected, but six hours later they'd managed to contain the blaze. While it wasn't the hardest challenge he'd ever faced, it had been a long day. He was desperate to get home, take off his prosthetic, slide into his tub and stay there until his muscles were lax and his washing-machine brain stopped churning.

Clint walked toward his vehicle and pulled off his jacket. He ran his forearm over his filthy face, grimacing at the streaks of dirt covering his arm. He'd have to take a shower before he sank into his tub. Man, he couldn't wait to get home. Clint looked around, saw many of his crew were also stripping down, guzzling water, all looking tired and played out. The *Secret Lives* van was gone and Clint sighed at his surge of disappointment.

Fee had, obviously, left as well.

Good thing he hadn't needed the list of evacuees from her. *Dammit, Fee, I trusted you with a task and when you got bored, you bailed. What if I had needed that information, what then?*

Annoyed with her, and with himself for believing in her, he flipped open the back door of his SUV and pulled out a cooler. Slamming the lid up, he yanked out a bottle of cold water and furiously cracked the top. This was why he shouldn't trust people, why he should keep to himself, be alone. Because people always, always let you down.

"Can I have one of those?"

Clint lowered the bottle from his mouth and turned around slowly, his eyes widening at the sight of the tiny figure in the fire suit. Her hair hung in strings down her face and her face was as dirty as his, possibly dirtier. The blue rings under her eyes told him she was beyond exhausted.

It looked like she'd been fighting the fire but that was impossible because he was in charge and he hadn't authorized her to fight the goddamn fire! He was going to find the person who put her out there and string him up by his balls! How dare he put her in danger?

"What the hell, Fee?" he roared, causing heads to turn and eyebrows to raise.

"You needed help, I helped," Fee said, placing her hands on her lower back and stretching. Her fire jacket hung past her knees and her boots were at least two sizes too big for her. "And, before you erupt like a volcano, I wasn't in any danger. I just went over ground the guys had already cleared, making doubly sure there were no sparks."

Okay, relief. Maybe he wouldn't have to kill any of his volunteers today.

"Still not happy," he told her, rubbing her cheekbone with his thumb. But he was relieved to know she hadn't bailed and that she'd taken his request to stick around seriously.

"I appreciate your willingness to help, Seraphina, I do. But I didn't know you were in the field and that's a problem. Firstly, because I need to know exactly who I'm responsible for so I can ensure that the head count I had at the beginning is accurate, that the people who walked into the path of the fire are the people who walked out. If you got into trouble, I wouldn't have known to even look for you."

"Dav—" Fee winced as she let slip the name of the volunteer who'd allowed her to work. Clint would deal with him later. "He knew I was there."

"And if he got into trouble and couldn't tell me?" Clint asked, trying to keep his tone conversational. He was trying to be reasonable, reminding himself she was a civilian and he couldn't rip her a new one like he would one of his unit.

She'd also, he admitted, had the best intentions at heart and didn't know any better. Still, she'd never learn if no one told her, so he continued his lecture.

"I have to take every variable into account, think ten steps ahead. And I needed to know where you were in case the fire got out of control and headed for the houses. You had information I might've needed."

"I knew where you were every minute," Fee said, lifting her chin. "I watched you, and I would've known if you were looking for me."

Well, that was something. And, really, they were argu-

ing—discussing—a possibility that hadn't, thankfully, ma-
terialized. And she had pitched in, gotten dirty, shed her
socialite skin to help when help was needed. He admired
and respected her for it.

Clint handed her his all but full bottle of water. "Drink.
And when you're done, drink some more."

"Aye, aye, Lieutenant."

"Smart-ass," Clint muttered as he reached for another
bottle.

Fee's eyes twinkled at him. "I thought you rather liked
my ass."

He did. And every other inch of her body. Fee chugged
back her water, wiping her mouth when she was done and
creating a new streak of dirt across her chin.

He grinned and shook his head. "You are something
else, Seraphina Martinez."

"I know," Fee replied, her tone jaunty. She arched a thin,
dirty eyebrow. "Think you can handle me, Rockwell?"

"I never start something I can't finish, Martinez," Clint
said, not caring the local media were milling about. He'd
spotted a cameraman from a nearby TV station hovering
around earlier but that didn't stop him from reaching for
the zipper on her fire suit and pulling it down.

Fee just laughed. "I wouldn't do that, cowboy."

"And why not?"

Fee laughed at him. "Look down."

Clint looked at her chest and saw she was only wearing
another sexy bra. This one was lacy and transparent and
the color of a tangerine. His mouth, dry from the fire, felt
like it hadn't tasted water in years. He looked again, he
couldn't not, and zipped her up.

"Why aren't you wearing anything under your jacket?"
he asked, sounding like someone had a very strong pair of
hands around his throat.

Fee looked at him as if he'd lost his mind. "Because I was a wearing a very expensive designer silk shirt and it would not survive the soot and dirt." She grinned at him. "You see, I was taking all the variables into account, thinking ten steps ahead."

"As I said, smart-ass."

"Yeah, but you like it."

God help him, he did. And, this time, he wasn't only talking about her very fine butt.

Six

They stripped off in the mudroom off Clint's kitchen and walked through his lovely house in their underwear. Fee was quite glad Clint held her hand and led the way; she wasn't sure whether she'd be able to find his bedroom again in the ridiculously large-for-one-person house.

Fee glanced through open doors as he tugged her along past a library, a study, a sunroom, a kick-ass media-slash-theater room. Another sitting room.

They all but sprinted past the gym containing the massage table where he'd made love to her. At the end of one wing, separate from the rest of the house, Clint pulled her into his bedroom and, once again, she looked around, enjoying the masculine space. The walls and floors were finished to look like concrete and two massive frames, splitting the canvas with a view of a snow-covered mountain, formed the headboard. The room itself was a study in gray and neutral colors but the focal point was the floor-to-ceiling views out over the paddocks to where Clint's award-winning Appaloosas grazed.

It suddenly occurred to Fee that they'd made love in this bed where anyone approaching the paddock could see them.

"While I'm not a prude, I don't feel comfortable standing in front of the window, dressed like this. Or naked."

Clint's teeth flashed white in his soot-covered face. "We can see out, they can't see in."

Thank God. There was reality TV and then there was providing sex shows to Clint's ranch hands. In her book, that was a step, or five hundred, too far.

"Let's get you cleaned up, Seraphina," Clint said, leading her into his gray-and-black bathroom. Stepping into the massive shower cubicle, he flipped the taps to one of the two shower heads and gestured her inside. "Take your time, there's plenty of water."

Fee immediately sensed he was uncomfortable. She saw a pair of crutches within easy reach of the shower stall and noticed the wooden bench running the length of the massive shower. She glanced at his prosthetic and realized Clint would have to remove it to shower. With all its electronics, it couldn't be waterproof.

She'd finally see him without his bionic leg. The last time they made love, he hadn't removed it but it was time. Fee tipped her head to one side and handed him a gentle smile. "Come and shower with me, Rockwell."

Clint looked indecisive and she could see the excuse on his lips. "Clint, c'mon. I'm dead on my feet and we can kill two birds with one stone. We can get clean together and have some fun."

"I—"

Fee placed her hand on his bare chest and sighed.

"We've been over this, Rockwell. I'm not going to faint and run screaming into the night. Trust me, just a little."

Clint scowled and stared at the stream of water falling inside the cubicle. When he cursed and sat down on the bench outside the shower, she knew she had won. The trick was, Fee decided, not to let him see a hint of surprise, a smidgen of doubt. If he did, he'd rabbit and they'd be back to square one.

She needed to distract him so she bent her head for a kiss. Clint pulled back from her and grimaced. "I'm filthy, Fee."

"So am I." She smiled against his lips. "I don't think I've ever been this dirty in my life but it's good dirt, you know? Dirt gathered while I did something important… or am I being silly?"

"I understand exactly what you mean," Clint replied, his eyes serious. "Good dirt is the sweat and dust after rounding up cattle, after spending the day checking fences, training horses."

"It's strange but nice," Fee said. Hearing the release of air, she looked down. Clint's bionic leg was in his hand and she could finally see what was left of his leg. Dropping to her haunches, she examined his injury. The top of his thigh was pure muscle, right down to where his leg ended, an inch or two above his knee. There were scars, sure, lots of them but…

It wasn't a big deal. It wasn't ugly or pretty or strange or unusual, it was…it just was. It was Clint. Fee risked placing her hand over the end of his leg, gently squeezed it and stood up. Handing him a crutch, she quickly stripped out of her underwear and ducked under the spray, groaning as she tipped her face up to receive the hot water.

Bliss.

After a minute, she opened her eyes and looked at Clint,

who looked shocked. She was not going to make this a big deal, because it wasn't. "Are you coming in? Because, you know, over here, I've got soap and skin and shower sex just waiting for you."

Clint gestured to the crutch tucked under his arm. "That's going to have to wait until I get you in my bed."

Fee ignored the tremble in his voice. God, someone had really done a number on his head. "Oh, we'll get to the bed but there's a bench in here. I rather fancy sitting on your lap…"

Clint groaned and pushed his boxer briefs down with one hand. "At the risk of repeating myself, you are something else, Seraphina Martinez."

Fee shot him a naughty grin. "So I've been told."

Turning as he stepped into the cubicle, she flipped on the other shower head and water pounded them from every direction. Fee felt like a dozen hands were massaging her muscles. "Oh, this is fabulous. I want a shower like this."

Clint pulled her to him, aligning their bodies so she was plastered against him, skin to skin. Fee ignored his crutch and lifted her hands to cup his face.

"You did good work today, Rockwell," she said, loving the gold in his hazel eyes. Gold meant he was turned on, feeling relaxed. Green was his hiding-from-the-world color. When his eyes turned gray, as they did earlier when he heard she'd been fighting the fire, she knew he was angry.

He was such a protector, such an alpha male. God, she adored him.

Shaking off the unsettling thought that she was allowing Clint to sneak too far under her skin, Fee lifted her mouth for a kiss and sighed when he covered her lips with his. Passion sparked, flared and exploded. His tongue wound around hers, demanding that she keep up as he feasted on her mouth. Fee fell, whirling and swirling, into this magical world he created, allowing their mutual fascination to take her on a magic carpet ride.

This was as close to love as she'd ever felt since those first heady days with her ex. A little scared but a lot turned on, Fee ran her hands down his sides, across his hard stomach and down to capture his hard cock between her hands. He used his free hand to hold one breast, his thumb swiping her nipple before running the backs of his fingers down her ribcage, and down her hip to a small patch of hair at the top of her sex. Then his long fingers parted her, tested her, and she whimpered as her magic carpet lifted her higher. Clint found her bundle of nerves and gently, so gently, stroked her. Fee dropped her forehead onto his sternum, panting softly. There were so many sensations hitting her—the hot, hard streams of water, the sooty scent of his fabulous skin, the harshness of his ragged breath as she stroked him from base to tip, his warm mouth on the ball of her shoulder.

It was all too much, too intense. She was so close and, judging by his soft curses and the urgency with which he thrust into her fist, so was he.

Fee let out a whimper as he slid a finger into her, then another and she released a low scream when he curled his fingers to hit a spot deep inside her. His thumb brushed her clit and she moaned against his chest, instinctively increasing the pressure on his cock, rubbing her thumb across the head every time he thrust his hips into her hard grip.

"So close, Fee," Clint muttered.

"Me too."

"Fly, sweetheart." Clint tapped her inner walls and Fee, flying on her magic carpet, hit the sun and shattered into a million sunbeams. From somewhere far away she realized Clint had also found his release and it felt like they were dancing on the rainbow, riding streams of sunlight.

The rainbow slowly disappeared and gray tiles and black walls replaced the shimmery sunbeams. Eventually, Fee blinked, realizing she had collapsed against Clint who, in turn, was using the wall to hold up their combined weight. He still held his crutch under one arm but the other was wrapped around her back, holding her tight. The side of his face rested on the top of her head.

"What the hell was that?" Clint muttered.

"Mutual madness," Fee sleepily replied. Now, if he could wash her, dress her and let her sleep, that would be great.

"Well said." Clint lifted his head up. Fee managed to raise her own head to smile at him.

"Was that amazingly good or was that just me?"

"It was good," Clint responded, dropping a quick kiss on her lips. He touched her lips with his fingers before pushing some wet curls off her forehead. "Let's get you clean and dressed, Martinez, and I'll see what I can heat up for supper."

Fee yawned and reached for the loofah and soap. "Don't worry about food. I'm too exhausted to eat."

"Food, then sleep."

"Sleep, then more sex—we can skip the food."

Clint smiled at her and her stomach rolled over. Really, the man should smile more since his smiles had the power to light up the sun. "I know my housekeeper cooked up some mole poblano earlier today."

Fee narrowed her eyes at him in mock outrage. "You're trying to tempt me to eat using Mexican food?"

"Well…yeah."

Fee was suddenly ravenous. "Well, it worked. I adore

mole. Let's get clean and eat. Okay, new plan, food, sex and sleep."

Clint sent her a look of mock horror. "Woman, you're insatiable."

She needed to remind them why they were here, what they were doing. "Well, if this is just our furlough together then I've got to get in as much as I can before I leave. Don't you agree?"

Clint's eyes took on a hint of green. "Absolutely." He reached for the shampoo and, using the wall for balance, dolloped some into his hand. "Because we're both not looking for a relationship."

Fee stared down at her pink toes. Exactly.

Because she wasn't...

Was she?

It was past midnight and Fee had yet to fall asleep. The moon was high in the sky and provided them with enough light to pick up the movement of the wind blowing in the trees, the individual slats of the white paddock fences.

It was a stunning night and if she only had a little time with Clint, she didn't want to waste it sleeping.

"Are you asleep?" Fee whispered, her words bouncing off Clint's chest. Her head was on his shoulder, her thigh rested across his leg, her knee tucked into it. She'd never felt so comfortable, so at peace, in her life.

"Nah. But if you want more sex, I doubt I can oblige. I'm done."

Fee doubted that. She was sure she could persuade him but she was too relaxed to make the effort. She just wanted to lie here, in his big arms, feeling happy and relaxed and, yes, protected.

Despite having parents, she'd been—mentally and emotionally—on her own for most of her life and she could count, on one hand, the number of people with whom she could fully relax. But Clint made her feel more than relaxed; he made her feel safe, like trouble would have to go through him before reaching her.

It was both a heady and a dangerous feeling. She couldn't allow herself to get used to it. She was leaving, sometime soon after the New Year's Eve bash at the famous, original TCC clubhouse. Within days she'd be gone and Clint would be nothing more than a delicious memory.

"I can hear you thinking," Clint said, his fingers running up and down her spine.

She couldn't tell him the truth so she hunted for another subject. "Did you ever think about following your mom into journalism?"

Clint tensed. "Hell, no."

Fee frowned, remembering she'd seen footage of him on one of his mom's shows. The research she'd done on him since their first time together had been extensive. And, no, she wasn't creepy. Or weird.

Just curious.

She might as well be upfront about it. "I like to know with whom I'm sleeping so I did a little research on you. For someone with no social media presence, there's a lot about you on the 'net."

Clint answered with a sleepy "yeah" but didn't sound like he cared much.

"I watched some old reruns of your mom's show. She often talks about you. She's even shown videos of your graduation ceremony and some from your childhood. She spoke about you often during her series about wounded soldiers and their heroism. They were heart-wrenching and rather wonderful."

"Yeah, my mom is a great BS artist."

Fee pulled her head off his chest to look up into his hard eyes. "What do you mean by *that*?"

Clint's sigh whispered over her hair. "My mom talks a good line but she doesn't like getting her hands dirty. Her sympathy and her patriotic spirit are all BS. She doesn't care about me, or about any of the veterans she interviewed for that series. She's all about her ratings and understands that wounded soldiers are a great way to get viewers."

He made the harsh statement in an ordering-coffee voice and Fee knew that she had to choose her next words carefully. "How do you know that, Clint?"

"Because she was in my room after I had my leg amputated and I overheard her telling her manager that I repulsed her. That she liked pretty and she liked perfect and I didn't hit either mark anymore. And she was happy I had a massive trust fund to fund me and a girlfriend to nurse me because she had no intention of helping my suddenly incapable ass." His voice was rough with disappointment and anger. "And I realized that if she couldn't care about me, how much can she care about the other vets?"

God, that explained so much. Fee suddenly understood why he was so independent, why he pushed himself so hard. It made her heart ache for him even as she reeled at his mother's callous attitude. While her parents had been a tad neglectful and a lot self-absorbed, they were never cruel.

His mother was a witch of epic proportions. "Man, that's cold."

Clint's fingers dug into her spine. "She really is. She's all about the packaging, not the gift."

"Is she the reason you keep to yourself, why you don't interact much with people? Why you don't…date?"

Fee knew there was more to his story, a lot more, and she wanted to know every detail.

"As I said, I had a girlfriend when I returned home," he admitted. "We'd been together for a while, but after the surgery, she moved in. She really looked after me. Saw to my every need…except one."

Fee winced. "Sex?"

"Yep."

Ah, no.

"She couldn't, with me, and after she left, I tried to date but that didn't turn out so well. So, I figured it was easier not to."

No wonder he'd had doubts about her reaction to seeing him naked. Who wouldn't?

"Between my mother and my ex and my inability to get lucky, I kind of lost my faith in people after that. I suppose that's also why I avoided Royal and people in general. I hate feeling less than, weak, incapable, disabled."

Fee tightened her arm across his chest and kissed his shoulder.

"I vowed I would do everything and anything I was able to do before. And I vowed I would never let anyone see me as anything other than fully capable."

And that was why he never allowed anyone to see his fake leg, to see him using crutches, to view him as being disabled. Because he wasn't disabled. He was one of the most able people she knew. "You've just lost half of your leg, that's all. To me it's no more important than a scar or a birthmark. It's a part of you but it doesn't define you."

Clint didn't reply—she hadn't expected him to—but she felt his appreciation in the way he tightened his grip on her, in the way he rested his lips in her hair. It was all she needed.

Clint's voice, when he spoke again minutes later, was rough with emotion. "How was your Christmas, by the way? Where did you go?"

Back on stable conversational ground. "I went to see my folks, in Florida. I gave them a cruise for Christmas, they gave me a voucher from Target. My mom bitched about my antics on *Secret Lives*, I tried to explain, again, that the show is scripted, that I'm playing a part. She doesn't get it."

"Not much reality in reality TV, huh?"

"Not so much, no," Fee replied. "But it's provided me with a healthy nest egg and a platform. I'm thinking about writing another cookbook, maybe trying to get a gig as a celebrity chef when the show ends."

"You cook?"

"I cook damn well," Fee told him. "I spent a lot of my childhood comfort eating and I wanted to learn how to make the foods I loved. We moved around too much for me to be able to revisit favorite restaurants or bakeries so I had to figure out how to cook everything myself. I make a mean red velvet cupcake and my fish tacos are to die for."

Clint moaned. "I love fish tacos." He pulled away from her to lie on his side, his head resting in his hand, facing her. "Why did you comfort eat?"

Time for her to get personal. Fee thought it wasn't clever to be exchanging confidences when she was leaving—but then, maybe that was what made it okay. In a few weeks, he'd just be a lovely memory, so what was the harm in telling him things she'd never told anyone before?

"We moved a lot and there was a new school—sometimes more than one—every year. Coming into a new school as a fat Latina was like putting a bull's-eye on your head and handing the kids a bow and arrow. I learned to fade into the walls, to make myself as invisible as possible. Even if I'd wanted to make friends, it wouldn't have been easy. And I didn't want to. Getting attached meant getting hurt... I don't allow myself to become attached, Clint."

"Because it hurts too much when you leave. And you always leave."

She nodded. "I tried to tell my parents I was unhappy, but they brushed me off. I told school counselors, and they did the bare minimum, which basically amounted to nothing."

Fee rested her head on the pillow, her hand on his chest. "I desperately wanted a stable base as a child but thanks to the way I grew up, I was equally terrified of being trapped. While I was going through hell at one school or another, the only way to survive was to believe I was only there for a set time, that the next school, town, situation would be better. I built up this idea that the grass is always greener just around the corner."

Clint stroked her from shoulder to hand and back up again. "Parents and the many ways they manage to mess with their kids' heads."

"Do you want kids, Clint?" Fee sleepily asked.

"Yeah, sort of. Bit difficult to do when I'm not so keen on the wife and the relationship that goes along with them. You?"

Fee yawned. "Sort of, for the same reasons." Her eyes drifted close. "I'm so tired, Clint."

Clint's fingers drifted across her jaw. "Then sleep, sweetheart. I've got you."

He did, but just for tonight. Because that was all she had, all she was allowed.

Situated in Royal, The Bellamy was the establishment all Fee's future visits to hotels would be measured against. Sitting on fifty or more acres of ruthless landscaping and lavish gardens, it had more than two hundred lusciously appointed suites, containing every gadget known to man. As well as staying at the resort while in Royal, she and her friends had been filmed dancing, and drinking, in The Silver Saddle bar and eating tapas from their award-winning menu. They'd eaten at the hotel's amazing farm-to-table restaurant The Glass House and today they were going to be filmed enjoying a spa day at Pure.

The Bellamy had it all.

After a night long on sex and short on sleep, Fee hoped she wouldn't snooze her way through the filming.

Deciding she needed coffee—preferably intravenously injected—she popped into the small, intimate coffee shop to the left of the dining room and smiled when she saw Lulu sitting at a small table by the French doors, scrolling through her phone. Kace LeBlanc sat at the table next to hers, reading a newspaper, and they were both studiously, deliberately ignoring each other.

What was their problem?

Pulling out a chair opposite Lu, Fee sat down, reached for Lu's coffee mug and took a large sip. Black and sweet, just the way she liked it.

"Hey!" Lu complained, her head jerking up.

"I need it," Fee told her, taking another drink. When the waitress approached them, she quickly ordered a stack of pancakes and a cup of coffee of her own.

"Nigel will freak if you put on weight," Lulu pointed out.

Fee smirked. "I worked it off last night and I'll go for a run later."

"God, I hate you," Lulu told her, raising her voice so the next part could be heard clear across the room. "I think I'm a born-again virgin, it's been so long."

Because Lulu was rarely so brash, and never at that volume, Fee quickly realized she was trying to make Kace feel uncomfortable. Fee darted a look at him but the man gave no indication he was listening to their conversation.

"I'm so jealous," Lulu told her. "I still haven't bagged a cowboy of my own."

Kace abruptly stood up and threw his linen napkin onto the table. They both watched as he quietly and deliberately folded his newspaper before finally tucking it under his arm. When he lifted his head, he only had eyes for Lulu.

"Can you, possibly, drop the reality star persona for five seconds?"

Lulu draped an elegant arm over the back of her chair. It was no accident that the movement made her chest lift. Kace's eyes dropped and he looked his fill. He shook his head when their gazes clashed again. "Like what you see, LeBlanc?"

"Any man with a pulse would," Kace replied. "But that's all surface, Ms. Sheppard. Is there anything beneath your pretty exterior? Like a brain? Or a heart?"

Lulu's eyes narrowed and Fee leaned back. She'd experienced Lulu's temper before and Kace was in her firing line. But instead of unloading, Lulu just stared at him with wide, round, hurt, eyes.

Worried that Lulu was genuinely upset, Fee opened her mouth to defend her friend against the stuffy lawyer, prepared to rip his heart out. But Lu shook her head and Fee shut her mouth.

Lulu had this.

One tear, perfect and devastating, rolled down Lulu's cheek. Fee hid her smile knowing Lulu could cry on demand and did it oh, so well. Lulu blinked, allowing another two tears to roll down her face.

"That's such a hurtful thing to say," Lulu whispered, her hand on her heart.

Instead of falling to his knees and begging her forgiveness, LeBlanc just arched one eyebrow, his brown eyes cool. "Cut the crap, Ms. Sheppard, your tears don't fool me."

Fee gasped, then winced. Nobody, and especially no man, had ever looked past Lu's tears. When she turned on the waterworks, every single one of them had begged for her forgiveness.

Huh.

So maybe the stuffy lawyer could see past Lu's particular brand of BS.

Lu's tears instantly cleared. "Well, well, well…you aren't just a pretty face."

Lulu resumed her languid, arm-over-the-back-of-her-chair pose. She crossed one long, gorgeous leg over the other and tipped her head to one side. "What is your problem, LeBlanc? With me, specifically?"

Kace shook his head. "Dammit, you're gorgeous. But you're also vain and superficial and shallow."

"So decisive in your opinions and we haven't even had a proper conversation," Lulu drawled. "Well, if we're making snap judgments, you're buttoned up, stuffy and have a stick up your ass."

Kace sent her a tight smile. "Glad to have that cleared up." Picking up his briefcase, he abruptly turned and marched out of the coffee shop.

Because she admired the back view of a built guy as much as the next girl, Fee sighed. "He's seriously hot."

Lulu reached across the table and pinched the skin on the back of her hand. Fee yelped and jerked her hand away. "What is wrong with you?"

"He's annoying, and stuffy, and condescending and annoying—"

"You said that."

"—and patronizing and buttoned up and very, very annoying."

"You're repeating yourself," Fee said, enjoying herself hugely. Lulu usually had men eating out of her hand and it was fun watching her deal with the one man who refused to grovel at her admittedly beautiful feet.

"You're attracted to him," she added.

"I. Am. Not," Lulu told her through gritted teeth.

"And you both love and hate the fact he's not super impressed by you."

Lulu glared at her. "Stop. Talking."

"You want what you can't have," Fee said, risking her friend's legendary temper.

"I hate you so much right now."

Fee leaned back as the waitress placed her plate in front of her. When the girl was gone, she dug into her pancakes.

"And you're jealous I spent the night having spectacular sex and you…didn't." Come to think of it, that really was strange. Even if she was trading barbs with the stuck-up lawyer, Lulu normally, at the very least, had a handful of men wrapped around her baby finger.

Fee chewed, swallowed and waved her fork around. "This town is full of sexy men and you're telling me you haven't managed to date one of them? Why is that, Miss Lulu?"

Lulu picked up a fork and Fee hoped she wouldn't use it as a weapon. "Nobody has caught my eye."

"Oh, someone has caught your eye and you're just pissed you can't bring him to heel, and worse, can't BS him," Fee told her, leaning back as Lu raised her fork. "Don't stab me."

"It's tempting but not today," Lulu retorted. "I am not attracted to LeBlanc. He's so not my type."

Fee hooted, amused. "He's smart, rich and stunningly good-looking. He's *so* your type."

Lulu's fork missed Fee's hand by half an inch and landed in her stack of pancakes. She cut through the fluffy stack with the back of her fork then lifted a huge mouthful and shoved it into her mouth.

Lulu glared at her as she chewed. When she was done, she narrowed her eyes at Fee. "You have me eating pancakes."

"Not me. You always comfort eat when you're upset."

Lulu went back for another bite and Fee whipped her plate away. "Prove LeBlanc didn't upset you by not having another bite."

Lulu held her stare but, after ten seconds, dropped her eyes and waved the waitress over. "Bring me my own pancakes please, heavy on the bacon and the syrup."

"Thought so," Fee said, smirking.

"Fee?" Lulu asked, super sweetly.

"Mmm?"

"Shut. The. Hell. Up."

Seven

What in the name of all things holy was he doing?

Clint stood in front of the door to Fee's home away from home, her suite at The Bellamy, and glared at his highly polished wingtips. He was dressed in a tuxedo, bow tie perfectly knotted, hair brushed and his face clean of its habitual scruff. He'd spent more time dressing for this one night than he had the entire week.

All because Fee had asked him to accompany her to the New Year's Eve ball at the Texas Cattleman's Club. He didn't do balls, the TCC or people, so why on God's great green wonderful earth was he standing outside her hotel door prepared to do all three?

All because a gorgeous brunette with a huge heart and wild curls asked him. And he couldn't blame a post-sex haze for his saying yes. They hadn't even been in the same room. She'd called him up, issued the invitation and he hadn't hesitated.

He was definitely losing his mind.

Clint jammed his hands into the pockets of his tuxedo pants and rocked on his heels. He and Fee had spent all their free time together lately—including very slow horse rides (Fee had never ridden before and was taking forever to learn), quiet dinners and sitting on the porch, drinking wine and talking—and it had been the best time of his life.

The Fee he was coming to know was nothing like the fast-talking, over-the-top character she played on the two episodes of *Secret Lives* he'd managed to watch. Oh, she was a firecracker in either incarnation, and wasn't scared to share her opinions, but one-on-one she was softer and gentler than her on-screen persona.

Clint raked his hand through his hair. She was… amazing.

Uncomfortable with that thought, Clint tried to distract himself by thinking how much had changed, in Royal and in himself.

The Blackwood siblings versus Miranda war was still raging, Kace LeBlanc was still, he presumed, doing what lawyers did to resolve the situation. The *Secret Lives* crew was still milking the drama for reality gold.

All the players in that saga would be present tonight and arguments and snide comments were, as he'd heard from Fee, expected. The situation was tense and everyone was on edge.

Not his problem.

But, at some point the buzz would die down—probably sooner rather than later—and Fee would return to Manhattan. That was a given.

He'd miss her, that much he knew. He also accepted they couldn't have a long-distance relationship. What they had wouldn't survive her leaving Royal. It was a long way from Manhattan to Texas, and if he could barely cope with the small town of Royal, he'd go mad visiting New York.

And, for Fee, Royal was a quirky place to visit but she was too much of a city girl to settle down in a smallish agricultural town.

Not that she had any plans to settle down anywhere. Fee, as she'd told him, liked having options, being able to move on when she needed to. Despite his career in the military, he'd always know he'd return to Royal and his land. He was emotionally tied to his ranch, to his grandfather's and great-grandfather's legacy. He belonged in Texas, on his ranch, raising cattle and horses and avoiding people as much as possible.

They were all the opposites—sun and moon, light and dark, city and country. They didn't have a hailstone's chance in hell of making a relationship work. He didn't want a relationship...

People, he reminded himself, hurt people.

So why was he standing here? Why wasn't he back on the ranch, listening to the wind whistling through the trees, sitting on his porch as one year rolled into another?

Because she'd asked him...

It was a short-term fling, a flash in the pan, a brief, fun affair. There was no need for self-analysis or deep introspection. He wasn't expecting more, neither was she. He was overthinking this...

Just stop, Rockwell. Right damn now.

Annoyed with himself, Clint rapped on the door and heard the click of heels on the tiled floor on the other side of the door. He heard the snick of a lock opening and, when he saw what she was wearing, reached for the doorframe to steady himself.

It was a dress, floor-length, embroidered, with long sleeves, the color of a fiery Rockwell ranch sunset.

The dress plunged to her navel in an enormous V, showing a considerable amount of her fantastic breasts. Clint couldn't decide whether he should rush her downstairs to show her off or take her back inside to see what that dress looked like on the floor. Instead, he just stared at her and reminded himself to breathe. *Holy crap.*

"Hi," Fee said, sounding a little shy. Clint pulled himself together and noticed the hesitancy in her eyes, her need for reassurance. Strange, because he'd never seen her question herself. She'd always seemed to be thoroughly confident in her body.

Could she, possibly, be waiting for his approval, wanting to hear whether he thought she looked good?

She didn't look good—she looked magnificent.

"Uh…um." He could think the words, apparently, but verbalizing them was giving him difficulty.

Fee stroked the lapel of his tuxedo. "You look wonderful, Rockwell. Very debonair."

Say something, dammit. "Thanks. You… Jesus, Fee, that's a helluva dress."

Fee held the edges of the skirt and winced. "Too much?"

He shook his head and ran his finger down the curve of one breast. "Yes, no… My head is spinning."

"In a good or bad way?" Fee asked and he caught her hesitancy again. *Get over yourself, Rockwell.*

Clint held her face in his hands and looked her in the eye. "You look amazing, perfect, gorgeous…too sexy for words. As you might have gathered."

Delight jumped into her brilliant eyes. "Really?"

"Oh, yeah," Clint answered her, looking at her mouth. "Can I kiss you or am I going to find myself wearing your particular shade of lipstick?"

Those plump lips curved up. "It's stay-fast so you should be good."

Clint touched his lips to hers, sighing when she grabbed the lapels of his jacket, holding on while he ravaged her mouth. Yeah, skipping the ball sounded like a fine idea. He'd take his time removing her dress. He'd leave her heels and her dangly earrings on while he kissed her from top to toe…

"Ah, get a room. But later, because we're going to be late."

Clint reluctantly pulled his mouth off Fee's to look over his shoulder at Lulu, who was closing the door to her own suite. She wore an aqua-colored dress with a coral band across one shoulder. Even to someone as fashion-challenged as him, the hues were a perfect complement to her warm Caribbean island-girl skin.

Fee stepped away from him and walked over to her friend, taking both her hands as they each gave the other a critical once-over.

"Love that color on you," Lulu said.

"Ditto. Your makeup is fantastic."

Clint had to smile at their mutual admiration society, appreciating how easily they communicated, how in tune they seemed to be. This was friendship, he realized. The give and take, the easy, genuine compliments. He didn't have a friend like hers, not anymore.

And whose fault was that? The vets who worked for him were his employees and he'd isolated himself after leaving the military, he'd brushed off offers of help, of company, the invitation to join the TCC. Fee had become his closest friend since leaving his unit and she'd be leaving soon and he'd go back to his solitary life.

Or maybe he didn't have to. Maybe, when she left, instead of brooding at home, he could invite some of the volunteer firefighters to Rockwell Ranch for a barbecue. He could join the TCC. He could start, slowly, to reintegrate himself into the community.

He'd need a distraction to keep him from missing Fee...

But, still...*people.*

He'd see. Fee needed to leave and then he'd re-evaluate his life. Hell, for all he knew he might just slide back into being the crotchety bastard he'd been before Hurricane Fee blew into his life. That was definitely the easier option—interacting with people took work...

But sometimes, like with Fee, the result—laughter, a connection, frickin' great sex—was worth it.

Fee's hand on his arm jerked him back to the present. He looked at her gorgeous, puzzled face. Did he have shaving cream on his cheek, something in his teeth? "What?"

"You just zoned out there for a minute," Fee replied, linking her fingers with his. "Ready to face the good citizens of Royal?"

Her hand felt right in his. Escorting her to the TCC clubhouse felt like it was something he was meant to do. But he did know his presence would set the gossip chain on fire.

Anything for Fee...

He smiled at her before returning his attention to Lulu. "Would you like to join us, Lulu?"

Lulu was opening her mouth to reply when they heard footsteps approaching them and Kace LeBlanc turned the corner, stopping abruptly when he caught sight of Lulu. Yep, that was what stunned looked like.

LeBlanc recovered a lot quicker than Clint had.

"Ladies, you look lovely," Kace said, approaching them with his hand outstretched for Clint to shake. He greeted Kace and returned his hand to Fee's back.

"Are you going to ride with us, Lulu?" Fee asked.

"I can give her a ride," Kace offered. "I came to collect

Miranda but she's left already. I have space for you two as well, if you'd prefer not to take your car," Kace told Clint.

Clint considered it for a minute, thinking it would be nice to have a couple of beers and not have to worry about going over the limit. Then he shook his head. "I appreciate the offer but I'd prefer to have my own vehicle in case another fire sparks and I have to leave quickly."

Kace nodded. "Understood." He looked at Lulu. "Ms. Sheppard?"

Even Clint, socially inept as he was, heard the challenge in Kace's voice. He looked at Fee and raised his eyebrows, silently asking whether he was imagining the electricity arcing between the tall lawyer and Fee's gorgeous friend.

Fee winked at him and they waited for Lulu's answer. Lulu eventually lifted her chin and nodded, with all the condescension of a Nubian queen.

"Thank you. Are you driving or do you have a driver?" Lulu demanded.

Ooh, snooty.

"I have a driver. Sorry, but you'll have to tolerate my presence for a very short time," Kace smoothly replied. "Just as I will have to tolerate yours."

Clint pulled a face at Fee, who was trying not to laugh.

Lulu looked at Fee. "Have bail money ready in case I kill him on the short drive from the resort to the club."

Fee struggle to keep her face impassive. "Always. Remember, jail orange is not your color."

Lulu picked up the skirts of her floor-length dress and arched an imperious eyebrow at LeBlanc "Shall we go?"

"Yes, your highness."

That wasn't a compliment, Clint thought as Kace and Lulu walked down the passage ahead of them. When they were out of earshot, he turned to Fee, laughter bubbling in his chest. "What the hell was that?" he asked.

Fee giggled. "Aren't they too precious for words? All growly and snarly and irritated because they are both too stubborn to admit they desperately want to see the other naked."

"Kind of like us when we first met," Clint said.

"Exactly like us," Fee cheerfully stated as she tucked her hand into the crook of his elbow. "I hope they eventually have the same fabulous time we've had. But they are running out of time—we're leaving Royal soon."

Yeah, did she have to remind him?

Miranda entered the ballroom at the TCC clubhouse by herself, choosing to make the silent statement that she was fine on her own, that she didn't need the acceptance of Royal residents, the members of the Texas Cattleman's Club or her stepchildren.

Stepchildren who were closer to her age than she'd been to their father's. Stepchildren who'd resented her role in their father's life even before he'd left her the inheritance they thought should be theirs.

Dammit, Buck, my life was perfect before you dropped this mess in my lap.

Miranda took a glass of champagne from a tray and caught a glimpse of her reflection in one of the many mirrors in this ballroom. She was pleased with her tight silver dress; it showed off her fantastic cleavage and the embroidered pattern between her breasts and hips highlighted her curves. The slit that came halfway up her thigh revealed her toned leg.

She looked good.

Looking good was great armor.

"Miranda."

Miranda turned and sighed at Kellan Blackwood's tight face. He'd found love with Buck's housekeeper and she looked around to see if she could spot the woman who'd been a faithful friend to her and Buck, in spite of Kellan's anger and resentment toward them both.

Not seeing Irina, Miranda forced a smile, knowing many eyes were watching their exchange. The cameras were also pointed in her direction, and she knew when the viewers watched this episode of *Secret Lives*, they'd wait in eager anticipation for the fireworks.

But, unlike some of her costars, she didn't seek notoriety. "Let's not make a scene, Kellan. It's New Year's Eve and this is supposed to be a happy event."

"I'm not the one who came back to Royal, determined to cheat a family out of their home and their father's wealth. I'm not the one who brought a camera crew with her to document the process," Kellan said, keeping his voice low.

He made it sound like she had complete control over the directors and producers, just as he apparently thought she'd controlled Buck. Miranda felt a headache building between her eyes. "Yeah, that's exactly what I did, Kellan. Where's Irina?"

"She's talking to Sophie." Miranda looked across the room to where her stepdaughter stood, tall and curvy, her dark hair and olive complexion the exact opposite of the Irina's pale skin, blond hair and blue eyes. Night and day, sun and moon, Miranda thought. Not unlike the way one of them liked and trusted her while the other passionately detested her.

Kellan also loathed her. So why was he talking to her? Why he was confronting her in front of everyone? He had to know their interaction would cause tongues to wag. Not that she cared about what the good residents of Royal thought, but he should.

"Say what you want to say, Kellan, and let's move on," Miranda said, giving him a tight smile.

Kellan's hand tightened around the tumbler of whiskey in his hand. "Irina and I were married in Nashville."

Whoa. Okay, then. "Congratulations?" Miranda posed the word as a question.

"We're very happy," Kellan stated, sounded defensive.

"Okay?" Another one-word answer, framed as a question. She saw the irritation flash in his eyes and smiled. These Blackwood children deserved to feel a little of the irritation, and annoyance, she constantly lived with.

"I want to make it perfectly clear I'm still going to fight you, tooth and nail, to win back my father's estate. We will claw back everything he gave you, Miranda."

This. Again. God, she was so tired. Instead of replying, Miranda just waited him out, knowing he would fill the silence she created.

"My wife wants to make Royal our base."

"What about your businesses in Nashville?"

"I'll travel back and forth to Nashville, as needed," Kellan said. "I just wanted you to know marriage hasn't made me soft. I still intend to fight you for everything you took from my siblings and me."

Same old same old. Miranda opened her mouth to blast him then remembered where she was and that the guests and the cameras were waiting for her to blow. She wouldn't give either audience the pleasure. "Noted."

Kellan waited for her to say more and when she just sipped her champagne, his frown deepened. "Is that all you have to say?"

Miranda nodded. "For now."

"What the hell does that mean?" Kellan demanded.

Just because it would make good TV, and because it would confuse the hell out of him, his siblings and everyone watching, Miranda reached up and placed a kiss on his cheek. Making sure her voice carried to both the guests, the cameras and the roving microphone held by the *Secret Lives* sound guy, she smiled at him as she wiped her lipstick off his cheek with her thumb.

"Congratulations, darling. I hope you and Irina are very happy together, like I was with your father."

Miranda heard the collective intake of breath, the murmurs following her controversial statement. Then she walked away, thinking the world couldn't prove or disprove her statement. Despite their divorce, nobody had known the true state of her marriage to Buck and she intended to keep it that way.

The cast of *Secret Lives* weren't the focus tonight and the cast wasn't miked so Fee didn't have to watch what she said. They'd been told the coverage of the ball would be minimal and they only needed to make a few direct-to-camera comments apiece and they'd be done.

And that meant Fee could have a quiet conversation with her best friend, who was, she reluctantly admitted, looking a little shell-shocked.

Leaving Clint talking to James Harrison, the TCC president—Clint being present at this party was causing a stir and everybody wanted a word with him—Fee walked over to where Lulu was standing on her own by a potted plant, looking a little dazed and a lot confused.

Fee walked up to her, put her arm around her friend's waist and gently turned her so they were both angled toward the wall and the room couldn't watch their interaction.

"Sweetie, are you okay?"

Lulu's lovely eyes met Fee's as she lifted a hand to her mouth and shook her head. "Not really."

Fee heard the panic in Lu's voice and instinctively went into mama-bear mode. Something was wrong and she was going to kick some lawyer's ass. She didn't think that Kace LeBlanc had hurt Lulu, she couldn't imagine him doing that. But something had happened...and she might have to get her ex-army ranger boyfriend—lover, fling, whatever—to knock him all the way across Texas.

"If said something that really hurt you, I will rip him apart," Fee muttered. "What did he say to you?"

Lulu shook her head and held up her hands. "Nothing."

Fee narrowed her eyes. "Then why are you looking all dazed and freaked out and crazy?"

Lulu placed her hand on her heart and gnawed on her inside of her cheek. "Because it was so damn fantastic, Fee. How can someone I loathe make me feel so...spacey?"

Okay, time to play catch-up. "What, exactly, happened on your five-minute drive, Miss Lulu?"

"Fastest, sexiest, craziest five minutes of my life," Lulu told her, pink in her cheeks.

"I swear, Lu, if you don't spill, I'm going to beat it out of you."

Lulu sighed and sighed again. "We didn't speak, at all, from the time we left you until we reached the limo waiting under the portico of The Bellamy. He opened the back door for me, I got in and he sat opposite me. The driver pulled off, Kace looked at me and...bam!"

Bam? What did that mean?

"I'm not sure whether he moved first or I did, but our eyes just connected and the next minute my dress was up around my waist and I was straddling his thighs and his hands were on my butt and his tongue was in my mouth and... *God.*"

Whoa. Hot damn.

"Not one word, we just kissed and kissed and..." Lulu saw a waiter carrying a tray of champagne and snapped her fingers to grab his attention. Lulu picked a glass up from the tray and downed the contents. She snagged the waiter's arm before he could walk away, handing Fee a glass before gulping a second one herself.

Fee stopped her from reaching for a third. "Nope, no throwing more liquor down your throat. Tell me what happened next."

The waiter finally escaped and Lu held her empty glass to her chest. "The limo stopped. Kace—" he was Kace now, Fee noticed, not Mr. Stick-Up-His-Ass as Lu normally called him "—put me back on the seat. He climbed out of the car, looking super cool, and helped me out. He walked me into the ballroom in complete silence, handed me a glass of champagne and a sarcastic smile and then walked away without looking back. I've been in a daze ever since."

Interesting. Lulu wasn't the type to lose her head over a man. "Wow. Just…wow."

Lulu frowned. "How can someone who irritates me so intensely set my panties alight? Fee…" She held her index finger and thumb an inch apart. "I was this close to letting him nail me in the back of the limo. It's stupid, and silly, and annoying and incomprehensible."

"It's chemistry."

"Or I have multiple personalities and the crazy woman inside me is making her presence known," Lulu muttered. "Maybe I'm simply psychotic."

"Chemistry," Fee insisted.

"I'd prefer to be psychotic," Lulu retorted. She tossed back her hair, straightened her spine and lifted her chin. Yep, Queen Lulu was back. "I will not let him affect me. I will not make a big deal about a hot kiss from a man who doesn't like me enough to try and make conversation. I deserve to be treated better."

"You do," Fee said. Then she looked past her friend to

see Kace watching Lulu with all the intensity of a Category 10 storm. He looked as flustered as Lu had earlier.

Yeah, she didn't think Kace was as unaffected as Lulu assumed.

Oh, this was going to be fun to watch.

"He's looking at you," Fee told her and Lu jerked her head around to scan the room. Kace had turned his attention back to the group of men surrounding him but his smirk told Fee he was very aware Lu's eyes were on him.

"This is so high school," Lu muttered, closing her eyes.

Nope, unlike Fee's experiences of high school, this was *fun*.

Eight

Sophie Blackwood stood between her two brothers, dwarfed as she always was by their height and good looks. It had always been the three of them and she was the baby, protected and, she guessed, cosseted. But now Kellan had his arm around the very beautiful Irina. While Sophie liked her brand-new sister-in-law, she felt like everything was changing too quickly and their lives were spinning out of control.

She wanted her dad to be alive, to be able to call Blackwood Hollow home again, to not have to fight Miranda Blackwood for what should be legally theirs. What the hell had their father been thinking leaving everything to Miranda and nothing to them? Had he really hated them that much?

Sophie looked across the room and watched the red-headed woman flirting with someone whose name she couldn't recall but whom she recognized as being a past president of the TCC. The man looked like his tongue was about to fall on the floor at her feet.

Miranda was a beautiful woman and beautiful women had always been her father's weakness. She'd been aware of his affairs from a young age, had met many potential stepmothers but Miranda, thirty years younger than Buck, was the one he'd married minutes after the ink on his divorce papers to Sophie's mom were signed.

Buck had moved on from his wife quickly and it seemed, by leaving everything to Miranda, he'd moved on from his kids as well. His relationship with all of them had been distant at best—problematic at worst—but she'd always thought they'd have a chance to resolve things. That chance was gone now. God, it hurt.

Sophie felt Vaughn's hand on her back and she looked at her brother, gorgeous with blue eyes and his sharp-enough-to-cut-glass jaw. She saw the worry on his face and tried to give him a reassuring smile.

When Vaughn asked her if she was okay, she knew he wasn't fooled.

Sophie shrugged. "As well as can be expected." She tapped her fingernail against the glass of her flute and frowned. "I'm so angry at him, Vaughn. And at her."

Vaughn knew exactly to whom she was referring. "I know, kiddo. We all are. And now we have to deal with meeting, at some point, a half-brother. Jesus."

He looked at Kellan and Irina, who were exchanging a long, loving look. Sophie rolled her eyes at Vaughn. "At least something good has come out of this mess."

"Yeah, they look happy."

Kellan turned his attention to them. "We are happy."

"Very happy," Irina said, laying her head on his shoulder.

Sophie, never having experienced love like that, tried to

control her jealousy. How amazing would it be to feel so at ease with someone, to find the one person you clicked with? She was happy for Kell, she really was, even if she wasn't happy about not being at their wedding.

"I cannot believe you got married on the sly," Sophie stated.

Kellan sighed. "Here we go again."

Sophie ignored him and looked at Irina. "Didn't you want the pretty dress and the vows said in front of a pastor?" Sophie demanded. "The presents and the first dance?"

"I just wanted Kellan," Irina said simply. "The rest is just icing on the cake."

"Icing on the wedding cake you never got to eat," Sophie muttered.

Vaughn laughed. "Give it up, Soph."

Sophie saw Kellan look across to Miranda and his eyes hardened. "I told her we were married and our fight is far from over."

"Good for you," Sophie replied. "Did you also tell her we think she's a classless, over-exercised fortune hunter and that we will wrest her grubby hands off Dad's assets if it's the last thing we do?"

Vaughn smiled at her bloodthirstiness but gestured to draw Sophie's attention toward Irina, who looked uncomfortable. "Easy there, tiger."

Irina excused herself to go to the ladies' room, and Sophie released a huff of exasperation. "I didn't mean to upset Irina—I just get so frustrated with this whole mess! The inheritance, the fact that we have a half-brother out there somewhere. I need answers to how this all happened. But we've only run into dead ends in Royal."

Kellan placed his hands on her shoulders and squeezed. "I understand your frustration, Soph, I'm equally pissed off. But, to be honest, I'm not sure how to unravel this mess."

"I could go to New York City and see if I could dig up some dirt on Miranda."

"And how would you do that, Soph? You're not exactly a PI," Vaughn scoffed.

"I have another idea," Sophie said, choosing her words carefully. "I've been researching reality show TV and I know they film everything and they have hours and hours of outtakes stored…somewhere. I'm pretty sure there will be some compromising footage somewhere. I just need a plan to get it," Sophie mused. "But I'll have to go to New York, I can't do anything from here."

"I don't think that's such a good idea," Kellan responded.

"Why not?" Sophie demanded.

"It's New York, Soph." Vaughn immediately sided with Kellan, both going into protective mode.

"And I'm twenty-seven years old, not a child," Sophie replied, her tone heated. "I need to do something, guys. I can't just sit on my hands, hoping something will change."

Vaughn rubbed the back of his neck. "I don't like it, Sophie."

"Me neither."

"You don't have to like it," Sophie informed them, her determination only growing in the face of their resistance. "I'm an adult and if I want to go to New York, or any other city, I can. If I want to try and track down some footage, that's my prerogative. All you can do is support me. And say thank you when I find something."

When, not if. She refused to accept any other option.

Clearly realizing that she wouldn't back down, Kellan sighed and gave in, shoulders slumping with resignation.

"Don't do anything stupid or illegal, Soph. And if you find yourself out of your depth, you come home."

Sophie rolled her eyes at his comment but she knew when to retreat, when to quit when she was ahead. "I'm a Blackwood," she reminded her brothers. "I'll do whatever is necessary—nothing more…and nothing less."

Fee loved her Bellamy hotel suite, from the bright purple door to the spacious hallway, the cool tones of the lavender-and-white color scheme and the natural light. She loved the French doors and high ceilings but she still would prefer to be on Rockwell Ranch, in Clint's gray-and-black bedroom, rolling around on his sheets.

Having sex in a hotel room brought home the impermanence of their relationship, made what they had feel more like a hookup and a fling…

But it *was* a hookup and a fling, wasn't it?

Fee kicked off her heels in the luxurious sitting area and switched on a lamp. She was leaving soon, leaving Royal and leaving him, and if she was thinking this could be more, that they could have more, she was setting herself up for a hard fall.

She would move on; it was what she did. Always.

She couldn't forget that.

Fee watched Clint shed his jacket and silently admitted a part of her loved the fantasy of being Clint's, of being one half of a whole. They'd had a magical evening and Clint, despite his loner personality, had seemed to enjoy himself, even slow dancing with her to one of her favorite songs. Despite the avid interest of the other guests, he'd kissed her—a kiss that was far too heated and went on for far too long for propriety—when the old year flipped over into the new.

The society columns and entertainment sites would be buzzing with speculation.

She hadn't cared then and she didn't care now. She was with Clint and that was all that mattered.

"Fun evening," Clint said, loosening his bow tie and flipping open the button holding his collar together. He looked around, saw the crystal decanters on a bar set up in the corner and his long strides covered the distance in a few steps. "Would you like a nightcap?"

"Cointreau, thanks," Fee answered him, sinking into the corner of the sofa and tucking her feet under her.

Clint handed her a drink and sat down next to her, pulling her legs over his thighs. He held her ankle as he sipped his drink.

"Happy New Year, Fee."

Fee smiled. "You too, Clint. I hope this year brings you so much happiness."

She wouldn't be around to witness what direction his life would take but she hoped he wouldn't retreat back into his lonely world—she hoped he'd make an effort to be more sociable. She could tell he'd had fun tonight; he'd enjoyed the company of his fellow ranchers, of the businesspeople in Royal, his town.

It wasn't hers. She'd like it to be but she wasn't the type to settle down, and she didn't think she could live in a small town where everyone knew each other's business, where you couldn't sneeze without someone across town sending a *bless you* your way. She'd hate it, she'd feel confined and hemmed in and claustrophobic…

But Clint was here and he made her feel free, accepted, protected.

What was the point in even considering it, though? Even if she could wrap her head around staying in one place—a massive "if"—Clint had never, not once, hinted he'd like her to stay. She was just a fling, someone to share a little of the holiday season with, some fun in the middle of a harsh winter.

Even if she wanted to, it wouldn't be fair to change the rules of the game on him now.

Fee rested her head on the back of the sofa and sighed, enjoying the way Clint's thumbs pressed into pressure points in her foot. She moaned, feeling heat slide into her veins and sparkles dance across her skin. They'd made love often but she still felt a hit of anticipation. He made her feel new, precious, undiscovered.

Even, she thought, *a little loved.*

But love was out of the question, and not something either of them was looking for. So why was she feeling this way? "You're looking a little pensive," Clint commented, placing his glass on the coffee table in front of them.

"It's a fresh start, a new year. A perfect time to feel pensive," Fee replied. She took a sip of her liqueur, sighing when the warmth hit her stomach.

Clint lifted her legs off his and stood up. Bending down, he pushed one hand under her thighs, another around her back and lifted her, with no effort at all, into his arms.

She still had her drink in her hand.

"Where's your bedroom?" Clint demanded.

Fee waved her glass in the direction of the hallway. "Last room on the right."

Clint carried her past the dining table and stepped into the dark hall while Fee continued to sip her drink, very confident in his ability to carry her. He kicked open her door and walked her across the luxurious room to lay her in the middle of her enormous, too-big-for-one-person bed. Clint took her drink from her hand, threw the last sip of Cointreau down his throat and placed the glass on the bureau behind him.

"I can't think of a better way to start a new year, Martinez," Clint stated, his voice extra growly. "You, a splash of orange on that white bed, eyes dark and mysterious in the shadows. Take down your hair."

Fee blinked at the unexpected command but she lifted her hands, pulling the pins out of the complicated knot her stylist had created at the back of her head. She placed the hairpins on the bedside table and allowed her heavy mass of curls to fall over her shoulders, down her back.

"You are so beautiful, Seraphina. I'm always going to remember this night."

She would too. She would remember him standing in front of her bay windows, moonlight highlighting the blond in his hair, turning his eyes from green to gold.

She'd remember the way his white shirt caressed those broad shoulders, how well he wore his tuxedo.

"I don't want this to end, Clint," Fee admitted, bending her legs and wrapping her arms around her knees.

"I know. I don't either," Clint said, coming to sit beside her on the bed, his fingers sliding into her hair. "But it has to end, sweetheart, because neither of us can change."

She could, maybe, if she tried hard enough. Clint shook his head when she suggested it.

"You're a beautiful butterfly who needs to experience the taste of different places and I need to be here, in Royal. Neither of us can—should—change."

His words hurt but the truth always did. "I know." Fee pushed her cheek into his palm, turning her head to kiss his calloused skin. "I just can't imagine not doing this again."

Clint held her cheek, his eyes a soft green-gold. "We've just got to enjoy the time we have and make some great memories."

He was right, they couldn't waste a second. Life was too short and their remaining time was minimal. Fee placed her hand on his knee, feeling the outline of his prosthetic under her fingers. Clint looked down and smiled. "You make me feel whole, Fee, normal."

Fee placed a gentle kiss on his lips. "You are whole, and you're better than normal—you're extraordinary."

Clint held her face and gently kissed her lips, in a caress that was as magical as it was erotic. "I want to make this last," he murmured against her lips, "I want to savor, to commit every caress to memory."

While that sounded wonderful, Fee knew herself all too well. "I'm not very patient, Clint."

"Suck it up, cupcake." Clint smiled against her mouth. Tipping her face, he changed the angle of his kiss and slid his tongue into her mouth, tangling with hers in a languid exchange that seemed to last for days, years.

Fee leaned back against the pillows and Clint covered her body with his as they kissed, fully dressed. This wasn't just sex; he was making love to her and Fee's heart expanded to explosion point.

She would take this night, and the memory, and thank God that, at least once, she'd known true passion.

Clint undressed her slowly, sliding her dress off her body and dropping the magnificent garment to the floor. She lay on the bed in her tiny flame-colored thong and gold spiked heels, her body flushed with pleasure. Clint stroked her from neck to foot, committing every curve, bump and freckle to memory. Fee tried to touch him in return but he moved her hands back to her sides, telling her this was his time to feast.

He loved her breasts, pulling her nipple between his teeth, easing the sting with his tongue. He buried his nose into her belly button, gently nipped her hip. He kissed the back of her knees, nibbled her ankle just below the strap of her heels.

Somewhere along the way he shed his clothes and allowed her to use her hands, her mouth, to torture him as he had her.

By the time she'd finished paying his body the same attention he'd paid hers, they were both vibrating with need, desperate to fly. Clint settled himself between her legs and rested his weight on his elbows next to her head. "Fee, look at me."

Fee lifted her heavy lids, sighing when he slid into her, hard and masculine, filling her, completing her.

"Remember this night…when you feel lonely or less than or sad, remember this night, remember me. Remember that I was profoundly, deeply grateful to share this with you. Remember that I think you are amazing and how your beauty makes my heart stutter. Remember this, remember me," Clint said, placing a hand under her butt to lift her up and into him.

Fee held his face as he rocked her up, and up. "I will. I always will. Will you remember too?"

Clint nodded, his eyes foggy with desire, his back tense from holding back. "I'll never forget you, Fee."

Fee smiled, nodded and closed her eyes as she followed him over the edge.

Nine

On the first day of the New Year, Fee, curled up against Clint's broad back, heard the beep of an incoming message on her phone and released a long groan. She gently banged her head against Clint's spine before rolling away from him to scoop her phone up off the bedside table. Pushing her hair out of her face, she squinted at the screen and cursed.

"Such ladylike language on the first day of the New Year," Clint teased, slinging a leg over her thigh and covering her breast with his big hand.

Fee dropped the phone onto the mattress and rolled her head to look into his pretty eyes. "We need to do some filming today, and I really don't want to. I'd rather spend the day in bed with you."

Clint lifted his wrist to look at his watch. "It's barely six. What time do you need to report for duty?"

"Ten."

"I need to get back to the ranch." He dropped his mouth

to her shoulder, nuzzling his cheek against her skin. "Do you want to come with me? I can check on my guys, the animals and I'll feed you breakfast. I'll have you back in town by ten."

She couldn't think of anything she'd like to do more. "Yes, please." She sighed as she rolled onto her side. "I'd much rather spend the day with you than filming."

"I don't know how you cope with having those cameras in your face all the time."

"You get used to it."

"It would be my worst nightmare." Clint stroked her arm from shoulder to elbow, his touch light and soothing. "Do you enjoy it?"

"Enjoy what?"

"Being a reality TV star? Having to look good all the time, being careful what you say and how you say it?"

Fee thought for a moment. Before she came to Royal, she would've quickly responded she loved it, that going to work every day was fun. And in many ways, it was—she'd had a lot of experiences she never could have had without the show opening doors for her, as she explained to Clint.

"I've traveled, a lot, seen places that would've been out of my budget on a normal salary. I've earned a lot of money over the years. Money that will allow me to keep traveling, to keep being able to see new places, do new things. To keep moving."

"And that's important to you, being on the move?"

Was it? She was no longer so sure. "It's what I know, Clint. As a kid, we moved every six to eight to ten months. The longest we stayed in one town was just over a year." Fee sat up and pulled the sheet over her breasts. "I like being with people, probably because I spent so much of my childhood and teenage years on my own. The show, the people working on it, are my family."

"But you will lose them if you leave the show and move on."

And that was something that still worried her... They'd been such a part of her life for so long. Could she could cope without being part of a group, not having people around her 24/7? Yeah, she thought she'd be okay. She'd miss her friends, miss the crew and the constant company, but she wouldn't be completely lost without them.

"Being here in Royal, learning the basics of ranching—"

Clint snorted. "Please. You didn't even scratch the surface of what it means to ranch..."

"Okay, point taken, we didn't take it very seriously."

"Or at all," Clint muttered.

Fee ignored his interruption. "But I would've like to have learned more. It's an interesting process. And I think I could be good at it."

"Mucking out a horse stall and counting cattle doesn't make you a rancher, Fee."

"I know that. I just said it's interesting. I like being in the fresh air, doing something with my hands, seeing immediate results. It's...life-affirming, I suppose." Fee looked through the open drapes at the day starting to unfurl outside. "I like the animals, the big sky, feeling grounded."

"Careful, you're starting to sound a little in love with Royal, with the ranching lifestyle," Clint teased.

That might be because Fee *had* fallen a little in love with Royal, with the town and the land and the relaxed lifestyle. And she was, terrifyingly, more than a little in love with Clint. Fee nibbled on the inside of her lip as she watched the sun's weak rays touch the huge lake she could see from her bed.

When had that happened? She couldn't tell; it had slowly crept up on her. Maybe it was his refusal to be pigeonholed by his disability. Maybe it was because he was strong and decisive and a natural leader. His superfine body played one part and his skill as a lover another. Under his taciturn exterior was a guy who just wanted the world to see him for what he was and not how he looked.

The residents of Royal did see him for what he was—it was only Clint who thought they were judging him by his disability.

They admired him and Clint still couldn't see it. He was still convinced they only saw the guy with the prosthetic. That was why he pushed himself so hard, why he was determined to fund the fire station, to act as their temporary Fire Chief. He wanted the world to see he was more than a guy who'd lost half his leg.

Fee could relate. She wanted the world to know she was more than a pretty face, a party animal, the high-spirited, loud-mouthed, fast-talking delight she was shown as on TV. Up until her visit to Royal she'd been content with the way the world saw her but after a few short weeks in this town, she understood, on a fundamental level, Clint's need to be recognized for who he was and not what he looked like.

She got it, she really did. Because the world didn't see her clearly either.

So was she confusing love with understanding, blowing their mutual connection out of proportion? She'd never been in love before so she wasn't sure, but it was something to think about. She also needed to give some thought to her future, to what she did next. But she'd need to leave Royal to do that. She needed to see if she still felt this way when she was back in New York, back in her apartment.

Back in Manhattan, she'd be able to think clearly again.

Turning back to Clint, she saw his eyes were closed and his breathing had evened out. His eyelashes were long on his cheeks and she could see hints of gold in his stubble. In sleep his lips were relaxed, his hair messy. Fee pulled back the sheet and looked down at the hard muscles of his stomach, his early morning erection, her eyes wandering down his thighs, over his knee and to his long, elegant foot.

His prosthetic was propped up against the bedside table and she was so thankful he had the money to pay for one of the most advanced systems in the world. She had no doubt Clint would've gotten by on a cheaper version, or on crutches, but his variety of robotic legs gave him amazing freedom of movement.

"You're thinking too loud," Clint muttered, kissing her shoulder again.

"I thought you were asleep," Fee replied.

"Dozing," Clint said, sitting up. He kneeled and, gripping her under her thighs, pulled her down the bed. Then he rolled on top of her, his cock settling within the V of her legs.

Fee lifted her eyebrows, instantly aroused. "I thought we didn't have time."

"We don't but I need you. I need to have you again."

Fee turned into his embrace and sighed when Clint kissed her.

Best way to start a New Year, bar none.

Clint heard the twang of a country song coming from the speakers of his SUV and hit the button on his steering wheel to mute the music. He smiled when Fee hit the radio to bring the song up again so he flipped the station to a heavy rock channel. "It's too early in the morning for slit-my-throat music, sweetheart."

"It's country—you're a rancher and a Texan, you're supposed to like country music."

"I don't," Clint replied, lifting his take-out cup of coffee to his mouth.

"It tells a story, and it's moving."

"It's depressing," Clint said, amused. His city slicker was really throwing herself into country living. He looked at her outfit and shook his head. Okay, it wasn't quite so over-the-top country as her first cowgirl outfit, but her jeans were tucked into a brand-new pair of tooled brown cowboy boots and she wore a sleeveless navy padded vest over a long-sleeved, pale pink T-shirt. The voluminous scarf in greens and blues made her eyes seemed darker and edgier.

She was the sexiest cowgirl he'd ever met...

Clint sipped his coffee and thought about their evening spent in Royal. Despite his bitching about the camera crews and dressing up in the tux, he'd had fun the previous night. He'd met several new members of the Texas Cattleman's Club and he'd enjoyed talking ranching and oil and beef prices. Despite the wealth, the glitz and the over-decorated ballroom, he'd felt more at home than he'd thought he would.

But the after-party in Fee's suite had been the highlight of the evening. He'd sipped champagne from her belly button, from the hollow of her back, trickled drops over her hard nipples. They'd loved and laughed and talked and loved and laughed and talked some more. He really wished they could spend the whole day on his ranch—saddle up two horses, go for a ride and, later, fall asleep, preferably naked, in the afternoon sun, hitting his bed in the middle of the afternoon.

He'd had little to no sleep and, God, he wasn't seventeen anymore. He needed to recharge...

"Clint?"

Something about Fee's voice jerked his attention back and he looked at her, frowning. "What is it?"

"Smoke."

The single word hit him with all the force of a bullet and Clint pulled his foot off the accelerator and looked toward where she was pointing. A massive black cloud hovered over the ridge and he cursed. That wasn't good, not at all.

Clint pulled over and reached for his cell phone. As he picked up the device to make a call, it rang. He swiped the screen to answer. "Jeff, yeah, I see the smoke. Blackwood Hollow?"

Jeff, one of his more experienced volunteers and the guy he wanted to be appointed as Royal's first permanent fire chief, didn't waste time with explanations. "The fire was started by kids smoking at the reservoir."

The reservoir was in a secluded area to the north of town where teenagers frequently met to party and let off steam. Clint cursed.

Jeff ignored him and continued. "These dry and windy conditions aren't helping. The fire is moving rapidly towards Blackwood Hollow. There are also fires north of Royal, and there's another one heading towards the TCC clubhouse."

Clint ignored Fee's big eyes and her inquisitive expression. He rapidly accelerated. "I'm heading toward Blackwood Hollow. When can I expect help?"

"Twenty minutes, maybe thirty?" Jeff replied.

"Tell them to hurry the hell up," Clint told him. He barked out another list of instructions, including a request for surrounding counties to send their people in to help. It was a crap start to the New Year but they'd have to deal.

And get the damn fire under control.

Clint cut his call to Jeff, made a few more calls and handed his phone to Fee. Keeping an eye on the column of smoke, which was to his left and growing bigger, he whipped into the driveway of Blackwood Hollow. He looked at the wind causing the trees to sway and felt dread curl in his stomach. The direction of the wind would push the fire directly toward Blackwood Hollow, and the house, stables and barn would be in its fiery path in no time at all.

"Is Rockwell Ranch safe?"

"Right now it is," Clint tersely replied. "The wind is sending the fire this direction, not toward my spread. But if the wind changes, everything could change."

"Don't you need to be there?" Fee asked, her hand on the dashboard in front of her.

"I spoke to my foreman. Brad has it under control. We go where the biggest threat is."

"Understood. What's the plan?"

"The plan is that you go into the underground bunker and stay put."

Fee's hard "No" shot out of her mouth. "That's not going to happen."

"Jesus, Fee, I can't be effective while worrying about you."

"Understood," Fee replied. "And I will get in the bunker when there's nothing more I can do, when I'm getting in the way. But there must be something I can help with now. I'll go mad sitting on my ass in a bunker."

Fair point. She could help, and it wasn't unsafe for her yet. Clint thought for a moment as he drove past the house toward the stables. He jerked to a stop and released his seat belt. "Okay, it's early so the horses should still be in the barn. We're going to get them out."

"And take them where?" Fee asked, following him out of the car. She unwrapped her scarf and threw it, and her vest, onto the passenger seat.

"We'll take them into the north pasture for starters.

Then I'll take the dirt bike and open a few gates and get them out of the paddocks and onto the range. Their instinct will take them away from the fire, to safety. We've just got to get them onto the open land and they'll head, hopefully, in the direction of Rockwell Ranch."

Clint saw the Blackwood hands pouring out of the bunkhouse and gestured them toward the other barn where all the working horses were stabled.

Clint headed to the second, smaller barn and Fee had to jog to keep up with his long legs. But he couldn't slow down, time was of the essence.

Clint headed into the first stall and ran his hand down the already sweaty neck of Buck's favorite stallion, Jack. "You can smell the smoke, can't you boy?" Clint kept his voice steady. "I need you to take your mares to safety. You can do that, can't you, Jack?"

Clint looked behind him to see Fee with her hands full of bridles. "Good thinking, sweetheart."

He quickly placed one over Jack's massive head and when he was done, handed the reins to Fee. "Lead him outside—do not let him bolt."

Fee took the reins and nodded, her eyes filled with fear. The horse was enormous next to her but Clint didn't have a choice, he needed to put bridles on the other ten horses.

His phone jangled and he pulled it out of his back pocket and didn't bother to greet Jeff again. "Yeah?"

"The intensity of the fire is building and it's quickly spreading. We need helicopters in the air, we need water dumps urgently. Blackwood Hollow is in immediate danger, Clint."

Clint ran over to the open door of the stable and saw the fire was so much closer than he'd believed. Smoke stung his eyes and he tasted the heat in the back of his throat.

They were out of time. Cursing, he retraced his steps and flipped open the latches to all the stalls.

"Unhook Jack's reins and slap his rump, tell him to go," Clint yelled at Fee. "And stay out of the damn way!"

He poked his head out of the stall, saw Fee following his directions. The horse bolted. Fee waited until the huge horse passed her and ducked into the stall opposite. A heartbeat later, another horse, this time a black filly, galloped out. Within minutes they managed to clear the stable. Clint grabbed Fee's hand and they ran out of the building. Clint watched as Jack led his mares away from the fire, all of them easily clearing the low white fences.

Yeah, they'd be fine.

They moved to the other stable block and helped the hands release the rest of the stock. In minutes the barn was finally cleared of animals but the air was getting thicker, smokier by the minute. They needed to burn a firebreak to keep the fire from hitting the house but he also needed to be up in the air. He was one of the few helicopter pilots in the area and before donating a few birds to the town of Royal, he'd made sure his certification was current.

Clint grabbed Fee's hand, heard her cough and knew she needed to get underground as soon as possible. The hands would start burning a firebreak but there was still a damn good chance that Blackwood Hollow would be burned to the ground.

"Are there any people or animals in the main house?" Fee asked, after coughing.

Clint thought for a minute. "Miranda? She's living here now, isn't she?"

Fee nodded.

"Can you call her, get her out here? Then both of you can go into the bunker."

Fee shook her head. "I left my phone in the car. I'll just run over to the house and get her out."

Clint saw a convoy of cars speeding up the long driveway and nodded. Thank God, help had arrived.

"You have ten minutes. I'm serious, Fee, ten minutes to get her out. Meet me by the front door."

Fee nodded and turned to sprint toward the main house. Clint fought the urge to run after her, to keep her at his side, and told himself she was running away from the fire, that he needed her to get Miranda out. She'd be fine, there was no need to worry.

Kellan Blackwood was the first person to exit a vehicle, closely followed by his brother, Vaughn, and Clint nodded, grateful. Despite having been estranged from Buck, they were, at heart, ranch boys who loved this land. They had an added incentive to save Blackwood Hollow. Gage, Buck's foreman, who'd spent the night in town with his honey, hopped out of the second vehicle and Clint sent up another prayer.

Gage was old school, had fought the massive fire of eighty-two and knew exactly what to do.

Running over to them, Clint spoke directly to Gage. "You're in charge. Burn a break, slow the fire down. If you can't fight it, get everybody to the bunker, make sure your people are safe. Human life is what's important, buildings are not."

"Got it." Gage nodded. "We need a bird up in the air."

"I'm on that. Jeff let me know he's got a pilot out of Deer Springs to fly the other chopper."

Gage nodded. "That'll work. Right, let's beat this bastard."

Okay, they had a plan. Clint raised his hands at the other volunteer firefighters as he jogged to his vehicle but didn't stop to talk. There was no time. He needed to get Fee and

Miranda into the bunker; she would be safe in the shelter Buck built to protect his people from tornadoes, storms and the end of the world, and Clint could do his job not worrying about his woman.

His woman...

Well, for now, today, she was.

Clint whipped his car around, punched the accelerator and drove up to the main house. He exited his SUV as the front door opened and he jogged up the steps to see Fee's white face. "She's not here. She must've stayed at The Bellamy last night."

"You sure?" Clint demanded, wondering whether he could spare the time to search the house himself.

Fee's look was sour. "I can search a house, Rockwell, even one as ridiculously big as this."

Point taken. "I trust you. Let's go."

Fee followed him into the kitchen and then down the stairs that led to a basement converted into a games room. Ignoring the massive TV and the billiards table, Clint headed for the far corner and twisted the painting to a forty-degree angle. Like magic, the wall slid away to reveal a steel door, complete with a brightly lit keypad. Clint punched in some numbers and light filled the room beyond the door.

"The code boots up the generator and filters the air coming into this safe room," Clint told her, gesturing her to step inside. It was a hell of a room, Clint thought. Couches, chairs and bookshelves filled the space. Bunk beds lined the far end of the room and, in the room adjoining this area were more bunks and a double bed.

If he didn't have a raging wildfire to fight, he could make good use of that bed.

"There's a shower and toilet through the door and drinks and nonperishables in the cupboards. Help yourself."

Fee folded her arms across her chest and looked apprehensive. Clint fought the urge to pull her into his arms, knowing he might not let her go. And he had to go.

"You'll be safe here, Fee. The fire, even if it takes the house, won't affect you. This room was built to hold twenty people, to keep them safe for three months or more. I promise you, you will be okay."

Fee rolled her eyes at him. "I'm not worried about me, you idiot, I'm worried about you. You're the one who's rushing into danger while I sit on my ass and do nothing."

Her obvious concern for his welfare touched his cold, shriveled heart. Clint clasped her face in his hands. "I'll be fine, sweetheart."

"Are you okay to fly the helicopter? You know, after having been in one that crashed?"

The crash was the reason he'd forced himself to learn to fly, getting back on the horse and all that...

"I've worked really hard to put that behind me, Fee."

"And you won't take any stupid risks just to prove you can?" Fee demanded. "I don't need a hero, Rockwell, I need you alive. To come back and get me."

"I won't be a hero." He'd do what he needed to do but he wouldn't take any unnecessary risks. Or he'd try not to. "And I've told Gage and the Blackwood boys, Kellan and Vaughn, you are in here. There's also a camera system for you to see whether the coast is clear. You can leave when you feel it's safe. I'd prefer for you to wait for me, though, so I'm asking you to wait for me to come and get you, Seraphina."

Fee nodded and Clint sighed at the tears in her eyes. "I'll be fine, Fee."

Fee smiled and knuckled the moisture away. "Of course, you will be. I, on the other hand, will be going crazy down here."

Clint kissed her nose.

Fee lifted herself up onto her tiptoes and brushed her lips across his. "Go now. Come back to me as soon as you can."

"That's a promise," Clint said, before dropping an open-mouthed kiss on her mouth. Allowing himself one last, quick taste, he pulled away and, without looking back, walked out of the safe room.

While he still could.

Ten

Fee stared at the TV screen, the image split into quarters, and wondered why she bothered. Twelve hours had passed since Clint pushed her into this underground bunker and night had long since fallen over Blackwood Hollow. Earlier, via the screen, she'd watched the fire reach the far barn, enveloping the structure in silky, almost pretty flames. The volunteers had allowed the structure to burn, choosing to put their efforts toward saving the newer stable block. She thought they might have succeeded, since the camera within that stable was still working while the other wasn't.

Fee folded her arms and looked at the solidly black screen. At least she couldn't see any more flames, and were those raindrops she saw on the lens of another camera?

God, she hoped so. It was time Mother Nature started working with them instead of against them.

Fee sat on the edge of one of the super-comfortable

couches and held her shaking hands between her knees, trying not to cry. Was Clint safe? Where was he? Was he still flying, fighting fires? She knew some helicopter pilots were night rated and wondered if he was too. She was in awe of his bravery and determination. If she'd been in a crash, and if said crash had killed a few of her teammates, she doubted she'd go anywhere near a helicopter, or a plane, again. Hell, she'd have trouble with anything more than two feet off the ground.

But not Clint. Clint had looked at himself, realized he was scared and instead of retreating—like a normal person would—rushed headfirst into resolving his problem. He was scared so he needed to conquer his fear by learning to fly the damned machine, exerting his control over the situation.

He was pretty damn amazing and a real inspiration and, yep, she was very definitely in love with her superhero cowboy.

Dammit.

But any woman would be. He was sexy, sure, good looking, sure, and possessed awesome bed skills. But he was also intelligent, hardworking, determined and reliable. He gave and gave and gave and all he wanted was for people to see him as capable. He didn't want medals, recognition or kudos, he just wanted people to see him, not his disability.

And they did. Clint just had to recognize that truth.

Fee stared down at the concrete floor, trying not to look at her watch again. Not ten minutes had passed since she last checked the time, and God knew, a watched clock didn't move any faster. She'd tried to read, she'd tried to sleep, but nothing kept her occupied for long.

She'd mostly just spent the past twelve hours pacing the floor, worrying.

Should she open the bunker? Was she safe? She didn't

know, but man, she needed to get out of here in the worst way. She needed to find Clint, to see if he was okay, to assess the damage done to this ranch, to Rockwell Ranch, to Royal itself. This might, after all, be her forever town.

But she didn't know what awaited her outside. The fire could still be raging off camera; she might be walking into hell itself. It was dark, and she didn't have transport.

She was, dammit, safe here. Safe and, since she couldn't find a phone or a radio, disconnected.

Fee tasted panic and forced it down. She'd fought occasional bouts of claustrophobia all afternoon and it had taken all she had not to wrench the door open and run out of the room.

But she wasn't a fool. She was safe here and she'd promised Clint to stay put.

He trusted her to keep her word, so she'd spend the night here, if necessary, and in the morning, she'd reassess the situation.

That meant spending more time in this box but she would deal...

Mostly because she didn't have a damn choice.

"Suck it up, cupcake." She repeated Clint's words and immediately felt steadier. Standing up, she walked into the bathroom and stared at her white face in the small mirror above the sink. There was nothing of Seraphina Martinez, reality TV star, in the mirror. She looked haggard, older, stressed.

Her man had been in danger all day; she had a right to look like crap. Fee splashed some water on her face and bent down to sip some out of her cupped hand. It slid down her tight throat and she felt a burning sensation in her eyes.

"You are not going to cry, dammit."

Fee headed into the main room, thinking of a way to

distract herself. Maybe if she pushed the couch to the side, she could do some yoga, find her Zen.

Well, she could try.

Fee bent down, put her shoulder to the heavy couch and pushed, relieved when the couch scraped, reluctantly, across the smooth concrete. There still wasn't enough space so she pushed it again, totally surprised when the couch easily glided across the floor this time.

Lifting her head, she saw his yellow trousers, his bare arm, and she squealed when she saw his sooty face, his white teeth flashing. Launching herself up, she gave him just enough time to straighten from his bent position before throwing herself into his arms, gripping his waist with her legs and raining kisses on his filthy face.

"Oh, God, you're here. You're safe."

"I'm safe." Clint pushed his hand into her hair and held the back of her head. "How are you? Doing okay?"

"Pfft." Fee waved his concern away. "I'm fine. Bored but fine. What's the damage? Is your ranch okay?"

"The fire touched some land bordering my ranch but we got lucky. It started to rain and stopped it from spreading."

"It's really raining?"

"Bucketing down. Thank God," Clint replied. "It'll kill the last few sparks, the small fires."

"What about Blackwood Hollow? How much damage is there?" Fee demanded, sliding down his body and ignoring the streaks of dirt on her clothing.

"The far barn is gone, as is one of the stables. The guest house lost a couple of rooms." Clint pushed the braces off his shoulders and allowing his pants to slide down his legs. He kicked them away and stood in his jeans and T-shirt, looking exhausted but satisfied.

"Is Royal ok?" Fee asked as she headed toward the big fridge on the far side of the room. She pulled out a cola and popped the tab, handing it to Clint, who sat down on the edge of the bed, clearly exhausted.

"We lost a few houses on the edge of town, the TCC clubhouse has been damaged and there's smoke damage to a few businesses on the outskirts. There's a lot of work to do, clearing up and rebuilding."

"I learned how to wield a drill and a hammer when I worked on a Habitat for Humanity project last spring," Fee told him, sitting cross-legged on the bed beside him. "I can help."

"I'm sure we can use your skills." Clint drank deeply from the can and looked down at his black hands. "I'm filthy."

"I thought you were flying—not fighting the flames up close and personal."

"I was," Clint said, standing up. "Then I landed and another small blaze kicked up not far from where I was. It was quicker to beat the fire back toward the firebreak than fly the chopper to pick up another load of water."

Clint strolled into the bathroom and Fee heard the shower. "Let me clean up and then we'll head out to my place."

Fee thought for a minute and followed him into the bathroom. He cursed when he looked down at his leg. "Shit. I don't have any crutches here."

"Hang tight," Fee said. Without giving him chance to argue, she stripped off and bent down in front of Clint to remove his leg. She heard the pop of the suction cup and gently removed his prosthetic, resting it against the bathroom cabinet. Clint leaned against the wall and Fee placed her shoulder under his armpit, letting him lean on her while he hopped into the shower, adjusting the stream of water to hit him as he rested against the wall.

He reached for the soap and loofah but jerked his hand

back to hold onto the edge of the shower door to keep his balance. "Crap, it's slippery in here."

Fee waited until she was sure he was balanced before leaving his side. She quickly stripped off her underwear and stepped into the shower. Grabbing the loofah, she dumped some liquid soap on it and started to wash Clint's body.

"Fee, I—"

Fee looked up at him, a frown on her face. "You've spent the past twelve hours helping your fellow ranchers, your fellow residents. You've fought fires, dumped water, flown a damned helicopter. You've helped and helped and served and served. Let me help you."

"I—"

"Just shut up, Rockwell," Fee told him, standing on her toes to drop a kiss on his mouth.

Not giving him more time to argue, she washed his shoulders, under his arms, across his chest and his stomach. She swiped the loofah over his private areas and down his leg, and then, equally clinically, over his short leg.

She took a washcloth, put soap on it and wiped his face. Seeing the dirty water streaming off his hair, she told him to duck his head. Picking up a bottle of shampoo, she washed his hair, once, then again.

"God, it feels so good to be clean," Clint told her, hot water pounding her head and his shoulders.

Fee wrinkled her nose. "Sorry, but you're going to have to get back into your dirty clothes."

Clint shook his head. "There's a cupboard full of clothes, different sizes and styles. I'll find something to wear."

"Buck really was prepared," Fee said, impressed.

"You have no idea." Clint wiped moisture off his face

with his hand and switched off the water. "Let's get dressed and we can go home."

Fee saw the exhaustion in his red-rimmed eyes. She touched his cheek. "Do you have to go back? Is there something you need to do on the ranch tonight?"

"No, my foreman has it covered," Clint replied. "Why?"

"Because there's a very nice bed in the adjoining bedroom and I think we could both do with a some sleep."

"I thought you would be sick of this place by now, that you'd want to get out."

Fee handed him the truth. He was a big boy and she was sure he could handle it. "You're here now and I'm fine. Let's go to bed, Rockwell. I need to hold you and be held."

Clint nuzzled his cheek into her palm. "Me too, Fee. I need to hold you too. But I can only sleep for an hour, maybe two. There's so much I still need to get to tonight."

Because, if there was work to be done, Clint was first in line to do it. Fee loved that, and everything, about him.

Sophie Blackwood, dressed in her most ragged pair of jeans and oldest, most battered sweatshirt, picked her way through the debris of what was once the original stables housing the Blackwood family horses. These days, her father's prize horseflesh was stabled in the new climate controlled, technologically advanced stable block but she'd loved the history of the original stables.

It was gone now. Annihilated. Burned to the ground.

She shouldn't be this upset about it, Sophie admitted to herself, blinking away hot tears.

Everything was changing and she didn't like it.

Sophie felt a big hand on her back and turned to see Vaughn standing next to her, concern in his expression and in his eyes. "You okay, Soph?"

She wanted to be able to tell him she was fine but couldn't speak the lie. "The hits keep coming."

He rubbed a big circle on her back. "It could've been worse. The house could've burned down."

Sophie managed a weak smile. "This stable block meant more to me than the house. I never felt at home there." Sophie pushed back her deep-brown Stetson with her wrist. She bit her bottom lip. "We owe Clint Rockwell our gratitude, Vaughn. His quick response saved Blackwood Hollow, even if it's not ours anymore."

"I tried to thank him but he brushed me off," Vaughn said, looking over to where Rockwell stood. Kace and Lulu were standing just behind him, for once not arguing. Clint looked dead on his feet, pale with exhaustion. He'd gone above and beyond and Sophie, when the time was right, would express her gratitude, in her own way.

"Blackwood Hollow will be ours again," Vaughn assured her. "We just have to find a way."

"From your lips to God's ears," Sophie murmured. "Here comes Kell."

Sophie took one of the bottles of water Kellan held out, giving him a grateful smile. Cracking the lid, she heard the arrival of an expensive vehicle. Her oldest brother rolled his eyes and Sophie turned to see the Step Witch pulling off her designer sunglasses and exiting the expensive two-door coupe. Her hair was pulled back into a ponytail, her makeup was understated and she wore jeans and a long-sleeved, emerald silk T-shirt. Despite her attempts to dress down, she still looked like the expensive trophy wife she was.

Sophie followed her two brothers as they approached their father's ex-wife.

Miranda tucked her keys into the back pocket of her jeans and sighed. "Oh, great, another inquisition."

Kellan ignored her sarcastic comment. "What are you doing here, Miranda?"

Miranda waited for a beat before replying. "I came to check on Blackwood Hollow."

"Aren't you supposed to be living here, as per the terms of the will?" Kellan demanded.

"I'm allowed to leave the property Kellan." Miranda didn't drop his eyes from his. "I had a late night and, probably, too many glasses of champagne at the New Year's Eve party. I wasn't drunk but I was over my limit and, because I am a responsible citizen, I chose to spend the night at The Bellamy." She gestured to the charred ruins. "I was told the stable block and an outbuilding burned down. Any other damage I should know about?"

"Like you actually care." Sophie snorted.

Miranda tapped her foot, obviously exasperated when none of them answered her. "Okay, I'll wake Gage up and get him to give me a status report."

Sophie knew Gage was exhausted and he'd just left, at Kellan's and Clint's insistence, to go home. He needed the rest. She'd stomach answering Miranda's questions if it meant Gage was able to sleep undisturbed.

"The stable block and outbuilding were, as you can see, destroyed. The guest house lost a few rooms but is mostly intact. We lost a lot of grazing land but you have Clint Rockwell to thank that you didn't lose more."

"I'll definitely extend my gratitude to him," Miranda answered, her expression and tone cool. She looked around. "What can I do?"

Three sets of Blackwood eyebrows rose. Vaughn spoke for all of them. "You're going to work?"

"I was planning on it."

"Hauling soggy bricks, trudging through the mud?" Kellan mocked her. "You'll last two seconds."

Miranda bared her teeth at him. "Try me."

Sophie caught the movement of a cameraman heading toward them, intent on capturing their exchange. None of them needed their harsh words to be caught on camera. "Tell your guy to back off, Miranda," she told her, steel in her voice.

Miranda turned and waved the guy away. "Sorry, they are overly inquisitive sometimes and have few boundaries."

"Oh, cut it out, Miranda," Vaughn snapped, sounding irritated. "We all know you are only here, pretending to care about Buck's ranch, as a publicity stunt, to garner more attention for your ridiculously inane show."

"Tell me how you really feel, Vaughn," Miranda murmured, a slight smile tipping up the corners of her mouth.

"They'll film here and they'll edit it to make your ten minutes of work look like you spent the day doing some serious labor. We're not fooled."

"Because nothing gets past you three."

Sophie couldn't decide whether that was sarcasm she heard in Miranda's voice or not. But the calm, smirky smile remained on her face. Miranda's smile widened as she made eye contact with all three of them. "So nice chatting with you all again. It's always a highlight of my day."

Yep, that was definitely sarcasm. Sophie watched her walk away and narrowed her eyes at Miranda's slim back and the cocky sway to her hips.

Oh, Sophie couldn't wait to get to New York City and find the footage she needed to take the bitch down.

Clint appreciated the *Secret Lives* stars' willingness to help with the cleanup of Blackwood Hollow, but honestly, they tended to create more problems than they solved. Lulu, Miranda and Fee, obviously, genuinely helped the process, but the blonde and the sultry brunette spent most of their time gossiping about the fire and chatting up any man with a pulse.

He was over it.

The rain had stopped and the wet ground had killed any embers that could spark into a problematic fire again. He was grateful for the rain, obviously, but now they were clearing waterlogged areas where mud and soot and water mixed together to create a horrible sludge.

He'd been shuttling between Royal and Blackwood Hollow since dawn and on arriving back at Buck's ranch, he found himself in the middle of a Blackwood family argument around the best way to clear the debris of the destroyed buildings.

Vaughn thought the best solution was to bring in backhoes and level the half-collapsed outbuilding and the listing stable. Kellan thought both structures could be shored up.

Both agreed they needed the insurance agent to visit the property before any decision was made.

Neither was thrilled when Miranda Blackwood reminded them that, as the owner, she would make the final decision about how to go forward.

Ugly words were exchanged and Clint walked away, not wanting to get involved in their family dynamics. They needed to work it out themselves, in their own way.

Clint tugged his heavy work gloves into place and walked back over to the burned-out barn where Fee and Lulu were hauling pieces of wood away to pile them neatly to the side. A cameraman followed their every move and their cast-mate Rafaela watched, her phone in hand.

The day was warmer than expected and his jeans were wet but he refused, like the other guys, to wear shorts. He was hot, uncomfortable and exhausted after he and Fee had spent most of the night burning up the sheets in a lovemaking session as hot as it was intense—a few hours of soul-touching, concentrated, breath-stealing emotion.

It had been magnificent, but today he was at the end of his rope: tired, mentally wiped and physically drained. He was also, he realized, peopled out. He needed to be alone, to soak in some silence, to recharge his batteries. He hadn't spent this much time with this many people since he was in the unit. He was done.

But he had work to do—his neighbor needed help, so did the town, and he would not let them down. He just didn't want to talk to anybody while he worked.

"Clint, how are you feeling this morning?"

Clint turned around at the strange voice and glared when he found a camera in his face. Putting his hand up, he shoved the camera away. "Get that out of my face."

The cameraman took a few steps back but didn't lower the device. "How do you feel about the fires, about the rain, about the mess Royal is in?"

Crap on a cracker. Clint rubbed the back of his wrist against his forehead to wipe away the perspiration.

"Any comment, Clint?"

Yeah, he had a comment. He looked directly into the camera and spoke with deadly intent. "Yeah, here it is…if you point that thing in my direction one more time, I am going to ram it down your throat. Clear enough?"

The camera lowered and he saw both fear and resentment in Jimmy's eyes. "Just trying to do my job, man."

"Do it somewhere far, far away from me," Clint told him before turning around to lift a piece of corrugated iron off a wooden beam. He walked it over to a pile he'd started and carefully placed it on top of another square piece of iron, trying to ignore the phantom pains shooting from his stump up his leg. It had been months since he'd experienced them and he'd thought they were behind him.

He'd pushed himself too hard and for too long. Clint needed to take a non-opiate painkiller—he had some in the car. Maybe the analgesic would disrupt the false signals his brain was receiving from his nonexistent limb.

He pulled off his gloves and walked toward his car, but before he'd taken a few steps, another camera appeared on the periphery of his vision. "Clint, can you comment on the cleanup?"

He was going to kill someone, he genuinely was. Clint stopped, clenched his fists and counted to ten. Then to twenty. When he thought he had his temper under control, he opened his eyes and nailed the cameraman with a hard look.

Before he had time to issue another threat, he saw Fee hurrying over to him, looking determined. Striding up to the camera, she pulled a jack from its connection and held it in her hand as the camera lowered.

"Vincent, back off. Leave Clint alone."

Vincent looked like he wanted to argue but the fierce look on Fee's face stopped him in his tracks. Fee wiggled her fingers. "Give me your radio."

Vincent dug a small two-way radio out of his back pocket and handed it over, resigned. Fee took the device, hit the button and spoke into the receiver. "This is Seraphina Martinez and I'm ordering you all to stay away from Clint Rockwell."

While he appreciated her intervention, Clint didn't need her to talk for him. He opened his mouth to blast her but a disembodied voice from the radio beat him to it. Clint recognized it as being the director's voice.

"You aren't the boss here, Seraphina. Rockwell is the hero of the hour—we need to get him on screen."

"I distinctly recall Nigel telling us all we shouldn't force cooperation from the Royal residents. Clint wants privacy, and he's entitled to it," Fee shot back.

God, he could fight his own battles. And by making her announcement, they'd attracted the interest of the *Secret Lives* cast, the Blackwood siblings and Kace LeBlanc, who was there, Clint presumed, to help with the cleanup.

"Seraphina, enough! I lost the use of my leg, not my brain or my mouth," Clint roared and he caught the hurt in Fee's eyes as she turned to face him.

Then a bright red flush climbed up her neck and into her face. Her humiliation was easy to see in her eyes as she said, "I was just trying to help, Clint."

"I don't need your goddamn help. I don't need anybody's help. All I want to do is go to my truck without tripping over a reality TV star or cameraman. I just want fifteen minutes of goddamn peace."

Fee lifted her hand and backed away as she sent him a princess-looking-at-a-peasant look. "Fine. Do what you need to do."

Shit, he'd screwed up. He started to call her back, to say—what? Apologize? Yeah, he could apologize, not for threatening the cameramen but for snapping at her in front of her friends and coworkers.

That had been badly done and he was ashamed of himself.

But Fee was out of hearing distance and his leg was killing him. Before he could make amends, he needed to take some pills and a mental break, calm the hell down. He needed to find a quiet place, maybe do some meditation exercises, to rest his body, his mind and his eyes.

He'd make amends later; right now he needed to be alone.

Clint dug his painkillers from the first aid box he kept in the car and chased them down with half a bottle of water. Walking away from the car, he skirted the damaged building and walked into the surviving stable block, welcoming the quiet shadows within the building. Yay, privacy. He saw a straw bale tucked into a dark corner and, feeling hot and miserable, decided to step out of his wet jeans for a little bit.

Sitting down on the bale, he stretched out his legs in front of him and debated whether to remove his prosthetic. Deciding to leave it on, he rested his head against the cool wall and closed his eyes, breathing deeply to calm his tumultuous brain.

It had been a tough few days but he'd endured many days a great deal worse.

Eighteen hours of fighting fires shouldn't wipe him out.

But it wasn't the fire—not really. No, what did make him feel tired, emotionally displaced and, yeah, terrified, was that he was so close to dropping to his knees—one knee—and begging Seraphina to stay in Royal.

To stay with him.

There, he'd admitted it. He wanted her to stay, on the ranch, with him. Which was, admittedly, crazy. Fee was a city girl, a TV star. She needed to be seen at restaurant openings, in clubs, dancing on bars in bohemian pubs. What could he offer her? He had wealth, sure, but comfort or even luxury couldn't turn Royal into a big, bustling city. She was not a rancher's wife, girlfriend or significant other. Jesus, the woman couldn't even ride a horse.

It didn't matter how unsuited she was to live on a ranch, on his ranch; he still wanted to beg her to stay. But that was a special type of madness.

Because, if she did, what would happen? They would have great sex for a few weeks, maybe a few months, before the isolation would get to her and she'd start to think she had someplace better to be.

Good sex would fade into dissatisfaction and her fascination with ranch life, with him, would fade too.

He refused to put himself in that position.

But, damn, it was a great dream. And because he was exhausted, and a little sad and a lot overwhelmed, he allowed himself to daydream about her cooking in his kitchen, teaching her to ride, making love to her in the flowers blooming in the high meadow in spring. He dreamed of her in his bed, in his shower...

In his life.

Later Clint realized how exhausted he must have been because he, a highly trained ex-army ranger, never once suspected someone stood in the shadows, watching him.

Eleven

The next day Fee was riding shotgun in one of Rockwell Ranch's pickups and she turned to face Clint as he drove up Blackwood Hollow's long drive. After a brief apology from Clint for his rudeness—which she readily accepted—and a solid night's sleep, he looked better than he had yesterday. He was back to being strong, fit and in control.

She needed to tell him shooting was scheduled to end in two days and she had a plane ticket back to the city that same evening. She wanted to tell him that, if he asked her to stay, she would. How did she tell him he was the only man who could persuade her not to move on, to plant her feet?

The only person she felt safe enough to risk her future on?

Clint had proved himself, over and over. He was steadfast, courageous and honorable.

She should tell him, she had to get the words out. But what if she was reading too much into the situation, seeing possibilities not there? What if he didn't want her...

like that? What if he was perfectly happy to see the back of her, to let her go?

What then?

She was driving herself crazy. Either way, one of them had to raise the subject, but seeing the entire cast and crew of *Secret Lives* waiting for them on the steps leading up to Blackwood Hollow's imposing front door, she knew their discussion would be delayed.

Fee wasn't sure whether to laugh or cry, to feel relieved or irritated. God, this falling in love business was hell on the nerves.

Clint parked his car and, seeing the excited faces of her colleagues, turned to her and raised his eyebrows. "What's going on?"

"No idea," Fee said, opening her door and jumping out. It was barely nine and nobody on set usually managed to crack a smile this early. They all needed at least four cups of coffee and a couple more hours before that happened.

Fee looked at Lulu and saw her smile was strained and she wasn't as excited as Rafaela or the producers. Gemma, their PR person, looked like she wanted to jump out of her skin with excitement.

"What's going on?" Fee asked Lulu.

Lulu didn't answer her, she just turned to Gemma and gestured for her to explain.

"Clint's photo has gone viral," Gemma gushed.

Okay, what photo? She didn't know what they were talking about. "Explain."

"Rafaela went around town yesterday, doing a photo essay of Royal, looking for the poignant, pertinent photos, the human-interest angle," Gemma responded.

Human interest? Fee almost snorted. Rafaela wasn't exactly the most empathetic or sensitive of the ex-wives.

The situation would be funny…if there hadn't been

mention of a photo of Clint. Fee felt ice invade her veins and, worse, she felt Clint stiffening behind her.

"What photo?" Fee demanded, between clenched teeth. Clint was so publicity averse, any photo of him hitting the tabloids or papers would piss him off. God, she hoped it was from a distance, and flattering.

Gemma waved her tablet around and it took all Fee had not to snatch it from her hands.

"Rafaela posted it to her social media accounts, then we shared it and it's had about half a million retweets and a million views. It's hot." Gemma sent a flirty smile Clint's way that had Fee grinding her teeth.

"Show it to me," Fee demanded.

Gemma held out her iPad and Fee took it, holding her breath. Fee looked down and read the headline first: News Anchor's Son a Local Hero, This Is What True Courage Looks Like.

In the photo, Clint sat on a hay bale, head against the wall, eyes closed. He wore plain black boxer shorts and a sleeveless tank, looking hot and sexy and dirty. He appeared utterly exhausted but a small smile played around his mouth and there was a hint of pride and satisfaction on his face.

It was a powerful photograph, soul gripping and intensely emotional, and she could see why it had gone viral. Clint looked like the hero he was.

Fee heard his sharp intake of air and immediately the atmosphere changed. She closed her eyes and waited for his explosion, for his temper to ignite. She instantly knew why he was upset—he never allowed anyone to see his prosthetic leg. He was intensely private and his disability was an off-limits subject.

But Rafaela had exposed him, showing what he tried to keep hidden from the world.

Fee turned around slowly and when she met his eyes, she saw the betrayal in his eyes, the sharp kick of shock. Then his expression turned bleak and she felt him slipping away from her.

Fee felt Lulu remove the tablet from her shaking fingers and felt her friend's hand on her back, steadying her.

Oh, God, this was bad.

This was so, so bad. Clint ignored her beseeching look and regarded her as if she were a brown recluse spider he'd found on his shoe. "Excellent work, Martinez. Fantastic publicity. Glad it all worked out for you."

Oh, no, now that was unfair. She didn't know anything about the photograph and she wouldn't be blamed for it. "I would've killed it if I'd known it would be used—or if I'd known she'd taken it in the first place."

"It's a great photo," Rafaela protested, "and it's very inspirational."

"Take it down," Clint told Gemma, whose excitement had turned to confusion. *"Now."*

Gemma exchanged a panicked look with Miranda. "I can take it down from our site but it's already out there on social media. Hundreds of thousands of people have reposted the picture, the news outlets have picked it up and interviewed the residents of Royal, who have nothing but amazing things to say about you."

She got increasingly flustered when Clint's face took on that robotic expression Fee so hated.

"I don't understand why you are mad," Gemma wailed.

"And I have no intention of explaining," Clint said, his voice a few degrees lower than freezing point. He turned his attention to Miranda. "I'm done. This stops, now… today. Either they leave or I do."

"Clint, don't do this," Miranda said, her voice soothing. "I understand you are angry, and it is a shocking invasion of your privacy, but maybe you should take a few days to cool down before you do or say something you'll regret."

Clint folded his arms and nailed her with a frigid look. "Either you get rid of them or I walk. That means no one will be around to oversee the lands, the cleanup, your hands, the stock."

Miranda held his eyes for ten seconds before nodding. She turned to the director and lifted her hand, dragging it across her throat. "We're done. Let's go."

"But I have a schedule! There are shots, interviews—"

Miranda narrowed her eyes. "I said...we're done."

Miranda told the crew and Fee's costars to head for their cars. Lulu gripped her hand and squeezed before walking away.

Clint jerked his head to Miranda. "You're going to miss your lift back to town," he told Fee.

Fee felt her anger bubble, way down deep in her stomach. "You know I'm not going to walk away without discussing this."

"I have nothing to say to you, Seraphina."

God, he'd never said her name in such a dismissive way, like he had acid on his tongue. "I did not know anything about the photograph, Clint."

"You're an integral part of the show. Are you seriously telling me nobody told you they were going to plaster a photograph of your disabled lover on social media? Please, tell me another lie! I dare you."

"Nobody told me." Fee lifted her hand when he started to interrupt her. "Maybe they didn't think they needed to because they saw what I did."

"Yeah, a goddamn cripple."

Fee grabbed his arm, trying not to feel hurt when he shook off her touch. "They saw a guy who went above and beyond the call of duty, who worked like a Trojan to make sure his community was safe, who still went to work the day after that grueling day. I saw a guy who can do everything a guy with two legs can do, and more. I saw a hot, sexy, tired guy who looked amazing."

"Bullshit, Seraphina. Stop trying to spin this!"

She was so over him putting himself down. "*You* stop! Stop assuming everyone is judging you. The only person who sees you as being disabled is you, Clint. You! No one else!"

Sparks of pure silver anger flashed in Clint's eyes. "Quit blowing smoke up my ass, Martinez. I know most women see me as only half a man. There's nothing I can do to make myself whole." He was just making her angrier and angrier.

Instead of yelling at him, Fee folded her arms and waited for him to look at her. "Are you done with the pity party?"

"What?"

She ignored the roar that had horses in the nearby paddock lifting their heads. "When you are done feeling sorry yourself, I have something to say."

"I'm not interested," Clint snapped back.

"You have yelled at me, embarrassed me in front of my friends and made a ton of assumptions that simply aren't true. You owe me the right to speak."

Clint hauled in a deep breath and she watched his big chest rise and fall. When she knew she had his attention, she pushed her words past her teeth.

"Fact, you have one leg. Fact, you are technically disabled. Fact, you lost your leg in an act of supreme bravery. Fact, your mother is a stone-cold bitch and those women you hooked up with who rejected you? Shallow and superficial. And how dare you compare what they said or did to me?"

Fee drilled a hole into his chest with her finger. "I am rude and loud-mouthed and outspoken but I am not fake, Rockwell, and that's what you're accusing me of being. I made love to you because I think you are the most amazing, inspiring, capable guy I've ever met. So, once again, the only person in the whole goddamn world who has an issue with you missing a limb is you."

"And my mother, and those women—"

"Again, superficial and shallow. Why are you even giving them headspace? I'm standing here telling you your town loves you, that I do too, and the people you are listening to are people who have proved themselves to be douches. What is wrong with *you*?"

"I hate that photo—it makes me look weak!"

"You look strong and brave."

Clint shook his head and Fee realized she was fighting a lost cause. She couldn't change his mind for him. He had to realize his worth, for himself, by himself. She held up her hand and blew air into her cheeks.

"I'm crazy about you Clint, head over heels in love with you, but I can't be with you. I can't spend the rest of my life reassuring you of your worth. I'm a strong woman. I need a man who's equally aware of his strength. Until you can accept yourself, love yourself, exactly as you are, as I do, I'm wasting my time."

Clint stared at her, obviously shocked by her honesty.

"I'm going back to New York, as soon as I can. This was fun but now it's not."

Clint nodded once. His short, sharp gesture was an exclamation point at the end of their conversation. "I think that's a very good idea. Even if I believed you about not being half a man—and I don't—we could never work. You're town, I'm country. We're exact opposites."

Fee felt like her heart was breaking but she forced a

smile onto her face. She placed her hand on his chest and felt him stiffen as she leaned into him, felt him pull back as she lifted herself onto her heels to speak in his ear.

"Coward. You can face down a band of terrorists intent on killing you and your team but you can't let people see your leg, you can't love me? Shame on you, Rockwell."

Fee was close to crying, but she refused to allow him to see her tears so she quickly turned and headed for the driveway, hoping against hope Lulu was waiting for her, that she wouldn't have to phone for a ride, leaving her waiting here with the gorgeous, broken man she loved with every fiber of her being.

Through her tears Fee saw her best friend sitting in the driver's seat of her rented Jeep, far enough away not to hear her conversation but close enough to intervene if their fight went south.

God bless her best friend, Fee thought as she slid into the passenger and burst into tears.

Lulu, because she was a goddess, just held her hand and let her weep before driving her back to a life she no longer wanted.

Twelve

Two weeks passed before Clint made a trip into Royal, and only because it was the grand opening of the new fire station. He'd dressed in a sharp white button-down shirt, a tie and black chinos, and desperately wished he was in his jeans and boots, and on one of his many horses. Or working on Tim's truck, having recently received the Chevy back from the body shop. He did not want to smile and shake hands with the Royal residents, to face their sympathetic and prying eyes, answer his questions about how he was doing.

He was alone. He was fine…

Which was all a steaming pile of bull crap.

He was alone but he wasn't fine, he was just holding on.

Ignoring the cars parked in the front of the building, Clint skirted around to the parking area at the back and slid his SUV between the two new, state-of-the-art fire engines he'd donated. The firefighting/rescue helicopters were parked at the regional airport, ready to be dispatched at a moment's notice. He had provided funds for two teams of permanent firefighters, a trained medic and a pilot, saying he would serve as backup to fly as and when he was needed.

He was giving back to his community—it was all he could do.

Clint exited his car, feeling like ants were crawling under his skin. He couldn't go anywhere in Royal without thinking about Fee and that, frankly, pissed him off. And he couldn't decide what he was most angry about— the invasion of his privacy or Fee lying to him by telling him she loved him...

Oh, wait, maybe it was the fact she'd called him a goddamn *coward*.

He'd snuck behind enemy lines in the dead of night, risked his skin a thousand times, suffered deprivations and starvation rations, endured mortar strikes and enemy fire, he'd earned medals—a goddamn Purple Heart!—and yet she'd still thrown the insult straight in his face.

How dare she judge him?

Walking into the large empty bay where the catering staff was setting up tables for drinks and food, he ran up the flight of stairs into the commander's office, hoping to hide out until he was needed. He'd say a few words and then fade away; nobody would even miss him.

Clint threw himself into the leather office chair behind the desk and rested his forearms on his thighs, staring down at the hard-wearing floor beneath his feet. His thoughts, as they always did, turned back to Fee. What she'd said was unforgivable, hurtful, cruel. This—this was why he should avoid relationships.

Because they sucked, dammit.

Well, like rehab and surgery and PTSD and everything

else he'd endured, it was over and he could put it behind him. He had work to do, a ranch to run, the fire station to oversee. All of that would keep him sane. He'd launch the fire station, and after it was up and running, he'd retreat and lick his wounds.

He'd tried, and failed, at a relationship. He should learn from it and move on.

Clint heard the sharp rap on his door and lifted his head to see Jeff, the about-to-be-appointed fire chief, standing in the doorway. Clint stood up and gestured to the chair. "Sorry, I should've asked you if I could be in here."

"Clint, you paid for everything here. You can be anywhere you like. And I don't have secrets to hide."

Clint sent him a tight smile and took a surreptitious look at his watch. The function wasn't supposed to start for another half hour so he walked over to the window and stared down at the cars streaming into the parking lot.

Damn, too many people…

Jeff sat down on the edge of his desk and picked up a signed baseball. "So, you must be pleased with the response you received from the photograph."

Yeah, *thrilled*. Not.

"I read a lot of the comments and the responses. Not sure how much of it you've seen, but hell, if it was me, I'd be floating near the ceiling," Jeff commented.

Clint frowned, confused. "What are you talking about?"

"Thousands of vets and paraplegics and disabled people—women, children and men—left comments saying you are a role model, an inspiration, and that you've given them hope. The story was picked up by a national news outlet and you're trending. God, your social media accounts must be blowing up."

He didn't have any social media accounts so he'd had

no idea of the extent of the reach of the photograph. "And the responses were mostly positive?" he asked, confused.

"They were *all* positive. You're the new poster boy for true American grit. And your mom has been hitting the radio stations and interview circuits, boasting about you and the fact she taught you everything you know."

She wished. And how typical it was for his mom to jump on the publicity he generated. But none of it mattered, not really, because he'd lost the person he loved.

It meant little without her.

"Talking about being an inspiration," Jeff said, "would you do me a favor and meet someone? He's in the gym."

Clint started to shake his head but Jeff held up his hand. "Ten minutes, Clint. Please?"

He didn't want to. He wanted to stay here and enjoy his solitude. *Coward*, a little voice inside him stated. It sounded like Fee.

Wanting to be alone wasn't an act of cowardice.

Sure it is...

Annoyed by the direction of his thoughts, Clint nodded abruptly and followed Jeff out of his office and down a floor to the gym the architects had tucked into the corner of the fire station. Clint had requested the workout room for the firefighters but had also suggested that it could be used by any veterans in the area who couldn't afford the fees at a normal fitness center.

Jeff was fully on board with his idea.

When Clint stepped into the gym, he saw a kid standing in the middle of the floor, his hand on a thick rope dangling from the ceiling. He sported a mop of bright blond hair but Clint's attention was immediately captured by his prosthetic leg.

Clint started to back away and hit Jeff's broad, solid chest.

"He's eleven years old, he's a cancer survivor and all he wants is to meet you. He won't say why or how you landed on his radar, but he's obsessed with you. His mom, a waitress, took a day off work to bring him here when they found out you'd be at the ceremony today. Apparently, it's the most excited she's seen him in months."

Clint felt Jeff's hand on his shoulder and his fingers dig into his skin. "You will not mess this day up for him, Clint."

Well, okay then.

Clint looked around and saw the boy's mom standing against the far wall, looking anxious. She also looked too thin and way too tired. A single mom, he realized, trying to cope as best she could with a kid who'd suffered through a horrible disease and was now physically challenged.

Sucked…

Clint jammed his hands into the pockets of his chinos and walked into the center of the gym, sighing when anxious bright-blue eyes met his. He held out his hand and waited for the kid to put his much smaller hand in his before giving it a gentle shake. "Hey, bud, I'm Clint."

"I'm Beck."

"I heard you wanted to speak to me."

Beck folded his arms across his chest and tipped his head to one side. "I've read every article about you and there were a lot."

Clint heard the challenging note in his voice and considered apologizing. If there were as many articles and comments about him as Jeff said, then the kid had spent a hell of a lot of his time reading.

Clint just held his gaze and lifted an eyebrow, waiting for Beck to continue.

"Did you really fight off terrorists by yourself, with half your leg missing?" Beck demanded.

Since he wasn't about to glamorize war, Clint just nodded. "If I hadn't, they would've killed me and my team."

"And they cut off your leg afterward?"

"They did."

"Were you mad?"

Out of the corner of his eye, he saw Beck's mother step forward and he held up his hand, telling her he had this. "At losing my leg? Sure I was. It was a shitty thing to happen."

Maybe he should apologize for his language but after enduring cancer and losing his leg, he was sure the kid could cope with some swearing.

"But you learned how to walk, to run, to ride a horse, to become a helicopter pilot with one leg."

"I did."

"How?" Beck looked at the rope in his hand and gave it a tug. "How did you know you could do it?"

"I didn't," Clint replied, keeping it honest. "But I knew I had to try. That trying and failing was better than not trying at all."

Beck shook his head. "I don't want to fail."

"Sometimes you do fail, that's life. But you have to give it your best shot. Not trying is being a coward and being a coward isn't something a soldier can be."

You had to give it your best shot. And he hadn't tried with Fee and, ergo, he *was* a coward.

Shit.

Of all the times to realize she was right and he was wrong. Clint ran a hand over his face and mentally released a stream of F-bombs. Saying them aloud would be more satisfying, but right now, he had a kid who was looking at him like he hung the moon, like he had all the answers to every question Beck had ever had.

A kid who was hurt, badly bruised and insecure.

He needed to restore some of Beck's confidence and he

needed to do it right now. Clint held up his finger and told Beck to stay put. Motioning Jeff over, he asked whether he could loan him some gear. He changed into a Royal Fire Department T-shirt, a pair of exercise shorts and running shoes, grateful he and Jeff were roughly the same size. He looked down at his bare prosthetic and shrugged off the wave of panic. If a kid could show the world his leg, Clint could too.

He jogged back into the gym and easily pulled himself up the dangling rope until he was close to the ceiling. He hung there for a sec, before sliding down and landing lightly on his feet.

He held the rope out to Beck. "Your turn."

"I can't. I don't know how. I only have one leg."

"You have just as many legs as me, and you won't know if you can do it until you try. One hand over the other, pull. Then wind the rope around your leg and pull up again."

Beck managed to pull himself up a few feet and grinned down at Clint, joy on his face. Clint high-fived him, then helped him down. "Twenty push-ups, soldier."

Beck sent him an uncertain look but copied Clint's stance, his toothpick arms managing five push-ups to Clint's quick twenty before he collapsed, his forehead on the floor. "I'm so bad at this."

"But are you trying?"

Beck turned his face. "Yeah, I am."

"I'm not asking you to be great at it. I'm asking you to try."

Clint worked with him for the next half hour, making Beck lift ropes, flip tires, practice squats and planks, vaguely aware he'd gathered an audience but keeping his sole attention on Beck. The kid's face was red and his hair was damp with sweat by the time he finished but his face radiated a sense of achievement and, yeah, pride.

Clint handed him a towel and a bottle of water and sat down next to him on a bench. "The kids at school, they call me a crip and a gimp," Beck told him, his voice soft.

Clint silently cursed at kids' cruelty. "Screw 'em. Work to be better than them and kick their asses when you're done. But don't tell your mom I said that."

Beck looked over to where his mom stood, talking to an olive-skinned brunette dressed in a flame-orange mini-dress and black knee-high boots.

She had her back to him, but he knew that body from any angle. Besides, only one person would have the audacity, the balls, to wear such a sexy pair of boots in Royal and look amazing doing it.

Clint raised his bottle to his lips, his heart stuttering. Fee was back.

Fee. Was. Back…

"Would you teach me to kick their asses? To defend myself?"

It took all he had to pull his attention back to Beck. "I'll talk to your mom, see if we can get you up here once or twice a month for some training, some lessons."

Clint darted another look at Fee and turned back to his new friend. "Look, Beck, I want you to remember you are allowed to fail, you're allowed to not be good at something—"

"What aren't you good at?" Beck interjected, his eyes bright with curiosity.

Clint didn't hesitate. "Dealing with people, checking my pride, allowing people in, being thoughtful toward the ones who matter to me. So, hug your mom, bud, I think she needs it now and again."

Beck nodded solemnly.

"I was saying you are allowed not to be good at something but you have to try. Promise me you will always try."

Beck tipped his head to the side. "Are you going to try with people?"

Clint grinned. "Touché, kid."

Yeah, he was going to try. And he was going to start with Fee.

Beck wrinkled his nose. "I don't know what that means."

Clint ruffled his hair and stood up. "It means you turned the tables on me."

He nodded toward the locker room. "Good job, bud. Go wash your face and hands."

Clint waited for Beck outside the locker room, thinking he hadn't even broken a sweat. He could go back in, change back into his clothes and carry on with his day. But he didn't want to waste a minute so when Beck walked out of the locker room, Clint placed his hand on the kid's shoulder and walked him back over to his teary-eyed mom. Fee gave Clint a brief nod of greeting and, being Fee and outgoing, immediately engaged Beck in conversation.

Beck's mom—she introduced herself as Jan—placed her hand on his arm. "Thank you for giving him your time. He's been struggling lately—he's been very sullen and uncommunicative. I haven't been able to talk to him for months and the only time he's really spoken to me was to ask to come see you."

Uncomfortable with her praise and thanks, Clint asked for her cell phone. Taking it, he programmed in his number and told Jan to call him when Beck was acting up. Or whenever she or Beck needed to talk.

Tears streamed down Jan's face. Fee handed her a tissue and she wiped her eyes as she turned her attention to her son.

"Did you see me, Mom? Did you see what I did? Clint said I have to try."

Clint watched them walk out of the now-empty gym and turned back to his biggest problem and his greatest joy. He didn't know what to say so he went for the obvious.

"I didn't expect to see you back in Royal, Fee." He looked past her, looking for the cameras. "I presume your crew is outside, filming this opening of the fire station. It's supposed to be more of an appreciation party for the volunteer firefighters, but we decided to hold both functions at once—"

"My crew isn't here," Fee interrupted him.

Clint frowned, puzzled. "I would've thought they would want to be here. It's a nice ending to the story."

"Since I'm leaving the show, I'm not part of the decision-making." She wrinkled her nose and Clint realized he wanted to watch her do that for the rest of his life. Could he ask her to give him another chance? What if he failed?

But he had to take his own advice.

But before he threw himself off a cliff, he wanted some more facts. "What, exactly, do you mean by that?"

"It means I am quitting the show," Fee told him, her tone still cool. "I still have to negotiate my exit, but I've made up my mind. I only came by today to tell you I've decided Royal is my town and I need to be here. I'm sorry if that doesn't suit you but Royal suits me."

Wait…what? What the hell?

"I'm sorry, what did you say?"

"I'm renting a cottage in Royal, working on a cookbook and I have feelers out to do a cooking show." She shrugged her slim shoulders. "Eventually I'll either buy or build a place but I felt I owed it to you to tell you I'm back. I'm not asking, or expecting, a damn thing from you."

Clint cocked his head. "Well, damn, now that's a pity."

Fee's eyes turned a shade of bitter chocolate. "You should also know I have no intention of climbing into your bed and being tossed out when you tire of me. Or when you get scared."

Fair point. "What if I just keep you in my bed, in my house, in my life for the rest of my life?"

Fee closed her eyes, color receding from her face. "That's such a cruel thing to say, Clint. You've been an ass and a jerk, but you were never once cruel. Congratulations, lieutenant, you've reached a new low."

Fee turned to walk away and Clint stared at her back, completely confused. He'd just tossed his heart at her feet and she thought he was taunting her by offering something he didn't intend to deliver? Yeah, he really, really, really needed to work on his communication skills. He might never be good at it but there was a lot of room for improvement.

"I missed you."

Fee stopped in her tracks and he heard her loud sigh. She started to walk again and he threw another truth her way. "You were right. I *am* a coward."

Oh, God, that hurt, but then the truth always did. Fee stopped again, slowly turned around and raised one dark eyebrow. "Sure, when it comes to me."

Typical Fee, never one to give an inch. But at least she wasn't walking away. She kept her eyes on him as she said, "But please, feel free to tell me how you came to that conclusion."

Sarcastic as well. He loved it. Loved her. "I worked my ass off to be capable, to show the world I could do anything I did before and more. But I didn't work at relationships and I didn't bother to work out how to deal with people. Because people are complicated, contrary, and they don't always react the way you want them to."

"We don't all jump when you bark an order, lieutenant."

He ignored her sarcasm. "So, I withdrew. I've always been solitary, Fee, always a loner. My ex, those women, their…insensitivity and my mother's comments about my disability, gave me the excuse I needed to not try, to not interact. It took a fast-talking, sexy, mouthy reality TV star to show me I'd stopped trying with people. That, when it came to relationships, I'm a coward." Clint shook his head. "It was a truth I didn't want to acknowledge."

Fee nodded. When Clint didn't say anything more, she lifted her hands before pointing to the door. "I'm going to go and I think people want to get this show on the road. James Harrison probably wants to get the formalities over with so he can have a beer."

"The president of the TCC can wait," Clint told her. "I'm not done."

"I don't know what there's left to say," Fee admitted.

Clint walked over to her and gently lifted a tendril off her cheek and tucked it behind her ear. "Oh, I have quite a bit still to say."

He saw the trepidation and the faint flicker of hope in her eyes. "Since when did you get to be Mr. Chatty?"

"Since I looked up and saw you across the room and I knew there was no way I was going to let you leave my life again." His fingers brushed her ear, ran down her neck, and he felt her shudder. "I wasn't joking earlier…stay in my house, stay in my life."

"Clint…" Fee begged him but he wasn't sure what she was asking.

So he kept talking. "I'm completely utterly, crazily in love with you, Seraphina. You brought color and warmth and a fair amount of craziness into my life and I don't want to go back to that colorless world again."

Fee's eyes glistened with tears and she finally, finally

touched him by placing her hand on his heart. "Do you mean that?"

"Those few, inadequate words don't even begin to cover the depth of my love for you." Clint cupped her beautiful face. "You just told me you are staying here, that this is your town. But did you mean it? Is this really where you want to be?"

"Why are you asking?" Fee asked, tipping her head.

"I don't want you to settle, just because I am here. I want you to be happy and if you're not going to be happy in Royal, then we'll find another place, any place." He shrugged. "I might have to buy a plane so I can come back regularly to keep an eye on the ranch but we can live anywhere."

"And you'd go with me?" Fee asked, a smile pulling her mouth up.

She was where he needed to be. Yeah, he'd miss his ranch but they'd make it work. "As long as you are happy," Clint murmured. "Making you happy is all I care about, Fee."

And it was. His life was now hers. Her happiness was everything.

"That's the sweetest thing anyone has ever said to me," Fee stated, looping her arms around his neck. "But might I remind you of one salient point you seem to have forgotten, Rockwell?"

"What's that?"

"I came back to Royal with no expectation of a relationship with you. I came back because I like this town, I like the people and I want to be part of this community. I want to live here, even though I thought I had no chance of being a part of your life."

"Oh." He was struggling to catch up, to make sense of

all of this, mostly because Fee was back and in his arms. "So, you're happy to move into my place?"

"More than," Fee said, her thumbs rubbing his jaw. "Tell me you love me before you kiss me senseless, Rockwell."

"Love you, sweetheart."

"Love you back, cowboy," Fee murmured against his lips, but before he could follow through on her command to kiss her senseless, he heard Jeff clearing his throat.

Jeff just grinned when Clint raised his head and gave him a piss-off-I'm-busy glare.

"James is chomping to get started since all the VIPs are present and accounted for."

Fee stepped back from him and Clint groaned his frustration. She slid her hand into his. "We can pick this up later, Clint." She rubbed his T-shirt between her fingers. "You need to change, darling."

Clint looked down at his exercise shorts and his faded T-shirt. Shrugging, he sent Jeff a wry grin. "Tell James I'm changing. I'll be there in five minutes."

Jeff nodded and left, but instead of heading toward the locker room, Clint pulled Fee back into his arms. "Now, where were we?"

"You're not going to change?" Fee asked him.

"I'd rather kiss you." Clint's mouth curved against hers. "Besides, it seems like the whole world has seen my leg and the planet didn't tilt off its axis."

Fee laughed and slapped her mouth against his.

And it was a good fifteen minutes before they made an appearance at the ceremony.

Epilogue

Fee looked at Clint posing for photographs with the mayor of Royal, Jeff, the new fire chief, and James Harrison, the president of the Texas Cattleman's Club, thinking Clint looked perfect in his exercise shorts and the tight fitting Royal FD T-shirt. Yeah, he should be more smartly dressed for such an important occasion, but most of the attendees had heard about his impromptu gym session with young Beck and applauded him for it.

Her man could walk down the main street of Royal buck naked and nobody would blink an eye. He was their own homegrown hero, one of their favorite sons and he could do no wrong.

When it came to her, though…well, she'd seen first-hand the challenges that faced anyone who loved this man.

Fee didn't have many stars in her eyes, and while she loved him with every strand of DNA she possessed, she wasn't naive enough to believe Life had just sprinkled a can of fairy dust over their lives. She fully accepted that, going forward, there would be problems and arguments and flared tempers and hurt feelings. That was just life. But there'd be love too. Happiness. Passion. Acceptance.

She'd found her happy place and it was here, in Royal, with Clint. And she'd told him the truth earlier. Even if Clint hadn't been part of the deal, she'd want to spend most of her time in Royal, make this town her home base. She felt at ease here, settled.

Royal was where the rest of her life began.

Having finished with the photographer, Clint made a beeline toward her, his hazel eyes more gold than green.

"You okay? Any second thoughts?" he teased, but Fee wasn't fooled by his light tone. He was worried and she couldn't blame him; this happiness was so new, it felt like it might disappear in a puff of smoke.

"Just catching my breath." Fee linked her fingers with his and rested her head on his shoulder, smiling when he dropped a kiss on her hair.

"I know. I keep feeling it's the most amazing dream and I'm going to wake up alone."

Clint took her glass from her hand and placed his mouth over the lipstick mark she'd left on the glass. He swallowed the rest of the chardonnay and handed the glass back to the waitress. He looked around and sent her a conspiratorial grin. "When can we leave? While I'm loving your dress, I sure as hell can't wait to get you out of it."

Fee grinned back. "Rockwell, really? We have to stay for a little while—it'll be rude to leave now."

"Ten minutes? Fifteen?" Clint asked, mischief in his eyes.

Fee rolled her eyes then allowed them to drift around the room, searching for a neutral subject to distract them from what they were both desperate to do. Soon…

"How are the cleanup operations going?"

"Slowly," Clint replied. "There's so much damage, Fee. More buildings were affected than we originally suspected, including the TCC clubhouse. By the way, James Harrison has asked me to join the Texas Cattleman's Club."

That didn't surprise her. "Of course he has. You're the town's hero."

"I wish everyone would stop calling me that. I just did what I needed to do," Clint replied, frustration in his voice. "I was able to help so I did."

He didn't realize many people wouldn't have, that lots of people threw money at a problem and then washed their hands of any responsibility, looking to others to find a solution. Clint used his money, and his time and his skills, and that was a rare and beautiful thing. But she liked the fact he was unaware of just how amazing he was.

"I'm surprised the Blackwood siblings aren't here," Fee commented, changing the subject.

"I heard Sophie Blackwood has left Royal for New York City." Clint shrugged. "Kellan is in Nashville, I think. I'm not sure where Vaughn is at present."

"Kace is here." Fee gestured to the lanky lawyer talking to James Harrison.

"And your friend isn't," Clint said. "Something happening between them?"

Fee was curious on that point too—but Lu had been uncharacteristically quiet lately. Then again, she'd been heartbroken and not really interested in anything but her own misery.

"I don't know. But I haven't been a great friend lately. I've been rather wrapped up in my own heartbreak," she admitted.

Clint turned her to face him and placed his hands on

her shoulder. "Hell, Fee, I have to apologize. Again. I acted like a jerk, and I'm really sorry."

"And I was a lot meaner than I needed to be but I was hurt. I'm sorry too. You're not a coward, Clint. I'm so sorry I insulted you like that," Fee said, her heart in her throat. She was still ashamed of herself, that of everything she could've said, she'd gone straight for his emotional jugular.

"But I was. When it came to you, and love, I was a total coward." Clint jerked his head at Beck, who stood by the table laden with desserts, stuffing his mouth. "I told him he had to try, that he could fail but he *had* to try. Then I realized I was crap at taking my own advice. And I looked up and there you were."

He smiled and Fee's heart jumped into her throat. Clint had an amazing smile and she was going to look at it for the rest of her life. How lucky was she?

"Your arrival damn near gave me a heart attack," Clint admitted. He looked at Beck and lifted one huge shoulder. "The fire station project is, obviously, over and we need to clean up Royal but—"

"But?" Fee asked, intrigued by the light she saw in his eyes.

"But I was thinking that, for my next project, I'd like to build a rehab center, a gym, something specifically designed for veterans and people struggling to come to terms with their disabilities. Maybe hire some physios, some counselors, have some skills training. A place of… acceptance."

Fee blinked away her tears. Oh God, that sounded perfect. "It sounds awesome, darling. You'll have my full support, Clint."

"Maybe we can call it Fee's Place, because you led me to a place of acceptance."

She was touched but…no.

"We'll find a name, a good name, but not that one." Fee rested her forehead on his chest before looking up at him, tears rolling down her face. "I'm so in love with you, Rockwell."

"As I am with you," Clint told her, spearing his fingers into her hair and tipping her jaw up to receive his kiss. "I only have one more thing to ask you…"

Oh God, it was too soon. What would she say? Yes, of course, but were they rushing things? Was she ready for a proposal?

"What?" Fee asked him, sounding a little breathless.

"Can we go home now?"

Fee released a long breath, a little disappointed. "Yeah, sure."

Clint took her hand and led her through the throngs of people, adroitly avoiding everyone who wanted to talk to them by telling them he'd catch up with them soon. Outside, in the cool evening air, he turned back to Fee and smiled at her. "So, would you have said yes?"

She didn't pretend to misunderstand him. "It's very soon but…yes. I would have said yes."

Clint brushed his lips across hers. "Good to know. Let's go home, my darling Fee."

She was already there. No matter where she was, if her hand was in his, she was home.

* * * * *

COMING SOON!

We really hope you enjoyed reading this book.
If you're looking for more romance
be sure to head to the shops when
new books are available on

Thursday 19th June

MILLS & BOON

MILLS & BOON

THE HEART OF ROMANCE

A ROMANCE FOR EVERY READER

MODERN
Prepare to be swept off your feet by sophisticated, sexy and seductive heroes, in some of the world's most glamourous and romantic locations, where power and passion collide.

HISTORICAL
Escape with historical heroes from time gone by. Whether your passion is for wicked Regency Rakes, muscled Vikings or rugged Highlanders, awaken the romance of the past.

MEDICAL
Set your pulse racing with dedicated, delectable doctors in the high-pressure world of medicine, where emotions run high and passion, comfort and love are the best medicine.

True Love
Celebrate true love with tender stories of heartfelt romance, from the rush of falling in love to the joy a new baby can bring, and a focus on the emotional heart of a relationship.

HEROES
The excitement of a gripping thriller, with intense romance at its heart. Resourceful, true-to-life women and strong, fearless men face danger and desire - a killer combination!

From showing up to glowing up, these characters are on the path to leading their best lives and finding romance along the way – with plenty of sizzling spice!

To see which titles are coming soon, please visit

millsandboon.co.uk/nextmonth

FOUR BRAND NEW BOOKS FROM
MILLS & BOON MODERN

The same great stories you love, a stylish new look!

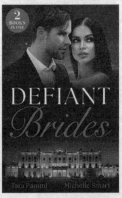
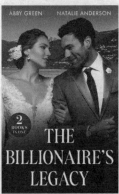

OUT NOW

Eight Modern stories published every month, find them all at:

millsandboon.co.uk

LET'S TALK

Romance

For exclusive extracts, competitions and special offers, find us online:

- **f** MillsandBoon
- **X** @MillsandBoon
- **O** @MillsandBoonUK
- **J** @MillsandBoonUK

Get in touch on 01413 063 232

Afterglow Books is a trend-led, trope-filled list of books with diverse, authentic and relatable characters, a wide array of voices and representations, plus real world trials and tribulations. Featuring all the tropes you could possibly want (think small-town settings, fake relationships, grumpy vs sunshine, enemies to lovers) and all with a generous dose of spice in every story.

♪ @millsandboonuk
⊙ @millsandboonuk
afterglowbooks.co.uk
#AfterglowBooks

For all the latest book news, exclusive content and giveaways scan the QR code below to sign up to the Afterglow newsletter:

afterglow BOOKS

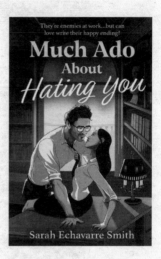

 Sports romance

🖤 Enemies to lovers

🌶 Spicy

💻 Workplace romance

🚫 Forbidden love

☯ Opposites attract

OUT NOW

Two stories published every month. Discover more at:
Afterglowbooks.co.uk

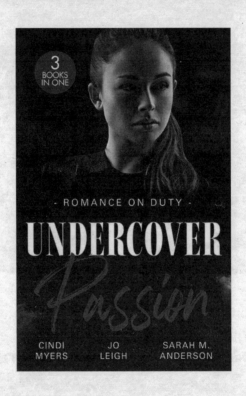

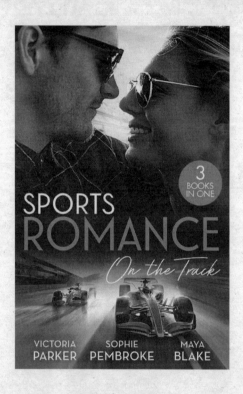